IMMORTAL ASCENDED

The story of Radoq Loxelsus Po-Fortisun

Toby Sanders

FROM THE AUTHOR

Thanks for looking at my book! I'm a passionate self-published author on a mission to share my unique tales with readers like you. If you've enjoyed the journey so far, I'd be honoured if you could take a moment to leave a review on Amazon. To connect with my Amazon page, simply follow me on Twitter (X) for a quick and easy link @Toby_Author.

For Sedge, Theo & Elba

CHAPTER 1

Thirst was the real cage. The sharpshooters that slouched in the shade of the great airships let their phasrs hang by the straps. The guards did not waste time patrolling the hot sand between the sweating lines of chained figures. They lounged in woven chairs beneath silk canopies, sipping tepid water from great iron-banded barrels. The pilots in the towering ships periodically adjusted their craft so that the shadows covered the crowds but, in the desert, the heat was inescapable.

Every hour or so a guard would stir themselves and uncuff a nearby slave. They would stand obediently with their head bowed as they were handed a wooden pail and a ladle. Then they'd fill it with clear water from the barrel, the guards watching their fellows like hawks for any sign of movement. Sips from the ladle would soothe cracked lips and loosen parched tongues but nothing more. Periodically, one of the thousands of grimy, ragged, chained figures would slump to the side or backwards, landing in the lap of the person behind them. The guards would curse, haul themselves over and revive the wretched soul, leaving them chained in their place. From the snarls of anger and the curling of their whips it was clear they begrudged every moment spent outside the shelter of their cool canopies but lives were profit here and the cargo of human flesh was worth more to the owners of the fleet of ships than the comfort of their employees.

This late in the afternoon, no-one tried to run. If they could slip their shackles, the slaves had the choice of sprinting off between the dunes. This was the one opportunity the guards had

1

to relieve their frustrations. A slave who failed to escape would, given the opportunity, try again. And next time, they might take others with them. To those who haggled in human lives, that was a loss of profit and the rules were clear. If a slave ran, they were fair game. Earlier in the day, two had taken the chance. Just two out of the thousands that sat in rows in the burning sand. One had fallen to the guards' coltacs, her blood long since dried a deep brown on the sand around her. The second, a burly soldier among the hundreds the slavers had scraped off the battlefield had made it almost to the top of the first dune before the plasma bolt from a phasr had taken the side of his head off. He'd been dragged back by the guards, grumbling and sweating to have his corpse lashed to a great iron post which now stood in plain view before the slaves.

The shackled thousands had lowered their eyes to the sand before them at this and throughout the long hours of the desert day, they'd kept their gaze low.

There was one oddity amongst the sea of misery. A lump, vaguely cuboid in shape beneath a white canvas cover stood out from the sun scorched rows. The faint breeze that the desert taunted its guests with would twitch the cloth at intervals, drawing the eyes of guards who would look away again quickly, as though avoiding some evil omen. In this hell where profit reigned supreme over comfort and safety, the rare luxury of the dirty canvas spoke to the value of that which lay beneath it.

A gust lifted one corner revealing the heavy chain that stretched between the bars of an iron cage. Lashed at one end to a hefty peg driven deep into the sand, the far end was hidden from sight but even the meanest slave noted that the guards gave it a wide berth when they chose to leave their shelters.

Movement...

A trio of guards walked slowly towards a canopy. They appeared from outside the camp, trudging over the sand and they bore the fatigue of those who had braved the desert. They made for the guards closest to the canvas covered cage and the occupants below it stirred, already calling ribald greetings to their fellow slavers.

Food was what the trio had brought and the guards gathered around the platter greedily. Across the camp others were appearing bearing the evening meal. One man, his chest bare and his voice cruel found a spur of energy from the meal and his loud voice carried as he gnawed a bone.

"Evening meal means we're nearly done! Get 'em loaded in what, two hours?"

"Two hours?" came the sarcastic response "Think you've been out in the sun, Haftan! We've got more'n four thousand head of slave-flesh to move here! Be dark long before we get 'em loaded!"

Haftan scoffed at the speaker "Ah, we move at your pace, Soldiran then yeah, might as well be here until the sun comes up!"

It was a weak joke but it was the first since the heat of the day had melted conversation away and the slavers chuckled, scraping the last of the meal from the bucket Soldiran and the two others had carried. Another guard, this one a sun scorched woman with a rusted berrett slung across her back began to taunt Soldiran, mocking his great sweating belly which brought jeers from his fellows. Haftan, chuckling at the banter tossed his bone carelessly over his shoulder into the sand.

Next to the cage that lurked beneath the canvas.

A crash rang out followed by the clanking of chains and Haftan spun around, whipping his coltac out with quick hands and levelling it at the cage. An oath died on his lips as he saw the bone resting by the canvas. He shook his head, slowly returning the coltac to the holster at his hip as Soldiran led the jeers.

"Cacked your shorts there, Haftan! Haven't seen you move that fast since that viral with the tits!"

The comment provoked howls of laughter at Haftan's expense. The slaver flushed red at the memory, his hand twitching to the hilt of his coltac but he made no real move to draw it.

"Anyway –" Soldiran had turned to scrape grease from the bottom of the bucket, licking his pudgy fingers as he did so "-

3

that one's Fallen! Scraped him off the 'field, last of his brigade I reckon!" he shot Haftan a softer look "He can't hurt you, Haftan. You could stop him with your coltac now."

The slavers began to turn away, breaking into other conversation as Haftan lurked on the edge of the shade provided by the canopy, nursing his wounded pride. His eyes passed unseeing over the nearest line of slaves, bound and miserable even as the temperature began to lower.

Movement...

"You!" Haftan's voice snapped like a shot from a gat and he strode forward onto the hot sand before the other slavers had registered where the sound had come from. His eyes were locked on a skinny young female with dark hair. The remnants of a dirty grey vest and breeches barely covered her skin and the flesh she was revealing had caught more than one leering glance that day. Haftan reached the slave who cowered visibly beneath the guard who stopped beside her and lowered himself into a squat, leaning close.

"Hello pretty." Haftan whispered to her. He reached out and took a lock of her greasy hair between his gloved fingers "You're a lovely one. Gonna get a good price for you in the flesh pots down in old Xeonison, eh?"

The girl had begun to shake with fear. Haftan smiled.

"Whats your name, pretty?"

She shook in response and Haftan twisted the strands of hair roughly, not enough to really hurt but enough to get her attention.

"Ju – Jucias." The slave stammered.

"Oh, surely not?" Haftan chuckled deep in his throat "Surely you aren't using a free name? You're a slave now, girly. You don't have a name!" he grinned in a vile manner.

Behind Haftan the other slavers were watching warily. Punishments were dealt out, sure enough but damaging the goods was something they'd all pay for.

"You don't get a name anymore. You get a number." Haftan's gloved hand shot out and grabbed the heavy metal collar that was clamped around Jucias' neck. She gagged as he twisted it, cutting into her throat. Tears were running down her cheeks leaving tracks in the dried dust and sand that caked her skin "You know what the punishment is for using a name?" Haftan's voice had not risen above a whisper but now there was a cruel, mocking tone to it.

Jucias shook her head, a whimper escaping her throat as she did so. Haftan smiled in response, pressing a bio-digit against the collar which popped open and hung suspended from the chain that ran the length of the row of slaves.

"Haftan!" someone called from beneath the canopy but Haftan ignored it. He stood, grabbing the manacles that bound Jucias' hands and began to drag her towards the canopy, ripping the remnants of her vest off as he did so to leave her chest bare. A mixture of whistles and worried murmurs came from beneath the canopy but aside from these guards, the only witnesses were other slaves. The next nearest canopy was far enough away that the desert wind ensured sound did not carry.

Haftan dragged the now half naked Jucias beneath the shade. He flung her roughly on her front onto the weaved rug that served as a floor. Someone leaned forward and slapped her skin provoking more jeers from the guards.

"By Chox, Haftan!" all humour had fled from Soldiran's voice. He stepped close to his younger colleague, sweat beading on his upper lip "If the bosses see this we'll all be fined! I'm not losing my delivery bonus so you can get your jolly on!"

Haftan snarled at the fat man, shoving him backwards "Ain't no-one but us here! No-one's getting fined, it's just a bit of discipline! Who's she gonna tell, anyway?" he leered at Soldiran who shook his head in dismay, stepping backwards.

On the floor, Jucias had rolled over onto her side, her knees drawn up to her chest with her manacled arms wrapped around them. She looked up at Haftan who gave a sadistic chuckle then dropped into a crouch again, this time taking a firm grip of her ragged breeches.

"Rip 'em off, Haftan!" shouted the voice of a younger guard,

5

quickly shushed by the others who glanced around warily. Haftan wasted a second to grin up at the spectators and that was when Jucias extended both her legs in a vicious two footed kick that knocked Haftan backwards, toppling him so that he rolled over in the sand.

A shout of laughter from the guards whose eyes followed his roll followed by curses and warnings as Jucias sprinted away from the canopy, violently swinging her bound hands from side to side as she struggled to make headway in the burning sand.

With an oath, Haftan was up and after her shoving the remaining guards out of his way. Someone bawled at him to use his coltac but he left the gat holstered, instead closing the distance to Jucias quickly, his desert boots gripping the sand efficiently and his long, well nourished legs outstripping her own staggering paces.

With a thump, he brought her down, both arms around her trunk in a flying tackle. She screamed in fear as he caught her and turned onto her back, trying to repeat her kick but Haftan straddled her, dropping his right elbow in a wickedly hard blow to her temple. Jucias sprawled in the hot sand, her body going limp as Haftan grinned, rolling Jucias over onto her front and tearing the last of her clothing away in a grotesque mockery of the act of love. He ignored the shouts from behind him, disregarded the sound of running feet, his eyes fixed on his helpless victim before him and he never saw the smooth skinned hand that reached out from beneath the dirty white canvas, never noticed that his bestial chase had led him close to the cage and its hidden contents...

Haftan flew sideways. To Soldiran, puffing and cursing still only halfway from the canopy to the brutal scene being enacted before him that was what it seemed like. What had a second before been a virile, muscled young man suddenly moved so fast that he could have been pulled by a cord. A metallic clang rang out as Haftan hit the bars of the cage. Then, like a child's doll, he lurched drunkenly sideways, still in a kneeling position only to be rammed back against the bars of the cage. Once, twice, a third time and now there was no mistaking the sickening crunching noise that could only come from human bones breaking.

"Get the chains! Get the Chox'd chains!" Soldiran was yelling to the desert but enough of his fellow slavers heard him and with shouts they surrounded the cage, reaching under the canvas and hauling on the four strands of iron link that were bolted into the sand. A snarl of animal fury sounded from within but the chain closest to Haftan went taught and the limp body of the slaver fell away, landing in the sand next to Jucias who was unmoving.

"Chox!" swore Soldiran hands out in front of him in an impotent gesture. Blood was coming from Haftan somewhere although he couldn't see the wound. His eyes met those of the nearest pair of slavers who were hauling on the end of a chain "Keep that Chox'd thing tight! You hear me?"

He stepped forward tentatively, towards Haftan. Inside the cage a low snarl sounded and he stopped, a small whimper escaping his throat. Feeling the eyes of the younger guards on him, Soldiran took a deep breath and closed in on Haftan. A glance told him that the man was dead, his neck broken and his eyes bulging in their sockets. Blood caked the sand beneath him and Soldiran swore "You in the cage! He's dead! You keep still now, hear me?" and he bent down, grabbing Haftan's boots and tugging him a few feet away from the cage, leaving a bloody smear in the sand.

"Is he alright?" a voice shouted and Soldiran flapped a hand at the inquirer but feet sounded in the sand and another slaver, the same sun scorched female that had jeered at Haftan turned to shout at the others.

"He's dead!"

The sound of coltacs and berretts being cocked filled the warm air. Barrels were levelled at the canvas and Soldiran cringed but a new voice, this one filled with authority cracked.

"Enough! *Enough!*" and Correlius was there, his eyes covered by his dust goggles and his bulging form seeming to fill the desert with the threat of punishment. Soldiran cursed under his breath as the other slavers hastily stowed their weapons.

"What in Chox's name is happening here?" there was no mistaking the fury in Correlius' voice. His eyes roved across the scene, taking in Jucias' naked rump and Haftan's blooded corpse. He stalked across to Soldiran, his grey eyes boring into Soldiran's own.

"He – Haftan tried to rape the girl." Gone was any loyalty to the dead man. Soldiran's thoughts now were on the delivery bonus to be paid in Xeonison. If the blame could be shifted to Haftan then perhaps they'd all be counting their coin at the end of the voyage...

"Chox'd Haftan." Correlius' voice was lowered but he turned away, roaring now at the rest of the guards "This is a Chox'd mess! I've half a mind to dock you all half your bonus!" he let the words sink in. A stunned silence filled the air "This thing you were all ready to fill with plasma bolts is Fallen! It can't hurt you, unless you're a stupid as this Chox'd fool!" he kicked out at Haftan's dead face "Let this be a lesson to you all! You mess with Domerus, even Fallen Domerus and this is what you get!"

The faces of the slavers were wary. Was he going to dock their pay? Surely Haftan's death was more than enough punishment? Correlius seemed to agree because he took a breath, lowering the tone of his voice "No more damage to the livestock. No more abuse than discipline dictates. These women –" he pointed a gloved hand at Jucias who was beginning to stir "- are not for you! They're for Domerus down in Xeonison! Good families who can pay decent coin for a bit of slave flesh1 Scum like you don't get to touch it! You want a bit of friendly bedtime, you visit a whorehouse like the rest of us!"

Like naughty children, the slavers stood avoiding eye contact. Correlius turned to the woman who still stood next to Soldiran "And that goes for you too, Mags! You Chox'd pervert!"

A roar of laughter at the joke. The atmosphere lifted a few notches. Their bonuses were intact and no-one would miss Haftan too dearly.

"Get a spade and bury him!" Soldiran called to a couple of the younger men who hastened to obey.

Correlius gripped his arm "Get the girl dressed and chain her up." He squeezed the layers of fat on Soldiran's upper arm "No-one touches her. Got it? She's worth a Chox'd fortune in Xeonison and I don't want another hair on her head harmed."

"Y – yes, Correlius." stammered Soldiran.

Correlius turned away from the flurry of activity, taking a few wary steps towards the cage. He cleared his throat, his hand resting on the butt of his coltac although he kept the gat in its holster "You there – in the cage. Do you hear me?"

Silence.

"The man is dead. Now listen, you keep your hands to yourself during the flight and don't go bothering my men any more. Do that and I'll see you go to a good family, got it?"

Silence from beneath the canvas. Correlius stood uncertainly. He wondered whether to rip the canvas from the cage and look the creature in the eye and his fingers twitched but he moved no further. He bared his teeth as the moment passed and he knew that he dared not step any closer. He spat in disgust, regretting it almost immediately as the wad of phlegm now evaporating on the sand left his mouth dry and he turned back to the canopy just as a deafening screech of metal brought every eye above the sand to the sky where the first of the great airships had turned and lowered its loading ramp to the cooling desert floor. It was time to load the slaves.

CHAPTER 2

"Are you Chox'd mad, Correlius? Bringing one of those things on my ship?" the Captain's voice echoed off the bare metal walls of the hold as Correlius resisted the urge to roll his eyes. He turned as the Captain, a beefy Xeonison named Attilur approached, one hand firmly gripping the handle of a high powered coltac.

"Good to see you, Attilur." Correlius greeted him.

"Do you know what'll happen if it gets loose?" Attilur watched as the cage, its canvas cover still intact was rolled on a heavy vakkor engine castor past the lines of slaves that were now chained in rows to sturdy bars that ran the length of the hold.

"It's Fallen, Attilur. We scraped it off the battlefield. It can't hurt you."

In response, Attilur pointed to a smear of Haftan's blood that stained one corner of the canvas "Looks like it hurt someone."

"Well, Haftan got too close. He was a young idiot."

"And I'm an old Ap am I?" Attilur roared with laughter, pounding Correlius on the back at the joke. Correlius mouth twitched in response but his eyes never left the cage.

"Keep it in the cage, keep it away from your crew and you'll be fine." He repeated.

Attilur was shaking his head "Can't keep the cage. It'll have to be cuffed like the others." He gestured around with a massive hand "Space is at a premium here, you know. Every inch we lose is another hit to our bonus."

"You want to take it out the cage?" Correlius couldn't keep the shock out of his voice.

"What? I thought it was Fallen?"

"Yes, but still! Have you seen a Domerus move?"

Attilur scoffed "I've heard stories! How dangerous can it be? Look, we'll get a set of aquar cuffs out and get his hands behind him!" he turned to Correlius "It is a 'he', I presume?"

Correlius nodded and called out for the canvas to be removed.

Dust and sand filled the air and Correlius reflexively wafted his hands before him, Attilur mirroring the movement. Before them, his chin drooping onto his bare chest knelt a man. His torso was caked in blood and he looked half dead. His legs were clad in tight fitting black cloth while his arms were hauled out to the side, the four chains that had been driven into the sand now wrapped securely around the bars of his prison.

Attilur whistled, stepping back "Look at the size of it!"

The kneeling man figure was easily a head taller than the Captain who was the tallest man on the ship. Broad muscles were visible even with the strain of the chains. The kneeling figure emanated a sense of power and danger that drew the eye of every slaver.

"Not sure I want this on my ship." Attilur was shaking his head.

"Don't be such a big girl!" Correlius pulled up a bio on a dusty handheld, scrolling through a manifest "Says here he's Radoq Loxelsus Su-Fortisun." He blinked in surprise "Bit of a mouthful these Domerus names.

"Po."

Correlius and Attilur looked at each other for a moment wondering where the sound had come from. Then understanding dawned.

"You what, slave?" Attilur called.

The man in the cage raised his head. Deep blue eyes, an inhuman intensity of colour met those of the Captain.

"I'm the Po of tritus Fortisun."

"Which one is Po again?" Attilur muttered to Correlius "Is that the head?"

Correlius shook his head "No. That's the Ji. Po is like second in command or something. Maybe the heir?"

"Which is it? And why's he saying Po if he's Su?" Attilur asked, peering at the handheld "Buyer will want to know the full history for one like this."

Correlius muttered under his breath as he flicked through a few screens on the handheld. He stopped, suddenly peering close and reading something intently before he gave a great shout of laughter "Tritus Fortisun? Looks like the whole family's been arrested! New Sheriff in town took the whole corrupt lot into custody! Must've done something to upset your Crown Prince, eh, Domerus?" Correlius guffawed as the slave dropped his chin back to his chest "Looks like you're Su after all! Still, you'll bring a good enough price in Xeonison. A Domerus is a Domerus, after all! Even a Fallen Su!"

Attilur burst out laughing at the insult and Correlius left to supervise the rest of the loading. Attilur gathered a ring of his crew around the cage, each of them pointing coltacs or berretts at the kneeling Domerus. A set of aquar cuffs, crackling with the blue energy were encased, one end on each outstretched arm before Attilur gave an order and the chains that bound Radoq were released. His arms dropped to his sides and the aquar snapped his wrists together, the bright light fading as the connection stabilised.

Attilur stared for a moment, seeming to wrestle with something in his mind "Bring another set! Bind his ankles too!" as an airman began to cinch the restraints he called out to the man "Make sure they're tight! That thing gets loose over the Dark Lands we can take our chances with the virals! Make 'em tight!"

Hours later and the cold night air was blowing into the hold. The slaves who had dreamed all day of cool nights and ice now shivered and shook. Attilur ignored their plight, checking the bonds of each line of the hundreds of human cargo that now filled his ship. He was slow and meticulous, despite the mutterings of his crew that wanted to be airborne, racing across the Dark Lands towards Xeonison. The first ship in the slave markets would demand the best prices and the crew felt their cut dwindling with every moment Attilur wasted. Surely the other ships were away by now? But Attilur would not be rushed and it was near midnight by the time he ordered the loading ramp closed with a squeal of rusted metal. The deep thrum of the engines soon filled the hold and the temperature began to rise, levelling off at a comfortable point which was no small measure of relief to the slaves, many of whom were soon in an exhausted sleep.

Attilur began to weave his way back through the lines of cargo, randomly checking chains and fastenings here and there until he drew level with the Domerus. Radoq still knelt only now the great cage had been removed around him. Blood still caked his torso and he alone amongst the slaves was not lashed to the metal fixings. Instead, the aquar held his hands fast before him, small movements in his muscles making the energy spit and crackle as the connection adjusted.

"Any trouble from you, Domerus?" Attilur had paused in front of Radoq.

"None."

"Have you eaten?"

"Not yet, Captain."

"You call me 'Sir'."

"Not yet, Sir." Radoq did not lift his chin from his chest.

Attilur grunted, looking around "Well, grub's on its way." He pointed and Radoq tilted his chin slightly to make out a slave who carried a steaming cauldron the contents of which he was ladling into small cups that were being passed out.

"Thank you."

Attilur chuckled "No need to thank me. You're valuable alive. Need you healthy for the auction in Xeonison." His tone turned sombre for a moment "They scraped you off the battlefield, eh?"

The chin dropped again. The shoulders slumped.

"Looks like you lost more than just your men out there. I've seen men defeated before. Lose their minds as the enemy destroys them." Attilur raised a finger in mild threat "I've seen men pull back from the edge of despair, too. Do stupid, heroic things. Not on my ship, understand? You give me any trouble and I've no problem opening a side hatch and pitching you into the Dark Lands. We'll see how well a Fallen Domerus fares with the virals."

Attilur waited but there was no response from the kneeling Domerus. After a while, he simply grunted and strode towards a flight of metal steps that led up to a gantry overlooking the hold. From here, a cluster of airmen stood guard, each of them armed with a phasr or a berrett. After a brief conversation, Attilur vanished through a small metal door that was the only passage to the rest of the great ship.

The food reached Radoq a few minutes later. He took the proffered bowl with a murmur of thanks, accepting a ladle of watery soup a moment later. He raised it to his lips and emptied the contents with a single swallow.

"Here..." the slave with the ladle was holding the utensil out again. In surprise, Radoq held the bowl up and the man filled it again.

"Thank you."

"Correlius was right you know." The slave avoided Radoq's eyes "Fortisul? Your home? The Domerus there were all taken into custody. A new Sheriff sent by the Crown Prince..." the man stepped away.

Radoq's hand shot out so fast the aquar snapped and flared. He seized the slave's cuff, stopping the man from moving.

"Let *go* of me!" the slave hissed.

"Please, I must know! A fair daughter of Hammun named Malain... What do you know of her?"

The slave wrenched his hand back with a curse and a worried look at the guards "You grab me like that again, *Domerus* and you'll go hungry until we reach Xeonison, I swear! We're all lun'erus now, you're mortal just like us!" he turned to move away.

"You know! You've heard..." Radoq pleaded as the man stepped away.

Spite filled the slave's voice as he turned back, safely out of reach of the grabbing Domerus "I've heard. I heard about your slut Malain, married off to one of the Sheriff's goons! If you thought she was waiting for you, Domerus, you're going to find her tupped and taken when you get home! Which you won't. You're one of us now, Fortisun!" he stalked away among the rows of slaves.

The black wave of misery crashed down over Radoq. His chin dropped back to his chest and his lids closed over the brilliantly blue eyes. Flashes of memory filled his mind. Malain warm in his arms. The tears in her eyes as he'd left for the battlefield. His promise to her...

I'll come back to you

He'd promised her. But he'd made so many promises that now lay broken on the bloody sands at the edge of the desert. Promises to his men. Promises to his father, the Ji. Oaths to his country, to the Crown Prince. All broken and in tatters.

I'll come back to you

Was this his punishment? To know that Malain was now happy in the arms of another man? To know that now and forever she was lost to him? To live with this knowledge the rest of his life as a slave in barbaric Xeonison, an oddity to be gawked at and trotted out to crowds. The Fallen Domerus. A freak. An oddity. A failure.

I'll come back to you

A fresh wave of misery washed over him. His men were dead. His tritus was gone and Malain had forgotten him. He deserved the aquar that bound his wrists. Radoq's head shook from side to side as he allowed his heavy body to slump forward. The cold metal floor of the hold was uncomfortable against his skin but he ignored it. Memories and pain filled his thoughts and burned like aquar through his mind.

Sleep was a surprise when it came, and a momentary relief. But now his dreams were filled with the fury of his father, the Ji. Loxel's face turned cold and furious as he, Radoq knelt before his sire, reporting his failure. His father turned away, hiding his face even as Radoq cried out for his parent not to leave him. Malain, dressed in an absurdly white gown wept in the arms of a rough faced stranger who leered at Radoq with Haftan's face.

"She's mine now."

Radoq could only kneel and shake his head. A pathetic excuse for a Domerus.

I'll come back to you

Another promise to break.

CHAPTER 3

The ship lurched to port in a sudden gust of wind. Moans of fear rose from the slaves, jerked from their sleep. Dim light filled the hold from glowing aquar lamps spread across the ceiling. Radoq woke to the sound of lun'erus fear feeling none himself. The Dark Lands over which they flew were prone to sudden storms and a gust of wind was nothing to be feared but for many slaves this would be their first time aboard a ship and he could understand their concern. The hull creaked alarmingly under the pressure and the voices rose again in muted fear.

On the raised gantry that held the bulk of the guards, a short, stocky man turned at the sound. A berrett was slung across his shoulders but it was his right hand that drew the eye. The long tines of a whip, infused with the same crackling aquar that bound Radoq's hands and feet was attached to his wrist by some manner. Clearly, the guard expected to use the whip frequently throughout the voyage. The second chorus of moans and screams drew his ire and he turned, stepping slowly across the metal gantry heading for the stairs that would lead down to the bound slaves.

Stamp – stamp – stamp

The brute stepped hard, his boots clanging against the floor with every step. Even from this distance, it was clear to Radoq that the man was intentionally stamping to exacerbate the sound his feet made. Perhaps he'd even stitched metal plates to the soles of his boots to make them produce the noise.

Around Radoq, slaves flinched at each step, fear raising shivers on their skin. The ship lurched and groaned again only this time there was silence from the bound figures.

The guard reached the bottom of the steps and paused, looking around at the sea of helpless victims before him. There was no sadistic smile on this man's face like Haftan had worn. Instead, his lips were twisted into a mask of cold fury. He began to stalk between the rows of slaves, the tines of the whip hanging from his wrist. The aquar crackled and popped every few seconds making the nearest flinch in fear.

"There will be discipline aboard this ship!" the guard suddenly roared in a leather throated voice that filled the hold "You are not free! You are not people! You are cargo, and cargo does as its told!".

It was a well-rehearsed speech, clearly a performance the guard had repeated on many occasions.

"I am Latian! You will remember me for one reason!" Latian raised his right hand, flicking some control which caused the tines of the whip to crackle with aquar and stiffen in front of him. Blue light reflected off terrified faces "The whip will teach you discipline, it will teach you to obey! It will teach you the fear necessary to learn your *place!*" he leaned on the final word, giving it weight. Every man and woman was staring down at the floor so hard they almost pressed their faces against it. Every slave wanted to show that they had discipline, that they knew their place and that they did not need the tines of the whip to strike them. Radoq felt his lip curl in disgust at the fear this bully was able to instil. Natural leadership was a quality to be admired but this was plain brutality.

Latian made a gesture to the guards who remained on the gantry and one of them nodded, moving to a control panel set into the wall. With a groan of screeching metal that seemed only too familiar, the cargo ramp began to lower. Radoq stared at the folly of the man who would attempt such a manoeuvre in flight but the slavers were calm, clearly used to this display. Freezing air rushed in as the black night sky outside was revealed.

"These are the Dark Lands!" Latian pointed with the whip "This is the home of the virals and the Dark Ji!" he stared around, letting the impact of his words settle "Monsters dwell here, death stalks the earth and sunlight never penetrates to the ground. We will not kill you on this ship! We have no need. Any man can kill you now under Xeonison law but here there is a far worse fate. You see – " Latian was getting into his stride now, clearly enjoying his speech "- there is a fate far worse than death or whipping! That fate is freedom!"

Stunned silence.

Latian was nodding "I see the confusion on your faces! Freedom is your greatest desire! But freedom here may not be to your taste..." he turned to face the dark sky and a second later there was a crash as aquar beams stabbed into the darkness. Radoq saw that the ship was low – far too low for safe flight but even as the lights illuminated the wasted ground of the Dark Lands the pilot pushed the throttle and the ship began to rise back into the sky, the effect being that the slaves were treated to a spectacular view of the Dark Lands, glowing in the aquar.

A view of the seething mass of thousands of virals that screeched and roared at the fleeing slaves before the aquar shut off and the cargo ramp slammed shut.

Radoq marvelled at the foolishness of the crew to fly so low over such a crush. He'd seen them leap at such a rashly piloted craft, overpowering the crew and bringing it crashing down to smoking ruin in the Dark Lands. He shook his head as the screams of the slaves rose again but Latian had been waiting for this. He was now close to Radoq, the whip crackling with blue aquar almost as though it were an extension of his mind, responding to the excitement he was surely feeling now he had provoked the slaves into flouting his rules.

"And now you show you have no discipline!" Latian roared "You scream and shriek like children at the sight of the realm of the Dark Ji! Let me warn you that the Dark Ji loves to claim freed slaves! He loves to feed them to his children and he begs us every time we pass to grant him the gift of some soft, warm flesh! Who are we to deny him? What right do we have?" Latian was striding as he spoke and he came to pause next to Radoq who wondered for a moment if he was to be thrown from the ship and he shrugged. It was nothing more than he deserved.

"You –" Latian had lowered his voice and was nudging another slave with his boot "Turn over onto your front." When the man began to beg Latian muttered in a quiet voice for him to get on with it and he'd make it quick. Radoq saw that it was the same lun'erus who'd fed him the extra ration earlier. He caught the man's gaze as he lay down on his belly, his hands shaking with fear.

"This is what happens when you lack discipline!" Latian placed a heavy boot on the slave's legs, pinning them to the deck and swung the whip back over his own head, letting the aquar crackle and burn for maximum effect before he slammed his hand down and laid the first stroke across the man's bare back.

The scream was like nothing human. The stink of burning flesh rose into Radoq's nostrils as Latian let the tines rest on the pale flesh, burning the skin away. He raised the whip again and the scream faded to a whimper.

Crack

The burning again. The slave appeared to have lost consciousness.

Crack

Radoq bowed his head to his chest, closing his eyes to the horror. But there was no respite. In his memory he saw his men incinerated once again by the pinzgats. Hot plasma searing their flesh and bone as they screamed and looked to him, their leader for help. He had miscalculated, a small blunder that in the war they'd fought had meant catastrophe. The lun'erus his father had bidden him protect and lead had looked to him and he had failed them. They had burned and he, solely by the fortune of his Domerus blood, had lived.

Crack

"Domerus…"

Was it a voice from his memory? Perhaps the woman who's hand he had clutched futilely as she died. She'd begged him for help and he'd tugged her towards the medical ship, shouting for a doctor but then he'd looked back and saw that the plasma had burned her away below the waist and she was already dead. Her eyes had stared up at him, still unseeing as he'd abandoned her, searching around for a lun'erus he could still help.

Crack

"Domerus..."

The slave had not blacked out. Instead, he was cursed with consciousness, with feeling every stroke of Latian's lash as it seared the flesh from his back. It was his eyes, burning with the aquar that stared at him. His weak voice that pleaded with Radoq to protect him. The same eyes the woman had looked at him with as he'd let her die.

His father's words filled his mind, spoken to him on the day of his ascension *"Your duty is to the lun'erus. They are why you live and breathe, Domerus."* The duty he'd failed in on the battlefield. The duty that had led him to become a slave, to allow his guilt to overcome him... A wave of resolve burned through Radoq. Malain may have forgotten him, he may have failed his men but here were hundreds who needed him.

Radoq caught the tines of the whip as they fell. It was an impossible stretch for him to grab them. Latian stared at him uncomprehendingly, seeing the inhuman shape of the Domerus' shoulder, understanding that he had dislocated the joint just to stretch around the restriction of the aquar cuffs. The stench of burning flesh was filling the air again but this time it was from Radoq's fingers. His eyes met Latian's and the slaver's widened in terror as he muttered "No..."

"Yes." Radoq tugged and Latian fell forward. The whip fell from Radoq's fingers and he stepped once, twice, his feet hampered by the thick cuffs but that did not stop him reaching around Latian's neck and leaning back, allowing his bodyweight to pull the whip wielding slaver into a classic Tal-Kan hold, his right forearm locked tightly around the man's neck and his legs pinning the whip.

Pandemonium erupted. Shouts, threats and contradictory orders.

"Drop it!"

"Drop him!"

"Shoot him!"

"Stand back!"

Radoq bared his white teeth in a snarl. Around him the slaves had flung themselves flat in expectation of a hail of plasma bolts from the gats of the guards.

"Release the cuffs!"

"Let him go!"

"Release the Chox'd cuffs!"

Radoq relaxed the pressure on Latian's neck one fraction of an inch and the man began to babble in terror "Release him! Do as he says! For Chox's sake, do as he says!"

With a whirr, the blue light vanished from the cuffs and Radoq flung them away from his skin. Latian began to speak but with a sickening crunch, Radoq popped the dislocated shoulder back into its socket, ignoring the pain. Latian flinched, and then died as Radoq gripped his chin and wrenched his neck through a half circle.

"Shoot it!"

Almost in response, Radoq grabbed the berrett that the dead man wore and blasted it towards the nearest pack of guards. He cursed in surprise. Whatever Latian had loaded the weapon with, it was incredibly powerful. A wide oval of plasma bolts erupted from the barrel, filling the air of the hold with heat and glow and the slavers scattered. One was too slow and the rounds impacted with his face, obliterating one side of his head. Radoq saw the glistening and smoking interior of the man's brain before the figure collapsed and suddenly the slavers were running for cover behind the metal of the gantry and any protruding struts.

An alarm began to sound, a repeating klaxon.

Chuk-chuk-chuk the sound of coltac rounds whipping past him flung Radoq to the ground. He saw the enemy, a young woman with beefy arms emptying the coltac with both hands towards him. He levelled the berrett but she was crouched in a cluster of slaves and the spread of his weapon was far too wide to risk firing. Enough lun'erus had died because of his carelessness and he snarled, instead lurching to his feet and running diagonally past her, firing the berrett over her head.

It worked, she flung herself flat imagining the rounds coming towards her and Radoq turned, sprinting the final few yards to close with her. Too late, she saw him coming and raised the coltac but he snatched it from her hand, relying on the Tal-Kan grip to disarm her and pressed the hot barrel to her temple.

Chuk

The superheated energy bolt blew the top half of the slaver into smoking ruin. Radoq, as ever when he killed felt the wave of disgust inside him. He clamped his jaw down hard, refusing to allow the emotions to take over. He ignored the dead woman, now turning her coltac to the other slavers. He fired, a single shot striking the exposed limb of a man who squinted along the barrel of an old fashioned phasr. The man roared in pain and reeled back, knocking the barrel of a slaver beside him who fired anyway, the round tearing into the slaves where screams came. Radoq shot the man with the phasr between the eyes, snarling his victory as he moved, running forward between the ranks of still bound slaves.

"Back! Move back!" a voice of command shouted and the klaxon alarm cut out mid wail. Slavers ran for the gantry, heading up and vanishing through the same metal door the Captain had passed through. A burst of gat fire forced Radoq to duck behind a thick, riveted stanchion and he crouched as the plasma dripped from the metal grinding his teeth in frustration as the slavers slipped one by one to safety.

A lull in the gat fire and Radoq leaned out, firing the coltac one handed. It was a long shot across the gloomy hold and the figure was moving sideways from Radoq's perspective but the plasma caught the slaver on the back, blowing a chunk out of his side and flinging him to lie before the door, blocking the way of the three who were desperately trying to follow him. They turned and spun, one having the presence of mind to fire his phasr at Radoq who was forced back into cover. The other two ran in opposite directions, finally throwing themselves flat on the gantry which provided the most cover.

Silence fell.

Plasma fumes filled Radoq's nostrils and the hot stink of blood was in the air. The slaves were unmoving as though a collective consciousness kept them down on the floor. Radoq quietly stole through their ranks, staring all the while unblinkingly at the remaining slavers who crouched miserably on the gantry. One made to stand and Radoq fired three shots from the stolen coltac which sent the man flat to the ground again and then he was beneath the gantry, able to make out through the holes in the metal where his enemies where.

Chuk

A scream, and then blood dripping down to the floor of the hold.

Two left.

One had moved, clearly able to see Radoq through the same gaps the Domerus used to see him and he stepped sideways, Radoq mirroring him on the ground below, both with barrels pointed at each other, neither able to fire through the angles of the metal.

Step

Step

Lean...

The slaver leaned too far, a simple mistake and Radoq killed him for it, the plasma bolt catching him in the face and flinging him backwards down the metal steps with a tumbling crash. The slaver had no time to scream.

Radoq stepped over the mutilated corpse, eyes fixed on the final slaver. A hissing snap sounded and he registered that the door to the hold had been sealed, the slavers abandoning their colleague to his fate.

Step

Step

And the man was facing the wrong way, thinking Radoq would come up the other stairs.

Chuk

And there were no more slavers in the hold.

Your duty is to the lun'erus

And the Ji was right. Radoq raced to the nearest line of slaves, seeing the heavy collars and chains. Remembering Jucias, he reached the nearest corpse and found the biodigit, pressing it against the collar which popped open.

"Thank you, Domerus –"

"No time. Here, free the others…"

It took time. Time that Radoq knew they didn't have but the slaves, smelling freedom took to the task with a will. Enough biodigits were scattered amongst the dead that the task became swift. Injured slaves were swiftly treated by those skilled in such matters. The dead were moved to one side and laid out the way. Radoq made to cover the door to the hold, putting himself between the lun'erus and any counter attack but to his surprise, a band of fifty or so freed men and women had gathered gats and plasma bolts and were already working on prising open the door.

"Domerus! Can you help?" someone called and Radoq approached, pressing against the thick metal of the door which was flush with the frame.

"I don't think –" he began but a slight woman elbowed him aside.

"All due respect, Domerus, you aren't qualified for this." The small girl shot him a grin filled with cheek and Radoq gave a small bow, conceding the task to her.

With a hiss, it sprang open and Radoq made to lead the charge but with a deafening war cry, the band of freed slaves charged through. The *chuk-chuk* of gatfire sounded quickly along with the screams of battle.

"Stay here, free the rest!" Radoq called to the slight woman who rolled her eyes as though he were stating the obvious.

Radoq charged down what proved to be a long metal walled corridor. A door loomed on his left and he burst through, coltac at the ready but the only living souls were the rebelling slaves. Radoq lowered his weapon and stared at the horror of the scene.

Bunk beds, presumably the crew quarters lined the space at even intervals. On them, between them and painted across them were the shattered and gore strewn remnants of perhaps half a dozen airmen who seemed to have been shot repeatedly with the plasma bolts, eviscerating them.

A woman, a hefty looking phasr clutched in her hands and her face covered in blood that was not her own grinned white teeth at Radoq "Lambs to the slaughter eh, Domerus?" and she vanished towards the sounds of battle.

Radoq followed at a slower pace. He still clutched the coltac but he lowered the barrel, sensing that the fury of the freed lun'erus would be more than enough. Blood and bits of body spattered the insides of the ship and he felt his stomach churning at the gore. Shots still sounded from around him in the maze of corridors and rooms. In each, there was death. Sometimes there were dead slaves but very few. It seemed the speed and ferocity of the assault was overwhelming the crew. Radoq tried to think how he could be the most use and headed for the bridge. Up a flight of metal stairs stepping carefully over a body that at first glance appeared to be undamaged but on closer inspection (coltac held ready) was missing the back of its head and a heavy door marked "Control" was wedged open.

He stepped inside. Attilur, the Captain was the last man alive. His face was bloody and one of his eyes appeared to have been gouged out. Panting and sweating freed slaves stood around him, arguing fiercely over what to do with him. Some were arguing that he was needed to pilot the ship whilst others had already opened a glass panel in the side of the bridge that gave access to the fighting deck and were insisting they toss him out into the Dark Lands.

"Domerus! You can fly the ship, can't you?" someone saw Radoq step into the bridge and he blinked in surprise. Attilur moaned at the sight of the freed Domerus and that seemed to be answer enough for the would-be slaves who with a roar dragged the man to the side of the ship and flung him unceremoniously overboard.

Radoq stared at the spot the Captain had just vacated with his heart racing. The crowd now milled uncertainly amongst the complex controls that made up the giant airship. They were leaderless, a rabble, a mob and voices called out suggestions.

"Where to?"

"The four cities!"

"Volanbuta!"

"Admirain! I've got family there!"

"Admirain!"

"May as well go to the four cities, they're closer!"

"Chox! Lets make a decision before we go down in the Dark Lands!"

"Domerus!" someone addressed Radoq "Where to?"

"Don't ask him! He's Fallen! We don't need a Domerus! We're free now!"

The slight woman who had freed them from the hold appeared in the same door Radoq had entered. She seemed completely unfazed by the death and destruction that filled the bridge "Oi! No point arguing over where we're going when we don't none of us know how to get there!"

Silence greeted her as every eye turned her way. She smiled sardonically before turning to Radoq "Domerus? You know how to fly this thing, don't'cha?"

Radoq bowed his head in agreement.

She smiled in victory "Right. So we do need him." She stalked across to the navigators table, eyeing the glass that tracked across the paper, marking their position "See here?" she glanced around as the shouting mob now gathered quietly and meekly around her "Smack in the middle of the Dark Lands. We go too far south, we hit the Southern Range and fly into a mountain in the dark. Same as if we go too far north." She pointed out the dark shapes of the Northern Massif on the map "Nearest free port is the Eyrie." She stabbed a finger down.

"That's in the Dark Lands!" someone protested "We can't land in the Dark Lands! The virals'll slaughter us!"

The girl with the attitude gave a derisive snort "Eyrie's not in the Dark Lands! It's *above* them! A free town, no virals there to speak of! No, we're going there. Domerus?"

There was arguing. Points were raised and shut down. Radoq watched with interest, remaining out of the debate. The slight girl managed the roughest of the blood spattered group with ease, her small stature and wicked tongue making her an unknown quantity. She wasn't physically threatening and that made most of the tougher figures back down, unsure how to combat her and she was clever which won over most of the rest. In the end, the decision was the same and Radoq obligingly set a course for the Eyrie. Once they were underway, most of the others began to slope out of the bridge, searching the hallways of the ship for any slavers unfortunate enough to miss the first wave of butchery. From the sporadic sound of shots and screams, Radoq gathered there were more than a few hidey-holes.

"Lucky we got you, eh?" the slight girl was standing next to him watching as the sunrise chased the gloom away from the great windows that lined the bridge.

"Indeed." Radoq made an adjustment.

"I'm Evie by the way."

"Radoq."

"Thanks for freeing us, I suppose."

"You're welcome."

Evie paused for a moment and Radoq readied himself for what he was sure was to be a joke at his expense.

"Maybe just let me do the talking with the others though, yeah? Can't say they teach you Domerus much in the way of people skills. No wonder you're all so miserable!" she chuckled at her own joke and vanished to adjust some piece of equipment.

CHAPTER 4

Evie, as it turned out, was a ships' engineer. For the first day as the slave ship trudged across the sky, she filled Radoq's mind with worry, bringing reports of rusted fuel lines, cracked bulkheads and tainted drinking water. Any one of these would have been reason to set down and risk the threat of the virals below them but when he suggested this course of action Evie looked surprised and reassurred him the ship was airworthy. He quickly came to realise that her sharp tongue and bleak prognoses were a defence mechanism to keep her mind focussed on the endless task of repair. There were calm moments though, where she would happily lean and chatter to him without bringing reports of their imminent doom which was a relief.

Her silence was a cause for concern as they leaned on the metal railings of the fighting deck outside the bridge and Radoq turned to her in concern "Problem?"

Evie pointed down to the blackened rock of the Dark Lands, thousands of feet below them. A great crowd of the virals was surging beneath them, climbing over one another as they did. They seemed to be tracking the progress of the ship, following their progress.

"They scare you?" Radoq asked.

Evie looked shocked "Of course! They'd slaughter me if they got close." She looked from the virals back to Radoq "They don't scare you?"

He paused "They didn't. I was raised to fight them. We used to hunt them, my brother and I."

"Chox!" cursed Evie "See, this slave route is why there're so many of them. Slaves die en route and they're chucked out for the virals. Then they get eaten."

"It's a grim business."

"You're right it's a grim business!" Evie's voice rose in consternation "Still, suppose we should be grateful they never cross the Western Hills. Never worked out why."

"My tritus keep those hills secure." Radoq told her "From Fortisul in the north we're charged with keeping the virals at bay from the forest to the foothills."

I'll come back to you

"Is that right?" Evie mused "I thought you were from Solisul in the south."

"No. You know Solisul?"

"Oh yeah! I was trained in Admirain – in the capital." Evie corrected herself "Started out as a lowly dockside techie then worked my way up to aircrew! If I don't know it about hull clamps, bracers and docking procedures it ain't worth knowing!"

She lapsed into a long lecture about her career and how she'd managed to gather the knowledge to climb each step in the ranks. Radoq was impressed. She was young to be so skilled although he sensed her youth and big mouth had held her back beyond her potential. He resolved to find her honest work when they reached the Eyrie, perhaps writing a letter of recommendation but then he remembered the arrest of his tritus and his defeat and his mind spiralled back into dark thoughts…

"Urgh." Evie had shivered. The temperature was well below freezing at this height and she was wearing a great coat several sizes too big. She cast a last look at the seething crush of virals below them "I'd rather fall into the Dark Ji's lap than into that mess!"

Radoq snorted in the failing light.

"What? You mocking me for being scared now, Domerus?"

"No." Radoq shook his head "This 'Dark Ji'. It's farcical."

"Gonna have to run that one by me again."

"Farcical – it's ridiculous. Fantastic. A joke. He isn't real –"

"Might be a she." Evie muttered.

"Might be a she." Radoq agreed "He – or she isn't real. There's never been a Ji who abandoned Wallanria for the Dark Lands. Why would they! The entire point of being a Ji is to lead and direct a tritus! A Ji without a tritus is pointless." He waved a hand dismissively "There's enough real danger in our lives to be afraid of, isn't there? Why go looking for ghosts that don't exist?"

Evie regarded him in silence for a long moment. Then she shook her head "You know, Domerus, that might be the first sensible thing I've heard you say! Come on, the ship won't fly itself you know."

As it happened, the ship *did* more or less fly itself. Radoq spent the hours of darkness as the lun'erus slept familiarising himself with the smaller controls, those that would make fine adjustments to their flight when they docked at the Eyrie. Such a big, bulky transport vessel was not agile and he allowed himself a moment to think mournfully of the sharp lines and gracefulness of the *Golden Kote*, his own ship now lost with his men...

The Eyrie was visible from miles away. As the sunrise filled the world with light, the towering crag rose up out of the Dark Lands like a beacon of life and hope. It was many years since Radoq had set foot upon the city and he drank in the sight greedily. Hundreds of feet high, the crag of dark rock was alone in a landscape of flat ground. Sheer cliff faces lined its sides making it inaccessible from the ground and unreachable by the virals that claimed the Dark Lands as their own. A single route, only wide enough in places for a man to shuffle along sideways, his hands clasping the thin guide rope tightly, led up to the bustling city and it was guarded by a trio of thick stone walls, manned day and night. It ran up the eastern side of the crag and with the benefit of the rising sun behind them, Radoq was treated to a spectacular view of the citadel and its defences.

"... ship... approaching ship. Identify..."

The communicator crackled and Radoq snatched up a handset relaying their identity to a pair of sleek, double hulled patrol ships that were streaking across the morning sky towards them. He was ordered to stop and he wound the engines down to an idle, an action heard across the ship that brought a yawning Evie stumbling into the glass fronted bridge.

"Wassgoinon?"

"We're here. Patrol coming in."

"Good." Evie yawned hugely as though the pinzgats on the patrol ships were not capable of blasting them from the sky "Mebbe they'll bring a pilot for us?"

"I can pilot us in." Radoq protested mildly.

Evie froze mid yawn, a comical sight and indeed, she burst into laughter at Radoq's words "No offence Domerus, but I'd rather someone else did it."

Radoq affected an air of wounded pride as one of the ships clamped itself to the fighting deck and a squad of phasr armed marines tramped across a narrow air bridge, seemingly unaware of the hundreds of feet that lay between them and the ground.

"Domerus – you and your crew are to exit the bridge and engine rooms immediately." The Sergeant was tall for a lun'erus, bearded and grizzled "Send the orders now."

"They aren't my crew, Sergeant." Radoq explained "We're freed slaves. We managed to overpower our captors."

"A Domerus was a slave?" The Sergeant sounded disbelieving and Radoq watched as in painful detail the implication of his own words dawned on the man's face.

Fallen

The respect in his voice tapered off a little and he unceremoniously seized the communicator himself. Radoq and Evie were ushered out of the bridge and a moment later, Radoq felt the thrum as the engines started again, presumably leading them into the Eyrie's skyport.

There followed a series of jerks and clangs which brought a stream of profanities, criticisms and oaths from Evie's lips as she mercilessly mocked the skill of the pilot. Radoq had to agree that he, despite his unfamiliarity with the slave ship would not have flown into the buffer strut of the dock which was surely what that heavy thump had been.

The cargo ramp opened and an authoritative voice began calling instructions. The slaves lined up obediently and filed past teams of clerks who took their names and nationalities down on handhelds, passing them on to waiting medics who rushed the injured off to treatment centres. The process was slow and Radoq forced his mind into stillness, avoiding thoughts of home and of Malain.

I'll come back to you

At odds with his dark thoughts was Evie who kept up a constant patter criticising the efficiency of the processing crew. When she stepped forward and stated her name and occupation to the clerk he looked surprised and sent her to stand with a slowly growing group of freed slaves all of whom were being questioned at length by Eyrie port officials who seemed to be interested in their various trades. Radoq nodded a goodbye to Evie, intending to see her once he'd been processed but as he approached the clerk who glanced once at the Domerus towering over him the man pressed a switch on his handheld before asking the questions.

"Name?"

"Radoq Loxelsus Po-Fortisun."

"From Fortisul?"

"Correct."

"Fallen?"

Radoq blinked at the intrusive question but before he could answer, a marine bearing the insignia of a Captain had approached with a cluster of phasr bearing soldiers.

"You – Domerus. You're to come with us."

The clerk looked askance at his incomplete handheld but the Captain ignored him, gesturing for Radoq to follow. It seemed he wasn't under arrest although as the marines avoided catching his eyes, Radoq couldn't help but feel concern. He glanced over at Evie but she was already deep in conversation with a dock master, gesticulating at the interior of the slave ship.

"This way." The Captain insisted and Radoq followed him

through the confusing crowd of refugees.

"Where are we going, Captain?"

"To the higher district." The Captain pointed up and Radoq saw the towering buildings of the Domerus. Set at the highest level of the Eyrie, long white columns faced each building which seemed to be stretching to tower over one another. The district, Radoq knew from memory contained more than the towering government buildings, the luxury villas of the Domerus were nestled there too as well as the smaller sky docks where the sleek racing yachts or outdated pleasure cruisers, their ancient gasbag and suspended sailboat hull looking as ridiculous as ever would be docked.

Down here in the main skyport, the common ships were visible as the Captain led them up a wide walkway along which cargo and people were hurrying to and fro. Great towering cargo ships with their distinctive tri-ball shaped hulls were moored next to cranes and stacks of goods. Modern, sleek delivery ships painted white and blue unloaded mail which was whisked away into the heart of the Eyrie. The battleships, bristling with troops and weighed down by pinzgats spoke to the fortitude of the mountain city. The Eyrie depended on trade to bring food and goods to the barren land and their sky force kept the trade routes open and free of pirates.

"Here." The Captain stopped abruptly at a transit point. They'd passed several of these already, small metal gondolas attached to a thin metal cable that snaked up into the higher tiers of the Eyrie. There were dozens, perhaps hundreds of these all interweaving in a complex tangle of guide lines that Radoq could see were built with mathematical precision. He watched with interest as the Captain and his men crammed into the small space. A chipped metal sign on one wall explained the limitations of the control panel reading 'NO MORE THAN 100 PFQ AT ANY TIME'. The Captain called a command and one of his men gently eased forward a control valve that spun the needle on a dial. The man's eyes never left the dial, watching to ensure it didn't exceed the stated 100 PFQ.

"Steady now." One of the other men called unnecessarily betraying perhaps a fear of flight because flight was now what was happening. Above them, Radoq knew, the small 'gasbag' atop the gondola would be rushing into a small vakkor engine which would enable the mechanism to become buoyant, lifting the gondola from the ground. The cable was simply to guide the vehicle up a pre-determined route and the maximum stated PFQ was a safety measure to prevent them straying into another cable line. Despite the uncertainty of his current predicament, Radoq found himself smiling at the efficiency of the system.

The upper tier was quiet after the bustle of the sky port. Here there were few people and the narrow streets were clean swept and the buildings smart. The Captain exited the gondola first, leading Radoq up a steep slope that had the marines sweating and stopping outside of an ornate building that sat in the shadow of a tower. A government building? Certainly, it was not a private residence, that much was clear from the armed guards posted to either side of the door. They allowed the Captain and Radoq through a heavy iron door that swung shut behind them. Radoq was marched down a long, sparsely decorated corridor and then through a maze of left and right turns until they reached a set of double wooden doors that, in this treeless land, must have cost a fortune to have made and shipped. The Captain knocked once, stepped back and marched away leaving Radoq alone in the corridor.

The door swung inwards and a lun'erus butler immediately began to offer Radoq refreshments. A table had been laid with great cuts of meat, stewed greens and thick cheeses. Radoq thanked the man but left the food, despite his hunger. Instead, he looked around the large room that had the appearance of an office. A smart print of a well-dressed Domerus hung over one wall and Radoq narrowed his eyes trying to think as a name hovered at the edge of his memory...

A second door this one smaller and lighter opened and the Domerus from the picture strode in. Older, with silvering hair but clearly the same man. He bowed in true Domerus fashion, with a wide gesturing arm.

"I have the honour to be Argan Pireunsus Ji-Trakkus."

Radoq returned the bow with less flourish "Radoq Loxelsus Po-Fortisun."

Argan smiled "We know of each other, I'm sure."

Radoq nodded. Any Domerus knew the name of Argan. An older man now, to be sure but fifty years ago he'd dominated the Tal-Kan duels, defeating Domerus from almost every tritus in Wallanria. He'd led troops against the virals that had erupted into Ychacha, making a name for himself at the last stand of the fallen City. His own father, then the Ji of the tritus had ordered him to retreat at the last minute, abandoning the city to the virals. As far as Radoq knew, the man had never duelled again but as a young man Radoq had watched countless hours of the man's sparring, trying to get inside the head of the master duellist.

"I was there five years ago in Admirain when you nearly tore that Wallsan girl's head off!" there was genuine admiration in Argan's voice "I saw the Crown Prince pin the golden kote on your biom myself." His eyes followed Radoq's down to the biom that had encased his left hand ever since his ascension. The kote still rested there although under the layers of grime and blood it was barely visible. A flicker of distaste covered Argan's face and his tone changed "My men tell me that you no longer hold the ascension of your tritus?".

Radoq simply held his gaze.

"I thought as much." Argan turned away, apparently affected by the awkwardness of the subject.

Radoq stayed standing still, wondering what subject the Ji was skirting around so delicately. The intrigue of tritus courts had never been his forte. His father had tried to instruct him on the various political machinations but Radoq struggled to see the layers of complex meaning and inference. He'd tended to rely instead on his charisma, intelligence and strength to outwit most adversaries and now he simply stood and waited, wondering what Argan would offer.

"I have a deal I would like to offer you." Argan had turned to face Radoq "I need you to perform a task. It is not a task of honour but one in your condition is not hampered by such frivolities." Radoq blinked at the insult "Your reward for completing this task – should you be successful – is that I will ascend you to my tritus. You will become Radoq Loxelsus Po-Trakkus."

"Po?" Radoq questioned.

"Yes. I have no living descendants. My Ji will pass to a distant cousin when I die. This way, I will make you my heir. It's a natural fit. The two of us hold golden kotes, people will assume we made an honourable deal."

Radoq nodded, simply waiting for the man to spit out whatever it was he was nervous to say.

Argan cleared his throat, puffing his chest out "I want you to kill a Domerus."

CHAPTER 5

Confusion. Why would Argan want a fellow Domerus dead? And more importantly, how?

"Do you want me to challenge them to a duel?"

Argan let out a derisive bark of laughter "No! No Domerus will duel you in this condition. Hah! You wouldn't be able to execute even the most basic Tal-Kan strike! Do your eyes even have the aurae anymore? No. No, my boy. I want you to take a coltac, sneak into the Ji's mansion and blow his brains out. Make it look like a lun'erus snuck in. Blame it on those slaves you freed."

"You want me to murder a Ji?" Radoq could not keep the disgust from his voice. He could not remember the last time a Domerus had been murdered. There were duels to the death of course and inter tritus wars broke out on the odd occasion but murder was so rare he could not think of when it had happened last.

Argan had the grace to look embarassed "I understand your reticence, Radoq. It's not the usual course of action but Oprain Radoqsus Ji-Brassul is a dishonourable man. He effectively rules the Eyrie despite never having been appointed to do so." Argan's lip curled "He's a Chox'd merchant! Nothing more. The man has never lifted a finger to fight the virals. Never done his duty as a Domerus. He's sat and made himself fat and rich for two centuries! You do this for me, Radoq and you will inherit the Eyrie when I die. What say you?"

Radoq blinked in surprise but as he suspected, his consent was not required. Instead, Argan reached under his desk and produced a smart looking black coltac. He showed Radoq the mechanism, demonstrating how to conceal it beneath his clothes.

"My men will get you into Oprain's office. You'll be a delivery boy bringing something from the sky port. It's a simple task, Radoq."

Entering the mansion was easy. Argan's lun'erus gave Radoq a heavy package to push on a vakkor engine trolley with a low handle, making him lean forward to push it. This hid his height from the staff of the mansion who barely spared him a glance. He was directed through a dozen corridors, taking in the opulence of the decoration before he stopped at the open door of a scholarly looking study.

"Yes?" A Domerus stood in the door looking surprised "You have a delivery for me?" he stood back, gesturing for Radoq to enter the room which was untidy, in contrast to the rest of the house. Books and scrolls lined the walls and were stacked on the dusty carpet. A writing desk, much like the one in Argan's office stood against one wall but was hidden beneath yet more books.

"Well?" the Domerus was becoming suspicious "Do you have a shipment manifest for me?"

Radoq stood to his full height for the first time and the Domerus frowned. Radoq smiled apologetically "No. I'm afraid I'm here to kill you."

The Domerus smiled as though waiting for the rest of the joke but his eyes took in Radoq's stature, his biom and the ragged state of his clothes "Have I done something to offend you young man?"

Radoq shook his head "No. Although I believe Argan Pireunsus Ji-Trakkus has taken something of an – ah – dislike to you."

"Argan!" the Domerus clenched a fist which Radoq noticed was lined and ancient. Oprain – presuming this was he – was an old man, at least three centuries if Radoq was any judge. He began to pace up and down in frustration "I suppose you're here to challenge me?"

Radoq shook his head "I'm here because I was brought here." He bowed formally "May I present myself. Radoq Loxelsus Po-

Fortisun."

Oprain stopped "Loxel? Of Fortisul? I know your father, young Radoq. Knew him well oh, fifty years ago? Ah – where are my manners?" he bowed stiffly "Oprain Radoqsus Ji-Brassul" Oprain smiled "My father is your namesake. I believe you were named for him."

Radoq started, marvelling at the coincidence "My father is a friend of yours still?"

"I'm afraid my books are my closest friends these days." Oprain gestured at the mess around them "But yes, Loxel and I were dear friends back when we were younger men. Loxel Jiquinsus Po-Fortisun as he was then." Oprain smiled "We used to nickname him 'Ji' because his name was Jiquinsus. It used to drive him mad!"

"You were with him at the fall of Ychacha?"

"Yes." Oprain nodded sadly "I gave up fighting after that defeat. An awful campaign. But your father proved his mettle there! His Tal-Kan was second to none – much like your own if I'm not mistaken?"

Radoq smiled modestly. Despite the conflict raging in his mind he found himself liking the old man.

"I suppose you aren't going to kill me?" Oprain smiled and Radoq shook his head. Oprain frowned "If you weren't to challenge me then by what method was I to be exterminated?"

Radoq slowly produced the coltac, laying it carefully on the messy desk.

"The scum! Murder? In the Eyrie? Agh!" Oprain seemed overcome with rage for a moment as he muttered incoherently. When he'd regained control he turned to Radoq "That man is as corrupt a Ji as any I've ever met. For two hundred years I've built the Eyrie from a filthy smuggling port to a bustling trade hub. It is my life's work! And at every turn Argan has bribed, corrupted and lied to block me! All he wants is control, power and status! As though he doesn't have that! The man is insane." Oprain shook his head "This is a step too far! I'll have him before the court by the time the day is out. What a fool!"

Radoq nodded dutifully.

"May I ask what Argan offered you in return for my death?"

"He offered to ascend me into his tritus. I was to be Po to him."

Oprain stared for a moment in disbelief before breaking out into a great guffaw of laughter "The fool! The power-blinded fool! Can he not see?"

"It would seem not."

Oprain laughed until tears ran down his face before he sent for a lun'erus servant and ordered him to report the scheme. The man hastened to the constabulary to report the attempted murder.

"You must tell me how you came to be here, dressed in such a manner!" Oprain demanded as he and Radoq sat at a dining table well laid with Domerus dishes. This time, Radoq gave in to his hunger and filled his stomach with the rich dishes. He recounted the tale as briefly as he could, telling of his defeat and his enslavement.

"The slave trade is a curse on these lands." Oprain scowled "If I had the agreement of the council I could destroy their vile business in a month! You've seen our sky port. We have ample ships and men! But they dither and argue and claim not to want to start a war. I ask you, what honour is there in claiming to be a civilised society if we allow that to happen just beyond our borders?"

A thought occurred to Radoq "Perhaps I could take the captured ship and attack them for you? I could –"

"You have a home of your own, Radoq." Oprain's tone was not harsh but it was firm.

Radoq lowered his eyes "I heard a rumour that my tritus was arrested."

"Arrested?" Oprain frowned "I had heard there was a new Sheriff appointed but your father? Arrested? It sounds unlikely." He summoned a servant and spoke to the man in hushed tones "I will make some enquiries, my friend but I suspect the rumours have been exaggerated. In any case, they will be delighted to know you are alive. Word of your death had passed through the

Eyrie –"

"They thought I was dead?" Radoq rose from his chair in shock as emotion surged through him.

Oprain peered at him as though he were dense "Radoq, your army was slaughtered, your ship captured and your body unaccounted for. What in the name of Chox did you think they would hear?"

"I –" Radoq sat down heavily. He couldn't bear the thought of the pain he had put his family through. To think he was dead? It was intolerable.

"I think I understand." Oprain had stood up and walked around the table to place a fatherly hand on Radoq's shoulder "I suffered a defeat once as a young man. Not as great as yours but I felt like a failure."

"I know what I did." Radoq started but Oprain cut him off.

"No. I'm not about to tell you that you didn't fail. Failure is a part of life." He cleared his throat "What I learned when I was in the position that you find yourself in now was that I sat and wallowed in my own misery, seeking recrimination and punishment for my actions. That seemed logical and worthy at the time. Am I close to what you're thinking?"

Radoq gave a single nod, fiddling with the cutlery on the table before him.

"Yes. And what I learned – aside from the specific mistake that I had made – was that self-pity is a fallacy that we put ourselves into to help with the guilt." Oprain placed his other hand on Radoq's shoulder so that he gripped the younger man firmly "The fact is, Radoq, you are hiding behind your self-pity and your guilt for your failure and you've forgotten that you're a Po of tritus Fortisun."

Radoq turned sharply at this "I've forgotten nothing!"

"Then why are you here, supping with me and being manipulated by Argan when your family needs you at home?"

Radoq stared at the older man. He was right, of course and a wave of frustration welled up inside of him. He stood, cursing as he did so.

"Take a moment, young Radoq."

He took a moment, nodding and closing his eyes as he understood "I'm still a Fortisun. My tritus and my people need me."

"And a certain young lady of the Hammuns if court gossip is anything to judge?" Oprain said with a sly smile.

I'll come back to you

Radoq did not smile "I hear she's married someone else."

"Really." Oprain did not sound like he cared "All the more reason to return to your home and win her back then, eh?"

"What if – what if the families of the lun'erus I failed want my blood? What if –"

"What if? What if? The men you led were soldiers, were they not? Men who volunteered to serve you and your tritus? Their families will be grieving, Radoq! Some may be angry but most will be broken. They will need you to tell them of their children, their husbands, their fathers! Tell them how they died valiantly in battle, without fear or pain! Support the families who can no longer afford to eat! Your duty is still to your men, even when they are dead! Chox, Radoq! The self-pity! It's blinding you!" Oprain's eyes flashed with anger. Radoq held his gaze, fresh guilt washing over him at his lack of action.

"I should go."

"Go! Of course you should go! You have a ship, do you not? I can arrange for it to be released to you. But before you go running off, wait for my man to return with information about Fortisun. Your people and your family will not thank you if this new Sheriff arrests you the moment you step foot in your home! Come, let us distract ourselves with the Great Game. Do you play Sagalm?"

"Of course." Radoq saw the sense in Oprain's tactic and he joined the man in front of the complex board, moving his pieces with strategy and cunning –"

"Not as well as you practice Tal-Kan!" Oprain exclaimed, taking Radoq's prince in a swift move and winning the game "Strategy has not been your strongest suit has it my friend?"

Radoq conceded that it had not. He was more at home facing his enemies down in the Tal-Kan ring or at the end of a phasr than outwitting them.

"Then may I suggest that on your return to Fortisul you do not change your current attire?" Oprain looked meaningfully at the grubby lun'erus clothes that Argan had given him to wear.

"For what –" Radoq nodded at his own question "I should be in disguise? To approach the situation with guile and subterfuge?"

"Well…" Oprain shrugged "At least to approach with some strategy. That seems to me to be a better approach than running in headfirst."

"Perhaps to you." Radoq muttered and Oprain affected not to hear as he cleared the board.

The sky port was reached in the sleek racing yacht that Oprain kept moored to his home. Radoq took the controls, bringing them in a wide arc around the Eyrie and into the shipping lane that allowed them to dock. He nestled the craft gently against an expensive mooring and a pair of dock techs greeted Oprain warmly.

"Oi! Domerus!" called a familiar voice and Radoq turned to see Evie waving to him.

"A friend of yours?" Oprain asked.

Radoq explained the part she'd played in reaching the Eyrie and Oprain greeted her politely, thanking her for taking part in the small reduction of the slave trade."

"Cheers." Was her laconic response. She looked up at Radoq "Where we going now then?"

Oprain blinked at the familiarity before turning away to hide a smile. Radoq glanced at the towering bulk of the slave ship they'd liberated "I need to go home."

"Oh yeah? Well you aren't walking are you?" Evie pointed out "When we flying?"

"We need a crew –"

"Got one! You're the Captain, I'm the chief engineer, just need half a dozen deck hands and we're away!"

"Indeed you are." Oprain had managed to control his humour

at Evie's personality "I can ensure the ship is registered in your name. Perhaps you'll take a shipment with you to Fortisul? There'd be no taxes to pay."

"'Course!" Evie responded for Radoq "Not running a ferry service are we? Need to make some coin to pay my chief engineer salary! Which we can talk about once we're underway..." she smiled evilly at Radoq.

"Very well. We have to wait for... some other information." He looked significantly at Oprain who nodded.

"Alright. She's not ready yet anyway." Evie turned to Oprain "Alright if we go first thing?"

Oprain nodded gravely and Evie smiled brightly.

Next morning brought strong winds blowing out of the Dark Lands which dampened even Evie's unfailing humour. In fact, she became positively depressed assuring Radoq that they'd be blown into the ground before they'd travelled an hour towards Fortisul.

"We'll wait another day then." Radoq promised, only to be thrown by Evie looking askance at him.

"Wait? Wait? We've already waited all night! Chox'd techies are done aren't they? You're just waiting for the all clear from your Domerus mate!"

"You said we'd crash!"

"I said we *might*! Chox, it's no wonder the country's in a shambles if you Domerus always miss the point like that." Evie rolled her eyes and stalked up the lowered cargo ramp to argue with the Eyrie's dockside tech's who'd spent a sleepless night bringing the hulking former slave transport up to their rigorous safety standards. Radoq shook his head at the impossibility of her behaviour then turned as a well dressed lun'erus approached him.

"Domerus, this is from Oprain Radoqsus Ji-Brassul." Radoq accepted a handheld from the man who bowed and left. Inside was a scrawled note from the Ji bidding him fair winds and fortune and instructing him to get underway as soon as practical. Radoq called out to Evie who rolled her eyes and shouted commands sending the Eyrie technicians scurrying for the dock. Minutes later, Radoq was steering the lumbering craft through the complex shipping lanes of the sky port and heading north west towards home.

"Take us a bit higher would you, Domerus?" Gul, a leading airman they'd hired on the dock looked an interesting shade of green next to Radoq on the bridge.

Radoq looked at the man in surprise, not having marked him for a fearful sort "Are you afraid the virals will reach us? We're at several hundred feet."

Gul shook his head instead pointing to the Dark Lands below them "It's the glowing rocks, Domerus. Cause tainting of the blood." He glanced awkwardly at Radoq's tatty, apparently Fallen appearance "For you too, now I'd guess."

Radoq stared at the man who suddenly blushed, realising he'd overstepped a boundary but Radoq dipped his head in acknowledgement, adjusting the controls and sending the ship's nose skywards. At this height the first of the Western Hills became a faint smudge on the horizon and Radoq gazed at them with a homesick longing, remembering wild hunts with Malain and his brother Gellian as they'd stalked and slaughtered the virals as they attempted to breach the border of the Dark Lands. As the ship levelled out and the first of the peaks that sheltered Fortisul appeared, Radoq's mood soured and he felt small beads of sweat form on his palms. He tried to calm himself with Oprain's words about duty and self pity but instead, all he could see was Malain's face as on the day he'd left Fortisul, holding her tears back and forcing a smile.

I'll come back to you

CHAPTER 6

As he stepped onto the dock Radoq took a deep breath, relishing the thin wisps of cloud that hung in the mountain air. The lun'erus on the dock were wrapped in thick cloaks and gloves against the chill but Radoq rejoiced as he felt the last of the scorching desert heat finally leave his lungs.

The dock lights had been dimmed as dawn chased the worst of the low cloud higher up the three peaks that surrounded the natural bowl of Fortisul. Unlike the Eyrie, Radoq's mountain home sprawled over a plateau worn by melting glaciers. A trio of icy mountain waterfalls cascaded into well-engineered channels that watered the city before tumbling over the edge, down, down, down to the lowlands of the valley floor. There, the lun'erus that farmed the land benefited from the purity of the water making Fortisul valley one of the greenest and most bountiful provinces in Wallanria.

Evie was suitably unimpressed when Radoq regaled her with this trivia but she gave an impressed grunt when she saw the channelled waterfalls and the complex network of pipes that ran at intervals under the city. She went quiet as Radoq, his face well concealed under a thick scarf wound around his mouth and nose, led her up a flight of carved steps to the top of the boundary wall, gesturing in silent amazement as they stared over the great expanse of eastern Wallanria.

"Is that the forest?" Evie pointed at the green-brown smudge many miles away and Radoq nodded pointing out the walls of Napp, just visible at the western extremity of the trees. Directly west of Fortisul, the trade road to Chrohold, the northernmost of the four cities was visible as a dark, twisting smear winding its way through farmlands and small towns.

"Oi!" a rough voice shouted and the two of them turned from the magnificent view to see a woman in the uniform of a customs agent looking at them expectantly "Did you two miss the sign or something?" she indicated the very prominent directions to the customs house that were set at regular intervals throughout the docks. Radoq ducked his head as the ire of the customs officer drew curious looks from the few lun'erus out this early. Hastily, he and Evie hurried down and filled out the necessary paperwork for the ship they'd named 'Freedman'.

"Got another ship of that name already." The customs agent grunted without looking up from the tattered handheld "Gonna call yours 'Freedman 2'."

Evie rolled her eyes at Radoq but he kept his face downcast, not wanting to be recognised however when she told them the docking fee he nearly choked in surprise.

"So cheap? Does the new Sheriff not like money?"

The customs woman shrugged "Sheriff doesn't have any say over docking fees. Fact is we can't get merchants to land here with that hovering over us." She jerked a gloved thumb up at the low cloud that still hid the three peaks.

Radoq followed her gaze with a small frown on his face, quickly turning to a gasp of wonderment as what he'd assumed were the half-visible hulls of patrol ships suddenly loomed through a gap in the rapidly shifting white mass and he found himself staring at an untidy mass of vakkor gondolas, tightly rigged cables and unevenly welded platforms that vanished back into the cloud.

"Volanbuta!" Evie cried in excitement, naming the famed flying city. Radoq could well understand the frustration of the customs agent. Volanbuta existed only for trade and was known as a hub for every type of goods, currency and desirable trinket in the known world. Radoq had never seen it docked at Fortisul, it usually stayed in the south, close to the Wallanrian sea over which it returned home to Xeonison at the end of every season.

"How long has it been here?" he asked the agent.

"Six weeks? The new Sheriff invited them from what I'm told."

"Six weeks? You lowered the docking fees already?"

"Things were going badly here long before old 'Volly turned up. New Sheriff hasn't a clue about how to run the place." She eyed Radoq for a moment "You a local?"

"We're from the Eyrie. I've spent time here though."

She nodded sagely "Chox'd Crown Prince sends us a new Sheriff without ever bothering to ask us. Didn't need a new one, need him even less now. Locked half the tritus up in the keep and now he's selling half the food in the province to those Chox'd fools!" rant over, the customs agent turned away still staring at her handheld.

Radoq let out a breath "Things are worse than I thought."

"Yeah." Evie agreed "Probably going to be a full scale rebellion on the streets. We should get up to Volanbuta and stay there. Best to be mobile if the whole town's going to tear itself apart."

Radoq rolled his eyes at her defeatism but even from the sky port he could see the towering white turrets of the Fortisun mansion and he could spare his friend no more patience and he bade Evie goodbye, stepping into the streets of his home.

Fortisul was filthy. Dirty strands of rotting straw filled the gutters along with scraps of shattered wood, more than a handful of dead rats and suspicious piles of debris that looked like they'd been placed intentionally to cover some hidden crime. Radoq wrinkled his nose at the stench of the place, an almost fruity smell of decay and filth. The lun'erus that passed him by walked quickly and purposefully, avoiding eye contact. That suited Radoq to a point beneath his hood and scarf but as he strode into the main square with its ornate waterfall fed fountain he became more and more concerned. Beggars dressed in rags were scattered in small groups crouched on piles of filthy blankets. A sight that Radoq had never seen in his hometown. Of course, there was always poverty in some form in such a densely populated space but his tritus had always stepped in to feed and house the most needy. No-one had ever lived on the streets in his memory and he wondered at the apathy of the new Sheriff that he would let the townspeople suffer in such a way. The sight of a pair of well dressed city guards strolling gently past the fountains, ignoring the suffering of the beggars sent a wave of anger surging through Radoq but he forced himself to remain calm.

He left the main square, following the street named for the capital city of Admirain, leaning forward as he climbed the steep slope. At the side of the smooth roadway were carved hundreds of shallow steps to enable the lun'erus to more easily climb to the higher districts. Remembering his disguise, Radoq stepped into them, finding himself regularly pressing his back to the stone walled buildings that lined the street to enable others to pass by on their way down the steps.

The cloud park loomed around the final steps in a tightly twisting staircase that was wide enough for a single figure to pass. A green expanse of well cultivated grass bordered by neat white stone walls on each side greeted Radoq and despite the squalor he'd seen below, he smiled at the luxury of the familiar sight. Long hours as a boy spent racing around the grass with his brother filled his mind and over there, just beyond the memorial to Ychacha was the quiet spot known as Lovers Leap where he'd made his final promise to Malain.

I'll come back to you

And he had. But of Malain, or indeed of any Domerus there was no sign. The cloud park itself was more or less empty although at this time of day that wasn't unusual. Still, the skies above them lay bare of the sleek racing yachts that would normally be skimming below the low cloud, their crews shrieking and laughing as the cold air blasted their faces. Radoq wondered if it was a measure put in place now that Volanbuta hung overhead. A safety precaution to prevent mid-air collisions.

"Up?" the laconic greeting came from a uniformed woman stood by a gondola not unlike those in the Eyrie although this one was tatty and lacked the smart glass windows of those in

Oprain's city. By her accent the woman was Xeonision which meant she lived and worked in Volanbuta. She also looked thoroughly uninterested when Radoq shook his head at her and went back to leaning on the side of her drab vehicle.

"Where is everyone?" Radoq questioned and she turned a surprised look on him.

"How the Chox should I know?"

"It's usually bustling up here."

She shrugged "Not since I've been here. Six weeks I've been stood here and I've got what, a dozen rides a week? You'd think old 'Volly was more interesting. Still, when it's as cold as this I can't blame people." She shivered for dramatic effect.

"Do you only go to Volanbuta?" he asked.

In response, she gestured at the slack cable that led into the cloud above "Singles and returns only. Why, where you tryna go?"

"Domerus tiers." Radoq muttered offhand, trying to look as lun'erus as possible.

The Xeonision girl sucked her teeth in surprise "Wouldn't go there today. Big protest again. Guards'll be looking to crack heads I shouldn't wonder."

"Protest?"

She looked at Radoq as though he were stupid "You just flown in or something?"

"Yes, actually."

"You saw all the dirt on your way up the hill though, yeah? Think people are happy about that?" she shuddered "I know I'm not going down there anytime soon! More'n my life's worth! One of our lads got a knife in his back from a beggar couple of weeks ago. Whole place is about to go off like a nuklera!"

Radoq blinked in surprise, thanking the girl and heading at a renewed pace along the length of the park. His mind whirled, he couldn't remember a lun'erus protest ever taking place en masse. Of course, there'd be the odd angry voice in the public assemblies, usually complaining about viral sightings in the Western Hills but they were satisfied quickly. For his entire life

Fortisul had been a peaceful and prosperous city.

"Watch it!" a voice close at hand snapped and Radoq stepped smartly aside as a lun'erus he didn't recognise dressed in the finery of a Fortisun servant marched past him. The northern end of the cloud park had a few more visitors now and as he watched the unknown servant stride away he suddenly sat down heavily on a nearby bench, his heart racing.

Striding along behind his servant, lines of stress and worry on his face was Gellian, Radoq's younger brother. Briefly, their eyes met before Radoq quickly bowed his head and Gellian carried on, apparently not feeling the shock of recognition that had burned through Radoq like the aquar of the slaver's whip. He watched as his brother and the servant exited the park up the white marble steps that led to the Domerus tiers. When they'd vanished from view, Radoq stood and headed after them.

The tiers were luxurious and a far cry from the dirt of the streets below. Radoq couldn't help but feel pride at the ornate architecture of his home, so much more decorative than the cramped spaces of the Eyrie. Here there were more Domerus and more than one glanced curiously at him, unused to seeing a lun'erus of such stature. Radoq slowed his pace, bending his head over to minimise his height but at the first opportunity he turned into a side street, avoiding the main walkways. Of his brother, he could see no sign but there were chanting voices coming from somewhere close at hand that drew his attention. Radoq headed ever upwards, following the now familiar paths towards his family home.

A figure rushed past him, heading towards the growing sound of chanting. Not a Domerus, instead this was a young and scruffy looking lun'erus, almost dressed as raggedly as the beggars in the lower tiers. Curiosity drew Radoq after the lad and he turned a corner back onto the main street and found himself at the back of a chanting crowd of lun'erus.

"Stop selling our grain! Stop selling our grain!"

The chant took a few repeats before he could discern the words but Radoq frowned in consternation when he worked it out. With his extra height he could see over the heads of the lun'erus but even so, he knew from memory they were only a short distance from the Sheriff's keep and surely well within earshot.

The crowd grew both in size and volume as lun'erus flowed in small groups from the surrounding streets. From their dress, Radoq could see they had come from the lower tiers and he wondered at the organisation it would have taken for them to gather in this spot. Surely there was a mastermind to this? He looked around him, now surrounded by the chanting figures but no-one seemed to be taking charge.

A rhythmic thumping began and he looked for a drum but instead, the sound came from an armoured squad of Sheriff's guards emerging from the keep at the far end of the street. Marching in regular step they headed directly for the protestors who only shouted louder as though their voices alone could halt the soldiers who stopped in neat ranks a stone's throw from the crowd.

"Friends!" a tall figure had stepped from the chanting ranks and turned to face them, his arms held high for silence. The chants died away as the man beamed at the lun'erus "My dear friends, thank you for coming to these higher tiers! Today, we let the Sheriff know that we will not stand for his greed!"

Raucous cheers at this. The chants began again and the speaker had to hold his hands up.

"This Xeonison rust heap is turning our city into a quagmire of poverty and hunger!" the speaker gestured at Volanbuta, now mostly visible through the receding clouds.

"Get rid of it!" shouted a voice to cheers of agreement.

"The Sheriff must remove it from our city! But he will never do so whilst he can line his fat pockets selling Fortisul's food to those flying brigands!"

Radoq raised an eyebrow. The Sheriff selling grain? He wondered how the man had managed to get control of the supply. Fortisul had a free market where the farmers sold their own produce. Mills and bakeries in town competed for the best price but there had never been a centralised store for crops.

"Get rid of him, Juraj!" roared a man close to Radoq and the crowd began to bay the name.

"*Juraj! Juraj! Juraj!*"

Juraj smiled at the sound, shooting a measured glance over his shoulder at the Sheriff's guards who stood silent "I am Juraj Aption! I am no Sheriff but I am here for you! I am here to say that today is *enough*!"

Apparently someone had had enough. Radoq saw a guard with the stripes of a Sergeant on his shoulder look at the screen of a handheld. He turned and snapped an order to his men and they began to march forward, great aquar tipped clubs in their hands.

"See!" Juraj was shouting "See how the Sheriff will protect himself! Brute force and thuggery! He will never let you be free! He will see us starve!"

The guards drew closer and lun'erus at the back of the crowd began to run, fleeing into side streets. Radoq stood his ground, eyes locked on the charismatic Juraj.

"Run, my friends! Run to fight another day!" a pair of guards struck Juraj simultaneously with their clubs and the aquar charge sent him crashing to the floor. As one, the protestors broke and surged backwards past Radoq who stepped forward instinctively to stop himself being knocked over. He found himself standing over the prostrate Juraj and bent down to help him to his feet. The man was white faced and shaking from the shock of the guard's clubs but he met Radoq's eyes and nodded his thanks.

"Enough!" the Sergeant had approached and Radoq saw that he and Juraj were part of a group of half a dozen lun'erus that had been cornered by the squad "These'll do. Get the cuffs."

"What about the others?" a guard asked but the Sergeant dismissed them.

"Leave 'em. Sheriff said take six. Now, you lot –" he addressed Radoq and the other prisoners "It's one night in the cells for you. Don't go making a fuss and it'll all be fine. 'Specially you." He pointed his club at Juraj who was still breathless from the shock.

The cuffs locked around Radoq's wrists with a crackle of aquar. He briefly considered escaping but Juraj was still leaning heavily on him and it didn't seem like he was in any immediate danger. Better, he thought, to speak to this man and to find out what had been happening in his home town. He remembered Oprain lecturing him over their Sagalm game and so he kept his mouth shut as the guards marched the six of them along the street and into the keep.

The cells were not uncomfortable with straw spread out across the floor and the prisoners that already occupied them looked simply bored rather than maltreated.

"One night, you're out in the morning." Called a jailer with heavy looking muscles "No-one give me any problems and we'll all part as chums." he left.

"My friend." Juraj was resting on the straw but he offered his hand to Radoq in a formal introduction "Thank you for your help. My name is Juraj Aption."

"Attilur." Radoq responded, grasping the name of the slave ship Captain at random.

Juraj shook his hand "A pleasure, Attilur. Are you local?"

"Yes. But I've been away for some time." Radoq made sure to sit down, the better to hide his height.

Juraj nodded "Then you'll know little of our plight!"

"In fact, I only arrived back in Fortisul this morning." Radoq admitted "It's fallen a great deal since I was last home."

Juraj's mouth twitched in something close to a smile.

"Something amusing?" Radoq questioned.

Juraj turned his head to one side to regard Radoq differently. He could sense the keen intellect behind the man's eyes and wondered at it. He noticed suddenly that the other prisoners in their cell were watching the exchange closely. No, not watching, *guarding* Juraj and he realised that these were the lun'erus' own men and they were wondering if he, Radoq was a threat.

"Not amusing, so much as ironic. You say the city has fallen but not as much as you have, Domerus."

CHAPTER 7

There was nothing to be said to that and Radoq shrugged in response, saying nothing.

"I'm sorry, I know amongst your kind its considered an impolite subject." Juraj smiled.

A second shrug seemed the most pertinent response.

Juraj gave a chuckle "I'll ask no more, my friend. Just know for now that I'm grateful for your help today and I look after those who help me."

"What is it that I'm helping you in?"

Juraj nodded as though he'd anticipated the question "You're right to ask. The new Sheriff Tricial Pulciasus Ap-Jatuh is Xeonision. He –"

"A Xeonision bastard is Sheriff?" Radoq was incredulous "Is he wealthy or something?"

Juraj shook his head "No. He won the favour of the Crown Prince in some trade negotiation with our neighbours to the south. His reward was stewardship over a city. He worked as a merchant for some years and all he thinks of is money. You saw the beggars in the lower tiers?"

Radoq nodded "That's never been seen before."

"Right. Fortisul has been blessed with good harvests for decades –"

"Centuries." Radoq interrupted.

"Yes." A flicker on Juraj's face "As a Domerus you'd know more about that than a humble lun'erus."

For some reason there was no humour in Juraj's smile. Radoq wondered at the ill feeling that lay behind the man's charisma.

He stored the information away for later.

"A city like Volanbuta can't grow its own food. Like the Eyrie in the Dark Lands, it relies on trade. But think of the size of the flying town compared to a province like Fortisul! They need far less food, there are far fewer mouths to feed and so they worked out a deal with our Sheriff. Of course, he isn't openly trading with them, its all done sneakily at night. A cart load here, a ship docking there and Tricial skims his take off the top of hard working farmers who can do nothing to stop the theft."

"Surely the city guard would step in?"

Juraj shrugged "They're as hungry as anyone else. When the Sheriff came, he brought his own men and they bullied, threatened and bribed enough of the city guard commanders in the beginning that by the time anyone realised what was happening, it was too late. What guard Captain would risk letting his family starve? No, they turn a blind eye as the gondolas haul our people's food away to Volanbuta."

Radoq remembered the girl he'd spoken to in the cloud park. Surely the vehicle she piloted was too small to lift a cart load of grain? And how would they get it up the narrow steps? He said as much to Juraj who shrugged.

"Your guess is as good as mine, Attilur. I aim to find out though." His gaze turned hard, meeting Radoq's own.

"Then what was the protest about today?"

"It was a declaration. Today we told the Sheriff and his guards that we will not stand idly by whilst he lets innocent people starve to fatten his own belly. In effect, we declared war."

"Do you think he got the message?" Radoq couldn't keep the scepticism from his voice "One night in the cells hardly seems like he took you seriously."

"An enemy who underestimates me is an enemy I crave." Juraj spoke with iron "The man may be a bastard but he underestimates lun'erus. Perhaps he has spent too little time in Wallanria."

Radoq considered for a moment then shook his head "You have to be a Wallanrian to serve the Crown Prince. No civil servant or Sheriff has ever been a foreigner."

"Desperate times, dear Attilur." Juraj laid back on the straw "The war in the east has gone badly and we all have less as a result. There are more in the eastern hills no doubt driven west by the Dark Ji."

"They've been seen west of the hills? What of tritus Fortisun?" Radoq managed to affect a nonchalant air as he asked the question he'd been burning to ask.

"Arrested. The elder son is dead, killed in the wars along with most of the tritus' men. The Ji is held under the Sheriff's arrest by an oath of honour."

Radoq nodded, understanding. If his father had sworn to the Sheriff not to leave his home then he would be bound as effectively as the iron cage that had held Radoq in the desert.

"What of the younger son? I saw him in the cloud park this morning."

"Oh?" Juraj leaned forward "You know Gellian?"

"I know of him." Radoq's mind raced to cover the mistake "A servant was with him in the livery of the tritus."

"Ah." Juraj lay back again "Gellian hasn't left the city in months. He certainly hasn't hunted and it's been left to local militias to fight the virals."

Radoq's lip curled in disgust. From before he could remember, his duty had been to keep the Western Hills clear of the virals and the thought of them running freely across those beautiful lands made him sick "If no-one is defending the hills then the Four Cities are exposed."

Juraj nodded "Yes."

"What do you intend to do about that?"

"Me?" Juraj looked genuinely surprised "I'm a lowly lun'erus. I can't fight the virals. That's what you're for, isn't it Domerus?"

Radoq blinked but Juraj appeared to close his eyes and fall asleep. Radoq had not slept in several days although fatigue was only just starting to creep in so he laid himself down on the floor and closed his eyes but his mind reeled with thoughts and the floor was hard. He turned over for the umpteenth time and Juraj groaned close at hand "What? For the love of Chox what is it?"

Radoq sighed "It's the whole system. It's undermined by a man like Tricial."

"Oh?" Juraj chuckled "A Domerus who thinks about politics? You're a rare breed, Attilur."

"The balance of power is delicate." Radoq explained "Who holds ultimate power in Wallanria?"

"It depends on your perspective but I suppose you mean the Crown Prince." Juraj replied.

"Yes. But he only holds power because the Domerus support him. If he alienated the Ji's and their tritus' then he'd be removed from power."

"The same goes for the Ji's alienating their tritus and the Domerus as a whole alienating the lun'erus."

"Right..." Radoq frowned at that last part but continued "The Sheriffs are the representatives of the Crown Prince. They have overall power and the Ji's bow to their laws."

"Yes, but Ji's have rebelled against Sheriffs before." Juraj pointed out.

"Mmm." Radoq grunted "But only in justified causes like protecting the lun'erus or to prevent danger from the virals."

"Are you saying Ji-Fortisun should have rebelled against the Sheriff?"

"No. Or maybe. I don't know what happened between the two of them that would cause the Ji to accept arrest." Radoq cracked his neck as he thought "But the Sheriff being corrupt affects the whole system. The Domerus lose authority and ultimately, it's just the lun'erus who lose."

Juraj sat up "A man of the people! I never thought to find a Domerus with such a point of view."

Radoq looked quizzically at Juraj "That's the point of view of every Domerus. That's what we're trained for from birth. It's what we're bred for and why we go through the ascension! You know that Domerus means 'to serve', don't you?"

Juraj laid back down slowly "Yes. Of course. But it also means to be powerful."

"The word doesn't mean that."

"No, but by default to be Domerus means to have power over us – over the lun'erus."

"It depends on your perspective." Radoq echoed Juraj's words "Power is only real when its exercised."

Juraj grunted at that, plainly disagreeing "You're immortal, bigger and stronger than us, you don't succumb to illness and you don't need to fear death. That's power."

"Long lived." Radoq corrected but otherwise did not see a counter argument. He'd lost the thread of what they were debating anyway, much like a game of Sagalm where his opponent's move had knocked his strategy from his mind.

"Maybe democracy is the answer?" Juraj suggested after a few minutes of silence.

"We have democracy. The lun'erus vote on their representatives."

"But we can't vote to become Domerus." Juraj pointed out quietly.

That effectively ended the debate although sleep eluded Radoq. The morning started with a clang of iron bars as their jailer set them free, warning them not to return in the near future.

Outside the keep, Radoq was at something of a loss. He looked up to the towering mansion of Fortisun but from what Juraj had said, his family were not there. He thought of other friends in the city he could call on but his hidden identity presented too much opportunity to learn more about the Sheriff, Tricial and Radoq vowed to use his anonymity to his advantage.

"Where to, Attilur?" Juraj was waiting for him.

Radoq shrugged "Around, I suppose."

Juraj clapped him on his shoulder, having to reach up to do so "Come to my house in the middle tiers. Whilst you're finding your feet you'll stay as my guest. It's the least I can do for throwing in your lot with me yesterday. I can't imagine a night in the cells is the best welcome home you've ever received." Juraj smiled and Radoq turned to follow him.

They strode through the streets and Radoq noticed immediately how Juraj's men spread out around him in a protective group. Lun'erus nodded to him as they passed, many greeting him by name and peering curiously at Radoq who tightened his scarf around his mouth.

"Cold, Attilur?" asked Juraj as he passed a handful of coins to a beggar.

"I've been in the desert for some time." Radoq explained "The cold gets to me more than it should."

"Ah." Juraj nodded "Good air here though, it'll clear that sand from your lungs."

More men were waiting for Juraj near to his home and they fell into step beside him as they strode through the middle tiers. Radoq didn't know these streets. It wasn't somewhere he'd have come before he left Fortisul and he looked around with interest seeing prosperous merchants' houses, overpriced tenements and ornate, if over filled green parks all fed by the mountain water piped across the city. They ducked through a market, Radoq eyeing the vakkor raised stalls warily, knowing that in the lower tiers the vakkor engines periodically failed, sending an entire stall crashing down to the street below but Juraj and his men seemed unfazed so Radoq relaxed.

A towering stone buttress cast a shadow across the street and Juraj stopped, turning to a neat brown door set into the stone. He knocked once and a small slat in the door opened and then shut swiftly. The door swung inwards and an elderly lun'erus dressed in working clothes embraced Juraj with obvious relief.

"Ptolm, this is my friend Attilur. He's to stay as our guest for as long as he needs!" Ptolm, clearly a butler or housekeeper bowed low to Radoq and ushered the two of them in.

"My love?" Juraj's house was decorated well with thoughtfully matched colours and furniture. Quite unlike what Radoq would have suspected. As Juraj called out again he wondered at the tastes of Juraj's wife or lover or whoever he was calling out to.

"Ah!" Juraj had leapt up a pair of decorative steps into a wide room almost filled with a round table "My love!" he greeted a woman who stood the same height as him, dark radiant beauty drawing Radoq's eye and making him stop so suddenly that Ptolm walked smack into him.

"Radoq?"

"Malain..."

For some reason, Radoq felt sick. His mind whirred as he took in Juraj, Malain and his own dishevelled state. What Malain was doing here with Juraj, a lun'erus, he could not imagine. And now she was striding towards him, Juraj forgotten and her hand was over her heart and she was real, before him, within reach and he hadn't broken his promise...

"Radoq?" Juraj's voice was harsh "You're Radoq? Radoq Loxelsus Po-Fortisun?"

Malain had stopped and as Radoq watched she squeezed her eyes shut hard before opening them and regarding him with a cold indifference that took the air from his lungs. She turned to Juraj who had approached her and took his hand "Did he not tell you, my love? This is he, Radoq. The one we thought dead."

Juraj smiled at Radoq who simply stood in shock, his heart pounding "Why did you not reveal yourself, my friend? Oh..." Juraj made the connection, his eyes casting over Radoq's shabby dress and dirty biom "Of course. Well, this is fine news, my love?" he phrased it as a question "An old friend returned from the dead?"

"I – yes. Of course." Malain's face was filled with an emotion that Radoq struggled to place. As ever, she was an enigma to him, keeping him waiting before she revealed her innermost thoughts to him.

"I –" he stammered. He had no idea what to say. She was married to Juraj? A ring was on her finger. A similar one on Juraj's. He saw the lun'erus glance at it and smile "Indeed, my friend. Newlyweds!"

Radoq needed to say something but words were stuck in his throat. He half expected a rage to wash over him and to slaughter Juraj where he stood but instead he felt only ridicule. How ridiculous he had been to think that she would wait for him! He'd allowed her to think he was dead and in the circumstances, his tritus and likely hers arrested by a corrupt Sheriff who could blame her for following her heart? Pain shuddered through him as he gave some meaningless congratulations.

"Your words are not needed, Fallen one." She spoke in icy tones.

Radoq felt her words physically strike him and he took an involuntary step backwards.

"Malain!" Juraj shot Radoq an apologetic glance "That's no way to speak to our guest!"

"He's not welcome." Malain grated, staring at Radoq with hatred in her eyes.

"I –" Juraj was clearly at a loss at her reaction "My love, perhaps you should allow us to talk?" he smiled at Malain until she abruptly turned and swept from the room leaving Juraj staring after her.

"My friend? I shall have to learn your name all over again." He smiled "Shall we sit?"

Radoq sat, before he fell.

"I'm sorry for her reaction." Juraj leaned forward, an earnest expression on his face "But now I know who you are, I must beg your help. We can work together you and I."

"How?" Radoq could not fathom working with this man, Malain's *husband* of all people.

I'll come back to you

She had not promised to be here when he got back.

"The Sheriff, Radoq. He's your enemy as much as he is mine. He has your tritus under arrest. If you and I can work together to bring him down then you can clear your family's name. Perhaps your father will even forgive you and ascend you once again?"

Radoq stared at the man, uncomprehending. He shook his head, not in refusal but in denial at the circumstances. Abruptly, he stood up, pacing up and down with a fervour.

"Radoq?"

He couldn't answer, couldn't think around the shock that rang his mind like a flicked glass.

"Radoq. We can work together. You can earn your honour back."

Honour

That was the key. If he could restore his tritus and free Malain's, she'd forgive him. He thought he could live with her as another man's wife if only she wouldn't stare at him with that hatred and disgust. Was this finally to be his punishment? To watch her be happy with another man? With a lun'erus? He thought it might be. Oprain's words about self-pity cut through the funk of his thoughts and Radoq forced his mind to think clearly. What was his duty? It was to his people. As Juraj was saying it was to free them from the tyranny of the Sheriff. If, along the way he could earn Malain's favour then that was all the better.

Radoq turned and sat down heavily at the table, looking into Juraj's face "What do you need me to do?"

CHAPTER 8

Juraj's followers were a motley band of rough looking lun'erus. Radoq might have mistaken them for a street gang if he hadn't been introduced by Juraj. He supposed that in effect they were although instead of extorting innocent passers-by, they were arguing over the most effective way to help their people. Radoq's people.

As the group had entered Juraj's house that evening, he'd introduced each of them in turn to Radoq who had questioned at first the good sense of this, wondering if the Sheriff would seek to arrest him if word of his return got out. Juraj had allayed his fears, promising that these were his inner circle, his closest friends and so Radoq had been accepted. He'd noted the surprised looks, quickly followed by the swift glances at his ragged clothes and appearance and the understanding in their faces. There were different reactions, one or two were sympathetic, some were amused. Most were ambivalent, simply shaking the hand of another ally in their struggle.

They sat around the wide round table in Juraj's house. Juraj led the conversation but as they debated strategy, Radoq was impressed by the man's leadership. He used charisma to flatter, intelligence to perceive hidden meanings and sometimes authority to flatten opposition. But what impressed Radoq the most was Juraj's ability to plant the seed of a thought in the debate and allow one of his acolytes to scoop up the idea, thinking it was their own. There was no clamour for recognition from Juraj, he simply smiled and coaxed the idea out into the open where it was picked apart, improved and critiqued until what had plainly been Juraj's intention all along, was solidified as a group decision. It was masterful, manipulative and impressive and Radoq was happy to take a quiet position of observation in the debate. But as the conversation moved onwards, Radoq began to suspect that there was a strategy for tackling the Sheriff that Juraj had already chosen, he was simply allowing his followers to convince themselves that his was the best option.

"The problem is –" Metary, a grey haired woman who sat next to her hulking and silent son, Rovi, "- the farmers in the province are facing more virals, less income and ultimately, starvation! Some of them have taken to sleeping in vakkor balloons above the ground just to stay safe at night! We have to tackle the problem at the source! If we attack the Sheriff and remove him from office then we can free the Domerus and solve every problem in one!"

Radoq cringed at the thought of such a course of action but Juraj had predicted it.

"It's a good plan, Metary, but whilst I know well how Rovi could hold off the Sheriff's guard single handed, removing Tricial by force would bring the Crown Prince's eye upon us. We'd be seen as rebels and he'd send a fleet to attack us. Even Rovi can't fight the Royal Guard and we don't want this to end with innocent blood on the streets."

Metary conceded the point with a disappointed shrug but Juraj kept speaking to her.

"It's the right direction though. We need to tackle the problem at the source. Tricial is the source, we need to hurt him but not make him feel attacked."

There was silence around the table. The small group looked confused and Radoq saw Juraj cast a significant look in his direction.

"If we try to stop the Sheriff's men, there'll be bloodshed." Radoq spoke and every eye turned to him "But, if we're careful, we can move in the darkness and let the Sheriff bring the stolen grain to us. After he's gone to the trouble of stealing it, we can intercept it as he's transferring it to Volanbuta. That'll cost him because he's already expended the effort to steal the grain but Volanbuta won't pay him if they don't receive the goods. That stops the trouble at the source." He sat back, seeing a small grin from Juraj in response.

"We should continue with the protests in the town." Metary replied and Juraj assured her they would.

"I like this idea, Radoq." Juraj spoke slowly, stroking his chin as though giving it great thought "We let the Sheriff waste his own time and effort and then we take the grain from under his nose." He frowned seriously "But how can we intercept them? Surely the Sheriff's men will be guarding it?"

"I don't think so." Radoq leaned forward affecting a similarly pensive air "Sure enough at the point they steal the grain they'll need a dozen or so armed men but after that, they'll send it on into the town with just a couple. They won't be armed either. That would attract too much attention. Remember Tricial is doing this discretely. He doesn't want people to notice carts of grain going into the city every night."

"Then how do you propose we take it from these one or two men?" Juraj leaned back as though he'd found the flaw in Radoq's plan.

"Bribes." A rat faced man named Cysan spoke up "Plenty of the guards are on the take. Particularly since food became so expensive. Sure, it'll cost us a bit for each cart load but we can afford it." He nodded around the group, several of whom were now nodding in agreement. Radoq considered amending his conclusion that they were not a street gang.

"And if the bribes fail?" Juraj asked.

"Force." Metary spoke now. Next to her, her son Rovi gave a single sharp nod "If they won't be taken, we'll force them to give it up. Rob the robbers, so to speak."

"We can't guarantee every cart falls to us like this." Pointed out Cysan.

"No." Juraj took over "But we can assume most will. Besides, there's always been theft here and there and a couple of carts going astray won't cripple the economy."

There was silence as the plan sank in. Voices spoke out with questions and further ideas and Radoq sat back, letting the conversation take its course once again. Juraj, he noticed took little part now, instead seeming to listen intently but Radoq suspected he had now got his way, all without seeming to propose any idea himself. It was a clever strategy but Radoq wondered at the intelligence of some of the group. A few were plainly old friends of Juraj who contributed little to the conversation whilst others were fervent, but lacking in insight. Radoq frowned to himself at the understanding that Juraj seemed to surround himself with those that he considered less intelligent than himself. It was easier for him to get his own way with them. Radoq shrugged to himself, admiring the leadership and welcoming the distraction from thoughts of Malain who he had not seen since she'd swept from the room earlier.

He saw nothing of her that evening nor the next morning when he woke from a couple of hours light sleep. Juraj was speaking to Ptolm in the meeting room as Radoq emerged.

"Radoq! Slept well? I understand you have little need of rest."

Radoq smiled modestly "I sleep a little. Less than most though."

"Good! I need your sharp mind around. You saw my council last night – fine people, all! But not perhaps the greatest minds in Wallanria." Juraj smiled to show he meant no insult.

"Indeed." Radoq nodded "You lead them well."

"Thank you." If Juraj felt any guilt for manipulating his friends he buried it deep. Instead, he was all business "I wonder if you might return to cloud park today? We're staging another protest there, against Volanbuta this time. We'll be massing around the gondola."

"You need me at a lun'erus protest?"

Juraj smiled "No. You're right. But I do need you to warn the gondola operator."

"Ah." Radoq frowned "You're expecting violence?"

"I'm expecting a peaceful protest." Juraj was serious "But

what we're doing here is rousing a rabble. People can behave in dangerous ways when they're part of a pack. I take great care to ensure no-one is in harm's way."

Radoq understood and he said so, resuming his hood and scarf disguise as he made his slow way to the cloud park. Still far emptier than he remembered, it now had a handful of occupants strolling through it or sitting on benches. This time there was no sign of his brother or indeed of any other Domerus in the park. Radoq frowned, wondering just how many had been arrested by the Sheriff and how many were simply afraid to leave their homes.

"You again!" the Xeonison girl greeted him "Still hiding your mug?"

"It's cold." Radoq explained.

"Shouldn't have come to the 'cloud park' then." She said, rolling her eyes.

"Look, you'd better get up to Volanbuta. There's going to be a protest here in a moment."

"Oh yeah? Another mob grousing about the Sheriff? You know no-one's seen him in weeks?"

"They've seen his guards though." Radoq retorted.

The girl spat "Sure! What's a city without guards though? Last I saw, they were being pretty lenient with Juraj and his gang."

"Gang?"

"You heard me."

Lun'erus had begun to drift into the park in ones and twos. Radoq glanced around, seeing them making a slow but definite way towards them.

"You'd better get going."

The girl opened her mouth to protest again or more likely, to deliver a cutting remark but she saw the numbers now in the park and thought better of it. She stepped into the gondola, speaking into a communicator and activating the vakkor that rocked the small vehicle.

"Oi, hood." She addressed Radoq, already six feet in the air "Your mate Juraj isn't all he's cracked up to be. Dunno what you're getting yourself into – that's your business – but my guess is you should watch your back."

"Oh yes?" Radoq called back to her "And who's watching the town's back whilst the Sheriff empties its coffers?"

The girl found this funny for some reason. She bent over the side of the gondola roaring with mirth "You damn fool! Can't you see it's the Sheriff?"

Radoq gaped at her but lost her meaning as she drifted towards Volanbuta that hung above them. A voice close at hand muttered his name and he turned to see Cysan, the rat faced bribe master had arrived with a posse of half a dozen rough looking lun'erus.

"Oi, Domerus. Time you made yourself scarce, eh?"

Radoq nodded at the man, walking unhurriedly away as the sound of chants filled the air. Almost as an echo as he made his way down the narrow staircase out of the park he heard a second set of chants coming from up the hill and turned to see a large crowd, their words unintelligible. Clearly, Juraj had given Metary free reign in planning the protests, keeping the Sheriff occupied.

As it transpired, Radoq himself was kept occupied in the coming weeks. He saw Evie only briefly to give her permission to hire a new pilot and make a series of short mercantile trips to the four cities. She returned each time, clearly hoping Radoq would provide her steady work and he leaned on Juraj to help. The would-be rebel was enthusiastic about helping her and soon had a regular route flying fresh water to the Eyrie which seemed to keep Evie happy although she constantly reminded Radoq that the ship was likely to break apart at any moment, pitching her and the crew into the Dark Lands.

Evie's concerns were not Radoq's though. The benefit of his Domerus blood meant he needed less sleep than the lun'erus and Juraj kept him busy, stalking carts of grain through the night and ambushing unsuspecting guards. Most were paid off quietly but Radoq had been treated to the sight of Rovi lifting two Sheriff's men who'd refused to take their bribe and smashing their heads together repeatedly until he'd pulled the bloodied men away. The recovered carts were then delivered to wherever Juraj had identified as a temporary safehouse, hidden from the Sheriff. Sometimes it was a dark alleyway with a rough stretch of canvas for a cover, others, an empty warehouse. Radoq would pass the carts to the team responsible for shipping the grain back to the farmers who would take it and leave with barely a word passing between them.

Until one night when they ambushed a cart which Juraj's men were already pushing. After a brief scuffle and hissed threats in the darkness the two groups managed to identify one another and Radoq worked out that Cysan, the rat faced bribe master had directed the cart in the wrong direction, sending it towards Volanbuta rather than away. After this, Juraj redirected him to bribing the guards during the day, allowing the meticulously planned protests to proceed unmolested.

Radoq returned to Juraj's house hopefully in the first few weeks, hoping to see Malain but aside from catching a glimpse of her once, she clearly made a point to avoid him. Radoq did his best to ignore the pain his chest, throwing himself into the task of liberating Fortisul.

"Sagalm, Radoq." Juraj said to him one night as they sat atop two 'liberated' carts of grain.

"The Great Game!" Radoq grinned "You've seen it played?"

"Seen it?" Juraj shocked Radoq by reaching into a waxed canvas pack he had carelessly dropped on the warehouse floor and producing a well worn board "I can never seem to get the knack of it."

Radoq eyed the board "Not through lack of trying, it would seem. Have you played a Domerus before?"

"No."

"Well, you'll not find a challenger of skill amongst the lun'erus." Radoq smiled to show he meant no offence "I mean when one learns, one should learn from a master in that particular subject."

"And Sagalm masters are all Domerus." Juraj grunted.

"Yes. Here…" Radoq began to lay out the pieces on the

board. He talked through a few of the basic attack and defence strategies he'd learned as a boy, demonstrating some common mistakes to Juraj who nodded, understanding quickly. Eager to test his new skills, he insisted they play for real without Radoq helping him.

"You must think further ahead." Radoq insisted, taking Juraj's Ji in a swift flurry of moves and winning yet again.

"Is that my flaw, Radoq? My inability to think several moves ahead?" Juraj was embarassed by the loss.

"To tell the truth, it's my own flaw." Radoq conceded "I'm perhaps breaking the rules here by trying to teach you. As I said, one should learn from an expert."

Juraj was controlling his temper but Radoq could see the effort "It's quite a game."

"Yes. There's a reason it's so highly prized amongst the Domerus."

"Because it shows off your genius?"

Radoq looked surprised "It can be used to show off, yes. But more importantly, it teaches you to think strategically. Each time we play and make a mistake like that one, exposing your Ji unintentionally, we learn not to do that." Radoq rapped the rickety table the board sat on "This game can be won in three moves. You know that? But only if your opponent doesn't see the moves coming. Watching two masters play this game is tedious to the untrained eye. They simply sit and predict, and hesitate and predict and finally one of them makes a move and then they sit again for hours, working through all the possibilities."

"Doesn't sound very fun."

Radoq laughed "It's not supposed to be! But it can be, if it's done right."

"You'll have to teach me again some other time."

"Practice, Juraj! That's all it takes. That and thinking several moves ahead of your opponent." He smiled.

Juraj, as it turned out had a curiosity about the Domerus that Radoq had never experienced from a lun'erus before. Frequently as they moved around Fortisul under cover of darkness he found moments to quiz Radoq on his upbringing.

"Your ascension, what was it like?"

"Painful."

"How old were you?"

"Oh, twenty one. Many are younger though."

"Did you choose when you were ascended?"

"No. My Ji – my father deemed me ready at that age."

"And the actual process, how long did it take?"

"How long? About two minutes I suppose? It felt an eternity whilst the change was taking place." Radoq shifted uncomfortably at the memory making the packing crate they crouched on creak alarmingly.

"It's a sort of technology, isn't it? Something to do with your biom."

Radoq raised his left hand with its ragged golden sheen. He stared at the ordinary looking flesh that held so much technology "Something like that. It's controlled from the biom though. That's how it enters the body."

"And it heals you? Stops you getting sick?"

"Well… some of it is certainly to stop illness. For example if an ascended Domerus were poisoned his biom would neutralise the effects. He'd likely still be quite unwell though. It's not a magic wand."

"Your natural speed and strength though…"

"Yes. We're almost a different species at this point. Domerus are bred stronger, faster and longer living. That's why a lun'erus can never ascend to be a Domerus. The ascension would kill them."

Juraj was silent for a long time at this point, picking at a splinter on the crate. Radoq hoped he hadn't offended the man. Lun'erus could be touchy when it came to discussing the divide between them, seeing only the inequity.

"Lun'erus can never become Domerus –" Juraj spoke slowly "but Domerus can become lun'erus?"

Radoq cleared his throat "Not exactly. A Domerus is born, you understand? Genetically distinct from a lun'erus. At a certain age if deemed ready by our Ji who is the head of the tritus –"

"Usually your father?"

"No. Plenty of Ji are female and another relative. An uncle perhaps, or a sibling is just as common. But the immature Domerus is ascended by their Ji, assuming they're ready."

"And the Ji can remove the ascension?"

Radoq began to fidget with a splinter of his own. It pressed too far under his nail, drawing blood and he swore quietly.

"Forgive me, Radoq. I'm being rude."

"No." Radoq shook his head in the darkness "It's a subject we should discuss more. I feel most lun'erus don't ask enough and most Domerus don't tell at all." He sighed "If a Domerus falls out of favour with their tritus or dishonours them in some way, the Ji can remove their ascension. It's not something that happens often and it's never taken lightly."

Silence filled the darkness.

"Then why did your father take your ascension?"

Radoq let out a long breath and opened his mouth to speak but one of Juraj's men, invisible in the darkness appeared next to them.

"The Sheriff has been sighted! He's in the keep!"

Juraj leapt to his feet his excitement palpable. Radoq didn't understand, why was the Sheriff being in the keep news? He tried to ask.

Juraj almost seemed to make to brush him aside but thought better of it. He clasped Radoq's arm in the darkness "I was going to tell you before we headed out, my friend. My men tell me the Sheriff has ordered our arrests. He means to hang us all from the walls of the keep."

"Chox!" Radoq cursed "What is he thinking? The people will tear the city apart!"

Juraj's grip was harder as he nodded fervently "If we're hanged they'll tear the city apart but they'll do just as much damage if they find out now that the Sheriff even gave the order!"

Radoq gaped. The man was right. The town was already a tinderbox waiting for a spark and the lun'erus' beloved leader

Juraj twitching at the end of a rope would ensure blood in the streets. Whether the Sheriff caught them or not was irrelevant. If word spread, the people would storm the keep.

"We can't kill the Sheriff, Juraj! That'll bring the royal guard!"

"I know! I know, my friend. This is my worst case scenario plan. We have to control the Sheriff, to storm the keep now and get him under our control."

Figures were racing around them in the darkness, the clunk of phasrs being loaded and the faint glow of plasma bolts everywhere.

"Chox!" Radoq breathed "Can we do it? Do we have the men?"

Juraj was silent for a long time. Too long. Then, "I can't see that we have any choice, Radoq." His face glowed faintly as someone handed him a berrett and he jerked a round into the chamber "Just think, by morning our city could be free!"

"Or we'll all be dead." Was Radoq's silent thought but he kept his dark thoughts to himself, instead clutching a borrowed phasr in his hands and following Juraj's men out into the dark, cold streets of Fortisul.

Which were, despite all his efforts, about to be bathed in innocent blood.

CHAPTER 9

The keep was an ominous shape at the end of the street. A rare clear night bathed Fortisul in moonlight. At any other time Radoq would happily have found a spot to perch and stare at the radiant beauty of the silver disk but now, he cursed the bright gleam that lit their every movement.

He stepped as lightly as he was able on the cobbles of the narrow side street. On either side, tall buildings with shuttered windows cast shadows in the moonlight, pools of darkness that Radoq and the band of darkly dressed lun'erus slipped between. It could have been any other night of the weeks Radoq had worked with Juraj. Moving after dark, avoiding the guards, keeping quiet so as not to disturb the curious citizens except now they were a warband.

The silhouettes of Juraj's men were disrupted by the multitude of weapons and assaulting equipment they carried. Two long ladders had been procured from some unknown source and were now each suspended between three men each who panted and puffed under their weight. Radoq, running behind them, found it hard not to criticise Juraj's lack of planning. It showed the man's lack of experience in violent ventures. The man was an excellent thief, a master of skulking, bribing and of sudden scuffles in dark alleyways but he was not a soldier. A military man would have found lighter ladders.

Perhaps a soldier would have chosen another plan. Attacking the keep was madness and Radoq rolled his eyes at the thought, scowling at the gleaming satellite above them. It was the right sort of night for lunacy.

"Here!" Juraj's voice, a restrained mutter rather than a carrying whisper brought the party to a halt. Soldiers they may not be but Radoq was impressed as the lun'erus instantly fanned out into a defensive formation, ensuring the all-important ladders were contained within a solid ring of armed men.

"Oi, Domerus…" someone nudged Radoq and he followed the guiding hands until he stood by Juraj and another man who, by his bulk could only be Rovi. The man was characteristically silent but as Radoq drew close he turned and spoke in a surprisingly gentle voice.

"Domerus – we're just around the corner from the keep. Sheriff has two men on guard, one inside and one outside."

Radoq nodded. He knew this.

"We've bribed the man on the inside but the outside is going to be a Chox'd problem." Ravi spoke in a matter of fact tone as Radoq frowned, wondering if Ravi was simply going to kill the man.

"What's your plan?"

"Distraction." Juraj spoke quietly as though overhearing Radoq's thoughts "If a Domerus walks down there and demands entry, the guard will call to our man on the inside who'll oblige us by opening the gate."

Radoq held his tongue for a moment, searching for tact "They won't suspect a Domerus appearing in the middle of the night isn't a trap?"

Ravi shrugged. An enormous movement "You lot don't sleep, do you? You come and go at all hours."

"Exactly!" Juraj encouraged.

Radoq stared "That can't be your only plan, Juraj!"

"Do you have a better one?"

"I –"

"No! You don't! So stop arguing, Radoq!" Juraj was angry and rightly so. Radoq dipped his head, acquiescing to the instruction. Above all, he knew, challenging Juraj's authority at such a critical juncture would only result in further strife, possibly putting Juraj and his men at even further risk of harm. No, the time for arguing was in the past. Juraj had made his decision and his men were loyal. He, Radoq, was not going to undermine the man's authority no matter how foolish the plan. He would just have to do what he could once they were inside the keep to prevent bloodshed.

"Go on!" Ravi tried to shove Radoq forward but despite his size, the Domerus was bigger still and Radoq looked significantly at the hand on his shoulder until Ravi hastily withdrew it.

"Do this for me, my friend." Juraj urged, the animosity gone from his voice to be replaced by a pleading tone.

Radoq nodded and the men in front of them moved aside to let him through. He stepped around the corner, the dark outline of the keep coming into plain view. A pair of towering smooth stone walls ended either side of a sturdy metal gate which was lit by a pair of aquar lamps that flickered in the gloom. The outline of a pacing sentry, the barrel of his phasr just visible above his shoulder could be seen and it was for this unfortunate lun'erus that Radoq made a beeline. His heart hammered in his chest as he approached, wondering what the wretched man's reaction would be. Radoq hoped he would simply bow and open the gate but it was more likely he'd level his phasr and order Radoq to leave.

Perhaps he'd shoot.

Radoq swallowed, forcing a slow pace. He walked in the middle of the cobbled street, keeping well away from the gutters which he noted were clean of the mess and detritus that plagued the lower tiers. Streetlights, aquar powered were dark beside Radoq. He knew that in the four cities and indeed in Admirain, the capital of Wallanria the streetlights burned all through the night. Not so in Fortisul where aquar production relied on the constant pounding of the mountain waterfalls and not on the nuklera power that fed the lowlands. The sentry would surely have a switch though and sure enough, as Radoq's footsteps drew nearer, the guard flooded the streets with light which crackled and popped. Radoq kept walking, his eyes now drawn to the squat, functional shape of the keep so out of tone with the ornate architecture of Fortisul. Two thick walls topped by aquar razor wire and unmanned pinzgats formed a circle only broken at the gate that Radoq walked towards. Provided by the capital for their appointed Sheriff, the funding for the construction had come solely from that city and Fortisul had been unable to stop the ugly building from elbowing its way into the street. Now it formed an intimidating barrier at the end of an otherwise residential street and as Radoq passed a home, a window opened in an upper floor and a curious lun'erus face peered out.

"Who are you?" called a voice but Radoq kept walking as the guard called out a greeting.

"Domerus, what business do you have with the Sheriff?"

Radoq walked a few more paces before he replied, now drawing almost level with the guard who now clutched his phasr with both hands, his brow furrowed "I wish to speak with the Sheriff. Immediately."

"No."

The tone was empty of any disrespect but Radoq blinked in surprise "I beg your pardon?"

"No. No entry to the keep after sundown."

"I am Radoq Loxelsus Po-Fortisun. I wish to speak to the Sheriff. Or perhaps to my brother, Gellian Loxelsus Su-Fortisun. Is he here?"

The guard's eyes widened in surprise "Er – I don't know –"

"Then order the gate opened so that I may enter and discover for myself!" Radoq snapped in an authoritative voice. As he suspected, the guard was well used to jumping at orders and he took a half step backwards, reaching out to give the signal to open the gate but he paused.

"I –"

That was as far as he got before Juraj (or more likely, one of his men) killed him.

Plasma bolts are superheated energy, fired from the barrel of a gat the blob of matter spins and gathers energy until it impacts on a solid object and burns through whatever it touches, cooling almost instantly thereafter. The phasr round struck the guard on the side of his head, just above his left ear. The blow staggered him sideways into the heavy metal of the gate which banged like a rusty gong. The plasma took the back of his head off, cleanly as though cut with a knife and a pool of dark gore slopped down the back of the dead man.

He dropped to his knees in front of Radoq who stared with fury and horror rising in him. The lun'erus' eyes were locked on his own although surely there could be no consciousness left. But there was a tightening of the small muscles around the eyes, a curling of the lips as the awful agony registered in what remained of the vital organ and then blood gushed from his mouth, the eyes rolled upwards and he slumped back to lie still.

Running footsteps and then the gate swung inwards. Radoq stared at the murdered man as Juraj appeared, grabbing him and urging him onwards into the keep.

"Why did you kill him?" he couldn't say if the question emerged from his mouth or was spoken in his head. Either way, Juraj didn't answer and now his men were flooding through the gate, firing phasrs and berretts provoking screams of pain. A harsh klaxon began to ring out and Radoq remembered the hold of the slave ship where plasma fumes had burned the air as the sound of alarms drew more to the fight.

To the meat grinder that was now the courtyard. Ravi, his bulk unmistakable had grabbed one of the ladders the attackers had carried and now propped it against the wall, anchoring the base firmly with his feet. He leaned back as Cysan, the rat faced bribe master scurried up it looking more like the pest he resembled than ever and hopped over the parapet, reaching the unmanned quadgat that covered the gate. He turned the contraption, straining against the mechanism until it pointed down into the courtyard where Sheriff's guards were now pouring into the space between the walls, firing their weapons at Juraj's men.

Chuk-chuk-chuk-chuk-chuk-chuk

The four barrels spat plasma into the soldiers, slaughtering three in the opening burst. Radoq heard a whoop from Cysan echoed by Ravi who had moved past Radoq into the courtyard and was firing a berrett from the hip, the widening oval of plasma bolts giving him little need to aim.

"Radoq! Get in the Chox'd fight!" Juraj crouched with two of his men behind a combat shield which the attackers had deployed. Already, the folding protection was beginning to smoke as plasma tore into it and Juraj had noticed, turning to scream at Radoq who had still not moved from where he stood by the murdered guard.

"No-one was supposed to get killed!" it was a stupid thing to say and a stupid time to say it but Radoq felt he was seeing Juraj for the first time in the battle stink of blood and plasma. Gone was the charismatic leader, in its place was a lying, desperately squirming beast which was pouring death into the keep.

"What did you think would happen?" when Radoq still failed to move Juraj turned fully away from the fight to bawl at Radoq "Chox! Haven't you failed enough of your men already?"

With a snarl, Radoq charged past him towards a cluster of Sheriff's guards who were hidden behind a combat shield of their own. On the turret, Cysan had painted them in plasma rounds and the heat was warping the air around them but the blasts stopped as Radoq sprinted ahead of the other attackers.

"Fortisun!" he shouted in a war cry as he vaulted the shield, kicking two men simultaneously as he spread his feet apart. Both flew back but were scrabbling for weapons a second later as the third brought a coltac to bear and then fell backwards as Radoq punched the weapon into his face.

"Move!" he heard Juraj yell behind him but he had no time to look as the two guards were up and one fired three quick shots from a short barrelled phasr and Radoq had to dive forward to avoid them, grabbing the man by the feet and toppling him.

"Chox'd Domerus!" snarled the man but Radoq drove an elbow into his temple and he went limp. Radoq turned to the final guard but the man had backed away and was running along with a cluster of his fellows into an open door that led into the inner rooms of the keep.

"Shoot them!" Ravi's voice was as surprisingly high as before although now it was deeper with battle fury and Radoq swore as Juraj's men, supported by Cysan with the quadgat on the roof slaughtered the guards, shooting them in the back and tearing them apart.

The door slammed shut.

"Cysan!" Juraj wheeled about immediately "Empty that thing into the door!"

Cysan grinned and fired at the hefty metal door as the attackers hastened to find positions they could fire from safely. The door began to glow with the heat. The stench of plasma fumes was overpowering and several men were coughing. Radoq moved so a stone pillar that supported a narrow balcony above them was between him and the door.

"Here it goes!" called Juraj and Radoq saw Cysan adjust his aim as the top corner of the metal door began to fold in on itself, literally melting with the heat.

"Stop!" an unfamiliar voice. Male. Old. Not one of theirs.

"Nearly there!" the door was beginning to fall. Juraj's men tensed.

"Stop! Stop this madness! In the name of the Prince!"

Above them. Radoq stepped backwards, wary of plasma bolts to see a grey haired, grey bearded Domerus dressed in civilian clothes bellowing down into the courtyard.

"Juraj!" he called and the man hastened over, shouting for his men to wait and for Cysan to stop firing.

"Sheriff!" Juraj sounded jubilant and indeed he had reason to "We seem to have taken you by surprise!"

"Juraj Aptoin!" the Sheriff thundered, a look of utter fury on his face "What, pray are you trying to achieve? If you kill me the Crown Prince will send an army! If you flout his authority like this, he'll destroy the whole town looking for you! This is the end of Fortisul, you Chox'd lun'erus fool!" spittle flew from the Sheriff's mouth.

Juraj laughed "Tricial! You worry so much! That's how we're able to overpower you so easily! I have a plan for this!"

A second figure appeared on the balcony and Radoq ducked his gaze, tugging his hood further over his face because the Domerus, looking surprised by the carnage below him was his brother, Gellian.

"Tricial?" he addressed the Sheriff "Has the keep fallen?"

"Yes!" shouted Juraj "And you, Master Gellian – you will return to your family's home and stay there!"

Gellian stared at the lun'erus with loathing but Juraj took a step forward as though threatening him.

"You recall your oath, Master Gellian? Or perhaps you'll break your word?"

Tricial, the Sheriff turned to Gellian and muttered something fast and quiet. Gellian spared Juraj a single withering glance and then turned, bending his legs and with the biom-given strength of the Domerus, leapt from the balcony, over the wall and into the dark streets.

Juraj grinned in victory then continued his smile as Tricial shouted to what remained of his guards to stand down, turning to vanish from sight. A moment later, he reappeared, shoving his way through the melted door to stand before Juraj, allowing a pair of aquar cuffs to be snapped around his wrists.

"You've gone too far, Juraj!" Tricial was furious, looking around at his dead men "This is murder and treason! The Crown Prince will want your head for this! I knew you were a crook but this is Chox'd foolish! I never took you for a fool, Juraj!"

"And you shouldn't now, Tricial! I promise you that no harm will come to you under my care – I need you alive, after all!" Juraj smiled as though he and the Sheriff were old friends meeting over a drink rather than captor and captured "You see, I've got it all worked out. Ravi!"

Arms loomed out of the darkness and grabbed Radoq. He turned his head, mildly surprised to see Ravi along with a pair of Juraj's bigger men attempting to wrestle his arms behind his back. He struggled, provoking a curse from Ravi.

"You see, we just need a scapegoat!" Juraj was saying, turning his cunning smile on Radoq "And we've got one here. A Fallen

Domerus, coming to reclaim his home, murdering, stealing and extorting the town! Why, the Crown Prince will give me a medal for unmasking him!"

The Sheriff stared at Radoq and then back to Juraj "You'll blame him for all the grain you stole? The money from Volanbuta?"

"I stole?" Juraj made gesture of innocence watching Radoq who was looking back at his erstwhile enemy as Ravi continued to struggle with his arms "But you stole the grain, didn't you Radoq? Took it from the Sheriff's men, led raiding parties against them in the dead of night? That was you these past few weeks, wasn't it?"

Radoq felt his stomach lurch at the words. Ice trickled through his veins and he ignored Ravi struggling to grasp his wrist. Could he really have been so blind to Juraj's true nature? Had he been duped by this lun'erus? What use was he if that was true? What point was there in him trying to help his home, to win Malain's love back if he was truly this foolish? He closed his eyes for a moment, screwing them shut against the truth of the words.

"That looks like a face of guilt to me!" Juraj crowed. His voice was loud, riven with hyperactive energy at his victory. His men were grinning all around him "That looks like the face of a Fallen Domerus, now fallen even lower! A criminal! Don't wallow in your self-pity too much, dear Radoq! Smarter men than you have been fooled by me!"

This provoked a chorus of jeers from Juraj's men and Radoq kept his eyes closed as the man rambled on, preaching to his followers.

"The self-pity, it's blinding you, Radoq!" Oprain's voice echoed in his mind and Radoq shook his head, knowing that the old man was right. The self-pity and recrimination fled leaving behind a clarity that left him suddenly fully aware of every detail, Ravi's hand still struggling for purchase on his wrist, Tricial's narrowed, suspicious eyes on his face and he realised with a start that he'd known Juraj's nature all along. He'd

allowed the man to sweet talk him despite realising that he was a master manipulator. Had he known he was stealing grain? Perhaps not but he'd avoided searching for the truth, fooling himself that in helping Juraj he was liberating himself in Malain's eyes.

Malain...

A wave of anger swept over him as her face swam in his mind, not at her but at himself. He'd allowed thoughts of her to drag him down under Juraj's power, to wallow in his own self pity at the terrible greeting she'd given him.

I'll come back to you

But he hadn't, really. Instead he'd crawled in front of her, all but clutching Juraj's hand for support, defeated, looking for nothing but pity to a woman who had lost everything. That had allowed Juraj to take the city, to arrest the Sheriff and now, to blame it on he, Radoq.

Behind him, Ravi suddenly went still. His eyes, a moment ago screwed up in fury went to the back of the Domerus' head and his palms, still holding tightly to Radoq were suddenly greasy with sweat.

"It's just like your Sagalm, Juraj." Radoq had to shout over the jeers and cheers but Juraj heard him, holding up a hand for silence and turning to Radoq.

"Sagalm?" Juraj didn't understand.

"You always failed to put yourself in your enemy's position, to see the board and their moves from their perspective." Radoq nodded at the carnage that surrounded them "You make your moves well, no-one can deny that but it's the moves you don't see that undo you."

"What in the name of Chox are you talking about, Radoq?" Juraj had drawn a coltac and was now advancing on the Domerus.

"The one thing I never told you but you always took for granted?" Radoq was smiling now although there was cruelty rather than humour in the expression.

"Which is...?" Juraj laboured the words, letting them hang

themselves in the air.

"You looked at the way I was dressed, at the way I carried myself?"

"And..." Juraj got it. He stopped, the coltac at his side suddenly seemed a thousand miles away as he looked into Radoq's eyes, seeing there a hardness he'd never seen.

Radoq didn't need to spell it out but as he effortlessly shook off Ravi's grip and activated his combat aurae, bathing the scene in a glow of heat signatures and metadata he couldn't resist leaning down to Juraj's level.

"I never said I was Fallen."

He smiled as he struck the rebel leader in the chest, watching with immense satisfaction as the lun'erus was plunged backwards by the fully ascended strength of a Domerus.

CHAPTER 10

A meaty thump sounded as Juraj crashed into an eviscerated corpse. Blood left a trail as he slid along the ground, coming to rest in a wet bundle that lay unmoving.

A pause.

Ravi was still behind Radoq and he stared up at the Domerus with wide eyes. Cysan, standing behind the Sheriff watched Radoq with tension in every line of his body. He twitched every few heartbeats as though ready to bolt into the nearest gutter.

"For Fortisul!" Radoq roared, bending his right knee and exploding his right elbow backwards against Ravi's skull. A meaty crack sounded and the big lun'erus fell to the ground. Radoq clapped his hands together and bellowed a wordless cry of challenge at Juraj's men, inviting them to come and die.

They came.

Cysan slipped past the Sheriff moving along the line of columns that supported the balcony above them. He stepped out from shadow, levelling his coltac and emptied the weapon.

With a snarl of contempt, Radoq was already behind him swinging a hammer fist into the rat faced man's spine which broke under the force of the strike. With a reedy rasping sound Cysan choked and heaved and died.

Chuk-chuk-chuk

The other rebels had snapped out of their funk now and were firing at Radoq. Hot plasma spattered across the stone columns as Radoq ducked back. His vision pulsed as the aurae warned him of movement.

There…

A hulking rebel leaned around the pillar and pointed his berrett. Radoq tugged the weapon forward pulling the man off balance and then placed a hand on his chest, launching him backwards off his feet and into the next two who were running forwards. As they spilled into a tangle on the floor he fired the berrett feeling the heavy weapon jerk in his hands. The plasma tore the three men to shreds and Radoq snarled.

"Back! Everyone back to the gate!"

The voice was vaguely familiar to Radoq but he couldn't recall the face. Still, Juraj's men were now edging back towards the still-open gate, weapons pointed towards Radoq. Several of them were carrying limp forms and Radoq spent a precious moment tweaking his aurae with his biom, checking the blood spattered faces in turn,

Juraj

The rebel leader was choking and pale but clearly alive. Two of his men had him between them and were hurrying for the gate whilst two more pointed phasrs towards Radoq, placing themselves between him and their leader.

"Radoq!" a shout close at hand and he turned to see Tricial, the Sheriff, his hands now free leading a charge of his own men towards Juraj's.

"Fortisul!" Radoq gave his war cry and erupted from behind the pillar. Two men loomed ahead of him and he ducked the coltac rounds that burned past him. He drove the heel of his hand into a soft throat feeling cartilage collapse and kicked the kneecap of the second, watching in grim satisfaction as the joint bent the wrong way and the man's screams filled the night air.

Chuk-chuk

The Sheriff's men were firing now and more of Juraj's men were down but Radoq had briefly lost sight of the party carrying the injured leader. Surely, they hadn't made it through the gate? But one of the Sheriff's guards was scaling the inside of the wall, using a ladder bolted there for that purpose and was heading for the quadgat Cysan had used to destroy the door and Radoq breathed a sigh of relief that the weapon could cover the street outside.

"Radoq!" the Sheriff was calling again and Radoq closed in on his fellow Domerus but the Sheriff suddenly dragged him down behind the remnants of a combat shield as quadgat rounds began strafing the floor.

Nightmare memories gripped Radoq's mind as he remembered the pinzgats of the enemy tearing into his men on the battlefield. He snarled in fury, risking a glance up to see the Sheriff's man had mounted the quadgat but was firing down at them.

"Juraj bribed one of your men!" he shouted to Tricial but the information was useless. Radoq cursed as two more Sheriff's guards sprawled beside them, one dead, one moaning weakly.

"Where's Juraj?"

"He's alive. They were carrying him out."

Tricial swore, looking around. He gestured to one of his men who nodded, stepped out of cover and took a carefully aimed shot with a phasr. The bolt passed through the corrupt guard atop the wall and the quadgat rounds stopped but the shooter was caught by a coltac round fired from the gate and was flung sideways to a snarl of fury from Tricial.

"Come on!" Radoq crossed the courtyard in one bound, relishing in the use of his biom which had lain dormant for weeks. The strength flowing through his body made him feel invincible but as he reached the threshold a sight met his eyes that made him pause.

"Radoq? What do you see?" Tricial was closing in, his own movements less graceful and powerful than those of Radoq.

Radoq gestured and together they stared in horror at the furiously chanting mob of hundreds that filled the space between the streetlights.

"Where's Juraj?" Tricial spoke at a normal volume over the chants and Radoq's Domerus hearing caught the sound clearly.

"I can't see him."

"This must have been his back up."

"Looks like the whole town is here."

"*Just-ice! Just-ice!*"

"*Jur-aj! Jur-aj!*"

The voices chanted and then, as the Sheriff was recognised, they gave a great roar and surged forward.

"Seal the keep!"

A great screech of metal and the fortress was secured again. Radoq looked around seeing the handful of the Sheriff's men that had survived. The fighting seemed to him to have lasted only a few minutes but already he could see the faint glow of dawn above the mountains.

"We should try and talk to them –"

"No point." Tricial shook his head "I've been trying to reason with the crowds for months. Juraj has roused them into a mob." He frowned at Radoq "And you've spent the past weeks ensuring his authority is absolute. The money he's made from all the grain…" Tricial shook his head.

"I'll make it right." Radoq promised, heading for the gate but Tricial stopped him.

"No! Enough lun'erus blood has been spilled tonight. I'll not see any more innocent lives taken and if you go out there, they'll attack."

As if in agreement, the first of a thrown series of missiles began to strike the gate, the muted boom of the metal reverberating off the survivors of the Sheriff's guard. More strikes followed as the chants increased in fervour. Were more of the townsfolk coming?

Radoq rounded on the Sheriff "Where is my family?"

"In their homes, as far as I know. Juraj bound them stay there with an oath of honour."

"I need to free them –"

"You can't. They won't leave and you'll be caught if you leave the keep."

"Chox!" Radoq swore, pacing in a circle "What do you suggest then?"

"Wait them out." Tricial's eyes were darting in small movements from the clanging against the gate to the ramparts of his small fortress "It takes energy to chant and shout like that. It's almost dawn, they'll have families to feed and jobs to go to."

"And then what?"

"Then we send a ship to the capital." Tricial swallowed nervously "We ask for the Crown Prince to intervene."

"You said yourself that he'd destroy the town!"

Tricial shook his head "What else can we do?"

Radoq had no better suggestions and he turned to the remnants of the Sheriff's guard, patching wounds and giving encouragement to those who needed it. They moved the bodies to one side, separating the rebels from the guards. Radoq counted twelve of Juraj's men dead, not an insignificant number. The guards had lost twenty men and a twenty first was vomiting blood and shaking in a corner, waiting his turn to be added to the pile. Tricial had twelve men left and each of them was tired, shaken and nervous. They would not be able to stop the mob outside.

Dawn lit the gore soaked courtyard with its glow giving full view of the small but violent battle. Pools of dried blood, chunks of flesh and organ meat spattered the floors and walls. Spent bolt cases littered the place and Radoq grimaced as they crunched underfoot, imagining bones breaking. The narrow walls of the fort once breached had served only to concentrate the violence into a narrow space and heighten the carnage. Few of the corpses now in a line against the wall were complete. Many were missing limbs or parts of the body and Radoq shook his head at the destructive power of the plasma bolts. He'd heard that other weapons used to be favoured, knives and arrows and the like and he wondered at the bloodlessness of such a style of warfare. Was it the lack of gore that had driven their ancestors to perfect the plasma style of weapon? Or was it simply through necessity, a thousand years of war forcing them to perfect the art of killing?

"Domerus?"

One of the Sheriffs guards, a middle aged woman with her name CHIRRUF stencilled on her chest approached Radoq. A bandage covered her left hand, and her voice was polite.

"Sheriff asked for you."

Radoq followed her out of the courtyard through the melted door and up a narrow flight of stairs to a small, bureaucratic looking office in which Tricial was hastily throwing objects into a waxed canvas travelling bag.

"Radoq. We need to leave. The entire town is filled with mobs."

"How do you know?"

Tricial cast a hand at the wall and Radoq had to step to see around an ornate statue of Chox to see the bank of dusty screens each of which showed a view of one street or another.

"You see everything from up here?" Radoq was appalled by the idea.

"Only in times of crisis." Tricial explained "I'll have to justify this use in court later. It's an emergency system but look." He pointed out a number of screens and Radoq could see the chanting and angry bands of men and women filling the streets. Juraj, he recalled, had turned the riots and protests almost into a business in the past few weeks and he could see the city guard simply standing by and watching, making no attempt to intervene.

"The sky port is more or less empty." Radoq noticed.

"Yes. But we don't have a ship."

Radoq turned in surprise "I do." He pointed to the former slave ship "It's that one. If we can get to the port, I can get us to the Eyrie."

"The Eyrie?" Tricial was surprised "What about the capital?"

"I have friends in the Eyrie. They'd help us. Won't you be arrested if we go to the capital?"

Tricial began to protest but eventually shrugged "Yes. Probably. For deserting my post."

"Well, if fleeing the mob is the only option then we should go somewhere nearby to plan our return."

"With twelve men?"

"That's what we can make plans for. We need more men for a start."

Tricial put his face in his hands "I'm not a warrior, Radoq. I'm an *ap* in case you hadn't noticed. Illegitimate. Barely a member of my tritus. I'm an administrator, I can't lead an army."

"I can."

"Oh, very well." Tricial turned to a handheld and pressed a complex series of keys "Lets get out of here first, then we can talk."

"How do you plan on getting to the sky port?"

Tricial glanced at him "Through the escape tunnel."

Radoq stared.

"Oh, don't look like that. I've got a bank of screens that allows me to see the entire town! An escape route isn't that hard to believe. Why do you think they insisted on building the keep above the sky port?" when Radoq didn't respond, Tricial continued "I'd imagine every Sheriff's quarters in every town has something similar. Our country isn't run by fools you know. Come on, Chirruf? Bring the men inside."

The handheld opened a narrow door in a basement, leading to a tunnel that was tall enough for a Domerus to walk without ducking. Radoq took a moment to examine the walls, seeing they were cut flawlessly from the rock of the mountain. He shook his head in wonderment, marvelling at the dedication of the administrators in Admirain to have such a route built. It must have cost a fortune.

"Radoq!"

Tricial was leading his men into the tunnel. Only eleven now, the injured man had breathed his last as they tried to move him and his friends had said their goodbyes. Aquar lighting buzzed and flickered as they headed down a long, smooth ramp. The tunnel twisted tightly, losing height rapidly as they traversed the high tiers of Fortisul. Sounds of chanting came at times as they passed by thin walls and Radoq marvelled at the skill of the engineers who had cut the passage from the rock. Then he noticed the walls here were rough in some places whilst the floor although smooth, was channelled and grooved and he nodded in understanding of the water that must have worn the original cave.

A door, this one the same colour as the surrounding rock. The Sheriff consulted his handheld, holding up a hand for silence. Outside, shouting voices sounded but they were moving and they quickly passed by.

"Let me to the front..." Radoq pushed past the guards, stepping in front of the Sheriff who nodded and gave way. Radoq opened the door. And started as he found himself under the same flight of steps he'd taken Evie up to show her the view the very day they'd landed in Fortisul. The passage led them right to the sky port, almost to the very dock the Freedman was anchored at.

"Come on!" Tricial pushed past seeing there were no dock workers nearby. Radoq jogged to overtake, seeing the looming sides of the former slave ship before them. Evie was lounging in a chair nearby, happily unaware of the carnage in the town.

"Alright?" she nodded as they drew close "Carnival in town is there?"

Quickly, Radoq related the events of the night telling her they needed to be underway immediately. In total disregard for his urgency, she shrugged and walked slowly up the gangway calling back over her shoulder as she went "Not much point. Whole ship'll probably break up as we clear the mountain. Either that, or your mate Juraj'll blow us out the air! Don't know why we bother..."

"Domerus!" Chirruf called to Radoq and he turned to see a mob at the far end of the dock. There were not many, a dozen or so men and women but they had spotted Tricial and were advancing.

Before Radoq could order her to stop, Chirruf had levelled her phasr and fired a trio of shots into the stone of the dock before them. That stopped the mob dead and Chirruf kept the phasr trained until Tricial was aboard and Evie had fired the engines.

"Go on, Domerus." Chirruf urged but Radoq shook his head, ordering her into the craft and staring at the mob who, seeing her leave were closing in although they were now walking warily and no longer shouted.

"Where's the Sheriff?" called a voice.

"He's leaving with me!" called back Radoq.

"And who are you, Domerus?"

"Radoq Loxelsus Po-Fortisun. I promise you that justice will return to Fortisul! No more thefts by Juraj, no more virals in the low lands. I'll be back to free you!"

A wet squelch and a sudden pulse of signals in his aurae and Radoq stepped smartly back as something flew through the air and landed on the gangway by his feet.

A rotten piece of food.

"Get out of here, Domerus! We don't need you! We're for Juraj! Juraj! Juraj! Juraj!"

With his enemy's name pounding in his ears Radoq waited only to hold their gaze a moment longer before he turned and made his way up the gangway.

"Alright?" Evie nodded to the controls "You gonna do the honours?"

She must have sensed his mood because she kept her mouth firmly shut as Radoq turned the Freedman at the dock and headed for the open sky. The city guard patrol ships hailed them over the communicator but at the sound of Tricial's voice, they backed off. The bulky ship picked up speed as it climbed out of the skyport into the flight lanes marked by flashing vakkbuoys but Radoq's mind was not on the pleasures of flight. Instead a weight sat on his shoulders, a burning sense of yet another failure.

Finally, as he set the ship on a wide banking turn to catch the easterly winds, he handed over to a silent Evie and headed out to the fighting deck. The wind rushed at him and his eyes watered until the aurae counteracted the effect and he ignored the elements, holding onto a strut and staring back at his homeland as the ship trudged further away.

I'll come back to you

Was it a broken promise? Or was it just one he had yet to fulfil? He vowed that it would be the latter.

It was then that Radoq saw it. Lun'erus eyes and perhaps

even those of Tricial would have missed it but Radoq's aurae was formidable and the small flash of light drew his gaze. He fumbled with the controls on his biom for a moment, bringing the image of Fortisul up higher and enhancing...

There!

Surely it couldn't be her? She'd be at the bedside of her husband, tending to him and cursing the name of Radoq Loxelsus Po-Fortisun! But she was on the middle tier, just visible beneath the stone buttress that shadowed the door...

Malain

A figure, staring up at the departing airship, watching him leave. Again.

"I'll come back to you!" he bellowed but the words were lost to the sky.

"I'll come back to you." Now they were only for him. His eyes never left hers. Was she watching him with anger? With relief? With hatred? With love?

He closed his eyes, screwing them tightly against the emotion that threatened to overwhelm him. When he opened them, the figure was gone.

"I'll come back to you." He murmured, the words barely a whisper.

But she was gone.

CHAPTER 11

Volanbuta was a hive of activity and energy that Radoq couldn't match. He felt drained, sapped of hope and energy and the vibrant colours and confusing tangle of people, airships and patched together streets served only to reflect from the dullness in his eyes. Even Evie let him be, her characteristic chatter still filling the bridge but muted. This served to ingratiate her with Tricial who'd blinked in surprise at the easy familiarity she'd had with Radoq. When the dour Domerus assumed a silent position staring out of the bridge, the two of them had assumed control of the ship, following Tricial's urging that they head for Volanbuta.

Below them, the vast green and brown of the Forest formed a horseshoe shape, hundreds of miles long around the shattered remnants of Ychacha. Evie had surreptitiously steered them on a course that avoided the fallen city but Volanbuta, dominating the sky before them was not beholden to Wallanrian superstitions and had passed right over the top on its journey south. Evie had set the *Freedman* to full power, vanishing down into the bowels of the engines to coax life from the ancient turbines but even as they began a gentle approach to the skyport, they were still moving at almost full speed.

"She flies well!"

Tricial started, turning to see if Evie had re-entered the bridge but of the coarse tongued lun'erus there was no sign. He looked to Radoq to see his fellow Domerus had finally broken from his silence although his expression was as dour as a funeral attendant.

"The city, you mean?"

"Yes. Volanbuta."

"Xeonison, you see. We build well in my country. Your own ship was from our lands, wasn't it?"

Radoq nodded once, a quick and painful dip of his head.

"Ah... But lost now?" Tricial searched for an escape from the difficult subject but Radoq beat him to it.

"How is it that a Xeonison comes to serve as Sheriff? I'd thought that only a Wallanrian could hold office in the civil service."

"I'm half Wallanrian. My mother was Xeonison. I'm fortunate to count myself a citizen of both countries."

"Oh?" Radoq glanced out the windows at the approaching city. A small tug had been released and was drifting back towards them slowly, a great stretch of cable holding it like an umbilical to the mass of the floating city.

"I grew up there, you know. Crossed the Wallanrian sea as a young man and found work in Solisul. My father's tritus were good enough to accept me and they found me positions in the service of the crown prince."

"How did your parents come to meet?"

Tricial gestured out the window "In Volanbuta. I lived here you know, oh a decade ago or more. I spent a few happy years here. It's quite the place." He looked meaningfully at Radoq "Plenty of distractions."

"Hmph."

Evie banged open the bridge door, seeing Radoq was speaking she resumed her usual patter as though nothing had changed "Alright, Domerus? That tug pilot gonna anchor us himself, is he?"

Cursing, Radoq jumped to the controls picking up the communicator to the sound of the irate tug pilot chattering in rapid Xeonison. Radoq attempted to stammer through a half dozen barely remembered phrases before Tricial, his face cringing at the butchery of his mother tongue seized the communicator and soothed the fiery tug pilot, guiding the connecting line that anchored the ship, pulling them in towards a gaudily painted dock.

Shadow blocked the bright sunlight from the bridge as the deck overhead covered them. Looking down, Radoq could see a second deck far below them and throughout the skyport, layers upon layers of vertically stacked docks, each marked with unique colour combinations in what he'd taken to be fantastic decorations were in fact a complex system of lanes and anchor points. Newcomers, it seemed were given no chance to make an error in docking and the tug deposited them at a mauve/green platform at which a sleek racing yacht rested. Evie, it transpired, was a racing enthusiast and she immediately began reeling off complex statistics and features of the craft as a smartly dressed customs officer waited for the gangway to swing open.

"... see the adamantine hull, Domerus? You'd think that'd make her slower, it's a heavy alloy after all but you know how canyon racing can get! A few bumps off a cliff face aren't going to put a dent in that whilst the competition will be scraping itself off the valley floor! Those stabilisers, too, they're corflye hide. Don't see that on any other ship, even you couldn't afford that, eh?"

Tricial blinked and stared.

"I had some corflye gloves." Radoq mused "My brother hunted the creature himself in the Northern Range."

"Domerus?" a Xeonison voice drew their attention and the next few minutes were spent in a tedious but efficient process of Tricial proving his citizenship which waived most of the docking fee and then listing each member of the crew before they were allowed to step foot on Volanbuta's solid deck.

"Well made." Radoq noted, looking down at his boot which felt sturdy on the deck.

"A metal structure, covered in insulation and then a thin soft layer to ease walking." Tricial turned and pointed across the dock where a cross section was visible "See the thickness? It's fire, weather and plasma resistant. Otherwise a gatfight would tear the place apart."

"So, it's more or less a giant airship?" Evie was bundled up in a greatcoat, hood and thick fur scarf so tightly that she looked twice her normal size. Radoq reflected that the air here was cool, attributable to the altitude.

"No." Tricial had spotted a sign down the dock and was leading them towards a well populated pathway that Radoq realised passed for a street in the flying city "It's more like an interconnected series of airships all lashed together. The connections..." he stopped at a wide junction, pointing at a narrow walkway, only wide enough for one person to cross and bordered only by a thin, well rusted mesh "The connections are flexible to allow for the air currents. Best not to fall off though."

"Best not." Agreed Evie, backing as far away from the treacherous walkway as she could.

Looking down, Radoq could see the ground far below them. It was true, a safety net was spread out at the bottom of the city but from this height it looked as though a human form would pass straight through and continue down to the forest thousands of feet below.

"Evie!" a lun'erus voice called and all three turned to see a cluster of dock technicians hurrying towards them. Radoq watched as embraces and back thumps were shared and then experienced the odd disconnect between lun'erus and unfamiliar Domerus. Evie's friends were Wallanrian, she'd met them in Admirain when training there but that was as far as Radoq got because the lun'erus left the two surprised Domerus, heading for a drink nearby.

"A drink sounds excellent." Radoq observed, watching Evie and the others vanish around a corner without so much as a backward glance.

"I know a place, its on the upper deck." Tricial gestured down the 'street', indicating an enormous metal tube that stood vertically, the top vanishing through the deck above them.

"Is that some kind of elevator?" Radoq asked, seeing the small line of Volanbutans waiting before a small gate set into the side of the tube.

It was and Tricial demonstrated, talking enthusiastically as they stepped onto the wide platform, a lun'erus attendant slamming the gate shut behind them. A whirr of a vakkor engine and the platform began to rise, passing straight up the tube. Radoq looked upwards as the local Volanbutans chattered or stood silent, clearly unamazed by the marvel of engineering. As they reached the deck above, he stared, watching as they passed through the thick layers of the deck and the platform slowed, arriving at the deck above. The unsmiling attendant banged open the gate and Radoq stepped out into a wondrous, if low ceilinged open deck filled with people moving to and fro across the space. Some wore work uniforms, others were clearly Xeonison Domerus who regarded Radoq warily but no-one, he noted, was stood still. No time for leisure aboard a flying city and he said as much to Tricial who agreed.

"When I was here it was the hardest I've worked in my long life. The city takes constant maintenance to stay airborne and then there's food, sanitation, all the issues a city would face normally but there's no single source of income. Trade is a great help but mostly the city relies on the settlements it docks near to."

"I see."

It was busy with a thrum of energy filling the air over the very perceptible thrum of the engines. Leisure did exist, it transpired although as a Wallanrian waiter ushered the two of them to a private booth in a wood panelled beer hall, Radoq noted that only non-natives were ordering drinks. Tricial ordered a stone pitcher of 'sky spirit', a clear, potent liquid that burned like fire on the way down but left a wondrously fruity taste on Radoq's lips.

They sat in a brooding silence for some time, working their way through the drink, ignoring the warnings from their bioms.

"I wonder –" Tricial began then stopped, considering his words. Overhead an aquar lamp crackled and spat blue sparks.

"Go on."

"I wonder if I might ask you, Radoq. Do you hold any

animosity towards me?"

Radoq was baffled "For what?"

"Fortisul was your home long before it was mine." Tricial was fidgeting with his empty glass. Radoq picked up the pitcher and dumped another load in.

"It's home to many."

"Including your family. Your tritus."

Radoq understood "Who you think you failed? No, Tricial, I don't hold a grudge against you. Juraj is a smart man, he fooled me well and as to his attack on your men, well, I never guessed he'd go to such a length."

"Do you know what provoked it?"

"Juraj told us that you'd ordered our arrest." Radoq shrugged "I suppose I should ask if you bear a grudge against me."

"You mean for stealing Fortisul's grain and selling it to Volanbuta?"

"Yes. For that."

"No." Tricial took a deep swig of the sky spirit, his eyes flicking upwards as the aquar bulb that lit the booth spat "Whoever is to blame for my failings, I'll take the responsibility myself. I should have seen earlier what Juraj was doing. I suppose he told you I was stealing the grain?"

Quickly, Radoq relayed his story to the Sheriff from his arrival in Fortisul to the fight in the keep. Tricial's eyes widened in shock and then shook his head in disgust.

"I negotiated with the aldermen here to stop buying the grain! I told them it was stolen and they agreed but the shipments continued, late at night. Juraj is a clever man." Tricial shook his head.

"He's a crook. An opportunist thief."

"No." Tricial reached across the table to grip Radoq's wrist "He's dangerous. Far more than a common criminal. He has ambitions, Radoq, beyond Fortisul. He wants power."

"Well, perhaps the crown prince will make him Sheriff now." The spirit had softened Radoq and the joke was poor but Tricial looked at him hard.

"Only a Domerus can serve as Sheriff. Even a lowly Ap like me."

"It was a joke –" Radoq protested but Tricial cut him off.

"No. That's what Juraj wants you see. That's why he would have kept you, a Fallen Domerus so close. Because you both want the same thing. He wants to Ascend."

The laugh started somewhere in Radoq's belly and shook his body all the way up until it burst from his mouth in a great guffaw. There was little humour in it though. Instead, in his mind's eye he saw Malain and Juraj, both as Domerus living together, happy together.

"Laugh you may, Radoq, but Juraj is serious about this. You know his surname?"

"Aptoin." Radoq remembered "But he's lun'erus. He can't ascend." A memory sparked and he winced, remembering the agony of his own ascension as his body burned with the power surging through his every cell "The transformation would kill him. Lun'erus aren't bred for it."

"I know that as well as you. But he's got it into his head that this 'Aptoin' means he's the long lost Ap of some tritus."

Radoq stared "That's madness."

"It may be. But if he's right? What if he ascended as a Domerus?"

"He'd need a Ji to ascend him –" Radoq cut himself off "And my father is still in the town, bound by an oath to remain there."

"And we can assume Juraj is now looking for a way to trick him into attempting an ascension."

Radoq sat back, blowing air out of his cheeks "Well, that makes it easier in some ways. As a Domerus I can openly challenge him to a duel. He can't refuse without losing honour and then my father would make him Fallen."

"And you, Radoq of the Golden Kote would best him in any fair fight."

The corner of Radoq's mouth twitched.

"In any case –" Tricial threw his hands in the air, sitting back to mirror Radoq "- we're still here and he's still there. As far as we know he's about as likely as becoming Domerus as he is of drinking sky spirit with the Dark Ji."

"And we're as close to liberating our home as Evie is to stopping talking."

"The crown prince will likely demand I return to Admirain." Tricial nudged his glass with his finger "Perhaps I'll be imprisoned? Punishment for my failure."

Radoq slapped a hand on the table, startling the older man "No. A wiser man than I once told me that self-pity was not the duty of Domerus. When we accept our failures and move on, we move forward. If we sit and wallow, we help no one." His eyes landed on the now empty pitcher between them "Except perhaps barkeeps the world over."

Tricial nodded slowly. He looked old and tired.

"You and I are still alive, in possession of a fine ship and we still have your men loyal to us. We're in a friendly city, drinking fine spirits and tonight we'll sleep soundly in a bed of our choosing. Who are we to complain and bemoan our losses? No." Radoq slapped the table again, drawing the attention of the other clientele in the bar whom he ignored "Tonight, we can wallow in our sorrows and this fine drink but only if we make a pact that tomorrow, we concentrate all our efforts on defeating Juraj and liberating Fortisul."

Tricial sighed.

"A deal, Tricial! Will you shake my hand on it?"

Another sigh "Oh, well at least this way I might keep my job. To Chox with it, Radoq, a pact! We'll retake our home!"

Both men stood, clasping their hands as Radoq called for a second pitcher. When it came, he filled their glasses and raised one in a toast "To a pact."

"To a pact."

"And to grief."

Tricial was confused "To grief? For your dead soldiers?"

"No." Radoq smiled sadly "To lost love, if you must know."

"Oh?" Tricial smiled now "What's her name, this lost girl of yours?"

"You'll know her tritus well. Malain Saxodas –"

"Po-Hammun." Finished Tricial, nodding "A beautiful woman if I'm any judge." He frowned, suddenly confused "But surely she's not lost to you? She's in Fortisul."

"With Juraj. *Married* to Juraj."

Tricial stared "Married? A Domerus of her status married to a lun'erus criminal? Have you taken leave of your senses, Radoq? A marriage like that has never happened! Domerus are not allowed to marry into the lun'erus! You know this!"

Radoq shrugged "A faux marriage then. An illegal marriage. Even so, she loves him, not me."

"No." Tricial was shaking his head stubbornly "I can't speak for Malain but I can speak for her tritus. They've not been seen in weeks. Word is Juraj took them. You've seen her mother the Ji? Saxo is an ancient woman. She couldn't resist a determined gang of lun'erus like Juraj's! No, Radoq. Malain's mother is held by Juraj. What you saw was nothing more than her attempts to keep her mother safe and well."

Radoq stood up so fast he knocked the table sideways sending both glasses and the pitcher crashing to the floor. Heads swivelled to them but the two Domerus ignored them.

"Then I have been played for a fool *again*."

Tricial started to say something reassuring but Radoq held up a hand.

"Enough. Enough foolishness. Enough losing, enough innocent death and enough failures."

Tricial stood slowly his eyes on Radoq's features which were set like stone. His eyes burned like the aquar lamp that sputtered above them.

"Tricial Pulciasus Ap-Jatuh." Radoq's tone was as formal as that of a Ji ascending a young Domerus "Will you bear witness as Sheriff of Fortisul to my blood oath?"

Eyes wide, Tricial nodded "I will."

Radoq tugged at the sleeve of the light shirt he'd worn since arriving in Fortisul, tearing the cloth with a savage jerk and shredding it so that he now wore one short sleeve on his right arm whilst his left stayed long. Discarding the torn cloth, he placed the nail of his forefinger on the skin of his bare forearm, just below the elbow. His biom suddenly glowed with a golden light as the power contained within it seethed and Radoq drew the tip of the fingernail down the skin, scoring a deep line in the flesh from which blood seeped. He finished just above the wrist, forming a deep, bloody score which formed a patch of gore on his skin. Already, the blood flow was stemming as the biom worked to close the wound but as soon as the liquid had stopped flowing, the healing process stopped and the wound remained.

"Then bear witness that I, Radoq Loxelsus *Po*-Fortisun swear by this blood oath that I will free my home from Juraj's tyranny. I will liberate my tritus, free my people and deliver Malain from Juraj's criminal grasp."

"I witness this blood oath." Tricial's voice was hoarse, deafened in the weight of the emotion on Radoq's face.

"By the laws of a blood oath, if I fail, my life will be forfeit." His eyes met Tricial's and the older man felt the shock of his gaze like a physical blow "You as witness will ensure this oath is fulfilled."

"I will."

Radoq smiled and the tension lessened somewhat. Lun'erus all around were staring at this Domerus pact, aware that something profound was happening in their midst but unable to fully comprehend the magnitude of Radoq's promise.

"The oath is sworn." Radoq finished.

"The oath is sworn." Tricial agreed.

CHAPTER 12

Radoq raised his hand in a final farewell as Alderman Kjall turned and vanished into the maze of Volanbuta's streets. The great engines that powered the city had already been roaring but now they increased to a fever pitch as the pilots on the bridge lifted the great behemoth into the grey sky, climbing higher and higher until they vanished through the clouds and all that was left was the fading throb of the engines.

The Eyrie seemed empty after the noise and bright colours of the flying city. For months the two had clung to the top of the craggy outcrop that supported the city passing trade and goods back and forth and drawing every mercantile ship in the country to the bountiful markets. Prices had been through the roof to the point where the Eyrie's council had stepped in and begun rationing food, issuing stamps to the lun'erus in their city lest families be forced from their homes. Now the great Xeonison marvel was leaving, things were beginning to settle and Radoq could understand the shouted insults and raised fists that chased Volanbuta into the now empty sky. The people of the Eyrie were glad to see it gone.

"I'm sorry that they feel that way." Tricial was sat on a stone bench, carved from the rock of the mountain. They were on a small natural ledge that the stonemasons of the Eyrie had long ago repurposed as a viewing platform overlooking the bustling sky port. Radoq was standing, one hand resting on the ornately carved railing while Tricial was resting to his right.

"It's been difficult for them." Radoq observed.

"We didn't come here to disrupt their lives."

"No. But the trade has been good for the economy. They'll benefit in the long term."

"I was glad when the council began issuing food." Tricial was troubled by the memory of beggars in Fortisul still. He'd petitioned the council at length, reminding them of what he'd seen in Fortisul and warning them it would happen in their city too.

"They're good people here. They look after their own. Besides –" Radoq pointed to a new, sleek looking cutter with distinctive black paint that was busily taking on joyriders "- some of them have done well."

"The merchants have."

"And some others. Think of the dock technicians."

It was true. The techs who would previously have been grimy and shabby as per their trade were now noticeably sporting brand new overalls and tools and as each shift ended, they could been seen in crowds around cleaning stations frantically scrubbing new stains from the cloth or scraping patches of rust from steel tools.

"Still." Radoq turned away from the port, leaning his back against the rail "We couldn't have achieved what we have without Volanbuta."

Implied was his thanks for Tricial's introductions and connections aboard the flying city. His Xeonison heritage had opened doors Radoq would never otherwise have passed through and the few months since he'd sworn his oath had been filled with a new kind of warfare, one that Radoq had struggled to learn.

Subterfuge.

Through bribes, well paid agents, rumours, informants and more than a few poorly told lies, Radoq had built a picture of Juraj, his history, his organisation, his strengths and next to it an ever evolving understanding of his position now in Fortisul and the forces he had at his disposal. Which were not inconsiderable. Since Tricial had sent by dispatch his report to the capital, their network of spies had told them of the would-be rebel's paranoia.

Certain that the crown prince would send a punitive expedition, he'd sent word across the Dark Lands and beyond the eastern desert for mercenaries to flock to Fortisul. Radoq had seen them, coming in ships or sometimes full squadrons, all of them streaking west past the Eyrie. None came back and the reports of the savage taxes Juraj was extorting from Fortisul explained the vast sums of money that would surely be needed to maintain such an army.

From the crown prince however, there was no word. No ships had flown from Admirain, no soldiers had marched and Radoq had finally turned to his friend Oprain Radoqsus Ji-Brassul in frustration.

"There could be a thousand reasons, Radoq." Oprain had counselled him, hardly looking up from the intense game of Sagalm that he and Tricial were battling over "Embarrassment for one – I can't remember the last time a Sheriff was overthrown by a lun'erus criminal." He looked up at Tricial "No offence, of course."

Tricial's eyes hadn't left the board "None taken."

"He could be hoping the situation will right itself which, if you have anything to do with it, it will." His eyes lingered on the blood of Radoq's forearm which he wore bare every day.

"Can we send agents to Admirain to find out?" Radoq wondered thinking of the quiet young man they'd dispatched that morning to Fortisul.

"No! No." Oprain turned away from the board for a moment "No, you must not do that. Admirain is a nest of spies, liars and politicians. Sending a spy into their midst is tantamount to declaring war to some of the powerful Domerus there. If word got back to the crown prince he'd demand your head."

"Then how do we find out what's happening?"

Oprain had spared a few moments to defeat Tricial in two more moves leaving the Sheriff sputtering with indignation before he'd turned back to Radoq "I shall go."

"You? You'll go and spy in Admirain?"

"Spy?" Oprain shook his head "I have to bear witness to the

high court as it is for my arrest of Argan." He smiled gratefully at Radoq "I intend to ask the crown prince outright what his plans are."

Radoq stared but Tricial chuckled "That may be the most sensible move you've ever made." He gestured at the board "You saw how he took my Ji there? Subterfuge and distraction up until that final move. Oprain is right."

And he had been. So, weeks prior Oprain had set out for Admirain leaving Radoq and Tricial to manage their ever increasing network of informants.

"Oh, Oprain left Admirain this morning." Tricial stood up to fish a small handheld from beneath his long coat and show Radoq the screen "He's headed this way."

Radoq frowned "Because of the attack?"

"No. See? He says his business is complete."

"Ah. We've had no word from Fortisul?"

"Nothing."

"Good."

The news was good because rumours had been flooding to them that Juraj planned to attack the Eyrie. They'd made no secret of their presence here, indeed, Radoq had made sure to spread word of his blood oath drawing in lun'erus who pledged themselves to his tritus in the fight. They now stood at the head of a full complement of fighting men, fifty soldiers all well experienced and armed spent their days in the east wing of Oprain's house, training, shooting and eating well. They were getting better every day, working more efficiently together and honing their skills. But still, Radoq was frustrated. Fifty men was not an army but the ever increasing numbers of ships swooping across the Dark Lands was becoming a formidable force and despite the data he'd collated, the knowledge he had of Juraj's every movement, Radoq was no closer to seizing Fortisul than he had been when he'd made his oath.

"Back to training?" Tricial suggested and Radoq nodded, leading the way around the thin path that led back down to the dockside. They headed to a gondola to the higher levels passing the bounty of Volanbuta's trade. Great stacks of dried food in crates, ammunition in thick lead boxes being watched hawkishly by air Marines, timber, fuel, cloths and strange foods were all around them and Radoq pointed them out as they passed as though proving to Tricial that Volanbuta had been helpful to the city.

The two of them stepped around the training yard carefully, wary of the sim-bolts their soldiers were firing at one another. The fifty soldiers were working out of two makeshift hulks which had been constructed to provide training in ship to ship combat. A trio of Air Marines had volunteered as instructors, two Sergeants and a Captain and Radoq had quickly learned to ignore the Captain instead watching with restrained amusement as the man made long winded and often nonsensical suggestions to which the Sergeants would listen politely before agreeing heartily and then suggesting a shorter, totally different set of orders to which the Captain would nod his agreement.

"Morning, Sir!" the closest of the Sergeants, a lun'erus with a luxurious beard named Staph snapped a crisp salute at Radoq who bowed in return, stepping up a flight of stairs to join Staph on the viewing platform that allowed them to look down into the roofless training hulks.

"Good morning, Sergeant." He looked down into the yard, eyes scanning the scenario the Marines had set "Ship A is attacking, B is defending?"

"That's right, Sir." Staph pointed at the hull marked B which was closest to them "Only A have got limited ammunition and B have got a thousand rounds apiece and a crate of stun pulsans."

As if on cue, the soldiers from A breached the gangway and a squad piled into B, phasrs and coltacs swinging this way and that. A concussive *BOOM* rocked the training yard and Radoq saw the hiss and crackle of aquar as jets of blue lightning shot into the air and Radoq felt Staph repress a chuckle as the boarding party fell to their knees clutching eyes and ears or simply collapsed.

Chuk-chuk-chuk-chuk

The sim-bolts erupted from the ambush, coating the stunned soldiers with plasma, albeit a significantly cooler version than the live bolts used. Still, the force of the impact was painful and shouts of fury rose from ship A as the soldiers rushed in to rescue their fellows. An exchange of bolts followed as the attacking force tried and failed to establish a hold on the enemy ship, the defenders of which simply poured gatfire into them. Soon, the commander of the attackers was forced to order a retreat and Rakr, the second Marine Sergeant bellowed an end to the exercise.

Radoq jumped down to the training yard for the debrief with Staph leaping down beside him, wincing at the impact even with his distinctive black leather jump boots.

"How did that go, troops?" Rakr and Staph had the same commanding presence from years of experience training soldiers that Radoq knew was invaluable.

A murmur of discontent from the stunned soldiers who were only now recovering.

"Speak up!" snapped Staph.

"Would have gone better with the Domerus." Someone muttered and Radoq saw it was Chirruf, one of the survivors of Tricial's guard they'd brought from Fortisul.

"Aye, that it would." Rakr nodded. He was from somewhere in the Northern Massif and his accent was so thick that Radoq had to concentrate to understand him "But the scenario didn't involve the Domerus, did it?"

The silence seemed to acknowledge that it did not.

"So, where's the commander? You, Chirruf?" the woman nodded "What else could you have done?"

She didn't have an answer. In her defence, Radoq could see she was still suffering the effects of the stun pulsan but he knew Staph and Rakr had no time for excuses. When Chirrut didn't answer they turned to the rest of the group for answers but the soldiers had no response.

A hand rose into the air and Staph grinned at Evie who'd

insisted on watching the bout "Miss?"

"Should've pulled back and took their engines out with pinzgats." She managed to make the point sound obvious, earning her a few filthy looks from the tired soldiers.

"Exactly!" Rakr nodded in approval "A good tactical move would've been to take the ship off a hundred metres and target the engines. That way they'd have to land and then you could breach 'em wherever you wanted. Avoid their ambush that way. Anything else?"

"Target the crew quarters. Thin their ranks." Radoq put in and Rakr raised his eyebrows at him.

"The Domerus says kill 'em all." He turned back to the troops managing to make a joke at Radoq's expense in the odd way the Sergeants had of doing so without giving offence "Up to you if you want to do that –" he paused for the soldiers to laugh "- but for those of us who haven't sworn a blood oath, engines and other critical structures are a good shout."

Radoq smiled at the joke but made a mental note to watch his mouth around the troops. Staph took over in a long explanation of how they now wanted the soldiers to start thinking outside their given parameters and to be innovative with their attacks. Radoq nodded but stepped away as Tricial waved to him from the observation balcony.

"It's Oprain." They headed inside the house to the communicator on which Oprain's face appeared.

"I have a job for you and your men, Radoq." He began after the usual greetings. On the screen, his face was fuzzy and the image lagged as he spoke. His voice had the crackling quality usual with in-flight transmissions "After the battle you fought in, we lost control of the western part of the desert."

Radoq knew this and thought of the slave encampment he'd been held in. The one benefit of Juraj shipping mercenaries in from the east was that the trade had more or less halted.

"This means there are now virals spreading out into the desert. Their numbers are increasing."

"We've seen them almost daily here." Radoq told the older

man remembering the sight of the creatures swarming around the crag.

"The Eyrie is safe." Oprain reassurred them "But this morning we had a report from a passing ship that the sightings in the Western Hills are increasing."

Radoq ground his teeth "That Chox'd fool Juraj is amassing an army and he won't chase virals out of the hills? The whole point in building Fortisul was to protect them! If they –"

Oprain spoke across him, either mishearing him over the communicator or simply to cut him off "Radoq, you must take those soldiers to the hills and fight the virals there. We can't have them crossing the River Tymere."

Radoq sighed "It's a Chox'd shame, Oprain that you wont let me arrest a few of those mercenary ships and force them to clear the hills out."

Oprain rolled his eyes, the image freezing on the screen for a moment so that he was left in a look of exasperation "Radoq, need I remind you that I am responsible for policing the air around the Eyrie? Those mercenaries have broken no laws in flying to Fortisul so I'd have to arrest you for air piracy. Secondly, attacking innocent men unprovoked is illegal and dishonourable so put those thoughts from your mind." He smiled to take the sting out of his words.

"We will, Oprain. Tell me, what did the Crown Prince say?"

"Very little. But you'll be pleased to hear Argan has been found guilty and will be sent to the capital as soon as I return."

"Excellent."

"You'll head for the Western Hills?"

"Yes, yes. But why are there so many now?"

"Ah." Oprain cleared his throat "After the battle the enemy lost a lot of troops."

Radoq leaned forward, suddenly interested.

"They've lost control of the desert completely. From the reports coming to Admirain, it's overrun with virals."

"Chox!" Radoq turned to Tricial "Then –"

"That's not your concern, Radoq. If this visit has assured me of anything, its that the soft landers are not like us. If the virals cross the River Tymere then they'll be in the four cities within a week. We can't have another Ychacha. Remember Radoq, you are not free like the lun'erus. Your duty is to your people."

"I know, Oprain."

The older man began another lecture and Radoq nudged the control of the communicator, ending the transmission.

CHAPTER 13

"He's right of course." Radoq admitted bitterly to Tricial later that day. They leaned on the terrace at the front of Oprain's house, looking down on the bustling splendour of the Eyrie as below them Evie ordered supplies onto the *Freedman*. White cloud surrounded the city, hiding the Dark Lands from sight and giving the impression that they sat aloft in the heavens. Far to the west, Radoq could just make out the tops of the Western Hills poking through the cloud and that was where his mind lay, his duty drawing him there even as he knew that below the cloud more mercenary ships would be speeding to Fortisul.

Word of the viral sightings had spread like wildfire through the town. The lower walls were not visible from this height but even above the clouds Radoq could see the increased patrols of Marines. Every ship that came in was greeted by an armed guard although, as Tricial pointed out who ever heard of *virals* being on a ship?

"The wind is picking up." Tricial observed and Radoq lifted his gaze from the tops of the hills to see that beyond them the great sheet of white cloud was breaking up.

"It'll be a strong headwind for us then."

"Sir?" Rakr and Staph had appeared "Ready for the troops to head down?

"Yes. But you two aren't coming are you?" Radoq looked askance at their weapons and body armour.

"Beg your pardon, Sir but we are." Staph told him.

"You're here to train these soldiers, not to fight."

Staph chewed his lip for a moment "Fighting virals is a

training exercise isn't it? Can't see it being that bad. Besides, Oprain will want Eyrie men on board."

Radoq tried to protest but he recognised the need for the two Sergeants to be with their troops and besides, they were probably the two best soldiers in the Eyrie so it wouldn't hurt.

The sky port was the usual cluster of activity and their small group of soldiers drew no particular attention as they trotted through the crowds to where Evie waited, her hands on her hips. A stream of ribald profanities issued from her as the soldiers ran past and Staph responded in kind prompting a rare cackle of genuine laughter from the engineer.

"Wind's picked up, Domerus." She called, her humour vanishing like a snuffed candle.

"I saw."

"Shipping's being diverted." She pointed to the shipping lanes that hung in the air. Indeed, incoming ships were approaching with the wind from the west whilst those craft leaving the sky port were heading east, some looping back around the city to join the correct lane.

"We'll have to swing around." Radoq nodded "That's no problem."

"Waste of time." Evie led the way up the cargo ramp into the same hold Radoq had been chained in. Now, stacks of cot beds and fighting gear lined the space between the walls where the soldiers were already claiming their own small havens. Small squabbles stopped and the lun'erus troops nodded to him as he passed, muttering 'Domerus' and moving kit out of his way.

"Chox!" Evie swore as they made their way through the narrow door that led towards the bridge "Have you actually made them like you?"

"What do you mean?"

"They shut their traps and jumped to it when you got in. That's respect if I know it."

Staph had caught up and of course, made a joke out of it "Yeah, you should hear him telling them to slaughter every last man! Chox forbid he ever get his hands on a nuklera or something!

We'd have another Dark Rain!"

"I was there when he said that." Evie called back to Staph "Are you having trouble remembering, old man? Is it past your bedtime? Domerus, I think this old codger should be left behind."

Radoq chuckled at the banter. Although Staph was probably twice Evie's age he moved with the grace of a far younger man, even when he wasn't wearing his highly polished jump boots. A thought occurred to him as they entered the bridge and Radoq ran through the startup protocols for the engines.

"Staph? Wouldn't a better solution to that scenario earlier be using jump boots? You'd get above the enemy then land on the top of the ship?"

Staph turned slowly with such withering condescension in his face that Radoq was taken aback "Domerus, how many of us do you see wearing these?" he lifted a boot with surprising dexterity and slammed it onto the control panel for Radoq to see.

"Just the two of you."

"Just the two of us." Staph nodded "And you think we'll just give out these boots to a bunch of land-leggers like them lot? You know how we earn our boots, right?"

Radoq confessed that he did not.

"First, we run from the ground all the way up to the higher tiers."

"The whole way up the city?"

"No. The whole way up the mountain. Got to do it in less than three hours with all your kit. Got that? Right, then we go back down and spend a night by ourselves in the Dark Lands. Just you, a coltac and five bolts. Sensible ones like me don't use 'em. Then its straight back up to the lower gate. Got an hour to make the run from the time the sun first rises. You get there late, they lock you out for another night." Staph grinned "Not many fail that run. Then you're into a cage with a viral. You, them and a knife. That's it. You manage all that without dying or running too slow and they'll *start* training you how to jump out of airships.

You don't keep up with the training, you do something wrong and it's back to the start. Back to the run from the ground. You pass everything and they'll give you the jump boots. Reckon you could do it, Domerus?"

Radoq blinked "Yes."

Rakr had entered the bridge and caught the last part of the conversation "Ah, but there's a version for Domerus you see." He grinned nastily "Obviously you can run up the mountain in ten minutes flat with your fancy biom so you have to switch it off. Dark Lands is a hard place even for Domerus."

"But then." Staph took back over "Just to make it really fair for you we give you less time for everything. And it's not one viral you fight, its five. And you don't have a knife."

"And we tie your hands behind your back –" Rakr lost it and cracked up provoking a roar of laughter from his fellow Sergeant who slapped a hand on the control console as Radoq released the docking clamps.

"Hah! Alright, maybe we exaggerate but you can't use your biom and you have less time than we do. There's been plenty Domerus who's failed it."

The challenge was there from the two men and Radoq could feel it tugging at him but the dried blood on his arm was a constant reminder of his oath and he pushed the information to the back of his mind, ignoring the sniggering of the Sergeants.

"Domerus? You getting us out of here or what?" Evie's sharp tones brought his mind back to the present and Radoq eased the fine adjustment control to pull the ship away from the dock. He cast a farewell look at the Eyrie, knowing that long, gruelling days lay ahead and the home comforts of the city lay behind. Ahead, the markers showed the way and he eased the *Freedman* out into the air currents. Already the cloud had been blown into small tufts leaving a clear picture of the blackened ground that stretched out before them. Radoq saw the two lun'erus Sergeants had gone silent, staring at the Dark Lands with looks of displeasure. He reflected that a night on the ground without the protection of his biom would be a formidable challenge and he nodded again in his appreciation of their fortitude.

"Staph." He called as they cleared the first marker, turning the rudder and letting the strong wind take them eastwards. The Sergeant glanced back at him.

"Sir?"

"Either of you two fail that run up the hill?"

Staph sniggered but Rakr looked mutinous and said nothing. Staph answered for his friend.

"Rakr here was ten seconds late for the morning run. Stopped for a lie in with his viral girlfriend."

"Chox'd pack of them came by my little hole I'd dug. Had to lie there like a corpse whilst they came past then ran faster than anyone's ever done that run."

"Still finished late." Staph chortled.

"Yeah." Rakr eyeballed his friend "Managed it the second time though, eh?"

"That you did." Staph nodded.

"So you spent two nights in the Dark Lands?" Radoq asked.

"Oh yeah." Rakr nodded importantly "Most experienced soldier in the Eyrie when it comes to the Dark Lands I am."

"Shortest life expectancy I bet." Evie interjected from beside Radoq at the control panel. She nodded at Staph "'Cept old man over here."

"You watch it." Staph warned and Evie threw a sheet of paper at him.

The banter carried them out of the Eyrie's shadow in a wider loop than Radoq had intended but the great bulk of the cargo ship caught the wind and the engines struggled to right them. Tricial stared out at the Dark Lands in a morbid fascination that Radoq had noticed the older man possessed ever since Volanbuta had crossed the Western Hills.

"It's odd to me that such a bleak place holds so much threat." the Sheriff called back to him from his position staring out over the fighting deck."

"It looks barren from here."

"Chox'd well is barren." Rakr muttered.

"I suppose we're lucky to have the mountains." Tricial pointed to the far north where the snow capped peaks of the Northern Massif reached the black rock below them.

"Lucky?" Rakr had crossed the bridge to stare out the same window as Tricial "S'not luck. Three mountain ranges protecting Wallanria?"

"Two." corrected Radoq quietly.

"Two and some big hills." Rakr agreed "But the hills, the mountains and the rivers are the reason they build Admirain in the first place. If it weren't protected by all that then it'd be further west, away from the Dark Lands."

"I see." Tricial said politely "And your people are from the Southern Range?"

"Northern Massif." Rakr pointed to the peaks "Southern Range is really part of the same mountain range only they got pushed further south when the Dark Lands was formed."

That didn't sound right to Radoq but Rakr was speaking with great pride and he didn't feel the need to correct him.

"'Course, we're not protected from the virals and the rocks like them in the Eyrie." Rakr continued, labouring the 'them' by indicating Staph "They's got walls and guards. We live on farms out in the valleys."

"In the vall-eys." Staph mimicked his friend's accent."

"Right. Sleep in balloons we do in case the virals come sweeping over us in the night. Many's the morning we woke to find our cattle been ravaged. Had to have a guard at night we did. Earliest memory is being sat with a phasr through the wee hours looking for virals."

"Is that why your chat's so weak?" Staph asked seriously prompting Rakr to seize a tin mug and throw it with shocking accuracy into the other Sergeant's face. Fortunately, Staph ducked and it glanced off his shoulder as both men cracked up.

"When you say the rocks, Sergeant, do you mean the black parts?" Tricial asked when the mirth had subsided.

"No, Sir." Rakr pointed then realised he couldn't see and turned to Radoq "You couldn't take us down a bit could you, Sir?"

Radoq obliged, adjusting the lift in the vakkor engine, and allowing the weight of the ship to drag them down towards the Dark Lands.

"That'll do." Rakr waved a hand "See them green bits there? That's the glowing rocks. See them all across the Dark Lands."

"Chox!" Tricial leaned forward in fascination "And are they always in a cluster like that?" he pointed and Radoq looked out to see the rocks which were more accurately boulders were stacked together emitting a faint greenish glow even in the daylight.

"Some of them are ridges." Rakr said still with a note of pride in his tone as though he were responsible for the creation of the Glowing Rocks "Some are little hills and some are just single rocks – oh! Look. Virals!"

And there they were. Radoq set the controls to hold them at their current position and joined the others at the window looking out to see a pod of thirty or forty of the twisted forms clambering over one another to get to the Rocks.

"Eurgh!" Evie grimaced "They almost look human!"

"They are human." Tricial observed casually.

"What?"

"Well, that is to say they *were* human." Tricial corrected himself. Evie was looking at him in horror whilst Radoq who knew this, stayed silent "Back long ago before the Dark Lands were formed there was a virus – that's why they're called the virals – and it transformed almost all of humanity into those things."

"But – but they've been around for thousands of years!" Evie exclaimed "They aren't the *same* humans, are they?"

"What? Oh, no. No, nothing like that. I think the lifespan of a viral is only a few years." Tricial, Radoq could see was pulling up some information on his biom "Here it is. Average lifespan is ten years although they've lived as long as twenty in captivity."

"Someone has them in a zoo?" Evie's incredulity had turned to disgust.

"Well, see the virus was incredibly contagious. In fact, that's why the Domerus were bred. We were made to be stronger, faster, bigger and healthier than normal humans. Then, when the biom technology was invented it protected us from the virus. Of course, by that point Domerus and lun'erus had become so separated in our development that the technology wouldn't work on normal humans – on lun'erus I mean."

There was a light in Evie's eye that Radoq didn't recognise. Gone was the usual exuberance and he thought for the first time he was catching a glimpse of what lay beneath the veneer "But the virus can't affect us now, can it?"

"Can do." Staph spoke up "We have quarantine procedures in the Eyrie. Still get a couple of people each year infected. Spreads fast, too."

"What happens?"

"Now they just die. The virus has mutated so it doesn't make you into one of them but it kills you just as well as one of them would."

"Urgh."

"I believe they reproduce now quite effectively –" Tricial began but Evie held up her hands.

"Alright! Alright! I don't need to hear about Virals bumping uglies!" she crossed to the other side of the bridge and busied herself with a chart, adjusting the glass that ran across it plotting their position.

"Do they always cluster on the rocks?" Tricial asked Rakr and the Sergeant nodded going off on a long winded description of the habits of virals which Radoq tuned out, crossing to Evie.

"You alright?"

"Fine." The mask was back up "See this?" she pointed at the chart. The glass that marked their position was suspended from a network of wires that tracked their movement. Next to it, a dusty screen flashed dark shapes which were supposed to show other ships but Radoq had never trusted the machines which were relics of ancient technology and notoriously inaccurate.

"What's that?" he pointed at a great dark mass somewhere south and west of them.

Evie spared him a withering glance "The Eyrie, oh great

leader."

Radoq blushed "Yes, of course."

"That's alright. I'm glad it's actually showing us something for once. Those, however, I'm not sure about." Evie tapped the screen showing three small dots which were north and east of them but heading west, hugging the base of the Northern Massif.

"Ships." Radoq didn't see the problem "They're more than likely mercenaries heading for Fortisul."

"Right. But why are they so low?" Evie tapped the readout next to the blips and Radoq saw they were just a few hundred feet off the ground.

"Oh." he leaned back in surprise and began plotting their position on the chart "They're only an hour north of us."

Evie grinned "So when you're done gawking at the wildlife shall we go have a look?"

Radoq sent them north and down, gaining speed as they soared across the wasteland. The wind had blown the clouds away and now from horizon to horizon stretched unbroken blue with a bright sun heating the bridge in response to which Evie buttoned her trench coat even tighter.

"Are you ever warm?" Radoq complained to her.

"Are you ever cold?" she countered to which Radoq had to admit, he wasn't. He looked down at the bare skin of his forearm where his blood oath was visible marvelling at the technology in his body that kept him from such discomforts.

"There!" Tricial, overhearing their conversation had been keeping watch and he spotted the three ships. Evie and Radoq joined him but the lun'erus could see nothing.

"Aurae?" Radoq asked and Tricial nodded holding up his biom for Radoq to mirror the settings.

"Try this." Radoq adjusted feeling the swoop of vertigo as his vision zoomed bringing the ground at the base of the mountains up to a fine detail.

"What setting?" Tricial was struggling to keep up with the minute changes Radoq was making and he read them out, hearing silence as the Sheriff tried to adjust "You're very skilled with the aurae, Radoq."

"I've always been very good with it."

"That goes some way to explain your skill as a duellist, no doubt?"

Radoq was silent. Tricial disengaged his aurae and turned to the younger man.

"Is everything alright?"

"That's my ship." Radoq said almost to himself.

Tricial turned back, fiddling with the settings and cursing as the mountains receded to tiny pinpricks in the distance.

"That's my ship. The Golden Kote."

Evie was at Radoq's side "The one you lost in the battle? I thought it was destroyed."

"No. Captured."

"Show me."

Radoq dropped his aurae and pulled up a projection on his biom watching the swirling shape of his beloved ship hover in front of him. Evie stared at the sleek lines of the battle ship before turning and abruptly stamping across to the defensive controls.

"Scanners up!" she called and brought up a vague, grainy image of the distant ships.

"We're too far away." Rakr muttered.

"That's not the *Kote* anyway." Radoq tapped the screen "That's – oh. There's three of them." They all peered closer at the screen, the images clearing as they drew closer "Oh!" Radoq exclaimed but everyone saw it at the same time "That's damaged. They must have run into a rival mercenary group."

Indeed, the reason the three ships ran so low was revealed as the two lead ships were towing the third which was leaking black smoke from its engines as it limped along.

"Radoq?" Tricial was closing "We're headed for the Western Hills."

Radoq turned to face his friend, the same fire in his eyes that Tricial had seen when he'd sworn the blood oath "Tricial, that is my ship. I swore no more failures. Here is one that I can fix. Forget the Western Hills. We're taking that ship."

CHAPTER 14

Radoq struck the alarm ringing the klaxon throughout the hold. Orders were shouted, armour was donned as Rakr and Staph vanished into the bowels of the ship.

"You need armour, Radoq." Tricial told him.

"Armour! To fight lun'erus?" Radoq was incredulous. A roaring energy filled him as they drew ever closer to the three craft.

"You have no idea what's aboard those ships. At best, they outnumber and outgun us three to one. Maybe more. And there are plenty of Domerus mercenaries so don't fool yourself, Radoq!"

"There's no Domerus armour in our hold. I'll be fine, Tricial! Remember this isn't my first fight!"

Tricial ground his teeth but allowed Radoq to leave the bridge, heading for the hold where their small force was gathered. To his surprise and pleasure, the soldiers were gathered in neat ranks, clad in their armour and helmets with phasrs held ready.

"Soldiers!" he paused, meeting their eyes pleased to see they held his gaze. He took strength from this "It's just like in the training yard." His eyes lingered on Chirruf, remembering her hesitation "Except now you have me –" he paused for the small chuckle "- and we make our own rules out here! We'll use the pinzgats to destroy their engines." His eyes met Staph's seeing the small nod of approval "Then we'll board them one by one. These aren't trained soldiers like us! They're criminals, thugs and brutes who aren't used to fighting together! Once we're on their deck they'll hesitate, looking around and waiting for each other to make the first move. So, don't let them! Keep the initiative, keep your momentum and aggression and put a bolt in them before they have the chance to think!"

A small cheer.

"Man the pinzgats! A pound of gold to every soldier who destroys an engine! The same to those who get a grappling line across! Let's do this!"

A rousing cheer this time as Staph and Rakr began to bark orders, sending the troops in a confusing maelstrom of back and forths. Radoq headed for the fighting deck, stepping out into the chill air. The pinzgats and quadgats were hooded with oilskin against the elements but the deck troops were now flooding out, wrapped in heavy greatcoats and masks against the chill they felt. Under Staph's lashing tongue the covers were removed, neatly folded and stowed before the great gats were warmed up, each barrel glowing with energy.

"All weapons ready, Sir!" Staph gave Radoq a thumbs up and he nodded, turning to adjust his aurae to see their enemy.

Who had stopped. He turned to shout to Evie in the bridge but she waved that she'd seen and he felt the engines hit their full power, driving them forwards and down to the static ship.

"They're abandoning ship!" he called to Staph who produced a telescope and peered through it. Radoq could see the smoking ship was now laid alongside the *Golden Kote* and the crew was being hastily disembarked. Clearly the Captain had decided that making it to Fortisul was out of the question in the face of the rapidly approaching *Freedman* and had chosen to preserve his men's lives. Even as they approached the maximum range for the pinzgats, Radoq saw the tow lines severed and the badly listing ship began to droop, settling down in the Dark Lands a moment later.

"Incoming!" Staph's warning came just in time as the first pinzgat round whipped across from the *Golden Kote*, shattering the windows on the port side of the bridge.

"Evie!" Radoq bellowed but she was safe at the controls. He saw Tricial beside her and reassurred himself that the Sheriff would be able to pull her out of harm's way.

"Permission to open fire, Sir?" Staph shouted and Radoq nodded although he suspected the Sergeant would have fired anyway judging by the speed at which he yelled the order to fire. With a cacophony of appallingly loud *chuk* sounds, the half dozen gats at the front of the fighting deck released their rounds and Radoq watched in mixed horror and fascination as the terrible plasma bolts, so much more destructive than those fired from phasrs or coltacs burned the space between the ships.

A blast of green flame and the *Golden Kote* turned directly towards them, racing across the open sky. Radoq shook his head in amazement at the stupidity or bravery of the unknown Captain who had turned so that only a single pinzgat could be brought to bear.

"Hit the engines!" he roared to remind the crew but those who could fire were doing so and a half dozen bolts impacted on the *Golden Kote*. Most were wasted on her thick armour plating but one struck the foredeck pinzgats and Radoq saw the crew managing it flung back in a spray of plasma and tangled limbs.

The first blood drawn.

"Sir? We've a casualty amidships. You need to man the gat!" Rakr had appeared on the fighting deck and without waiting for an answer he turned and vanished around the corner of the bridge.

Radoq tore after him, catching up to the lun'erus Sergeant in a few paces. The fighting deck ran the entire way around the superstructure giving a full field of fire but it was narrow here, the mounted pinzgats giving barely enough room to squeeze past. A figure was twitching beside the deck, smoke coming from the hull beside them where the round from the *Golden Kote* had struck.

"Chirruf!" Radoq shouted but Rakr was already blocking him, beckoning to two more soldiers who carried an aquar stretcher.

"Get some ice under her armour before you take it off – make sure she's sedated!" Rakr bellowed after them as the aquar crackled and lifted her into the air.

Radoq clambered into the turret, kicking the adjustment panel that moved it between lun'erus and Domerus occupants. He racked the cocking lever only then noticing that Rakr was still watching him, evidently confirming to himself that Radoq was competent. He wasted a moment wondering who was really in charge here before the *Golden Kote* was drawing level and the Captain, either realising his foolishness or danger had swung around to bring the main gats to bear but Evie, anticipating the move had already climbed high and so neither ship was able to fire and then they were past, leaving the battle ship to slow and turn in an ungainly manoeuvre that spoke volumes to the inexperience of her Captain.

Radoq looked to the front expecting open sky but now the second mercenary ship was sideways on to them and the pinzgats were belching green fire at them and he swore, wrenching his turret to face and pumping the trigger.

CHUK

The superheated plasma tore across the sky, impacting on the armoured flank of the ship. Radoq cursed again, racked the weapon again and aimed, this time sighting on the engine.

CHUK

His round impacted but not before another fired from the *Freedman* had torn the protective cowling aside revealing the complex tangle of wires and tubing. A muted cheer from the aft fighting deck but Radoq had no time to see who had struck the first blow because the engine had exploded, catching fire but almost immediately a suppressant had kicked in and now the fire was out.

The mercenary ship lurched drunkenly now down to only one engine. The suddenly uneven force caused it to spin wildly in the sky. The pilot had the presence of mind to wrench the throttle on the remaining engine back but it was too late and Radoq could hear Staph bellowing for grappling lines. As the ship turned, he saw mercenaries running from the open fighting deck into the cabin and the door was wide, enough for five or six armoured figures to squeeze through at once and his lip curled in battle fury as he sighted the heavy pinzgat.

CHUK

Screams carried over the sound of the wind and their own engines. Two more rounds from other turrets tore into the cabin prompting green flame to belch from the small opening but now a grappling cable had anchored to the mercenary ship and they were pulling it in. Radoq fired a last round and then leapt from the turret, sprinting to the boarding ramp.

"Alright! Berretts in first, use your pulsans!" Staph was bellowing "Remember not to shoot the Domerus in the back either! That'll make him Chox'd annoyed with you! Once you're in, move fast and don't stop! Get to the bridge and put a bolt in the Captain's face! Here we go!"

But here they didn't go because fire had burst from the cabin door. Radoq felt the heat on his own skin and the lun'erus ducked although his biom protected him. He turned and bellowed for the grappling lines to be cut, the panic in his voice lending urgency to the crew's movements.

BOOM

The mercenary ship exploded. Hot flame smothered the side of the *Freedman* even as Evie swung her hard away. Three of the boarding party collapsed, coughing hard and even Staph was sweating badly. Radoq shouted for stretchers, making sure the injured were moved quickly then turned to see the enemy ship plummeting to the ground, her vakkor engines clearly destroyed in the explosion. He couldn't see to lean over the railing of the fighting deck because an injured man was in his way so he scooped up the soldier, passing him to the stretcher bearers as Rakr hauled Staph to his feet, checking his friend for wounds.

"... alright... burned –" Staph was standing although his voice was hoarse. Rakr seemed to double his own voice in volume as he bellowed for the pinzgats to be manned again.

"Sir! Back to your turret!"

But Radoq had felt a change in the motion of the *Freedman* and he sprinted to the bridge where a white faced Evie was wrestling with the controls whilst Tricial read numbers from a screen.

"What happened?" Radoq demanded.

"Starboard engine failed. I'm restarting!" Evie frantically thumped the start sequence while Radoq sprinted back to the fighting deck, leaning dangerously far out over the railing to see the huge engine at the rear of the ship.

The turbines were still, the engine cowling smothered with plasma rounds. Clearly, the mercenary ship had taken its final revenge and Radoq wasted a moment to look for the wreckage seeing the fiercely burning crash site well below them.

"It's been hit! It's non-functional!" he shouted into the bridge seeing the horror on Evie's face. She abandoned the startup sequence, instead beginning the laborious task of flying the giant ship on one engine.

"Incoming!"

The *Golden Kote* had finished its lumbering turn and was now side on to the stricken *Freedman*. Radoq stared in stupefied horror as the pinzgats began to hurl plasma at them. He remembered the battle, how powerful he'd felt when he commanded those same gats but now, on the receiving end he felt helpless.

"Inside! Everyone inside!" he ordered the crew off the fighting deck. His mind spun with the beginnings of a plan even as Rakr looked askance at him.

"What you doing, Sir?"

Radoq rounded on the man "Winning this fight, Sergeant! Now get the men inside!"

"Aye, Sir." He didn't look happy about it but such a change in strategy was Radoq's job and the Sergeant was too much a professional to question orders at such a crucial moment.

CHUK-CHUK-CHUK

Radoq twisted aside, flinging himself out the way as three enormous plasma bolts impacted with the hull. The armoured hull held, dissipating the energy and leaving smoke streaming backwards with the momentum of the ship.

"Domerus!" Evie's voice sounded and he turned to see smoke now issuing from the bridge. Hauling himself up, Radoq sprinted into the control room to see the glass shattered and the controls obliterated. Tricial was pulling Evie out from a shattered panel and there was blood on her scalp.

"Chox!" Radoq stared around at the destruction. There was no way they could fly the ship now "Get down to the hold! Get yourself a coltac! Tricial, make sure she's alright!"

The Sheriff nodded, his own eyes twitching with the panic of one not used to violence. Radoq had to remind himself that his fellow Domerus was not used to battle, had not been in the presence of other men who were actively seeking to kill him before. It was natural that he'd feel fear and struggle to respond.

But Radoq felt alive. More alive than he'd felt since the pinzgats of the enemy had pounded his army. The ship may be shattered, the enemy may be closing in but his blood boiled like aquar and as the *Golden Kote* began to turn to bring more gats to bear he showed his teeth in a savage grin.

"Sir!" Rakr came into the bridge staring appalled at the damage "Everyone's inside!"

"Good! Standby to repel borders! Follow my lead, Sergeant!"

"Sir!" Rakr vanished down the stairs into the hold as Radoq raced back to the fighting deck, resuming his position in the turret and racking the pinzgat with another round.

In the sky before him his beloved *Golden Kote* hung as though suspended from space itself. The pinzgats had stopped firing in anticipation of a boarding party and he thanked Chox the *Freedman* had been a cargo ship with its heavily armoured flanks protecting them from the worst of the plasma bolts. Radoq carefully adjusted the turret, relying on the inexperience of the crew that they would not spot him, instead wasting time on grappling lines that by his judgement should already have been attached. If he'd been at the controls of the ship he'd have taken out the *Freedman's* remaining engine before attacking and would have a lookout at each end of the ship looking for an enemy airman attempting what he himself was attempting now. It was because of this that he'd thought of taking such a risk as he tried to conceal his face behind the fat barrel of the pinzgat as much as possible.

No-one saw him. No-one looked. Instead, thick grappling lines crossed the space between them, the first, badly aimed lines simply bouncing off the armoured hull. Radoq gave a humourless bark of laughter at the ineptitude before making an adjustment to the sight of his turret. Would the moment never come?

The boarding hatch in the side of the *Golden Kote* swung open, a gross breach of procedures that showed the mercenaries aboard had not learned from the demise of their fellow ship as the inside of the ship was now exposed. Radoq had the perfect opportunity to fire round after round through the hatch turning the boarding party into red ruin but he held back, waiting for his moment.

He angled the turret so that the muzzle faced towards the bridge, hidden behind a thick wall of armour that was pulled down for battle manoeuvres, leaving only tiny viewing holes for the crew to peer through or the dusty images on screens to make adjustments to their flight path.

"Bring her in! Let's get ready, lads!" the chief of the boarding party on the stolen ship was shouting encouragement to his own men and Radoq peered at them, seeing a motley band of men and women with mismatched weapons and armour.

A lot of weapons and armour.

"Here we go!"

And it was then, as the ship began to lay alongside that the small, dark object mounted below the bridge came into Radoq's sights and he fired.

CHUK

Shouts of fear from the boarding party who dived back into the hold but the shot wasn't aimed at them. Instead, Radoq was frantically readjusting his aim, seeing the small node he'd shot away was gone and he knew that in the bridge, the pilot would be staring at an empty screen no longer connected to its source.

There

The pilot risked cracking open the armour on the starboard

side, just enough for them to see the *Freedman* and to judge when to cut the engines and Radoq hit the trigger, firing the enormous plasma bolt at the small space where the life saving armour had been just moments before...

CHUK

A roar of pain and fury and Radoq sprinted from the turret, racing back into the bridge, sealing the door behind him and down into the hold where the crew and soldiers crouched, weapons ready as a heavy thump announced the *Golden Kote* slamming against their side.

"What did you do?" Tricial wanted to know.

"Killed their pilot. Hopefully their Captain too."

"Will that stop them?"

"No."

"Then why?"

Radoq turned to bare his teeth at the Sheriff, the madness of battle on his face "Because that's *my* ship!"

The crackling of aquar drew their attention away from conversation as every eye turned to the burning hole being torn in the side of the ship.

"Spread out!" Staph was giving the orders, his voice still hoarse from the explosion "A fire team up there, another over there! You, you and you – get up on the gantry! Someone kill the lights!" all of this in a muted hiss because they could now hear voices outside on the fighting deck and orders being snapped. With the engines of both ships stopped, there was no sound, not even the wind as both vessels drifted with the breeze.

"Here they come!" indeed, the cutting sound had increased and now a red line of melted metal stretched the height of a man and even as Radoq watched, he saw the boarder wielding the tool turn a right angle and begin cutting to the side. Next would come a second vertical cut and the chunk of metal would fall outwards.

"Stun pulsans!" Rakr had suddenly remembered and he frantically began tugging them from a storage crate, pressing them into the hands of the soldiers who had now taken cover behind any available object, all of them concealing themselves as much as possible beneath canvas and tarpaulins.

"I said, lights!" hissed Staph and there was a clunk as someone pulled a switch and the hold was plunged into darkness.

Radoq adjusted his aurae, giving him clear vision even in the gloom but there was no need because the vertical cut was complete and the piece of the hull hung teetering for a moment, still held at the bottom.

Then, a sharp order and it was wrenched outwards with a groan of protest.

The enemy poured into the hull.

CHAPTER 15

"Wait for it, wait!" Radoq didn't dare speak the words aloud but his thoughts were so loud in his head that surely the hidden troops must have heard them. They surrounded the breach on both sides, forming an irregular tunnel of weapons at the end of which was Radoq. He crouched in a Tal-Kan posture, knees bent and ready to leap forward as the first of the enemy crew, nothing but a dark silhouette against the brightness of the breach stepped through. Then another, and another quickly fanning out trying to cover as much ground as possible before the inevitable ambush.

"Now!"

Chuk-chuk-chuk-chuk-chuk

Gatfire tore into the boarders. Screams filled the gloom of the hull and the reek of burning plasma. Heat blurred the air as the first of the boarders died terribly, torn to shreds by the concentrated fire. Surely the attackers would hesitate before trying again?

The stun pulsan sent jagged forks of aquar into Radoq's troops. He saw men reeling back, clawing at their eyes. The device must have fallen beneath a dead man because he'd missed it.

And now more figures were pouring through the breach firing into the stunned soldiers and Radoq snarled as he saw his own men fall.

A leap, a sickening sensation of crushed bones beneath him and then he was flowing in the complex movements of Tal-Kan. A martial art built for Domerus and therefore reliant on strength and power he locked his left hand in a vice like grip on an armour clad shoulder, ducking easily under a coltac bolt he drove his elbow up and forward connecting with the mercenary's chin snapping the head back and severing the spine.

"Domerus!"

The shout was a warning, a call to the party that remained outside on the fighting deck and at once the other attackers began to pull back. The man who'd shouted was within Radoq's reach with a phasr pointed in shaking hands but he let him retreat, watching the man back towards the breach.

Chuk

Radoq couldn't fault whoever had chosen to kill the man. Some of his own troops were lying still behind him and the fight had become a grim bloodbath.

"Sir?" Staph was alive, looking for orders and Radoq held up a warning hand as voices sounded from outside.

"In there, who are you to slaughter innocent lun'erus like a coward? What crime have these men committed that you attack them like some savage pirate?"

It was a Domerus, no doubt. A male and deep sounding with a tinge of an accent that wasn't Wallanrian.

"You call me pirate yet you fly in my ship! The *Golden Kote* belongs to me!"

An intake of breath enhanced by his biom. Radoq didn't care to miss a word the mysterious Domerus said.

"I fly as a crew member, not a Captain aboard this vessel!" the voice was accompanied this time by a bearded face that peered into the hold and immediately whipped back out of sight "As to the ownership of the vessel, I cannot say."

"It belongs to me!" Radoq grated back.

"As you say. But the Captain here would say differently!"

"Lun'erus do not own battle ships like that." Radoq stated flatly.

"This one does."

"Enough!" Radoq snarled, losing his patience "To whom am I

speaking? Identify yourself!"

The bearded face dipped back once, moving just as fast out of sight "I have the honour to present myself, Sijun Kaymsus Su-Camrouak!" he finished his name and tritus with relish as though Radoq should have heard it before.

Radoq bowed in response, good manners forcing him into the habit even though Sijun couldn't see him "Radoq Loxelsus Po-Fortisun."

"I thought so!" Sijun's voice had a note of excitement in it "I see you, Radoq Loxelsus, I see the Golden Kote on your biom! I would claim it for my own! A duel! What do you say?"

A duel. Radoq looked at his troops who were battered and bleeding but still armed and more than capable of winning the fight. He bared his teeth but Oprain's voice in his head reminded him of his duty to the lun'erus, including those aboard the *Golden Kote.* A duel might mean no more deaths.

"On what terms?" he called back.

"The cessation of this fight." Called back Sijun "I presume the victor will be free to claim their rival's ship."

A voice outside seemed to disagree and Evie hissed in indignation but Radoq nodded.

"Our duty as Domerus decides it! No more needless death."

"A duel then! To the death! *Haast!*" Sijun cried and leapt through the breach in a blinding rush of speed.

"Lights!" Radoq heard Staph shout not to afford spectators a better view but to allow the lun'erus to move out of the way as Sijun surged forward, displaying a body that was a full head taller than Radoq who was considered large even among Domerus. He felt an instant dislike at the hearty faced young man with his heavy beard and snarling jaw as Sijun tried to end the duel before it had begun, raising his left hand so the biom glowed green with energy and then exploded outwards towards Radoq.

CHUK

The berrett bolt missed Radoq as he turned to the side sweeping his left foot forward in a simple strike. Sijun had reckoned on his speed overwhelming Radoq but Radoq had anticipated the shot from the biom and now he punished Sijun for his assumption sweeping the bigger man's legs out from under him with a sickening, bone jarring crash.

Sijun crashed onto the floor of the hold skidding into a pile of soldier's cots which tangled him. Instantly, Radoq was atop his back striking the back of his head with the heel of his hand in an attempt at a quick kill but Sijun's hip was raised by a crushed camp cot and he tugged the crumpled metal aside, giving himself leverage which flipped Radoq off his back.

And sent him flying across the hold, slamming into the opposite wall. White lights flashed in his eyes as his biom told him three ribs were cracked and offering a painkiller which he ignored. Domerus did not heal themselves mid duel. Bellowing to overcome the pain he waited for Sijun to make a second charge, rolling forwards over his shoulder at the last moment to seize the man's left foot in both hands. There was a heart beat of a pause as Sijun registered what was about to happen and then Radoq twisted, rolling slightly to force the bone past its breaking point. Sijun roared in agony as the tibia splintered along its length. He rolled over, trying to drag himself up to his knees but the pain, Radoq knew was like aquar in the veins. An instructor his father had hired had done the same thing to him once, punishing a mistake to make a point. Breaks like that took *days* to heal properly.

Sijun was far from beaten though although he would make no more great charges. He raised himself to one knee, placing his uninjured foot flat on the ground and rotating as Radoq began stepping around him in a circle.

"Come, see how I can crush you against my chest!" Sijun jibed, thumping a closed fist against his torso. Radoq ignored the talk, watching for small movement in Sijun's muscles that would betray a weakness.

He leapt without warning, jumping over Sijun's outstretched arm and coming down to land behind the bigger man. He landed on the shattered tibia, eliciting a scream of mixed agony and frustration from Sijun as the man realised what was happening and slammed his chin against his chest to protect his neck as Radoq reached calmly down, pinning Sijun's arm with his leg, wrapping his right arm around the chin and placing the glowing green biom on his left hand against the Domerus' temple.

"Lights!" called someone again in the sudden stillness and the switch was thrown revealing the two men immobile.

"You have me!" Sijun called "The soul grip!"

So called because it held the soul of a Domerus in its grasp. The berrett within Radoq's biom whirled with deadly intent as he snarled at his enemy. Sijun could not move from this position without being shot and indeed, most duels ended at this point with the victor firing the fatal shot but Radoq wanted to give the man a chance.

"You can yield, Sijun Kaymsus Su-Camrouak. Keep your life and let men know everywhere you go that you were beaten by Radoq Loxelsus Po-Fortisun! That you lost your ship to him and kept your honour."

There was silence. A cluster of the mercenaries had stepped in to watch the brief but intense duel while Radoq's own troops were staring in mixed shock and pride at the destruction that had unfolded.

The vibration started beneath Radoq's arms and he thought for a wild moment that Sijun had some terrible device attached to him that would destroy them both in a cloud of pulse energy and he snarled at the lack of propriety in this death and then Sijun started to shake and he realised the man was laughing.

Guffawing with tears streaming down his cheeks. Had he lost his mind? Was this him losing control at the moment of his death?

"Forgive me! Forgive me." Sijun could hardly move let alone wipe his eyes "I accept my defeat Radoq, Po of tritus Fortisun and your honourable terms! Oh, to be beaten by the man who bears the golden kote, I can live with that!"

Satisfied, Radoq released the man and stood by in confusion as he continued to howl with mirth "What is so funny?"

Sijun shook his head, looking up at him "Nothing! Please take no offence. I merely laugh at the thought of my mother who, when I told her I was going adventuring told me I would end my days at the feet of a great champion, the victim of my own foolishness! Oh! What an adventure! What a day!"

Radoq was nonplussed but tried to take the moment in his stride "I see. Your leg is injured."

"Shattered! Broken!" Sijun started laughing all over again.

"Perhaps some pain relief?"

"Oh. Yes, I'll begin the healing." Sijun's biom began to glow as the technology began to set the bone. He remained on the floor as Tricial approached and introduced himself formally.

"You're an adventurer?"

"Yes." Sijun was distracted by the pain now the battle adrenaline was fading "And you, Radoq are a conduit of adventure." He smiled.

"I don't intend to be. I'm only trying to do what's right."

Sijun fixed Radoq with a hard stare at these words. There was a sort of madness in his eyes that matched the impulsive laughter and his wild appearance. It made Radoq wary, he didn't trust this sort of dangerous impulsiveness. He preferred to carefully watch and calculate before taking action but the younger man before him had no such misgivings.

"Radoq! I can see on your arm the mark of a blood oath! Tell me, is this battle the culmination of the oath you've sworn? Is there something in that ship that you felt it important enough to give your life for?"

"No. Not here. I'm on a path to fulfil my oath." Radoq explained "The ship was mine, I lost it in battle. This is me reclaiming it."

Sijun's eyes grew wide with a burning desire "Fascinating!" he still knelt as his ankle continued to right itself with a series of painful crunches "But you have yet to fulfil your oath? The quest is still ongoing?"

Radoq dipped his head in acknowledgement.

"Then, friend Radoq I would pledge myself to your service. I will swear to serve you in whatever capacity you may choose until such time as your blood oath is complete. Will you have me?"

To his surprise, Radoq found himself touched by the oath which he could see was not lightly given although he suspected Sijun was more interested in adventure than Radoq's own aims but then his problems were his own, not Sijun's and the man was a formidable duellist.

"Very well. I accept your oath, Sijun." Radoq responded formally "I swear to you that I will use you to the best of your abilities and not lead you into dishonourable actions."

"Fine!" Sijun managed to stand although pain was written on his massive features "Then, I believe your ship awaits!"

He gestured to the breach but a harsh voice called through "My ship!"

The handful of mercenaries that had boarded *Freedman* took several careful steps backward as a figure ducked into the hold.

"This is my ship and I don't care what some uppity Domerus says!" the voice was familiar, a harsh tone that Radoq placed immediately "You and you –" the figure pointed at Radoq and Sijun "You like making rules so much then I'll do you a favour. The two of you can have this wreck and I'll take whats left of your men to the markets. Chox knows you owe me after I lost that delivery bonus!"

Correlius. Radoq almost smiled at the sight of the man still trying to assert his authority. The mercenaries were backing away from him, clearly intimidated by the man but Sijun wasted no time. He stumped forward on his injured foot, limping until he drew level with the former slaver and then shoved him bodily through the breach and into the thin gap between *Golden Kote* and *Freedman*. Correlius vanished without a scream, plunging down to his death far below. Sijun turned back to the mixed crowd of mercenaries and soldiers.

"Does anyone else have a problem serving Fortisun?"

No-one did and Correlius stayed silent on the Dark Lands far below. Satisfied, Radoq began issuing orders as Staph and Rakr gathered their troops.

"Bill, Sir?" Rakr approached.

"Bill? Oh…" Radoq understood and he took a deep breath.

"Three dead. Chirruf needs the surgeon at the Eyrie pretty soon or she'll be number four."

"Who are the dead?"

Rakr named them. All men, all who had signed up in the Eyrie and trained with them. Radoq hadn't been close to any of them although he remembered talking to them and felt absurdly guilty that he hadn't known them better when they'd died for him. He said as much to Rakr who understood.

"They didn't die for you, Sir. They died to protect themselves and their mates around them. They didn't have to be here and they knew what they signed up for. Dying like that is the way we can all hope to go. Chox knows there's got to be a reward in the afterlife for dying a warrior's death."

Radoq nodded, seeing the sense of not blaming himself but he ensured the bodies were carefully placed on stretchers and covered neatly.

Aboard the *Golden Kote* was another matter. Radoq's shot into the bridge had beheaded the helmsman steering the ship and torn through two more men who were scattered across the bridge in a gory mess of body parts. Feeling his stomach churn he distracted himself by asking Sijun about the loyalties aboard the ship. Interestingly, only Correlius and a handful of the crew knew one another. The rest had been loaded on after hearing Juraj's call for mercenaries and were a mixed bunch, mostly looking for coin. They eyed Radoq warily but he spoke to them, assuring them that they were free to leave the ship at the Eyrie unless they wanted to join him. Most merely nodded although a few seemed interested and he turned away to find Evie only to find her standing behind him, her brash tone returned as though their ship was not in ruins and a bandage wasn't worn tightly around her head.

"Alright? We've got problems."

"Go on."

"*Freedman* has had it. Reckon she's going down whatever we do. Vakkor engine has taken some damage and we've had a fuel leak."

Radoq cursed "Can we tow her?"

"Probably. Question is whether we want to or not. She's in bad shape."

"Surely we can repair her at the Eyrie?" Radoq was surprised at Evie's reticence "Is there anything you can do to get the engines running?"

"With no controls? No. She's dead in the air. If you want to tow her, we can rig some lines but she'll be scrap when we get back to the Eyrie."

Radoq felt a sense of loyalty to the ship remembering all that had taken place in this very hold and so Evie went off to cast tow lines as Staph supervised the transfer of everything salvageable to the *Golden Kote*.

"She's a Hyperion class battle ship." He told Tricial and Sijun enthusiastically on the gore spattered bridge "Laid down only five years ago she's a crew of twenty although we can carry more than two hundred aboard."

"Surely you didn't have that many here?" Tricial asked Sijun.

"No, just a skeleton crew. Correlius barely got her out of port. He had a young pilot – " he stopped, looking at the blood soaked chair the young man had been decapitated in "Shame."

"Shame." Radoq echoed, unable to feel guilt for the man's death. He continued speaking to cover the moment "She's plasma turrets down each flank, a battery fore and aft and carries over a hundred pulse torpedoes. That's our main armament."

"A wonder they didn't use them on us!" Tricial looked concerned "I think you might have warned us about such a threat?"

"There are none onboard." Radoq pointed to a screen which flashed faintly with a warning about empty magazines "I know because I shot them all personally and the chances of mercenaries getting hold of pulse torpedoes is slim to none."

Tricial still looked askance but Evie burst into the bridge with a second engineer she'd located amongst the mercenaries following hot on her heels.

"Problem."

"What?"

"*Freedman* fuel wasn't drained, it flowed into the bilges."

"The bilges –" Radoq turned and bellowed for the grappling lines to be cast off. He roared for Evie to take the helm and sprinted back through the ship past stunned mercenaries to the open boarding hatch which they'd used to move between the ships "Is everyone off?"

Staph piled through closely followed by Rakr "Yes, Sir. Last man."

Radoq slammed the hatch shut and roared at a communicator on the wall, praying Evie would be monitoring the ship's network from the bridge and it seemed she was because a moment later the *Golden Kote* swung to the side, her movement as smooth as the *Freedman* was rough but just as Radoq was marvelling at the smoothness of the ship (*his* ship) an explosion rocked them and *Golden Kote* lurched dangerously across the sky, tipping so far she almost rolled.

"Evie!" he crashed into the bridge seeing the small lun'erus wrestling with the controls as warning lights and alarms flashed and howled.

"Shut that noise up, would you?" she snapped and he hurried to the closest console.

"Engine two is overheating!"

"Initiate shutdown!"

"One has stopped!"

"Switch it off!"

"It's already off!"

"Then stop bothering me!" the ship lurched downwards drunkenly and Radoq stumbled, landing close to the screen that gave readings from the all-important vakkor engine that kept them aloft. Another warning and he frantically tapped controls, beginning a stabilising sequence that righted the ship and silenced a few alarms.

"Chox!" Evie was breathing hard. Tricial was reading data from another screen and Radoq took some small measure of relief that the hull was still intact.

"Life support?" he called.

"All fine."

"Fuel?"

"That too."

Evie turned and caught his eye, raising an eyebrow "Not our day for engines, eh?"

Sijun piped up from across the bridge "Statistically, engines are the most likely part of an airship to be damaged. They're exposed to the elements, at risk of bad maintenance and hold the greatest strain of anywhere in the structure of a craft. It's no surprise that they've been damaged whilst the rest of the hull is intact."

Everyone stared at him in shock. He shrugged.

"I like reading."

"Domerus? Can you take over?" Evie handed over the controls which to Radoq were sluggish "I'll go take a look at the engines."

A minute or so later she called over a communicator "Domerus, how's the lining on this ship?"

"How do you – oh." Radoq shook his head "We can't put down in the Dark Lands."

"Seems to me we don't have a choice." Evie was as matter of fact as always "Engines might explode if we push them too hard and I've had enough of that for one lifetime."

Radoq couldn't fault her logic.

"Find the highest spot we can and hope we don't draw attention?"

Sijun spoke up "You and I can handle the virals. If needed we can set up firing lines and a perimeter. We're close to the Northern Massif here, there are no large packs. They stay in the low lands in the middle."

Radoq nodded "There should be masks the soldiers can wear. That'll help protect from the glow."

"The glow?" Sijun was confused "Ah! The rocks. I forget they're dangerous."

Radoq steered them as far north as he could before Evie called and told him to stop before he blew them all up. He bade Tricial lower the craft gently downwards which was the most control they had without engines and headed aft to offer his help.

The dark confines of the engine room were already exposed to the elements. Evie had wasted no time removing the armoured panels that lead from the interior power to the turbines that drove the craft on the exterior and Radoq cautioned her about the danger from the rocks.

"Can't do much without getting outside, can I?" she chastened "You just get out there and keep them virals off my back."

He leaned through the hole she'd made, peering out at the black rock they were heading towards.

"Question." Evie was stretched up to a complex array of switches, pulling a tangle of wires out whilst her new assistant who's name, Evie had explained, was Baxl handed her tools.

"Go on."

"That berrett the other Domerus shot at you. D'you all have that?"

Radoq coloured "Yes. A Domerus' last line of defence. That's why that grip I had him in is called the soul grip. I held his soul in my hands."

"It's just used for duelling then? I never saw it on the competitions."

"In a duel to the death, yes. You won't have seen it in the competitions. We don't talk about it much. It's a way of ensuring you die with honour."

Evie leaned back to stare at him "You mean kill yourself?"

"Well, yes."

She laughed and shook her head "You Domerus are impossible. Kill yourself! And it's built right into your hand. Madness! Chox'd madness.

Then even she went silent as a distinct thump sounded and the ship rocked as the ship set down in the Dark Lands.

CHAPTER 16

Fear was palpable throughout the ship. Dusk came quickly in the Dark Lands, the black rocks that gave the land its name muffling any ambient light so that night was on them quickly. Radoq stepped through the decks of the *Golden Kote* giving quiet words of praise for the actions of the day or introducing himself to the mercenaries who had gathered together in an uncertain group, separate from Radoq's soldiers. Tricial, he noticed had moved to sit with them and was earnestly in conversation with a small knot of shabbily dressed lun'erus apparently discussing the politics of Admirain which left Radoq bored after a few brief exchanges.

Golden Kote was large, bigger even than the *Freedman* although as she was a fighting ship every inch of space was crammed with equipment and components leaving only a small space in each of the corridors tall enough for Radoq to walk without striking his head. Sijun had no such luck and as he limped after Radoq, the pain in his leg apparently dulled sufficiently he kept up a constant stream of profanities as his skull impacted with exposed corners and bulkheads.

"Why don't they think about head room in these things?" he grumbled as they climbed a steep flight of steps up past the communications deck where Staph was busy attempting to signal the Eyrie.

"They did! It's just not built for giants." Radoq thought guiltily of the dislike he'd felt the first time he'd seen Sijun. In just a few short hours his opinion of the young Domerus had shifted drastically and he found himself laughing often as

Sijun's irascible energy filled every silence with a joke or titbit of information.

"You know, the standard ceiling height of a military grade airship is set to eight feet." Sijun piped up unexpectedly as Radoq lead the way to the upper decks.

"How do you know that?"

Sijun looked surprised "It's published everywhere... Don't you read?"

"Sometimes." Radoq tried and failed to remember the last book he'd opened. He thought of Oprain and the clutter of his study in the Eyrie and made a mental note to borrow one of his many tomes when they finally returned to the sky port.

"Are we going on deck? Excellent. Some fresh air will do us good." Sijun held open the top hatch for Radoq who vaulted up the ladder onto the flat open space of the upper fighting deck.

"Bleak." Sijun hobbled to stand by Radoq looking out at the poisonous looking rock the *Golden Kote* rested on.

"We need to set up a perimeter." Radoq reminded him of the real reason for visiting the upper deck.

"Say, a firing position there." Sijun gestured to an outcrop of black rocks with a loose scree slope on the far side "The lun'erus can shelter behind it and the loose stone will give them warning if virals try to flank them."

Radoq nodded his approval "Did they find the breathing masks?"

"Yes. Only a dozen though."

"Chox." Radoq breathed, thinking of the harm the poisonous air would do to his men. He looked down at Sijun's injured leg "Can you stand with them? It'll boost their morale if we're seen outside."

Sijun slapped his knee "Right as rain."

Radoq pretended not to see his wince and turned to the other side of the ship pointing out a likely location for a second sentry position "We'll have men in the turrets too. The pinzgats will give them fire support should we get any visitors."

"Are there floodlights?"

Radoq cast around before pointing at a series of thin lights that ran the length of the hull "Those are landing lights. They aren't too bright though."

"Flares?"

"Some. We'll issue them but only use them in an attack."

"I'll go and ask the Sergeants." Sijun hobbled back to the hatch, vanishing into the depths of the ship. Radoq looked around the open deck, seeing the scuffs left on the armour from plasma impacts. The last time he'd stood here the deck had heaved with soldiers, the greatest fighting force he'd ever seen. Or so he'd thought at the time. A simple misjudgement in navigation had led to the enemy cruisers sweeping down out of the sun, raking the deck with their pinzgats and slaughtering his men. The pulse weapon had blasted him off the deck, flinging him backwards into the dusty land where he'd lain in shock, seeing his ship plough a furrow in the ground as enemy shock troops had swarmed through the hatches, slaughtering Fortisun soldiers who were unprepared for the boarding party. His communicator had been destroyed in the blast and the gatfire was too thick for him to board the ship and it was all over so fast. The screams of the dying had not needed the communicator though...

"Sir?" Rakr had poked his head out of a hatch although Radoq noticed the lun'erus took pains not to expose any more of his body to the glow "Time to set the sentries out I think."

Radoq nodded and busied himself organising protective clothing and weapons. To his pleasure, several of the mercenaries had their own masks and heavy armour to combat the effects of the glow and they readily agreed to stand guard with his own troops. It was full dark outside by now but Staph had laid a ring of luminescent orbs around the ship and they provided some light for the nervous troops who stood silent, weapons pointing outwards.

Evie was making progress but snapped at Radoq to let her work when he pressed her for an estimated time of completion. Rolling his eyes he made for the gunnery deck, ensuring the pinzgats turrets were all manned.

"We're low on plasma bolts, Sir." A mercenary, a thuggish looking Xeonison named Armlu turned out to have served as a gunnery Sergeant aboard a Xeonison cruiser and it was he who took stock of the magazine, even producing a half dozen rounds for the pulse cannons although as he pointed out unnecessarily to Radoq they were no use at this range "They'd blow us to Chox and back, Sir. I'll keep 'em for another day. But we're down to fourteen shots per turret."

"Chox!" Radoq breathed "What about the quadgats?"

"Doing alright there." Armlu nodded showing Radoq the crates of ammunition "Besides, we can load phasr bolts in there if we need to."

"Fine. Let's hope we don't have to rely on that." Pleased, Radoq headed to find Tricial who was crouched in the communicator room attempting to signal the Eyrie.

"Any joy?"

"Yes. They can't get a ship out to us until dawn at least though."

"So we're stuck here?"

"Looks that way."

"I wonder –"

Radoq never finished his sentence because shouts of alarm and the unmistakeable *chuk-chuk* of frantic gatfire filled the night and he turned, racing through the narrow decks for the open air.

"Lights!" he bellowed at a pair of startled looking soldiers who stared stupidly at him "The landing lights! Switch them on!" they hastened to the bridge whilst Radoq raced up a flight of stairs shoving open the hatch at the top of a ladder and leaping onto the fighting deck just as the lights crashed on with a crackle of aquar.

Illuminating the seething mass of virals that reeled around the outer marker Staph had so carefully laid.

Vaguely human with hairless skin, distended bellies and deep black eyes the virals howled in a bestial cry as they raced on all fours up to the cordon of light where they hesitated, clearly afraid of the glow and the soldiers at the sentry post drew a dear price from them as rapid gatfire tore into their mass, dropping them in a spray of dark gore.

"Fire support!" Rakr's voice carried in a leather throated bellow from where he crouched behind the shooters. Understanding, Radoq leapt into a turret racking the pinzgat, sighting and feeling the hot *CHUK* as the bolt leapt into the night air.

Screams, a vague flash of bodies pinwheeling through the air and the virals retreated, screeching a disappointed hunting cry as they vanished.

Adjusting his aurae, Radoq watched them go losing sight of them after a few seconds as they dipped into a hidden ravine. Below, Rakr's voice was loud but calm, ordering the soldiers and mercenaries to reload and prepare for a second wave.

"Report, Sergeant!" Radoq shouted down from the deck and Rakr turned, craning his neck to stare up at the Domerus far above him.

"Ten, fifteen enemy destroyed, Sir. All good down here."

Radoq nodded and turned to the far side of the ship, pleased to see Staph had mirrored Rakr's position on this side. He called reassurance to the men, scanning with his aurae to check the ground.

"All well?" Sijun had approached silently and Radoq spared a moment to marvel at the ability of him to move in such a way despite the injury. He nodded.

"Shall we hunt?"

Intrigued, Radoq turned to the younger man "That's an idea."

Sijun gave a short bark of a laugh "Thought your mind would have been elsewhere! Come, when will we have a finer opportunity?"

Without waiting for an answer, he turned and pushed off his uninjured leg making a giant bound that landed him outside the ring of light the Sergeants had placed.

Radoq flung himself after, sticking the landing and staggering a few metres much to Sijun's amusement "You duel like a master but a simple leap perplexes you?"

"I prefer to keep my feet on the ground." Radoq growled, adjusting his aurae so the world appeared in a whirl of colours. He pointed towards the hidden ravine "Over there."

"What? What do you see?"

"Do you not see the heat? That's a nest of them or I'll be Chox'd!"

A second passed where Sijun adjusted his own aurae, murmuring as he found the correct setting "You're Chox'd good with your vision." He sounded vaguely unhappy about it.

"We all have our strengths." Radoq set off at a run which would have left the lun'erus behind them gasping if they could see it. Sijun's leg finally hampered him and he struggled to match Radoq's pace, finally resorting to bounding in more great leaps as they closed in on the spot.

A great crack in the rock some ten metres wide yawned before them. In Radoq's aurae it was like looking down into a lava flow from an erupting volcano, such was the concentration of heat signatures.

"Chox!" breathed Sijun staring at the mass of virals "What a pit!"

He flung himself forward, permitting a howl of fury as he landed amongst the beasts and Radoq spared a moment to grin as he mirrored the move, diving forward and rolling in mid-air to land feet first on the back of a viral, crushing the creature beneath him.

The shriek of their hunting cry filled his ears as Radoq began to flow through the basic forms of Tal-Kan, stepping smartly past charging virals, driving elbows, knees and hammer fists into vital organs feeling flesh and bone crumple beneath his hands.

"*Hast!*" Sijun cried a Tal-Kan challenge as a knot of the creatures seemed to hesitate, drawing back and turning as though to run up the sides of the ravine. Their pause was their undoing as Sijun exploded forward, crushing two of them against the rock with nothing but his bodyweight, swiftly turning to dispatch another with a savage chop to the throat.

Radoq nodded in approval, seeing the skill of the younger Domerus but noting a few flaws in his technique. No matter. Tal-Kan became complex when fighting another Domerus but the art had been designed to fight the virals and against them it was brutally efficient. The swarm seemed to recognise the danger and moved as one, seeming as always to Radoq like a single mind controlled the mass. They swept past him, scrabbling and jostling against one another in their haste to flee the predators and vanished around a corner in the canyon.

"How many?" Sijun called.

Radoq counted "Twenty one – no! Twenty two!" he called proudly.

"Ah! Bested again! Fifteen for me!"

"A fine score!" the two men grinned at one another, black viral blood covering their faces.

Sijun gestured back towards the ship and Radoq nodded as they made their way slowly back, hampered by Sijun's injured leg.

"You move well through the forms." Radoq complimented Sijun's Tal-Kan "If anything you rely too much on strength and speed."

"Surely not! Tal-Kan is based on strength and speed." Sijun argued.

"Tal-Kan is based on forms and technique." Radoq corrected firmly "It takes advantage of our strength and speed to execute those forms. That's why it is useless to the lun'erus."

Sijun brooded in something approximating a sulky silence for a few paces before speaking again with a sigh "First the glow, now the virals! There isn't much the lun'erus can do for themselves, is there?"

Radoq drew up sharply, the outer ring of luminescent light now visible "They can do plenty, Sijun." He spoke sharply.

The big man looked at him with surprise "Have I given offence? I meant none."

"Yet you disparage the lun'erus so easily." Radoq felt venom in his voice "They place their trust in you and I and men like Tricial and you make so little of them?"

Sijun paused, considering his next words before he spoke "But we are so much more than them."

Radoq gripped Sijun's biom in an iron grip "We are! And that is the point! No lun'erus could do what we just did, could walk with an injury like yours! Of my entire army, only I survive and not only live, but thrive! We are different to them in ways they cannot even conceive!"

Sijun was nonplussed "Then how have I caused such offence?"

Radoq shook his fellow Domerus' biom "Our duty, Sijun is to them! Have you never thought why our lives are so different to the lun'erus? They live and die in freedom, choosing their own paths whilst we are bound to the duties of our tritus! Even you adventuring as you are, find yourself bound by honour, mere words that you will allow to define your life!"

"To live with honour is –"

Radoq cut him off "Is a Domerus' life! Lun'erus like Evie, like Staph and Rakr care nothing for honour! It's meaningless to them! They'll make promises to friends and loved ones, sure enough and work hard not to break them but they're free to break them if they wish! What would happen to you if you broke your oath to me?"

"I wouldn't." Sijun didn't get it.

"But why?"

He considered "If I did I'd…" he looked at Radoq "I'd dishonour myself and my tritus."

"And?"

"And I'd destroy myself. Suicide."

"But do you see why we are taught to be like that? It's exactly because we can do so much more than the lun'erus. Have you seen the slave camps in the desert? I have. I've watched what happens when power is corrupted. You and I even though we come from different lands are taught the same way from birth. Tritus, duty, *integrity*. They're among the first words our kind learn and it's to stop us becoming tyrants! If you and I wanted we could slaughter every man and woman on that ship – you know we could! But we don't and we expend our own energy hunting the virals and protecting them. Why?"

Sijun was silent.

"Why?" Radoq insisted again, forcing an answer from Sijun.

"Because it's the honourable thing to do." He answered lamely, frowning.

"So, ages past when the ancient Domerus decided to split the strata of humanity, they created this concept of honour! Otherwise, we'd be a race of slaves and masters with the one never able to become the other!"

"But we *do* rule them, Radoq." Sijun pointed out.

"To an extent. Our tritus protect their lands and organise the defences of their settlements. We lead their armies and command them then but otherwise we set no laws and have no say over their existence."

"But in Wallanria, much the same as my own country your Crown Prince makes laws and sends Sheriffs to ensure they're not broken."

"But the laws are proposed by the council in Admirain. The *lun'erus* council. The Crown Prince merely approves their laws."

"He controls the armies and the fleet."

"But he doesn't use them against his own people. He swears the same oath you did at your ascension to serve and to protect."

Sijun threw up his hands in frustration "So, what is your point, Radoq? I should kow-tow to my lessers? I should bow to them as a servant?"

"No." Radoq shook his head, his ardour cooling a little "No. I don't mean that. We are proud, us Domerus and rightly so."

Sijun began to limp slowly back towards the lights "There is a balance to our power, is that what you're saying."

Radoq considered "I suppose in a way, yes."

"And I should not insult the lun'erus in your presence again." It was meant as a joke but there was resentment in Sijun's tone. Radoq stopped again, turning to the man.

"No. Do what you will, say what you will. I don't seek to control your thoughts, Sijun. The point of my words is to help you to want *not* to disparage them. If you think less of them, that's your business but I think by spending time amongst them, getting to know their lives will change your perspective."

Sijun's face suddenly brightened "Like an adventure?"

Radoq rolled his eyes "Sure. Like that."

Shouts sounded from ahead and they closed the final distance in bounds and a fast run. Staph almost shot Radoq when they loomed in the darkness but quickly recovered himself pointing at the far side of the ship where Rakr and his men crouched. Radoq leapt to the side of the ship, bounding to the flat fighting deck at the top and manipulated his aurae, gasping as he saw the long line of virals watching, waiting.

"This isn't right!" it was one of the mercenaries, a grizzled looking man who despite his appearance was shaking with fear "They never come back like this!" Rakr was trying to silence the man but he was insisting "They never come back after a slaughter like that! This is the Dark Ji..."

"Enough!" Radoq snarled, leaping down to join the men, silencing the merc who shuffled out of Radoq's way looking embarassed but the damage was done and fear was rippling through the small group. He cursed silently "Listen to me! We'll get you out of here alive, I promise! Dark Ji or no, by morning we'll be on the way to the Eyrie, safe! Keep your weapons ready and remember, they're just animals! They can't outthink, outflank or outfight us! We've got an entire battle ship and an army to keep them at bay!" he saw some nodding and a few weak smiles. In the darkness a viral shrieked and the smiles vanished "Hear that? They're taunting us! Let's return the favour! Let them know we aren't afraid!"

The roar of the soldiers filled the air as in the darkness just out of their sight, the virals seethed, ready to strike.

CHAPTER 17

"Think we should engage, Sir." Rakr didn't take his eyes off the perimeter lights for a second.

"They aren't attacking us. It might provoke another wave."

A grunt from the Sergeant.

"Anyway, they're at long range as it is."

"The pulse cannons then?"

"We'd need to move the ship to bring them to bear. We've only a couple of rounds left as it is."

A shrieking cry split the night making every man stiffen with fear. Rakr spat onto the black rocks beneath them "Chox'd things."

Radoq lowered his voice, gesturing for Rakr to drift away from the other lun'erus with him "Do you know why they've come back? You must know their behaviour well."

Rakr shrugged "They aren't that predictable. Fella over there was right, they don't usually come back after they've been hit that badly."

"Usually?"

"It happens. Sometimes." Rakr shrugged again.

"When was the last time you saw them return after being frightened away?"

Rakr started to speak, hesitated then stopped "Can't remember, Sir."

"Chox."

"Right?"

Movement in the faint glow of the luminescence but the viral that had stepped into the light whipped its foot back as though stung.

"Does the light hurt them?" Radoq wondered.

"No." Rakr was emphatic.

"Any idea why they're stopping there, then?"

"None. Can't say I'm complaining though."

"No." Radoq agreed seriously.

After a moments silence Rakr spoke again "How far would we need to move the ship to get those pulse cannons aimed straight?"

"Too far. Ninety degrees or more. It'd be easier to lure the virals into our sights."

Rakr turned away from the perimeter for the first time to look up at Radoq "You could do that, couldn't you?"

Radoq stammered "I – I could. But I don't want to provoke them."

Rakr ground his teeth, his training forcing him to lower his tone "Sir, as it stands, we're gonna have half our lads losing their minds long before first light. This is like a torture chamber just sitting here watching them. If they come, we can take 'em."

Radoq sighed, nodding at the advice "Alright. But I'll go back up top and do a proper reconnaissance first." Without waiting for a response, he turned and bounded back up to the fighting deck where Sijun was watching as Tricial redeployed a group of mercenaries to the fighting deck. A dozen or so, moving in pairs with an oversized phasr between them.

"Sharpshooters?" Radoq asked one duo, both stocky looking women who were muttering to one another in accents from the Northern Massif.

"Sir. Want us to start taking 'em out?"

"Not yet." He smiled and watched as the teams set up positions, laying out thick mats and covering themselves in layers of camouflage.

Sijun approached, having limped his way across the deck stopping to inspect the sharpshooters. He drew close to Radoq, leading him away from the closest team.

"What do you know of the Dark Ji?" Sijun's voice was so low

that only Radoq and possibly Tricial could hear him although the Sheriff was tactful enough to appear in deep conversation with a sharpshooter.

Radoq turned a cold expression on Sijun "Is this the conversation you really want to be having? Now?"

"I'm serious, Radoq! Now is as important a time as any!" Sijun stared out at the virals, held back as though by an invisible barrier.

"What, you think some boogey man is controlling the virals? Holding them back for what?"

"Maybe to protect us."

"If the Dark Ji had that much control, then wouldn't he steer them away from us?" Radoq couldn't believe he was having this discussion when the threat was so close.

"Do you know the legend behind him?"

"No!" Radoq lowered his voice to a furious hiss "And now isn't the time for ghost stories, Sijun!" as if giving credence to his argument a viral howl filled the night. Murmurs of fear came from the men behind their barricade.

Sijun jabbed a thick finger towards the sound "When else should we be telling them? Anyway, it's not a ghost story, the Dark Ji is – or *was* – a real Ji! His name is Guysil Chirrutsus Ji-Kanata."

Radoq stopped dead. For the legend to have an actual legitimate Domerus name he was not prepared. Sijun saw he had Radoq's attention and pressed on.

"He was a Ji much like any other. Decades ago, there was a scandal. He was found to be using his power to take advantage of lun'erus women."

"Take advantage..." Radoq got it. He felt sick at the thought of Domerus power being so abused "That's disgusting."

"Isn't it? Society thought so too and if it were anyone else, a Po, a Su or even an Ap then they'd lose their ascension for good. No Ji would willingly ascend a Fallen Domerus that had done that."

"But he was a Ji?"

"Exactly. He held the title and he was the last of his tritus.

You know how it is, there was a cousin of a cousin by marriage somewhere down the line but they were in another tritus and no-one wanted to touch the Kanata name."

"Was this in Wallanria?"

"Yes." Sijun gestured west, towards Radoq's country "As I say, it was decades ago. Long before the fall of Ychacha."

"What happened to Guysil?"

"The King – your King, at the time anyway – was given the task of punishing him. Of course, he couldn't remove the Ji's power so instead he found another Domerus who'd been convicted of some other minor offence and ordered that he have his power removed by his own tritus. It was quite the shock, the Domerus all thought that a harsh punishment for a minor offence and there were plenty of cries for leniency."

Radoq had forgotten the virals temporarily.

"See, the King had Guysil under arrest and he forced him to ascend this other Domerus. I heard he tortured him to make him do it but I don't suppose there's any record of that. Anyway, now there was a Po in the tritus but Guysil was still Ji. The King wanted his Ji status."

"He couldn't just execute the man?"

"No, because it wasn't a capital crime. Besides, he'd tried to send a challenger against Guysil to kill him in a duel and Guysil tore the woman to shreds. Literally. So now they had to get Guysil to make this new Po the Ji but he wouldn't. They tortured him, he refused. They threatened to cut his biom away but he still refused."

Sijun paused and Radoq pressed him "What did they do?"

"They brought the lun'erus woman he'd been accused of abusing in front of him. The King put a coltac to her head and told Guysil to release the Ji title to this Po or he'd kill her. Anyway, Guysil agreed and the woman was killed anyway to keep the little scene secret."

Radoq scoffed "The King murdered a lun'erus woman? That didn't happen. Besides, how did the story get out?"

"Maybe some details got lost in translation." Sijun admitted.

"I'll say! Anyway, you said he was taking advantage of lun'erus women, not falling in love with them! Why would he care about her if it was the other way around?"

"Look, the point of the story is that this Ji, Guysil was now a Po and the new Ji immediately rescinded his power. He was Fallen. So, they banish him from Wallanria and pack him aboard a ship to my country."

"What happened to the Ji?"

"I'm getting there! He's on the ship but the ship goes down over the Dark Lands. There's a third Domerus aboard and he makes it safely to the Eyrie no problem but the crew all die in the Dark Lands. So does Guysil, they assume and that's what everyone thinks. Ships from the Eyrie go out and see the crash site and confirm its swarming with virals, right next to the glowing rocks so no lun'erus and no Fallen Domerus are surviving that. No chance." Sijun chopped a hand down to illustrate the point.

"So, cut ahead a few years and the new Ji – the one who the King forced to take the tritus has had family and now has a Po and lots of Su of his own. Society is gradually forgetting that Kanata was a bad name at all until one day the tritus wakes up to find the Po dead, his head on a spike in their tritus home."

"It was Guysil?" Radoq was impatient.

"Right. But Guysil was last seen in the Dark Lands surrounded by virals. Besides, he's Fallen and the Po when they find his body was killed by Tal-Kan. He died in a soul grip but he wasn't shot."

"Oh?" Radoq was intrigued.

"So one by one all the Su and the new Po are killed until it's just this Ji with his stolen power. He appeals to the King who brings him to Admirain for shelter but his ship never arrives. They find the crash in the forest, years later and his body is there, well preserved but missing the head. So, we have a dead Ji."

"And that's the end of the tritus." Radoq nodded.

"Well, that's where facts end and rumours start." Sijun admitted "But this Fallen man, Guysil managed not only to survive the Dark Lands and the virals but to slaughter an entire tritus single handed including the Ji. How many lun'erus can do that?"

"He wasn't lun'erus though." Radoq pointed out "Fallen or not, we're still stronger than they are. Bigger, faster, longer living."

Sijun rolled his eyes "My point is that he clearly found a way to survive in the Dark Lands and it made him stronger."

Radoq rolled his eyes at that "That's a stretch of logic, Sijun. I can buy that a man of his years and skill could survive the Dark Lands even if he was Fallen but that doesn't mean he found some hidden source of power. Domerus power is technology, not magic. We know how it works and we control it in infinite detail. If he managed to kill the entire tritus then the Ji power died with them. Even if he's the most dangerous Fallen Domerus to have ever existed, he's still Fallen."

Radoq finished, realising his tone had turned harsh and an awkward silence passed between them.

Sijun turned and gestured at the milling virals, still held back as though by an invisible hand "How do you explain that, then?"

Radoq shrugged "Something. Some force of nature. They know we're a threat. They don't like the lights." Seeing the expression on Sijun's face he sighed in exasperation "Oh, Sijun! If there were a mysterious Ji stalking us from the darkness, what would you have us do? Challenge him?"

"Talk to him! Domerus to Domerus! He bears us no ill will. He was Fallen before we were born! We could strike a deal with him to keep the virals away from our lun'erus!"

"Enough!" Radoq's temper flared and he turned to jump back to the ground where Staph stood with his men. This side of the ship was at least clear of virals and he found the soldiers here in better spirits.

Sijun followed him but Radoq ignored him as he spoke to the troops, gauging their morale and trying to encourage them. He spoke briefly with Staph who, like his counterpart on the far side of the ship did not take his eyes off the perimeter the entire time they spoke.

"I'm thinking about trying to lead them off." Radoq told Staph quietly wanting the man's opinion.

The grizzled Sergeant considered "Not a bad shout, Sir. Only thing is you might lead more back to us doing that."

"Rakr practically begged me to do it."

"Can't speak for him, Sir. He's got them in his face over there so maybe it's different for him. I'd say we need you here though. If they do attack, maybe you can try then. As it stands though, Sir, my opinion is to hold fast. Can't be more than six hours until dawn."

Radoq went to check on Evie, Sijun following like a shadow through the decks which were filled now with prone figures who stirred and shifted rather than sleeping.

"Chox'd things!" Evie swore as Radoq entered the engine room. She'd covered the panel to the outside but was now hard at work burning some gears together with an aquar torch whilst Baxl passed her parts.

"How long, Evie?"

"As long as it takes!" she snapped "We've got four circuits out on engine one, that'll take two more hours and I haven't even started on engine two! What time is it?"

"After midnight. Six hours to dawn?" Radoq estimated and Evie swore foully.

"Gonna be here until daylight, Domerus. Unless your pal Oprain can send us a tug?"

"He is but the tugs aren't fast. It'll be here first thing but not before."

"Chox. I hate Chox'd tugs." Evie began a rant which accompanied her feverish work as sweat dripped down her face. Radoq left her to it, stepping out into the narrow corridor beyond it only to have Sijun grip his shoulder.

"I apologise, Radoq."

"No need. I should have held my temper."

"The story is one that I heard as a boy. I've always held the Dark Ji to be something of a legend. It's an enticing thought, don't you think?" seeing Radoq's expression he hastened to add "Not the part about lun'erus women! Never that. But to live as a rebel alone amongst the virals. It's something!"

"It's miserable."

"Maybe! Maybe it's the perfect life. No world to interfere, living life on your own terms." Sijun began a happy soliloquy as his imagination spun dreams of living as a hermit in a cave, practicing Tal-Kan and exploring the limits of their Domerus power.

There was no escaping the virals though and as the guards were changed over, Radoq headed back to Rakr's side of the ship where they still roiled just beyond the light.

"You need some sleep, Sergeant."

"Beg your pardon, Sir, but no I don't. I've kept longer vigils than this before."

He didn't argue. Instead, Rakr repeated his request for Radoq to lead the virals away and he relayed Staph's thoughts.

"He's not wrong, Sir, but if you do manage to lead them away then it removes the problem. We get another load coming at us we can handle them. It's the waiting that's doing everyone's head in." the Sergeant shrugged "It's your call, Sir."

And it was. Radoq gathered Sijun and Tricial, telling them what he intended. The two of them agreed to stand watch atop the ship, looking out for any further incursions by the virals and Radoq took a small communicator with him, posting Armlu, the former gunnery Sergeant from Xeonison in the communicator room.

"… hear me, Sir?"

"Just about."

"Smashing. Have a good trip. Shout if you need me to come running." Armlu went silent as Radoq repressed a laugh.

A great bound took him over Rakr and his men, landing beyond the virals and the perimeter of weak lights. As he passed over them, Radoq tried to analyse their patterns of movement (they were never still) to sense some kind of meaning or purpose but the roiling mass climbed over one another heedless of cries of discomfort only to be climbed over again in turn.

He concentrated on his landing this time, coming down

silently and staying still in a crouch. The virals were now behind him and he froze as a screech sounded but there was no movement towards him and he turned slowly, watching them from the back. *Golden Kote* was a beacon of light in the blackness that surrounded them and he could see at once that they were visible for miles around. Perhaps it was the light that held the virals back because the difference between where he now crouched and the ship was night and day. Surely the artificial light had both drawn them in and frightened them off. Perhaps that was why they reeled and climbed over one another.

Movement behind him and Radoq saw a lone viral moving quickly towards him. He tensed for a fight but the beast changed its direction to pass him by, apparently unaware of his presence. He stared at the pink skin, flicking his aurae so that it appeared almost like daylight. Aside from the distended belly, the creature had the same basic structure as a lun'erus. The arms ended in hands and the legs in feet although the hands were hooked into claws and Radoq could see a hard, callous like substance had formed on the palms. The heads were hairless and round and a faint sheen hung across the skin as though they exuded an oil. None were clothed, their genitals and breasts the only palpable difference between the genders and bearing little resemblance to anything human.

The creature paused, a few metres from its fellows and turned, raising its face to sniff the air. Radoq caught a glimpse of a flat nose, cracked and yellow teeth and deep black eyeballs filling the socket like two wells of darkness.

Then the creature ploughed on, vanishing into the midst of the pack. Radoq turned, looking to see where it had come from and spotted more movement, one, two, a handful moving as a pack all drawn in from across the Dark Lands.

Cursing, he realised the light that was keeping them at bay was serving only to draw in more and, in the hours remaining until dawn, they'd attract many hundreds and when the light of day came, their flimsy perimeter would fail and the virals would wash over his men.

As the next pair drew near to Radoq he sprang forward, kicking his toe into the throat of one and leaving it choking to death on the black rocks. The second he seized, flinging it to the ground breaking both arms with casual blows. He pressed the monster down, leaning over until his face was level with the snapping jaws and his eyes stared into the black pits of the viral.

"What do you want? What are you?"

A shriek rose from the pinned creature and he raised his fist in a hammer blow to shatter the skull when a cultured voice sounded close at hand in a polite tone.

"Would you please not do that, Radoq?"

CHAPTER 18

A figure, unmistakeably a Domerus by his height and build, was standing beside him. Dressed in dark clothes with a thick black cape across one shoulder, Radoq could make out a greying beard and a hard looking face with eyes that were locked on him.

Radoq straightened slowly, allowing the viral to wriggle to its feet, apparently unburdened by the loss of its arms.

"How do you know my name?"

The man smiled "I know a great deal. The *children* whisper it to me."

The Dark Ji

"Are you Guysil?"

A snatch of laughter then a hand clapped over his own mouth as though to stifle the sound "Yes! I was. I am. I will be again!"

He's insane Radoq thought to himself. He felt for his communicator, trying to press the button that would transmit his voice but when he pushed, there was no accompanying static. The message wasn't transmitting.

"How do you know my name?" Radoq asked again.

Guysil took his hand away from his mouth. The viral had scurried away, ignoring the two Domerus. Under the guise of watching it, Radoq shifted his feet subtly so that he was in a Tal-Kan stance, hands loose by his sides and shoulders tensed.

The same cackle of laughter, this one not cut off issued from Guysil's mouth "You would fight me? Duel with the Dark Ji?"

Radoq raised his left hand to display the golden kote that adorned his biom but Guysil merely chuckled.

"I know! I know, I know, I know. The children told me!"

"You mean the virals?"

"The wretched ones, the virals, the children of the glow!" Guysil suddenly turned and began to walk away from the ship and the massing virals, into the depths of the Dark Lands.

"Wait!" Radoq shouted after him but Guysil simply made a beckoning gesture. After a moment of hesitation, Radoq followed.

Seeing he was playing along, Guysil broke into a run. Actually, it was more of a sprint and Radoq began to see flashing warnings in his aurae as his biom failed to cycle oxygen fast enough. An unfamiliar sensation began to build in his chest and legs.

Pain.

Fatigue.

He couldn't breathe. No, that wasn't quite right. He couldn't catch his breath. He tried to distract himself as he pumped his arms and legs, determined not to fall behind Guysil who loped along seemingly effortlessly with his black cape streaming out behind him. When was the last time he'd run so hard? Before his ascension, surely. Years ago. Decades maybe. He could recall a training session where he and Gellian having earned the wrath of a new tutor had been forced to run repeats up the steep mountain slopes outside Fortisul. The instructor had chosen a section of loose scree, just shallow enough that the boys could run rather than be forced to crawl. Up they sprinted, turning to their left at the top and running along the flat ground until a second, steeper rock strewn slope opened and they sprinted down it, arms windmilling frantically to maintain their balance and then back along the bottom, past the instructor watching him closely for any sign, an indication that the torture was almost over.

Gellian had the longer legs but Radoq had the will to continue and as his brother tumbled down the slope coming to rest in a panting, heaving pile at the bottom, he'd continued, sprinting once more past the instructor, up the scree slope until white lights flashed in his vision and he came too, lying on his back whilst the instructor poured some type of harsh spirit into his throat which made him gag and retch but restored his breath in an instant.

Now he felt he'd give his arm for a sip of the spirit, anything to tear free the iron band that seemed to have tightened around his lungs. Sweat poured into his eyes, cold shivers ran down his spine, he thought he might vomit and his bowels had turned to water. His legs felt as if they weighed a thousand tonnes each and his feet dragged as though he were moving through deep sand rather than over hard rock.

I will not stop

His mind took over, willing his body to continue. As long as he could think, he could run but his eyes never left Guysil's cloak, watching for the first indication that the man would slow, just as he'd begged the instructor with his eyes.

"Here!" Guysil appeared not to have noticed Radoq's suffering and indeed, he barely seemed out of breath. Radoq tried to estimate how far they'd travelled. He turned back the way they'd come but the lights of the ship were nowhere to be seen. He switched his aurae through different settings, searching the bleak landscape but the *Golden Kote* and his men were gone.

"Will the virals attack my men?"

Guysil was on one knee, busying himself with something on the ground. He looked up sharply "No. I will keep them at bay."

"If you can control them, can't you call them off? When it gets light, they'll attack."

Guysil cocked his head at Radoq, peering at his face as though searching for some quality. Evidently satisfied, he gave a short cackle before responding "The lun'erus in your town, Fortisul. Could you call them off if an oddity landed within your walls? If you stood on the ramparts and called 'I am Radoq! Return to your homes! Leave this place and don't gawp at the visitors!', would they listen?"

Radoq shook his head, now bent over with his hands on his knees as he fought to regain his breath.

"No. But if they formed a mob with gats and torches you could stop them killing the guest?"

Radoq got the point "So –" a violent cough "So they're your lun'erus? The Dark Ji and his virals?"

Guysil's head jerked up at that giving Radoq the distinct impression he had insulted the man. He slowly straightened up feeling nausea surge through him.

"Do not mock the virals, Radoq."

Radoq bowed his head in acknowledgement "I will endeavour not to."

"Wonderful!" the mad tone had returned and Guysil's cloak flapped and snapped as he leapt to his feet, hauling open a hidden door set flat into the rock, reminding Radoq of the hatches atop the *Golden Kote.* Guysil was gesturing for him to enter but he held out a hand, allowing the caped figure to lead the way and Guysil gracefully flowed forward, jumping down into the hole and vanishing from view.

Radoq stepped close to the edge, adjusting his aurae for the pitch blackness within.

"Come, Radoq!" Guysil called from below and Radoq suddenly spotted him, stood at the bottom of a deep natural cave.

Radoq took a deep breath and jumped. His stomach lurched for a moment before his biom steadied him and then he bent his knees in time for the landing. He straightened up, seeing Guysil had already moved into the cave as above them the hatch crashed shut. The space was vast, more of an underground cavern really and whilst most of it was bare rock, a good portion was lined with the glowing green rocks that Radoq had seen from the air. A smaller portion was filled with human furniture, a bed, a wash basin, several chests. Everything was ordered neatly, the bedclothes folded back and crisply arranged and chairs facing each other with mathematical precision.

"Is this your home?"

"Home! Home, home, home." Guysil cackled, filling a glass "This is the realm of the Dark Ji!"

"Where you live alone?" Radoq hoped that the man's lunatic behaviour was simply the result of so many years alone and that some normal conversation with a fellow Domerus might cause his temperament to settle. Otherwise, he was unpredictable and after that run Radoq had no illusions that any fight between them would be certain to end in his victory. Besides, he had no idea where his ship lay. He thumbed the communicator in his pocket but again, no burst of static greeted his ears.

"Drink!" Guysil thrust a glass into his hand and Radoq caught the strong whiff of sky spirit. He raised the glass in salute and Guysil mirrored it, both tipping back the contents.

"Where do you get it all from?" Radoq indicated the trappings of human life.

Guysil grinned hugely "From the sky! Men fall, Guysil finds." He cackled again.

"Is that your sigil?" he pointed to a great cloth banner that hung towards the top of the cave. It was torn through the middle.

"Was! Was, was, was. The sigil of tritus Kanata!"

"Are you the Ji?"

"I am the Dark Ji!"

"But of tritus Kanata, are you the Ji of that tritus?"

Guysil ignored him, instead swigging his drink and disrobing his cape in a sweeping motion of his hand. It fell onto the floor and he abandoned it, at odds with the neatness of the cave.

Seeing his host was not going to answer, Radoq strode across to the lowest of the glowing rocks Fascinated, he peered at them from every angle, touching them, feeling the faint heat that filled them. The luminosity was limited. The centre of each stone seemed to be the brightest part and the light faded the closer to the edge it got. It was a murky green in colour, almost turning the rock translucent.

It looked dirty and Radoq found his nose wrinkling as he examined it.

"Beautiful." Guysil had approached as silently as he had on the surface and was gazing enraptured at the rocks "Utterly beautiful."

"It's poisonous, isn't it?" Radoq asked "Left over from the nuklera."

Guysil's head snapped around at the word "What poison would allow you and I to stand here and admire it, Radoq? What poison doesn't harm those who touch it?"

"No – I mean its poisonous to lun'erus."

"Lun'erus! Lun'erus, lun'erus, lun'erus. The dregs of our species, the children, the weak, the weight that pulls humanity down into the dirt." Guysil suddenly spat on the cave floor in disgust, an uncharacteristic action for a Domerus.

Radoq remembered his conversation with Sijun only hours before. He'd spoken harshly to his new friend then but he adopted a more pacifying tone with Guysil "Our duty as Domerus is to our lun'erus."

"Oh, it is! But what of their duty to us, Radoq?"

Radoq was nonplussed "What?"

"What do they do in return for our service? What do they provide us with?"

Radoq frowned "Food, production, manufacturing. All those are done by the lun'erus." He knew the Dark Ji knew this but the man was labouring towards a point and a fascination filled Radoq.

"All tasks any Domerus could perform a hundred, no, a thousand times more efficiently! They're slaves, Radoq! Nothing but slaves, as you were when you passed over my home those many moons ago."

Radoq started "How –" he stopped, knowing the answer "The virals told you?"

"Ha!" Gusyil cackled delightedly "You know! You know, you know, you know!" he danced a few steps with joy "They tell me everything!"

"They told you I was in a slave ship? Thousands of feet above you? I think not."

"But you came down, all the way down to their level and the ship showed its belly to the virals and they saw a Domerus, pretending he had Fallen, bound by restraints he could have shattered in an instant whilst around him those who he swore to protect were shipped into bondage."

"I freed them."

"Oh, to what end? To grow food? To produce goods? To manufacture a new ship for you?" humour had left Guysil's face "Tell me, Radoq. What exactly did you do for those lun'erus? And what exactly did they do for you?"

Radoq took a few tentative steps away from the rocks, peering around at Guysil's other possessions as he collected his thoughts. His father, Loxel would have been far better at this, his swift tongue nearly always the master of any debate. Radoq found himself instinctively disagreeing with Gusyil but he found it hard to put his thoughts into words. As though sensing this, Guysil allowed him to think.

"I think that we live in a careful balance, Domerus and lun'erus." He picked up an ornate sword, engraved with the sigil of Kanata "The one cannot exist without the other and each has its role."

"And what is our role, dear Radoq?"

"To protect the lun'erus. To fight for them. To lead them when they require it."

Guysil had closed in again, firmly taking the sword from Radoq's grasp and placing it back where it had rested atop an iron bound trunk. He leaned in close to Radoq's face, his pale skin reflecting the ghastly green pallor of the rocks "Protect them from what, Radoq?"

"From the – virals."

"Aaah..." Guysil sighed in immense satisfaction, stepping away to throw himself into a plush armchair set over a thick woven rug.

"You see a fault with the system?"

"Fault?" Guysil sounded appalled at the mediocrity of the word "I see no fault. I see failure. Lies and corruption. I see no system, in fact, Radoq. I see only ruin and deceit."

"Deceit?"

"The lun'erus!" Guysil slammed his hands down on the arms of the chair. A small part of Radoq's mind noted how little dust shot from the fabric and he wondered how the man kept his furniture so clean out here.

"What have the lun'erus done to deceive you?"

"You? Me? Us? We stand as their protectors, no? What does history tell you, Radoq? At some point, around a millennium ago after terrible destruction humanity split into two distinct castes." The madness had fled from Guysil's tone to be replaced with lucid anger "Two castes, lun'erus and Domerus. Domerus were descended from the strongest, fastest and healthiest, no? Bound in service all their lives to live and die at the behest of their Ji. And all the rest? Lun'erus. Common people. The free folk. The Domerus serve the lun'erus as payment for their privilege."

"No." Radoq shook his head "The Domerus serve because it is our responsibility."

"*Whom* do we serve, Radoq?"

Radoq opened his mouth and closed it again.

"Exactly! We serve the lun'erus. We are the slaves."

It was madness. Utter madness. Guysil was insane, driven so by the years of isolation talking only to the virals whilst he scavenged crashed airships. Nothing he was saying was logical.

"But how did I know about the slave ship?" Guysil had watched his face closely.

"You were there. You saw me." Radoq shrugged. It wasn't complicated.

"I was by the Eyrie, carrying my children away from the guards."

Radoq made a dismissive sound "Fine. So the virals told you? What else did they tell you?" it was hard to keep the scepticism from his voice.

"That we should serve *them*. Not your lun'erus."

Madness. Radoq didn't bother to argue knowing a lost cause when he saw one. Instead, he began to look around for a way out.

"Think of it, Radoq! There are not two species of human but three! Lun'erus, Domerus and the virals! Three distinct species! Why should the virals be persecuted? Why should they be slaughtered? Why should it be to hunt them that we exist?"

"Because they're feral and they kill people." Radoq felt he

shouldn't antagonise the clearly unstable man but he couldn't help but call out the dross that Guysil was spinning.

"Do they? Or are they merely curious like children?"

"No."

"But they are, Radoq! All they want is to see and to understand! They're us, Radoq, an innocent, untainted version of humanity broken down into its most savage form! They don't care for politics, for hate or love or anger! They move as one, sharing thoughts with each other as if they were one person! They are the future, Radoq, not us! Not the lun'erus!"

Radoq raised his hands and dropped them again in a gesture of defeat "Fine. They're the future. What future?"

"The future lun'erus! Oh, of course they'll need guiding and protecting! That's our role! But since I ascended again I've been able to see as no other man has ever seen! I understand them, Radoq! They're lost, all they need is our guidance." He stood and the green light of the rocks reflected off his skin again and understanding clicked in Radoq's mind. He took several steps back, his heart suddenly hammering in his chest.

"You're not ascended like a Domerus."

Guysil smiled "No."

"You're like them."

A huge, maniacal nod.

"You're a viral."

"Oh, but I am so much more! Think of how I approached you, you never heard or saw me coming! And our run here? I jogged, Radoq, slowly enough to let you keep up with me and yet your heart pounded so loudly it echoed from the mountains in the north to the Southern Range! You say I'm not ascended but I laugh in your face! To me, Radoq, it is you who are not ascended! *I* am the true Domerus!"

You're a Chox'd brain rotted madman Radoq thought but he forced himself to nod as if he understood.

"You're fast, I'll give you that." He began but Guysil was out of the chair before he'd finished speaking, kicking Radoq's legs from under him and pinning him. Before he had time to do little more than lower his chin, Radoq found himself pinned in the soul grip.

"Fast? Fast? There is nothing in this world as fast as me! You think yourself strong with your ascension but I promise you, Radoq, there is far more than your mind can comprehend!"

Radoq could not reply. He couldn't breathe and his eyes felt as though they were bulging from his head. Abruptly, Guysil released him and Radoq sprang away, hands raising in a defensive stance although his heart hammered wildly, unable to remember a time when he'd been bested so thoroughly.

"I didn't bring you here to fight, Radoq."

"Then what am I here for? To hear you preach your ideology at me? For you to infect me with this virus?"

"Infect you?" Guysil sounded surprised "No. I cannot infect you." He shook his head, frowning as though annoyed the conversation had got away from him. He paused, clearly collecting his thoughts.

Radoq watched warily, wondering what madness he'd be subjected to next.

"I brought you here because I wish to strike a deal with you. I believe we can help one another."

CHAPTER 19

Dawn was breaking by the time Radoq got a signal on his communicator. A frantic Tricial was on the other end demanding to know where he'd been. Radoq shouted over his irate voice, ordering the Sheriff to check the virals and indeed a moment later, Tricial reported that they'd gone. There followed a tedious round of sending and receiving signals as Radoq navigated along the bottom of the Northern Massif, covering miles and miles before he came upon the *Golden Kote* and the shocked faces of his crew.

"Sergeant!" he called to Rakr receiving a nod of greeting from the taciturn man who seemed utterly unflustered by his commander's disappearance but it was Sijun who leapt from the fighting deck, staggering as his injured foot gave way.

"Radoq! We'd thought you lost!"

"I'm well, Sijun. No call for alarm."

"But where've you been?" curiosity certainly spurred the question from the big man but Radoq also detected a bitter disappointment that Sijun had not been included in what he surely felt was a great adventure. Fortunately, Radoq was spared an explanation as Tricial emerged from the ship, shouting that the tug from the Eyrie had made contact and every eye turned to the west to see the squat, ugly shape of the ship that chugged towards them.

"Chox'd thing." Radoq turned to see Evie, a smear of something black down the side of her face and exhaustion written into every line of her body.

Elation at their rescue filled him and so Radoq jibed "Didn't manage to fix it?"

She turned a furious look on him, ready to lambast him but the sight of her sent Radoq into a guffaw, turning away from her and a moment later he heard her higher peals of mirth too.

"Chox'd bearings were all bust on engine two. Can't get the relay firing without new ones." She shook her head.

"Well, sounds like you had a productive night." Radoq loaded sarcasm into his tone as Evie made an obscene hand gesture.

"Where did you go last night, anyway?" she asked but Radoq shook his head, indicating to discuss it later.

The tug came to a halt close by and a gangway lowered into the Dark Lands to disgorge a squad of air Marines who then stood somewhat lamely, seeing the professional layout of the perimeter. Staph greeted their commander by name and a moment later, the soldiers were milling about aimlessly swapping stories and noisy jokes as soldiers will do when there is no enemy to fight.

"Radoq!" the familiar voice brought a smile of recognition to Radoq's face and a moment later he was shaking Oprain's hand warmly as the elderly Domerus stepped gingerly onto the nuklera blackened rocks "All well?"

"All well. Three men killed in the air combat."

"I see." Oprain was eyeing the ship, his gaze resting on the embossed name at the stern "Your missing ship?" he raised an eyebrow leaving Radoq impressed at the man's ability to recall small details.

"A legitimate re-appropriation of dishonestly taken property."

"Ah." Oprain turned to a small, bookish looking lun'erus who stood beside him with a nervous expression "We'll forgive the air piracy charge, then."

Radoq smiled at the joke but the lun'erus made a note on a small handheld and he blinked in surprise.

"*Golden Kote* is my ship. It was taken in battle."

"As I said, all is forgiven." Oprain smiled "The law must be upheld though, Radoq and you destroyed three ships yesterday. That could be seen as a crime by some."

"A legitimate –" he began again but Oprain cut him off with a wave.

"Oh, enough. It's done now. It'd likely have only been a formality anyway, Radoq but I don't take matters of law lightly. Anyway, introduce me to your friend."

Sijun had been politely standing behind Radoq and when he and Oprain had made their formal bows and introductions they struck up a conversation about the intricacies of aviation law so tediously detailed that Radoq swore he could actually feel his mental faculties dying off. Making an excuse, he turned to oversee the embarkation of the crew, mercenaries and soldiers back onto the ship but Staph and Rakr had already given the necessary orders and he found himself speaking inane words to exhausted men who did not need to hear his voice. Instead, he watched in fascination as Evie took control of the tug technicians, her sharp tongue sending them scurrying to and fro with tow cables.

Soon, the *Golden Kote* was ready to move and Evie all but ordered Radoq into the bridge to start the vakkor engine and give them lift. Slowly, the slack was taken out of the towing cables and the ship began to climb steadily towards the Eyrie.

"And not a viral to be seen." Tricial was facing away from Radoq, looking out over the Dark Lands. He turned, a knowing look in his eyes. They were alone in the bridge although the door that led down the companionway into the bowels of the ship was ajar.

"Strange." Radoq murmured in a non-committal voice.

"Strange. As strange as how you knew those virals would be gone this morning." Tricial raised an eyebrow.

"Indeed!" Sijun's booming voice sounded and Radoq turned in surprise, thinking the young Domerus had boarded the tug with Oprain. Of the 'Light Ji', there was nothing to be seen suggesting he had reboarded the Eyrie ship now ahead of them "Perhaps you care to share your secrets with us, dear Radoq?"

Radoq grinned hugely as he got up to seal the bridge door, turning so his back was pressed to it.

"Well, out with it!" Sijun's already scanty patience had vanished and the big man looked as though he were about to burst with anticipation.

"I met the Dark Ji."

"*What?*" Sijun's voice boomed from the enclosed space as Radoq fought not to smile.

"He's real, then?" Tricial asked in a wary tone.

"Oh yes."

Sijun turned to Tricial "Of course he's real! Guysil Chirrutsus Ji-Kanata!"

Tricial's eyes widened in shock "Kanata? *That's* the Dark Ji?"

"You know the story?" Radoq asked in surprise having never heard it before Sijun had told him.

"The story?" Tricial sounded shocked "I was there, Radoq! I was in Admirain when the King seized him! It was the greatest scandal Wallanria has ever seen!"

"Of course." Radoq had forgotten the Sheriff was decades older than him and would remember it well.

"He was killed, though. Or so we thought. Vanished into the Dark Lands." Tricial shrugged "I suppose it's feasible he could have survived."

"But he was Fallen?" Sijun asked earnestly.

"Oh yes. That was the point of sending him into exile rather than killing him." Tricial seemed to peer into the depths of his memory "It's part of the reason we now have a Crown Prince rather than a King. He lost a lot of credibility amongst the Domerus for his actions. Most thought he should have taken Kanata's head."

"Well?" Sijun demanded "Was he Fallen or not? Did he reclaim his Ji title?"

"I –" Radoq hesitated, wondering how much to say. The babbling manifesto Guysil had proclaimed last night was madness and he thought it best left behind in the Dark Lands as a bad memory. Then again, the deal he'd struck with the madman weighed heavily on him and filled his mind with the burning excitement that only a new, wondrous idea can.

Sijun let out an exasperated noise and Radoq cleared his throat.

"I can't say. I can tell you that he's mad, utterly insane."

"Decades of living in the Dark Lands would do that." Tricial nodded.

"That's what I thought. But he approached me last night as I was heading out to lead the virals away."

"And you didn't think to tell us?" Sijun was indignant.

"He caught me by surprise." Radoq explained.

"And? You could still have called to us."

"No, I mean he approached without me seeing him."

Sijun frowned. The idea of anything approaching a Domerus without being spotted was utterly alien. The biom that protected them and enhanced their senses did not miss even small details let alone a full grown Domerus approaching over open ground "Was he hidden?"

"I don't think so." It was Radoq's turn to frown, remembering the cape Guysil had worn "He could have had a stealth device." He explained the cape to the two Domerus.

Tricial looked uncertain "I've never heard of stealth technology being woven into fabric like that." He shook his head "I imagine it was just a cape, nothing more."

"But you didn't see him coming?" Sijun urged, fascinated.

"No. And there's more. He told me to follow him and he ran faster than anything I've ever seen. Racing yachts would have struggled to keep up with him."

Sijun scoffed "But you kept pace?"

"Barely"

"And you can run as fast as a racing yacht, can you?"

Radoq scowled "A small exaggeration then. But he was fast. I know I'm no runner but... Chox he ran fast! And when we arrived at his home, he wasn't short of breath at all!"

"Then he's been training his body all this time." Sijun shrugged and Radoq sensed his friend was desperate to find a normal explanation for the frightening things he was saying.

"Perhaps." Radoq nodded slowly "But this was something

else."

"A Ji is always going to be stronger than a Po or a Su." Tricial pointed out "Or an Ap for that matter."

"Lun'erus are faster than an Ap." Sijun joked scornfully before looking in contrition at Tricial "My dear Tricial."

Tricial waved the insult aside "But there are limits. You would still have noticed a Ji approaching you. Especially with the virals all around. I'll wager you had your aurae on the sharpest setting?"

Radoq nodded.

"Then what?" Sijun demanded in exasperation "What was the edge he had?"

"The virus." Radoq shrugged, realising how lame the words sounded "He was infected."

"He was a viral?" Tricial sounded disbelieving.

"In a way. He was still human, we spoke at great length and although he was mad there were periods where he was lucid."

"Well, perhaps the virus made him stronger?" Sijun was still trying to rationalise things but he went pale as the significance of what he'd said struck him.

"Stronger than Radoq?" Tricial was playing Chox's advocate but Radoq could hear the nervousness in his voice "I flatter you Radoq that you're among the fastest and strongest of our kind." He indicated the golden kote that adorned Radoq's left hand "I doubt there are many who could best you like that. Certainly not those of us cursed with old age and Guysil is centuries older than you."

"So –" Sijun had stood and began pacing up and down, his limp noticeably lessened since the night before "He's what, some type of viral Ji?"

"A Dark Ji indeed." Tricial murmured.

Sijun snorted but there was little humour in the action "Let's try to work this out." He bent his head, now still and looking down at the floor of the bridge still stained with the helmsman's blood "Decades ago, a Fallen Ji vanishes into the Dark Lands. The ship crashes, correct?"

Radoq and Tricial nodded.

"But we know he is more than your average Fallen Domerus because he's already slaughtered the rest of the tritus including the Ji. How many lun'erus can do that?"

"He wouldn't have been lun'erus." Tricial reminded Sijun but the big waved an impatient hand.

"I know, I know but he would have lost his ascension strength."

"No." Tricial leaned forward "It's a crucial point, actually. When the three of us were ascended we each took on exponential growth through the technology in our bioms but since then have we remained the same?"

He looked at Radoq who shook his head and at Sijun who shrugged.

"No. We've each got stronger, faster and more skilled in our various disciplines. Of course, the biom makes us what we are but strip away the power and there is still the raw strength of a Domerus beneath it. All those years of training and learning make us far more dangerous than we'd give credit for. Radoq, when you were disguised as a Fallen Domerus you didn't use your biom did you?"

Radoq admitted that he had not.

"But you were still a cut above the lun'erus surrounding you? The slavers had to lock you in an iron cage, didn't they?"

Radoq shrugged, then nodded.

"But that doesn't make Guysil as strong as a Ji." Sijun still wasn't buying it.

"No. But he was a clever man and it doesn't stretch credulity all that much to assume he used guile and cunning to destroy the tritus." Tricial saw the expression on Sijun's face and sighed "I'm saying it's a possibility, not a reality."

"The man I saw last night was faster and stronger than any Ji I've ever met." Radoq shook his head "He got me in a soul grip."

"Chox!" Sijun swore "How?"

"I barely even saw him move. I had no chance."

"He was a champion of Tal-Kan before his fall." Tricial

remembered.

"Yes. But this was more than just a skilled Tal-Kan practitioner, Tricial. This was blindingly fast."

A silence filled the air between the three Domerus as they considered the possibilities. Sijun broke it as a though occurred to him.

"The virals – he had some type of control over them?"

"Yes." Radoq frowned "It was hard to get an answer through the babbling but he likened it to us staying a mob of lun'erus from a crashed ship."

"Oh yes." Tricial nodded "That's that old parable, the one from nursery books about the Domerus who prevent the townsfolk from murdering the crashed pilot."

"Exactly." Radoq nodded.

"So he was able to stop them attacking us?" Sijun asked and Radoq nodded "I suppose we should be grateful."

"Indeed." Tricial looked anything but. His eyes lingered on Radoq as Sijun turned to stare out at the tug that bobbed on the air currents before them.

Feeling the Sheriff's gaze on him, Radoq's mind filled with the idea that had borne him from Guysil's lair. He fought to keep the smile from his face.

"There's something else, isn't there?" Tricial was watching him expectantly and Radoq had to remind himself that the man was a seasoned politician, well used to reading behind expressions.

Sijun turned back "What?"

Radoq smiled, taking a deep breath "I made a deal with him. With Guysil. A plan to retake Fortisul."

Sijun and Tricial's faces displayed anything but excitement. Tricial looked concerned whilst Sijun was appalled.

"With that? With a mad viral?"

"What was the deal, Radoq?"

Radoq laughed at the expression on their faces "All in good time, friends! All in good time!" when neither man smiled he shook his head in exasperation "Look, all I ask is that you trust me. You've followed me this far, haven't you?"

"Trust? I've pledged my trust to you, Radoq." Sijun reminded him "But don't keep us in the dark."

Radoq dipped his head in acknowledgement and scooped up a communicator to summon Evie to the bridge. When the caustic lun'erus arrived a few minutes later, Sijun was practically vibrating with anticipation.

Radoq told them the deal he had struck with Guysil.

"You're sure it was him that was mad, not you?" Evie's sharp tongue broke the silence that followed his words "You didn't hit your head last night? Maybe the old biom took a battering in the explosion?" she seized his left hand and turned it over and over as though checking for signs of damage "Maybe those glowing rocks got to you after all, same as they did to us?"

"I promise I'm in my right mind." Radoq assured her prompting a stream of her usual profanities. He looked to Tricial for his reaction. The Sheriff's brow was furrowed in consternation.

"It's such a risk, Radoq. You realise that if this fails, if we're discovered then the Crown Prince will take all our heads and perhaps those of our respective tritus' too?"

"Not to mention the virals breaching the Western Hills en-masse for the first time since Ychacha!" Evie pointed out.

"I know the risks." Radoq stood, meeting his friend's eyes. He needed their support for this but more than that he wanted their honest counsel "Believe me, I do. But every day we are in the Eyrie or in the Dark Lands is another day that Fortisul suffers! Juraj gets stronger with every ship that comes to him and so far, we've less than fifty men – maybe a handful more now and we've got the *Golden Kote* but this is one ship and it can't fight an army! Besides, what would our plan be? Attack Fortisul? Slaughter my own people? Never. That's never going to work."

"But that's been our only strategy, Radoq!" Tricial argued "That's what we've been working towards! This is why you swore the blood oath!" he gestured to the gory mark on Radoq's arm.

"But this is another way, Tricial! One that doesn't mean more innocent deaths! If we do this right, no-one need die!"

"And Guysil? Will he follow through?"

"Yes."

"You have no guarantee. The word of a madman."

"The word of a Ji, Tricial." Radoq reminded him "He swore an oath to me."

"And you to him?"

Radoq looked uncomfortable "In a manner of speaking."

"Ah." Tricial nodded "You avoided a full oath?"

Radoq sighed "He promised me. I... skirted around the promise."

"That was not an honourable thing to do." Tricial murmured gently.

"No." Radoq agreed "But it wasn't strictly *dis*honourable. I think, given the circumstances it was the moral thing to do."

"Hah!" Sijun, who had been silent suddenly boomed with laughter. He thumped a fist against his chest as a grin spread across his face "I think it a fine plan, Radoq! High risk, high reward! If we pull this off we'll be the greatest adventurers of the age!"

"And if we fail, I'll kill you myself." Evie threatened drawing a snort of laughter from Sijun who was still unused to the lun'erus' manner and seemed to draw endless entertainment from it.

"Well? Are you with me?" Radoq grinned at his friends.

"Always!" Sijun didn't hesitate.

Tricial sighed, slowly levering himself to his feet and holding out his hand "Evie may be right, Radoq. You could well be the madman and Guysil the sane one. But I'll stick around long enough to find out." He smiled and they shook.

"Then –" Radoq's jubilant declaration was cut off by a frantically buzzing communicator which Evie leaned over a console to peer at.

"From the tug." She handed the handset to Radoq.

"Radoq? Oprain. I've had a signal from the Eyrie. The ship

carrying Argan went down at the northern edge of the Western Hills. Our rescue crews are there now but Argan's body isn't."

"North of the Western Hills..." Sijun, not familiar with the geography hastened to the map, peering. His finger stabbed down and he looked up with horror on his face "That's Fortisul."

Radoq nodded, a grim look of understanding passing between him and Tricial "Juraj. And now he has a Ji."

CHAPTER 20

There was nothing to be done. The *Golden Kote* needed repairs and Radoq had already explained the flaws in any attack on Fortisul.

"We have to assume that Juraj will be attempting an ascension." he leaned over a chart in Oprain's cluttered office as Tricial, Sijun, Evie and Oprain gathered for a council of war.

"Well, perhaps that'll kill him." Sijun suggested.

"If I may –" Oprain leaned forward "For all Argan's faults, he is still a Ji. His honour would not permit him to ascend a lun'erus."

"It didn't stop him trying to have you murdered." Tricial pointed out.

"True." Oprain nodded "But I think there is a great difference between personal greed and such a gross breach of – of…" he floundered for a word.

"Tradition?" Tricial suggested and the Ji nodded.

"Yes. Or protocol. Or common sense." Oprain seemed certain.

"If Juraj is ascended –" Radoq began.

"We don't know that." Evie cut in "Besides, if he's ascended then so what? All of you were last time I checked and it doesn't make him any better. He's still a crook at the head of a bunch of mercenaries."

"It legitimises him if he's Domerus." Oprain said.

Evie gave an exasperated sigh "Aren't there laws against this? Won't this bring the Crown Prince down on his head?"

"No!" Oprain sounded shocked "There are no laws preventing a Ji from performing an ascension. That would be… tyrannical."

Evie fixed him with a hard glare that Oprain seemed not to

heed. Radoq noticed it with a frown, wondering what thoughts were hidden behind his friend's face.

"Perhaps it simplifies things." Sijun had a pensive expression on his face "If he announces his ascension, you can call him out and duel him."

"Argan can refuse to let him duel." Oprain interjected.

"But you can put it in such a way that he can't refuse without losing face." Sijun was becoming excited with the idea "We were just talking about how much stronger the years of experience make us. Ascended or not, Radoq will tear him apart in a fight."

"That's true." Tricial nodded seriously "But we've still received no word from our agents in Fortisul?"

"No." Oprain shook his head "But these things take time. It would be foolish to assume that Argan has gone anywhere other than to Juraj, though. My men tell me the ship carrying him was shot down by a pulse torpedo."

"Not a pirate then." Radoq murmured.

"No. And pirates capture ships, they don't destroy them."

Sijun seemed exasperated. Radoq was beginning to learn that the man's patience was paper thin at the best of times.

"Sijun?"

"It seems to me that demanding a duel with him is the simplest, most effective plan. It's far simpler than what you spoke to –"

He cut himself off with a wary glance at Oprain.

"What?" the Ji stared at Radoq "What are you planning, Radoq?"

Radoq sighed "As you say, Oprain, you're responsible for the rule of law in these lands. What I am planning breaks a great deal of those laws. It's probably best if you don't know."

Oprain's eyes narrowed and he considered Radoq for a few tense moments before he sighed, turning to the window that gave a spectacular view of the Eyrie "I suppose you're probably right, Radoq. So long as no-one is going to get hurt?"

"Juraj, if all goes well."

He snorted "And Argan won't fare too well either? I thought

not. Well, keep your schemes to yourself then. I'll make sure to visit your cell next time I find myself in Admirain."

There were chuckles and more discussion but ultimately without news from their network of informants they could take no action. As they strolled around the grounds of his house, Radoq informed Oprain that as soon as *Golden Kote* was airworthy they would be flying on a mission to the west.

"To the hills, I hope?"

"Not quite, Oprain." Radoq hesitated, making sure not to reveal too much to the old Ji "What I'm planning will protect the hills. It may be that the virals cease to be a threat anymore."

Oprain stared at him, a cluster of emotions spreading across his face as the weight of Radoq's declaration settled. Finally, concern won out "You know what powers you're playing with here, Radoq? There are more dangers in the world than the ire of the capital and the Crown Prince."

"I know –"

"Just for a moment, pretend that you don't." Oprain glanced around but they stood alone in the empty training yard of his house "I of course would like to see nothing more than the destruction of the virals. It would free humanity from millennia of war and suffering." He gripped Radoq's arm "I don't know how you hope to achieve such an end but know that if you choose to go on such a path what it is that Domerus exist for."

Radoq narrowed his eyes, remembering Guysil's ramblings in the Dark Lands.

"I hesitate to caution you against such a path but think of the dangers of..." Oprain searched for a word "... *invalidating* the existence of thousands of people. Domerus are here to protect the lun'erus from the virals. If there are no more virals..." he left the sentence hanging.

"I understand." Radoq nodded, feeling more than a little impatience at the old man's caution. If he could remove the viral threat then they'd be freer than humans had been in living memory! What was a little danger in the face of such a goal?

"You're leaving soon?"

"Evie is just making the final repairs. Thank you for the ammunition, by the way."

"No bother." Oprain waved away the stacks of plasma bolts and pulse torpedoes he'd had delivered to the *Golden Kote*. The man made light of it but Radoq knew the expense had come from his own purse and he'd refused to even hear of being recompensed "I only hope you won't need it."

"We won't." Radoq smiled and Oprain shook his head before laughing.

"Oh, to be young and without doubts! Forgive an old man his caution, Radoq! I've lived too many years and seen too much to not worry. Perhaps I should not voice my fears."

"I appreciate your counsel."

"I know. And I appreciate you seeking it out. Go, Radoq! Fulfil your mad plan but when you're done, remember who you are. Po of tritus Fortisun. Your people need you. Malain needs you."

I'll come back to you

How long was it since he'd thought of that promise? Guilt flashed through his mind as he thought of his blood oath. Could he really say that this was the best path? Was the risk he was taking too high? Was he needlessly putting his friend's lives at risk? After all, if he failed in even one step of his journey the entire scheme would come crashing down.

Oprain clapped him on the shoulder and left him to make his way slowly down through the mountaintop city towards the skyport.

"Alright?" Evie was her usual unflustered self as though what they were undertaking was a casual mercantile flight and not the boldest theft Wallanria had ever seen.

"How's the ship?"

"Beautiful." For once, there was no sarcasm in Evie's voice and Radoq looked at her in surprise to see what looked like genuine love as she stared at the armoured hull of *Golden Kote*.

"She's a fine vessel."

"She's the finest." Agreed Evie "It's odd because she's smaller than *Freedman* but she feels so... big."

"Better laid down. Plus, she's tougher and faster."

Evie grunted in response.

"I'm sorry about losing *Freedman*."

"Me too. She had a good run and served her purpose but let's be honest, Domerus, she was a tub."

Radoq snorted and they shared a chuckle as Staph ushered the last of the crew aboard. He turned to look for Radoq and making eye contact, signalled that the embarking process was complete.

Radoq and Evie followed him up the gangway, the bright light of the morning vanishing as the armoured hatch sealed behind them. Evie led the way to the bridge where Tricial was already chattering to the port master through the communicator. He looked up as they entered from the luxurious new seat Evie had installed behind the main command console.

"Departure when we're ready. Lane alpha via beta two."

"Alpha via beta two, confirm." Radoq exchanged seats with Tricial.

"Are you making a speech to the crew?" Evie asked as Radoq fired the engines, feeling a pleasurable shudder as the smooth new bearings filled the ship with a thrumming vibration.

"Sure, but not until we're underway. I want to make sure no-one's following us."

"Oh?" Evie sounded sceptical "What'll you do if they are? Try out the new torpedoes?"

"No. And stop sounding excited about the torpedoes. Technically we shouldn't even be carrying them over the soft lands but I'm not anticipating an inspector coming aboard."

Evie as usual found a point to scoff at "Just because we're not from a freezing mountain top doesn't mean we're soft! The four cities are the heart of the country! You try going into a bar in Napp and calling them soft!"

Radoq rolled his eyes, deftly adjusting their course so they crept from lane beta two into alpha, heading out of the Eyrie's enclosed embrace.

"Anyway, you didn't answer the question about if we're followed."

"Didn't get a chance to." Radoq muttered.

"Well?"

He shot Evie a savage grin, wiggling his eyebrows "We'll lose them. How about making yourself useful and telling the crew to sit down?"

Watchers on the dock in the sky port behind them turned in amazement as the *Golden Kote,* her stern barely clearing the final stretch of lane alpha two roared in a blaze of noise, the immense power of the dual engines sending her rocketing into the sky. A second later, the slipstream caught the port and rocked the lane markers, sending dust and debris into unprotected eyes provoking much cursing and gesticulating that Radoq, grinning at the helm saw nothing of.

"All systems go, eh?" Evie spat through a clenched jaw, locked back into her seat as Radoq drove the battle ship into the blue sky. He lifted the nose, climbing thousands of feet before banking sharply to the north, sending them scurrying away from the Eyrie in the direction of Fortisul.

"Are you lost, Domerus?" Evie's voice was slightly less strained as he backed the engines down to a fast cruise.

"I'm above the shipping lanes but if anyone sees us, they'll think we're headed for Fortisul. Why do you think Oprain made such a big deal about the torpedoes? It looks like we're going to attack them."

"Right, but we're not. And they might not be ready for us now but we've got to come this way on the way back." Evie pointed out "And given what we'll be carrying, I don't think getting into a scrap is the best idea." She clung onto the seat as Radoq nosedived to skim the Dark Lands which whipped by in a black blur.

"Noted."

Evie grumbled but Radoq felt alive at the helm. If this had been a racing yacht, he'd have rolled it a few times or dipped into the deeper canyons that yawned across the blackened ground but despite her performance, *Golden Kote* was not built for theatrics and as they passed out of sight of the Eyrie, he reluctantly climbed into the upper shipping lane, slowing the engines and setting the controls to automatic.

"The crew." Tricial reminded him as Sijun entered the bridge, cursing Radoq's flying before flopping into the weapons officer's seat.

Radoq took a moment to think about his words before he picked up the communicator. Of the forty seven surviving soldiers they'd recruited in the Eyrie they had forty five remaining. Chirruf, the former Sherrif's guard was under Oprain's care being treated for her wounds but she would live. Oprain had already secured her a place in the city guard as a Lieutenant, a rank she had only dreamed of but already she was out speaking to the guards, getting to know her new command. One more, a sturdy lun'erus from Napp had declined to continue on with Radoq complaining that the exposure to the glow in the Dark Lands had already shortened his life.

Privately, Radoq though the man had lost his nerve at the sight of the virals around them but he couldn't blame him and paid him off.

Rakr and Staph had simply refused when he told them to return to the Marine barracks and no-one had come looking for them. Between the two of them Radoq reckoned they counted for as much as any army and he hadn't argued although he'd increased their pay to double the agreed price.

Fifteen of the mercenaries that had flown on *Golden Kote* under Correlius had elected to join Radoq, each of them being interviewed by he and Tricial on their experiences and past combat. He'd rejected four initially believing them to be little more than well-armed thugs but those that he had welcomed fit well with the other soldiers.

Armlu, the former gunnery Sergeant had point blank refused to leave the magazine when he saw the pulse torpedoes insisting he would work for free if only Radoq would let him stay. In response, he now proudly wore the three stripes and crossed gats of his old rank and when he wasn't chasing the four assistants he'd been given around the ship, Radoq presumed he was polishing the torpedoes. The man was obsessed.

That made fifty nine, plus Evie, her new assistant Baxl and the three Domerus. A sizeable enough ship's crew and Tricial had been given the task of finding everyone a job. Despite Evie's formidable efforts there was always work to do to maintain a ship of this complexity or the two lun'erus Sergeants would have the soldiers out on the fighting deck practicing drills or simply running endless laps.

"Crew of the *Golden Kote*. This is Radoq." All around the ship he knew the crew would be pausing, looking up at the loud hailers connected to the communicator he held. He pressed the button to talk again "All of you will be wondering where we're going. Of necessity, I've kept this a secret from you until now."

Radoq turned so he wouldn't see the expressions on his friend's faces "North of the capital Admirain, in a place called Khafon is a small facility protected by the Royal Guard."

He could imagine the first stages of unease sinking into soldier's minds at the mention of the crack troops that answered only to the Crown Prince.

"This facility uses nuklera to provide aquar for the four cities. It also holds the only nuklera weapons in existence. We are going to steal one and detonate it in the Dark Lands."

Even now, after explaining the plan in detail in Oprain's study countless times the words sounded foolish to Radoq. Dangerous, idiotic, irresponsible. Still, the next part would be the hardest for everyone.

"This may come as a shock to some of you but I assure you I have worked out this mission in the finest detail. We will enter the facility in disguise and retrieve the device. Then we will return east, detonating the device at a pre-arranged spot in the Dark Lands, well east of the Eyrie. For those of you concerned about the glow travelling into Wallanria, I ask you to remember the wind blowing us ever eastward as we fought there. The prevailing wind is always that direction and the glow will travel over and dissipate in the desert."

He paused, listening for any sign of discontent but the crew seemed silent.

"I understand that some of you may not want to be included in this mission. Well, that's tough. You signed on and you'll follow orders. If you wish to leave my company after this then fine. But until then, no soldier or airman will leave the ship without my express permission."

"As you know, I made contact in the Dark Lands with Guysil Chirrutsus Ji-Kanata, sometimes called the Dark Ji. I struck a deal with him to help us in our fight to liberate Fortisul from the criminal Juraj. He has managed to gain control over the virals, this was demonstrated when he stopped them from attacking and overrunning our ship when we sat grounded in the Dark Lands."

Radoq swallowed nervously.

"Guysil wishes to detonate the nuklera because the glow it releases gives life to the virals. In return, he will summon the virals to a spot close by to Fortisul, forcing Juraj to leave the town with the army he's amassed and there we will destroy him utterly."

Now he thought he could hear a few murmurs of discontent but he ploughed on.

"We'll reach Khafon tomorrow morning. When we get there, every man will stand-to, ready to repel boarders should we be discovered. I will enter the facility along with our engineer and a personal guard of ten lun'erus. Any volunteers are to let Sergeant Staph know."

That was a joke, he thought. At this point it would be a miracle if the crew didn't toss him out the boarding hatch.

"Until then, keep sharp, follow orders and maintain discipline. This is still a fighting ship and you are all under orders. Questions are to be directed up the chain of command. That is all."

"Wheeeew!" Evie didn't give him time to catch his breath "Anyone ever tell you a leader's job is to incentivise, not to direct?"

Radoq regarded her coldly "Sometimes a directive attitude is what's needed."

"Sir?" Rakr was at the door to the bridge with a pair of soldiers behind him. The first of the mutineers, Radoq thought with a thrill of fear as he moved to speak to them.

"What is it, Sergeant?" his tone was hostile.

Rakr blinked at the coldness "Beg your pardon, Sir but these lads say they're from Khafon. They know the facility well. Thought they could help."

A surge of surprise, quickly followed by pleasure filled Radoq as he ushered the two men in where they immediately began an earnest conversation with Sijun who seemed to have swallowed a treatise on the safe handling and storage of nuklera. Radoq made to join them but Rakr murmured to him.

"Sir? They took it well. The crew, I mean."

"Thanks, Sergeant." The relief in his voice was palpable and he turned away but Rakr caught his sleeve in a not impolite manner.

"Beg pardon, Sir but it might go some way if you chatted to the crew, let them know if this goes south they won't be held responsible?"

"Of course."

"Maybe lay it on a bit thick. Make 'em think you'll be to blame and they'll – I dunno, eviscerate you in public or something? Always find that helps morale."

"Thank you." Radoq wasn't sure if he was being mocked but Rakr was watching him with knowing eyes "I'm starting to trust you, Sir. From where I stand, there's more'n meets the eye to this plan."

When Radoq began to protest the grizzled soldier held up a hand, shaking his head.

"No need to tell me, Sir. S'above my pay grade anyhow. But just food for thought, I suppose. I'd sleep better in my cot at night knowing you weren't putting the human race in jeopardy. You know what I mean, Sir?"

"I think so, Sergeant."

"Cheers, then."

Rakr left, leaving Radoq staring after him not entirely certain what he'd just promised.

CHAPTER 21

"The Royal Guard are there sure enough but they're hardly the Tempest Legion." Nimel, the older of the two locals of Khafon was speaking. They were gathered around the navigation chart in the bridge although it was barely needed as they knew their destination. Instead, Radoq was picking the two young lun'erus' brains for every titbit.

"It's an easy posting?" Radoq guessed and Cirmad, the younger man nodded enthusiastically.

"Greybeards and the injured. The Crown Prince gives commands there as a reward sometimes. The Guard calls it the best kept secret in Wallanria. Easiest soldiering job there is."

"That's not to say it isn't secure." Nimel began sketching the shape of it on a rugged handheld "See, it's set in a bowl in the ground because of the glow but then the buildings are quite high because they need the size to fit in all the technology. The skyport is here –" he indicated on the sketch "- and that's busy. They bring a lot of supplies in and out and people come and go all the time. It's always being inspected and visited. Lots of people incoming."

"Shouldn't stand out too much then." Evie thought out loud.

"How many guards?" Radoq asked Nimel.

"Oh, five hundred? They call it a legion but it's well understrength. They have that many because they rotate around in shifts. Some are on at night, others during the day and all that."

"How many at one time?"

"Fifty? Sixty? Like I say, Domerus, the buildings are tall but the whole thing isn't huge."

"What about the aquar?" Tricial asked "How is that transported out?"

"By ship." Cirmad took over "My pa was a mate on one of them. They load the aquar up into those great big spools you sometimes see in the cities – you know the ones I mean?"

Radoq nodded, remembering the great sealed cylinders that could for safety's sake cause an entire district of a city to be shut down when they were being transported. Aquar was generally safe but was prone to bursts of energy which made people rightly wary of it.

"They chuck two of 'em in the back of the specially designed ships. They're like Aldmerin class cargo birds but modified so the aquar don't spark and blow 'em to Chox."

"And the fuel coming in? What they use to make the nuklera do they come on the same ships?"

"Oh yeah." Cirmad nodded proudly as though it were he who carried the substance "Big business that is. The mines is well west of Admirain you know. So the ships go from Khafon down to the capital then west across to the mines and back to Khafon. Three day round trip then the crews get three days off." he added unhelpfully.

"Wouldn't we be better off trying to steal some from the mines and making our own?" Tricial asked.

"Absolutely not!" Sijun sounded appalled "The glow would tear the *Golden Kote* apart before we were halfway across the forest! The stuff may not harm Domerus but it's deadly to any other human or life form for that matter! We've all seen what nuklera did to the Dark Lands." He shook his head "Even stealing a weapon in a secure state is incredibly fraught with risk. All lun'erus coming close to it will have to wear protective gear –"

"We've got that." Radoq pointed out.

"– and the compartment or hold its carried in will have to be scrubbed afterwards lest we poison unsuspecting crew members."

Radoq waited but Sijun was apparently done. He looked

around in surprise at the silence.

"So, it has to be the facility itself." Radoq rapped his knuckles on the sketch "What else can you tell us?"

"We used to joke in the tavern about how we'd rob the place." Nimel looked vaguely guilty but Radoq encouraged him, relishing in the bounty the two of them were giving him.

"How?"

"Storm the place with a legion and a fleet." Cirmad piped up earning a booming encouragement from Sijun.

"That's the best option! Pulse torpedoes to blast the doors open, drop-troops through the main entrance and slaughter everyone in sight!"

"No-one is going to slaughter anyone." Radoq declared in an icy tone "And why is everyone so obsessed with these torpedoes?"

"A pulse torpedo would level the place." Evie pointed out "And probably cause the nuklera to detonate. Can't say I want that happening whilst *Kote* is within range."

"*Golden Kote.*" Radoq corrected sharply earning a scowl from the engineer.

They kept talking and the two lun'erus provided detail that Radoq could only have dreamed of but each plan they came up with seemed more unlikely than the last. Sijun had drifted away from the conversation, apparently out of ideas beyond a violent storming of the place which Radoq would not allow.

"Who commands the Guard?" Tricial suddenly asked.

"Er – like we said, Sheriff. It's given as a reward for good service."

"No, but I mean which Domerus tritus has responsibility?"

Nimel and Cirmad exchanged a glance which was half amusement, half awkwardness.

"What?" Radoq couldn't guess the meaning.

"Thing is, the old King – current Crown Prince's father ruled that only lun'erus were to protect it. Said that –" Cirmad faltered and turned to Nimel.

"He said that Domerus are too prone to flights of romantic

adventure and couldn't be trusted after what happened in the Dark Lands."

Sijun practically had a fit at that, doubling over and thumping his great fist on the floor as tears streamed from his eyes. Cirmad and Nimel tried to restrain the mirth but they too had to turn away from Radoq who felt his cheeks burn at the irony.

"How does that help us?"

"It means storming the place would be a Chox'd sight easier!" Sijun declared, still chuckling.

"Enough –"

"Look, if there's no Domerus there, why don't you just disguise yourself, turn up and pretend you're doing an inspection of the docks?" Evie piped up.

Radoq looked at her in surprise. Usually, her ideas were worth listening to "I don't think that's how it works."

She turned a stony gaze to him "Oh? Lots of experience of dockside life have you, Domerus?"

Radoq admitted that he had not.

"When I was on the Royal Dock in Admirain, it happened all the time. 'Course, no Domerus is bothering themselves with dock techies because there's no need for 'em. We get on with our stuff and don't need them telling us what to do."

Radoq spared a moment's sympathy for those unfortunate Domerus who had been placed in charge of dock technicians in ages past.

"Every now and then, though, some passing politician or dignitary would swing by and 'inspect'." Evie loaded the word with sarcasm "Not that they ever knew what we were doing, but it made them feel good. Point is, no-one ever refused them. Wasn't any need to. They want to come and waste their time, that's their business."

A stunned silence met her words. The plan was absurdly simplistic and Radoq said so.

Evie shrugged "Simple works for me."

No-one else had any better ideas and there was fatigue on the two lun'erus' faces so Radoq thanked them and dismissed them.

Tricial began voicing half formed ideas but Radoq stopped him.

"We've still time. There's no point in forcing ourselves to innovate. That never works. As it stands, we'll attempt to gain entry by disguising me or Sijun and at least manage a reconnaissance which will give us an understanding of what we're dealing with."

"Not me." Sijun declared and Radoq remembered the faint accent that marked him as a foreigner.

"Right. Me then. In the meantime, lets take our mind off things."

Evie seemed eager to do just that, throwing herself into the helmsman's chair and resting her feet on the control panel "You know that game, Domerus, the one you're always losing?"

"Sagalm?"

"That one. Teach me?"

Tricial had his set out and ready almost as soon as she'd finished speaking. Eagerly, he talked her through the basic moves as Sijun rested his behind on a nearby console to watch.

"Do you play, Sijun?"

"Of course! But I watch much better than I participate." He smiled at Evie who was nodding to Tricial's explanation.

"Radoq? You'll play her and I'll guide her through the first few?"

Radoq took his place, making a customary opening move seeing Evie's eyes flicker across the board like a hawk. Tricial gave her a couple of pointers but after those, she asked him to stop and soon made a few daring strategic moves that cleared a third of Radoq's pieces.

"See –" Radoq moved his Ji into an attacking stance, surrendering a Su to Evie's next move "It's all about thinking several moves ahead and anticipating the different directions an attack can come from. Sometimes you set up a formidable attack only to forget your defence. Others, you miss a move from across the board and you –"

Evie moved her Ji and took Radoq's, defeating him. He stared at the board before he swore foully, taking Chox's name in vain until even Evie raised an eyebrow.

"Simplest is best, eh?" she winked as Radoq coloured.

"Again!"

Sijun howled with laughter at the sight, shaking his head in disbelief as they rearranged the pieces. Tricial kept his lips pressed together as he restrained his own mirth and indeed, Radoq beat her swiftly in the second match. Any thought that she was relying on beginner's luck was dispelled however when she beat him again, this time in only eight moves.

"Simplest, Domerus!" she grinned.

To his surprise, Radoq felt himself grinning back, enjoying the challenge. They played until the sun began to set out the bridge windows and Radoq eventually won the most games although his pride had taken a dent. They peered out the windows, seeing the walls of Napp below them as they discussed strategy and techniques.

"Simpler is better, Domerus. You lot always overcomplicate things. Same as for tomorrow! Simpler. Let me come with you, we'll do the inspection. At worst they'll just show you the dock and chase you out the door as quick as they can. No-one is going to refuse a Domerus entry. Got it?"

Radoq let her persuade him, looking out into the darkness long after Evie had retired to sleep. Sijun came up behind him, wordlessly handing him a small glass of sky spirit.

"Misgivings?" he asked.

"Plenty." Radoq sipped the spirit which was cheap and burned "What concerns me most is being recognised."

"Because of the taboo?"

Ever since the Dark Lands had been blasted by nuklera in a desperate bid to keep the virals at bay, the use of the weapons had disgusted Domerus and lun'erus alike. Though the Crown Prince kept them secure, the notion of him or indeed, any other nation deploying them in battle was unthinkable. It was an unspoken agreement that superseded treaties and agreements, keeping the awful destructive power secured.

"If my name is ever associated with this then I'll be an

outcast." Radoq murmured "The Crown Prince will make an example of me."

"Is it worth the risk?"

Radoq looked at his friend, seeing the concern in his eyes "Yes. I know it's a wild plan but it'll work." He nodded as if reassuring himself.

"And the Dark Ji?"

"What about him?"

Sijun snorted and shook his head, finishing his drink "I'm with you, Radoq. Know that."

As dawn spread over the eastern horizon behind them, they set the *Golden Kote* down in an empty valley north of the road that ran between Chrohold and Admirain. There the entire crew worked to disguise the ship. The name at the stern was covered over and a new ship *Spirit of Chox* was born, a nod to the Royal tradition of naming their ships with religious themes.

A red and gold banner was fashioned from cloth Oprain had procured for them and draped across the hull in a diagonal line down the middle where it flapped in a faint breeze until Staph, at Nimel's direction began ordering troops to gather up armfuls of a thin brush that grew on the slopes of the hill and crushing it.

"See?" Nimel crunched his fist around some, spitting into it and demonstrating the adhesive effect it had "Foalweed. Use it all the time to stick stuff."

"Good thinking."

Foalweed smeared the sides of the ship leaving Radoq and Evie wincing at the thought of clearing it off but the banner looked vaguely Royal. No-one amongst the crew could think of the last time they'd seen a ship flying the Royal colours and Radoq banked on this being common to all lun'erus, especially those at an outpost like Khafon.

"She looks alright." Tricial nodded in appreciation at their handiwork which was not insignificant. As much as a battle ship could be disguised, the *Golden Kote* was unrecognisable. Of course, anyone who knew anything about flying would spot her as a Hyperion class but then there were plenty of those in the

Royal Fleet.

Or so Radoq hoped.

His own disguise was grander. Tricial was the last to visit the Royal Court before taking his position as Sheriff and he led the design, changing Radoq's shabby tunic for a long robe in red and gold.

"You'll have to hide that." He indicated the blood oath at which Radoq ground his teeth but there was nothing for it and he dropped a sleeve over it.

"I need a good name." he told Sijun and Tricial and the two of them read out various tritus, questioning him on their ancestry but Radoq found his memory lacking and realised that any of their suggestions would fall to the most basic scrutiny.

"Who was the girl you defeated to win the kote?" Tricial suddenly piped up "From a respectable tritus if I remember."

"Wallsan. Can't remember her first name. She was a Su-Wallsan. A very old tritus. From the west country."

"Good. What about a first name?"

"Gellian?" Radoq suggested his brother's name but Tricial shook his head.

"Too obvious."

"How about Evie?"

Radoq shot her a withering look but Tricial was nodding "Evieus. That could work."

"That's a girl's name!"

Tricial shrugged "It's both. It's a fine name."

"Evieus Guysilsus?"

"Not bad. Evieus Guysilsus Wallsan. Something of a mouthful." Tricial made a face.

"Aren't they all?"

The disguise complete, Evie searched the ship for a smart uniform to match the station of a Chief Engineer which, she reminded Radoq, was her correct title that her salary should match.

Even she stopped her usual patter as the facility came into sight and Radoq slowed the engines to a gentle approach. Tricial handled the communicator spinning a yarn to the ground controller who sounded uninterested, giving them a landing lane and dock assignment. Radoq made sure to turn the ship and show the Royal sigil on the flanks and sure enough, as they landed a small delegation of uniformed lun'erus were hurrying to meet them.

"You go out first." Radoq told Evie and she picked a half dozen of the youngest crew to form a small guard before marching down the gangway with her chest thrown out importantly.

"Thank Chox for her." He muttered, watching her on the screen as she immediately began to browbeat the officers who quailed before her. One, dressed himself in an engineers uniform turned pale as Evie pointed out some minor detail on the dock besides them. Radoq hoped she'd tone it down a bit but as she stepped aside to wait for him expectantly at the bottom of the gangway the lead member of the group, a sweaty lun'erus who introduced himself as Commander Gaiul ushered him onto the dock, practically gushing in his attempt to impress Radoq. From what he could discern, it was not the presence of the dignitary that he assumed Radoq to be but the fact that such a figure had dared to attend with an engineer! Nervousness filled Gaiul's voice and although he directed his words to Radoq, his attention was on Evie pacing slowly behind them, her eyes flickering over every surface.

"Hmph!" she stopped by a docking clamp which even Radoq could see was in poor repair "Has this dock been de-laned, Commander?"

Gaiul turned helplessly to the engineer who'd accompanied him, an enormously fat woman with pasty skin. She hurried forward with a sickly smile and attempted to shake Evie's hand introducing herself as Yannon but Evie managed to turn smartly aside to rap her knuckles on the clamp.

"De-laned? Or do you not follow sky-code procedures here?"

Yannon stammered but it was clear there was a lapse in protocol and Evie took out a handheld, pretending to make a detailed note on it.

"If – this way, Domerus." a chastened Gaiul tried to regain the initiative by leading them out of the main dock and further into the skyport. Radoq gazed up above them at what he now saw was an enormously tall building, easily protruding above the natural dip in the land that the facility sat in. At multiple levels docks were stacked, many with airships moored to them. Radoq felt his heart rate increase as he saw a cruiser bearing the Royal sigil far above them.

They moved around the dock area, Gaiul trying to lead them but really following Evie who cast a critical eye over everything, finding half a dozen faults all of which Radoq could tell from the expression on Yannon's face were serious slip ups.

"Perhaps after we're done this could be discussed at length somewhere more private?" he suggested in a soothing tone of voice.

Gaiul latched onto the faint sign of friendliness like a drowning man clutching at a straw "Yes, my office is just off the dock..." he led them away at a rapid pace, forcing Evie to follow. Radoq shot her a warning look.

Steady!

She seemed to get the message and allowed them to be led up a flight of metal and stone steps where bare walls echoed their footsteps back at them. Gaiul's office was sparsely furnished although Radoq noted a pair of chairs suited to the bulk of a Domerus.

"Ah – you sit here, Domerus. Madam? Over here. A drink? I've a fine sky spirit but –" his face fell as Evie started "That would be against sky-code."

"Indeed." Evie took a seat, crossing her legs with her gaze never leaving Gaiul's face. Yannon had scarpered, closing the office door behind them as she headed in a different direction.

"Would –" Radoq began in a conciliatory tone, meaning to make an excuse for Evie to leave the office and find a way into the rest of the facility whilst he distracted Gaiul but the door crashed inwards revealing the reason Gaiul had two Domerus sized chairs in his office and the explanation for the cruiser bearing the Royal Sigil.

Staring in surprise at Radoq were two men, both Domerus, both dressed in the red and gold tunics of the Royal Guard.

CHAPTER 22

Domerus, Royal Guards, staring first with shock and then with increasing suspicion at Radoq and his bad disguise.

Gaiul, clearly unaware of the tension passing between the Domerus tried to make introductions "Domerus, this is Evieus Guysilsus Wallsan here to inspect the docks."

Badly dressed or not, Radoq was still a Domerus and courtesy forced the two Royal Guard's into a formal introduction.

"I have the honour to be Vallance." The elder of the two, a hard faced woman whose bare arms were thick with muscle. Radoq knew when Domerus joined the Royal Guard they shed their tritus names, keeping only their given name as a mark of their service to the monarch.

"I am Wipjan." The second Domerus was male, shorter than his companion and younger. His eyes locked on Radoq unblinking.

Radoq bowed formally "Evieus Guysilsus Wallsan. And as you can see, I am not a member of your order." He smiled as though his deception was merely mischievous, not sinister.

"Come, out with who you really are." Vallance's voice cracked like a whip. Gaiul had finally realised something was afoot and was leaning back in his chair as far away from the three Domerus as he could get.

Radoq racked his brain feverishly and Evie's harsh words returned to his mind, floating on a providential fluke of memory as he bowed, acknowledging the deception "Forgive my theatrics. I meant only to use this – ah – childish garb to gain access to the skyport for my colleague here." He indicated Evie who leapt to her feet, her face and manner as confident and harsh as they had been on the dock.

Vallance spared Evie a single glance, taking in her Chief Engineer uniform and confident gaze and a frown came over her.

"Vallance..." Wipjan had worked it out. A frown of concern rested on his face and he placed a hand on his companion's shoulder.

"You're from the sky-code." She finally got it.

"Air Marshallry." Evie corrected in a voice like iron "We provide the sky-code in order to keep lun'erus and Domerus alike safe."

Vallance blanched visibly, realising she had made a bad error but her reaction was nothing to Gaiul who having already been shaken now looked on the edge of a dead faint and a small squeak left his throat as he registered an authority that trumped even the Royal Guard.

Radoq's mind whirled with elaborations to the tale but he forced himself to say nothing, allowing the two Guards' imaginations to do the work for him. The Air Marshallry was an authority that transcended even the dominance of the Crown Prince. They set and enforced safety protocols and procedures across all air routes in the doctrine known as the sky-code. Radoq had never come into contact with their agents but he knew from horror stories other aviators shared that they were a bureaucratic machine, filled with faceless, unsympathetic automatons whose sole purpose was to enforce the sky-code. Radoq had never heard of them disguising themselves to gain entry to a facility but then, this was an extremely *secure* facility.

Vallance and Wipjan seemed to have mirrored Radoq's thoughts. They looked from the sheepish Radoq to the icy Evie and seemed to make a decision.

"Is there anything that we can do to assist in your inspection?" Vallance's tone changed to courteous.

Radoq's head swam with their change in fortune. He smiled warmly but as he made to speak, Evie cut across him "Domerus? I should get going. A lot to cover."

"Of course. Gaiul? You don't mind my associate continuing, do you? We can remain here. We've a great deal to discuss."

Gaiul almost hit the floor with relief as Evie strode out the door peering at the screen of her handheld. Radoq wondered what the two Royal Guards would do if they realised the device did nothing more than display the exhaust temperature on engine two.

"I have to say, I disapprove of your methods." Vallance softened the complaint with a smile "Very effective though. Perhaps Gaiul here should look to his security?"

"Oh, I don't think there's anything to worry about." Radoq returned the smile, gesturing for Vallance to sit. He took the other Domerus seat leaving Wipjan standing "Any ship could access the dock in an emergency. The rest of the facility is secured, I'm sure?" he phrased it as a question, to the red faced Gaiul.

"Yes! Of course. We have strict protocols." To Radoq's delight, the nervous lun'erus began to laboriously explain the exact protocols although he retained the presence of mind not to reveal access codes. A series of interlocking doors, each controlled by a secure handheld granted access to the weapons facility. Every lun'erus in the building was issued one and carried them at all times. He demonstrated his own device, Radoq eyeing it hungrily but there was no chance of him taking it. As the lun'erus went on, his heart began to sink. How foolish he'd been to think he could waltz in here and steal a nuklera of all things! The place was likely the most secure in the kingdom. His only hope now rested with Evie and he willed her to find a weakness.

"Perhaps a tour of the facility?" either Wipjan was bored or endeavouring to flatter Radoq with the suggestion. Gaiul stammered about protocols but Vallance reminded him Radoq was in the presence of the Royal Guard and the facility was as safe as any. Bowing to pressure, Gaiul saw them out of his office with obvious relief.

Too prone to flights of romantic adventure, indeed!

Radoq kept up a constant chatter as the Domerus unwittingly led him past the security measures, casually using her handheld to breach the complex security.

"I understood the facility was staffed solely by lun'erus?" he asked.

"Of course. We aren't a permanent feature of the place although no doubt it's improved by our presence." Vallance shot Radoq a knowing glance and he caught a strong sense of the kind of snobbery rife in the Capital.

"Oh? Then what brings you here?"

"Duty." Wipjan spoke from behind Radoq "We periodically check the facility is secure. Make sure the lun'erus aren't getting above their station. You understand what's stored here, of course."

"Yes." Radoq nodded as though having a profound thought "It's reassuring that you do visit."

"Regularly." Vallance confirmed "The posting here is considered an easy one for our lun'erus in the Guard. It's our responsibility as Domerus to keep them on their toes."

"Indeed!"

"Domerus?" Evie called out and Radoq turned to see her hurrying through the closing door.

"Ah, you don't mind if my associate joins us, do you?"

Eager to please, the Royal Guards said they did not although he caught the flicker of distaste and they ceased to chatter as much in her presence. Vallance led them down a straight corridor, marked with a thick red line on the floor. The walls were bare stone, lacking any style or design. Indeed, the whole facility was utilitarian to a fault, feeling unwelcoming. Radoq commented on it to Vallance who snorted.

"Why waste good taste on those who have none?" she flicked a glance at Evie who was peering intently at the empty screen of her handheld and deigning not to hear the insult.

They turned right, heading, judging by Radoq's internal compass to the extreme east of the building. He tried to think of the sketch drawn by Nimel, matching it to the view from the bridge as they'd flown in and reasoned that they must be at one of the great domes housing the actual machine that produced the nuklera. As they stepped through a door, a lun'erus guard sprang to attention although Radoq noticed he surveyed the strangers intently, lacking any sign of restlessness or slackness. This was a Guard who took his position seriously.

"You'll have to wear a suit in the next chamber." was his only comment, aimed at Evie who looked up in surprise, seeing a warning painted above a thick iron door set into the bare stone. Evie scrambled into a protective suit as Vallance unsealed the entrance, leading them into a narrow corridor that snaked to the right. Radoq thought that this part of the building curved around the side of the tall section that housed the skyport. At the very least they were surely now at the outer edge of the building and Evie nudged him, pointing at an exit set into the outer wall with a heavy seal.

"The glow in here is very dangerous to your kind." Vallance didn't bother to hide the condescension in her tone as she spoke to Evie "These escape routes are for you to leave in the event of a disaster."

Evie chose not to respond and at the end of the narrow corridor, Vallance stopped before a thick glass window which overlooked a vast room.

"Nuklera." She seemed to reflect the vivid glow that emanated from the room. Radoq moved to stand beside her, staring in at the chamber which housed three vast black tanks from which thick pipes ran into the ground.

"Quite impressive." Radoq commented but his eyes raced around the chamber, coming to rest on a small series of metal chests that were stacked against one wall.

Aside from the nefarious looking tanks and chests, the chamber was empty and Radoq mentioned it.

"Of course. Lun'erus can't stay in there more than a few minutes. It's incredibly dangerous." Even as Vallance spoke, a deafening hiss swept through the room and the image behind the glass vanished in a great mountain of steam as the top of one of the tanks opened.

"You'd better step away from the glass." Wipjan warned Evie and the slight lun'erus backed up, moving around the corner of the corridor and out of sight.

"Impressive, no?" Vallance was looking at Radoq and he filled the silence with a patter of inane compliments which Vallance seemed to take in her stride as she led them back through the secure doors, pausing only for Evie to clamber out of her suit, her own clothes now crumpled.

Radoq could not help but be dismayed. Although he'd reached close enough to the nuklera themselves to see them, he was as far from getting to them as he had been in the Eyrie. Disconsolate, he barely shrugged as Vallance with forced manners asked Evie if she was complete in her inspection, perhaps understanding that if they really were from the Air Marshallry, Radoq was simply there to open doors for Evie, the real inspector. He shook his head at the hypocrisy of the Royal Guard, unable to see her logic in holding such opinions on lun'erus when she fully understood such an arrangement.

They boarded the *Golden Kote* slowly as Radoq called polite goodbyes to the Domerus. Gaiul had hidden himself in his office and did not see them off. Radoq could hardly blame the man. Instead, he nodded to the crew as the boarding hatch sealed behind him and strode to the bridge where Sijun and Tricial waited with tension in every line of their faces.

"Well?"

"Disaster." Radoq pulled the makeshift tunic over his head, tossing it into the corner "I was actually close enough to see the Chox'd things." He held out a clenched fist as though seizing the nuklera "Ran into two Domerus of the Royal Guard. Evie saved the day as always. Maybe you should be an actor if this doesn't work out?"

"Maybe you Domerus should shut your holes and listen to the little lun'erus?" anger flashed in her eyes.

"Steady now." Tricial murmured and Evie shot him a look but cooled her temper "Can't see why you think it's a disaster. Think we saw our way in clear as day."

"What? What did you see?" Radoq rounded on her, his mind filling with images of stolen security handhelds or overseen code entries.

She shot him a quizzical look "Same as you did, Domerus. I saw a door."

He frowned "The emergency door? Sealed tighter than a tomb. From the *inside.*"

She smiled in a condescending manner, really putting some energy into it "Oh, you small minded Domerus. Where would you be without me?"

As it transpired, the emergency doors were sealed by an aquar lock. This was different to the security doors, Evie explained because they had a six point, metallurgically transitioning device to secure them "And you won't get through one of those without your Chox'd torpedoes!"

Radoq rolled his eyes at yet another mention of the torpedoes.

"But those doors aren't designed by Domerus. They're built by and for lun'erus and no Crown Prince is ever going to consider them as important as his sec-ur-ity." She drew out the word sarcastically.

"Well? How do we open it from the outside?" Sijun demanded.

"We hack it." Evie held up the handheld she'd carried inside. After a moment she looked at it "Although not with this one. I've got a proper one down in the engine room."

"It's as simple as that?" Radoq didn't believe her.

She rounded on him, a fire behind her eyes that he'd never seen before "It's like the game, Domerus." she shrugged "Simplest is always best."

They made a plan. Radoq fired up the engines, warned the crew to stay alert and as Tricial signalled the port master for permission to leave, Evie called up from the engine room that she was ready.

"Lane danfo via alpha." Tricial called and Radoq echoed the command back, flying slowly out past the markers.

"Tell Evie we're clear!" he called and Tricial sent the message.

A second later, a crash shook the ship from end to end and Radoq felt the controls lurch sickeningly.

"Port master is asking for an update." Tricial managed to sound smooth and calm even under the circumstances.

"Must have been watching us." Radoq spun the controls, sending the *Golden Kote* into a lurching skid through the air, turning her nose firmly towards the left and the extreme edge of the wide dome that housed the nuklera.

"He's asking if we need a tug."

"Give it here!" Evie appeared in the bridge, breathless as she'd run from the engine room. She snatched up the communicator "Listen here! We're having a technical malfunction in our engines, probably caused by your code-breaching lane system!" when the port master began to argue she shouted him down "You give your pal Gaiul a call right now and ask him if we need help. Go on!"

There was a pause as Radoq gently nosed the stern buffer against the building, applying the necessary reverse thrust and sending the ship spinning around its own length towards the outer edge of the eastern dome as if they'd lost all control. As they turned, he saw the wide, black trail of smoke they were spewing behind them and flinched at the damage Evie had done.

The port master came back a moment later, his voice now shaking and his tone full of faux warmth. Evidently, Gaiul had frightened him.

"There!" Radoq stabbed a finger forward and Evie hissed as the faint square shape on the outside of the building appeared "Tell Sijun to be ready!"

"He's ready!" she argued but Tricial hailed the giant Domerus over the communicator anyway.

"Here we go..." Radoq felt the controls lightly in his hands and judged the moment as the ship completed its final skidding swing and the stern impacted gently with the wall of the dome "Now!" he shut the power off, leaving the engines idling.

"Alright, lets do it!" Evie clenched her fists, staring out the bridge window.

Smoke filled the space between the ship and the dome but Radoq adjusted his aurae, seeing Sijun's bulk crouched beside the door.

"Come on..." he hissed, seeing his friend working feverishly with the handheld Evie had given him.

"Engage the aquar current, release the clamps and bypass the manual release." Evie was muttering under her breath, every muscle tense.

Radoq saw the ship drifting closer and fired the engines for a brief burst, sending a fresh cloud of smoke over Sijun.

"I can't see!" Evie complained.

"Good. Neither can they."

"Port master is sending a tug." Tricial announced.

"No!" Evie rounded on him "Tell him..." She thought frantically.

"Tell him we're anchoring here as per sky-code procedures." Radoq instructed "That should shut him up."

It worked. The tug did not materialise and every eye turned to Sijun his massive form standing out against the white stone of the dome.

"How long does it take?" Evie raged but Radoq could see Sijun was stuck. The big man was becoming frustrated, repeatedly entering the same protocol into the handheld.

"It's not working." Radoq told Evie.

"It has to work!"

Tricial pressed a switch on the communicator console and a supercilious voice replaced that of the port master.

"This is the Royal Guard." Vallance's tones were clipped "We're sending a support vessel to recover you. Standby for assistance."

"Chox!" Radoq swore "Tell him to abandon and get back!"

Tricial shouted to Sijun over the communicator but the big man merely turned to the bridge, frustration visible in every line of his body. The hack, for all Evie's planning and reassurances, had failed.

"We need to leave." Radoq's heart began to race. If the Royal Guard boarded the ship, they'd see that this was not an Air

Marshallry vessel. They'd find out his true identity and then he, Radoq, would be known from the Western Hills to Admirain as the Domerus who broke the taboo.

"What's he doing now?" Evie hissed "Get him back in the ship!"

Radoq turned to see Sijun had dropped the handheld, apparently abandoning it. He stepped back from the door, raising his left hand.

"Chox!" swore Evie.

Sijun's biom glowed with a green burst of plasma, so similar to the glowing rocks in the Dark Lands. His entire body jerked back as the berrett within his left hand fired.

"What's he thinking?" Evie cursed "That won't work, the rock is too –"

The door swung open.

Evie was silent. Radoq could feel every fibre of his being straining to see Sijun who had vanished through the door in a blur.

"The tug." Tricial pointed out the port side windows and Radoq turned, feeling his stomach drop. A squat little craft was just clearing the sky port and making its slow way towards them. Radoq snatched up the communicator.

"Vallance? Evieus here. We're grateful for your assistance but there's really no need. It's rather embarrassing really..." he tailed off, hoping the other Domerus would allow courtesy to take hold.

But apparently the security of remote communication overcame the Guard's inhibitions as she merely repeated that the tug was on its way.

"There!" Evie shrieked the word in her excitement and Radoq turned to see Sijun, clutching one of the great iron chests in his hands. He leapt through the door, dropping the chest with a thump which made Radoq's heart come into his mouth but the big man only paused long enough to slam the door shut, ignoring the gaping hole in the locking mechanism. Then, he sprinted for the boarding hatch and a moment later, his voice crackled over the communicator.

"Port master, this is *Spirit of Chox*. Thank you for your hospitality, we'll be re-joining our lane."

With a whoop of elation, Radoq punched the throttle, surging *Golden Kote* forward and up into a clear, unbroken blue sky.

CHAPTER 23

"It's so small. Is that it?" Sijun held the device, no bigger than a baby's head in his enormous palm.

"Isn't it enough?" Evie's voice was muffled from behind the thick protective suit she wore.

"So much power in such a small object..." Sijun's spoke with awe.

"Our ancestors refined this technology to an art." Tricial was as enraptured as Sijun "They made devices powerful enough to destroy the entire world."

"Ugh." Evie did not share their reverence. Despite the protection of the suit, she would not stand anywhere in the small containment area other than with her back pressed firmly against the wall. Still, Radoq thought, no-one had forced her to come into the room.

"What happened with the hack?" he asked Sijun who was flushed with the success of his adventure.

"I – " he looked apologetically at Evie "I couldn't do it."

She nodded in understanding "Not your fault. It was your first time."

Sijun shot her a grin of thanks and she shrugged, the folds of the suit massively magnifying the movement. "Your way worked better, anyway."

"I saw the lock mechanism was exposed and thought I may as well try."

They left the containment room as Evie hovered in the decontamination chamber, running the cycle of the chemical wash no fewer than six times.

"You know that wash probably shortened your life more than being near the Glow?" Radoq jibed as the others headed for the bridge.

Evie shot him a look as deadly as any nuklera "You leave us mere mortals to ourselves."

"I'm just saying there's a sharp knife in the galley, maybe you should take a layer of skin off?"

Evie put her hands on her hips and faced him "You know, Domerus, next time you're in the sights of a phasr and I'm holding it –" she stopped, rolling her eyes in exasperation "Why d'you always make that face when I say 'phasr'?"

Radoq chuckled, looking away for a second "Sorry. I'm being pedantic really."

"Go on!"

"You know 'phasr' is the name of the maker, it's not an actual type of weapon?"

"Oh? And what's the actual type?"

"Long gat."

Evie nodded sarcastically "Right. And so why do we use the word phasr?"

Radoq scowled "I'm just saying it's not the correct terminology."

"I'm just saying" Evie mocked in a childish tone of voice.

"You're impossible."

"And you spent too long in Domerus school, learning about... Oh I don't know, how to be better than lowly lun'erus."

Radoq turned sharply, remembering the earlier bitterness in her voice. He realised there was more to this than her customary bad temper and concern softened his features although he felt himself grow wary of a looming disagreement "Doesn't what happened back there prove that there is no better or worse when it comes to the divide between us?"

"Divide." Evie spat "It should have a capital on it. Like 'Divide'." She sketched marks in the air with her fingers "It's its own 'thing' like a subject or an object with rules and feelings."

Radoq narrowed his eyes "Is this because of the Royal Guards?

They were Chox'd snobs. That's typical of-"

"Of Domerus in the capital, I know." Evie interrupted "Remember I've lived there? It's the most Chox'd disgusting way to live."

Radoq made a despairing gesture "But I'm not like that, nor is Tricial and nor is Sijun."

"That's not true!" Evie turned and shouted, taking Radoq by surprise "I heard you talking out in the Dark Lands! You left your communicator on –"

"Chox!" Radoq swore, half with guilt and half with anger "That was a private conversation, Evie! Between –"

"Between Domerus?" her own anger was fiery now "So I shouldn't have listened with my lowly lun'erus ears? Am I not worthy to hear two great immortal titans converse? Well, you Chox'd fool! Turn your communicator off! Otherwise some pathetic little nothing like me might be listening!"

"I didn't –"

"Yes you did! You were going to say Domerus! Don't lie!"

"I do not lie!" Radoq thundered, losing his temper "I *was* going to say it was a conversation between Domerus, what I meant was that – like –" he searched for the words to convey his meaning "- like a conversation between men. Between friends. It was a private discussion, within the boundaries of which Sijun was free to speak his mind and I mine, trusting that the conversation would go no further!"

"Oh? So you could be sure that we'd never find out great secrets like, oh, lun'erus have no honour?" Evie's eyes were shining with fury.

"That's not what I said." Radoq lowered his tone "I said lun'erus are not bound by honour and integrity in the same way Sijun and I are. We swear oaths that can end our lives as easily as a – *phasr* bolt. That was the point I was making." The anger proved it hadn't left him because he narrowed his eyes "I think you know that."

"Hah!" Evie turned away in frustration, slapping her open palm against the smooth bulkhead outside the containment room. There was a moment of silence as she faced away from him. Radoq tried to breathe, to marshal his temper but he felt the justness of his argument.

"And what about your duty, Radoq?" Radoq thought that was the first time she'd used his given name "What about your *responsibility* to protect us? To rule us?"

He sighed "We don't rule you."

"Who is in command of this ship?"

He pressed his lips together in a hard line.

"Exactly. And the chances of me ever being captain?"

"If I die –"

"If you die! And the same applies to our whole society! Not just Wallanria but the whole world! If Domerus died, lun'erus would rule!"

"Chox, Evie! Is that it then? You show your true colours! You want me and all my kind dead? I thought we were friends!"

"I work for you in your engine room!" she bellowed "I'm no better than a slave!"

Radoq stared at her, appalled. Tears were now spilling down her cheeks but she made no move to conceal them. He sat down heavily on the floor, knees bent before him "Is that how you really feel?"

"Is that not the truth of the matter?"

"No." he shook his head but there was little conviction in his voice "I don't see you as a slave. If you want to leave, I'll fly you to any of the four cities. To Admirain if you like. Or Xeonison –"

"Where I can live as a slave? What's the highest I can rise, Radoq? Supreme Engineer, fixing the racing yachts of the elite Domerus?"

Radoq snorted in derision "You could own your own racing yacht if you wanted."

"But I can't fly it half as well as you could! I don't have the reactions, no aurae to help me. I'll always be second class!"

"Physically, maybe. But you're short. And a woman. You'll always be weaker physically. And that has nothing to do with Domerus or lun'erus. Look at Staph! He's lun'erus and he's huge!"

"That's not the point!" Evie shouted "If I was born a Domerus I'd be bigger, faster and stronger than him! Like you! You never did anything to earn your strength or speed or agility! You were given it by technology!"

"If that's true then how did I best Sijun? Why isn't Oprain as fast and strong as me?"

"He's old!"

"And Sijun?"

Evie snarled but Radoq thought he had her.

"You stand there furious at the rough hand you perceive that life has dealt you but you know nothing of being Domerus!"

"I see enough!"

"Is that it then, Evie? You want to be ascended? You want to be _"

"I want to be the person you see standing before you! I just want it to come with some justice!"

Silence fell between them. Radoq found himself regretting his anger. Evie looked calmer for a moment. The corridor they stood in remained pointedly empty, the crew giving them a wide berth.

"I don't want to be a Domerus." Evie spoke in a calmer voice although still laden with emotion "I just want us to be more equal."

Frustration drove the anger back to the surface and Radoq found himself standing without remembering doing so "More equal *how*? You say we rule you but I say we don't! You say you could never captain this ship but you saw Correlius leading his crew, not Sijun! And you sit there preaching about the injustice of our divide having never tried to see it from our perspective!"

"And you have from ours?"

"No!" Radoq shouted "But I don't pretend to understand what being a lun'erus is!"

"But it's fine for you, you'd never trade your life for ours!"

Radoq stared at her "I'd give it up in a heartbeat."

Evie looked incredulous, then disbelieving "You – the paragon of honour and integrity would abandon everything you –"

"No. No, no, no." Radoq shook his head "I mean in principle. If I could be born again a lun'erus I would. I don't mean now. If that was how I felt now I'd give up my power and live Fallen the rest of my days. No, I mean I'd live my life free as a lun'erus."

"Free?"

"You know what lun'erus means, don't you?"

Evie rolled her eyes "You mean Luntefiderius? 'The free ones'? Please. Don't make me pull a cringe muscle!"

Radoq held out a hand to illustrate the point "But you are free."

"Free to be slaves!"

"Fine. Free to be slaves. Maybe you're right." Radoq shrugged as though ignoring the point "But you aren't bound by duty or by custom or by honour. That's what I meant in the Dark Lands." As Evie made to interrupt, he held up a hand "Let me say this. My life – our lives are lives of service. From the moment we're born we're coached in service."

"To your tritus?"

"No." he spoke more sharply than he intended "No. Not to our tritus – or, it *is* to our tritus but the tritus only exists in the service of lun'erus."

"But you don't *serve* us."

Radoq could see her point. With perfect clarity he understood her frustration and he wondered why he had never thought of it like this before. It was obvious that she'd feel this way, growing up in the four cities, working in the snobbish luxury of Admirain and then falling prey to the slavers…

"Had you ever left Wallanria before you met the slavers?"

She blinked in surprise "No."

"Never seen the Dark Lands?"

"Yeah! Flown by them plenty of times. Been to the Eyrie before, too." Her eyes narrowed "What's your point?"

"My point is you – and maybe this is true of most disaffected lun'erus – only see the two strata. You only see the divide between Domerus and lun'erus. Even Juraj can only see that, that's probably why he's so bent on becoming one of us."

"There are only two!"

"No! There are three! There are the virals!"

She narrowed her eyes in disgust "That's rubbish! That's lies made up to justify your existence!"

A moment ago, Radoq would have exploded with anger but now he understood and he looked at her with pity "You've never seen a real mass of them, have you?"

"I was with you when *Kote* went down, wasn't I?"

He shook his head "I'm talking thousands. Millions of virals, even. Swarming towards the Western Hills and the River Tymere." His eyes softened "There used to be a small farming village in the hills. The lun'erus had a name for it but my brother and I always just called it 'Viral Town'. Constantly being attacked but the ground there was excellent, a little valley between two of the higher peaks and they grew crops like a factory produces machines. They made so much gold they could afford a pinzgat and after that they didn't need the Domerus so much. You'd have liked living there by the sounds of it. Still, one pinzgat was like throwing stones at the ocean when they swept out of the Dark Lands. We got word from the Eyrie and my whole tritus, along with every other Domerus in the four cities headed to the hills. We met some stragglers on the way and got bogged down in fighting and by the time we got to Viral Town the virals were just in range of their pinzgat."

He paused, the memory still a dark stain in his mind.

"They overran the settlement just as the Domerus got there. We engaged straight away and the Eyrie had sent a fleet so they were strafing them from the air. My brother and I thought it was the greatest sport we'd ever found. I remember laughing as we tore down the slopes and smashed into them but my father was furious. He brought us back into formation and made us stay there as the other Domerus formed up around us. I thought it was stupid – probably like you, Evie, I thought we were immortal!" Radoq shook his head.

"That was the first time I saw a Domerus die outside of a duel. It was a Po from one of the Aldrahan tritus. He knew his business, he'd served with the Royal Guard for a century or more before returning home but he stepped out of his formation for a moment and the virals got hold of him. Everyone tried to get to him but the Ji – this Domerus' own father called them back into formation. He abandoned the Po. I thought that was madness but my own Ji stopped me doing anything and we saw the virals kill him."

"They tore him apart?" all mockery was gone from Evie's voice.

"They played with him." Radoq's face was frozen in a snarl of disgust "They kept him alive whilst they tore him to bits. Fingers, then his hand and then they eviscerated him. One of the problems with our biom –" he held up his left hand "- is that it's very good at keeping us alive so it prolonged his death. And he screamed for a very long time."

Radoq shrugged.

"Anyway, the point is that we were overwhelmed. The tritus' held their positions and killed anything that came towards us but there were thousands now getting past us and the ships above couldn't cover them. One of them was dispatched west to warn the capital but the virals outran it. They got to Viral Town and my father saw. The Western Hills are our lands so he risked all our lives by breaking formation. We all ran back, jumping over their heads. Two more of our tritus – my cousins – were killed on the way back and it was all for nothing. See, the virals can tell the difference between you and me, Evie. With Domerus they know to swarm us, try to overwhelm us with numbers and move on when we're dead but with lun'erus, they outmatch you in size and strength and ferocity so they go for you one on one."

Evie looked faintly sick.

"They chucked the lun'erus around like child's dolls. There was blood on every blade of grass in that valley. We were too late to do anything and so we moved on, kept getting ahead of the virals until we got to the River Tymere which is when the Royal Guard got there and we wiped them out." Radoq shrugged as though the lameness of his words didn't conceal the death, pain and slaughter that had occurred.

"How many Domerus died?"

"Thirty eight in total. The most killed in one setting since the fall of Ychacha."

"And the lun'erus in Viral Town?"

"Twenty four. Five families. All their animals, too. We thought there were a hundred thousand virals in the swarm but a lot fled into the Dark Lands."

Evie tried to speak but paused to clear her throat instead.

"The point isn't about the battle, Evie. The point is that the virals would have swept over the river, through the forest and then straight into the four cities. That would have been it. No more Wallanria."

Evie said nothing.

"I'm not in charge because I want to rule over you, Evie, I'm in charge because that's what I was born to do so that we – our *species* could survive. When it comes to survival at any costs, I don't care about principles and freedom. I care about one thing. And that's what I was born to do."

Evie was still silent. Radoq wanted her to speak but he'd had enough of arguing with her. He sensed that she was trying to avoid a feeling of defeat and he had no desire to claim a victory in the disagreement so he stood and made to head away down the corridor.

"Domerus –" she stopped him.

"Yes?"

"You don't make me feel like a slave."

Radoq nodded.

"I don't feel free though, either."

He sighed "Well, what is it that you want? To feel freer?"

She blinked "I'll have to let you know."

"Alright. When you've figured it out, I'll help you find it. If that's what you want."

She nodded stiffly in acknowledgement, but not in acceptance. Something about her expression stirred a faint, final ember of anger in Radoq and as she turned away it was his turn to call her back.

"Evie? Don't ever eavesdrop on my private conversations again."

CHAPTER 24

A cordial peace formed between Evie and Radoq as they flew with the wind towards the sanctuary of the Eyrie but they didn't slip back into their usual banter. The rest of the crew noticed and to Radoq's relief, no-one brought it up. He sensed Evie had a great deal more to say and knew that sometime in the future they would have to fly at each other again but for now, he tried to focus on the task at hand.

"How will we know when they find out it's gone?" Tricial wondered.

"The lun'erus council will know already." Sijun supplied as though it were obvious.

"How?"

"The nuklera storage is checked twice per day by the Royal Guard so the hole I blasted in the wall will have already been discovered. The question is whether they'll work out how or by whom."

Tricial stared at the younger man "If you know so much then why didn't you say so before we went in?"

Sijun looked surprised "Nimel told us! Weren't you listening?"

"Apparently I lack your ability to retain such detail."

"Ah. Superior breeding, you know."

Tricial threw a cup at the big man's head, just missing Radoq.

"Thank you, Sheriff."

Tricial bowed "Trying to teach this young ruffian a lesson."

"You make a good point though." Radoq nodded seeing Sijun's eyes widen in indignation "About the Guard! How will we know when they're on our tail?"

"Assuming they know it was us."

Radoq nodded "Assuming they do. What's the quickest course of action?"

"They could follow us."

Radoq glanced at the control console "Not at this speed. With our head start and this wind there isn't a craft flying that could cut us off."

"I suppose once we're seen crossing the Hills, they'll think we're headed to the Eyrie?"

"That's right." Radoq nodded at Sijun "We're already past Chrohold and Napp. The only thing that will slow us down is heading south to avoid ships from Fortisul."

"We've the torpedoes now if that happens." Sijun reminded him.

"Right." Radoq nodded "But let's avoid that if we can."

Evie entered the bridge and sprawled in the engineer's chair "All systems normal." she reported brusquely.

"Thank you. We were just discussing how to avoid being caught by the Royal Guard."

Evie raised an eyebrow "Getting rid of that little bundle of death seems the smartest option. Isn't that the plan now?"

"We aren't going to the Eyrie?" Sijun asked in surprise.

"No." Radoq said almost apologetically "We're heading out into the Dark Lands. It's time to end this."

Sijun sat forward "You mean to strike your deal? We'll deliver the nuklera and then straight to Fortisul?"

"I think it will take Guysil some time to mass the virals, but yes." Radoq nodded firmly "This is it!"

The silence that followed his words belied the overpowering lack of enthusiasm in the bridge. Evie raised an eyebrow whilst Tricial fidgeted awkwardly with his biom.

"Sheriff?" Radoq turned to the elder man who met his gaze wearily.

"Radoq."

"Speak your mind."

Tricial sighed "It's not just mine, Radoq. It's all our thoughts.

I suppose we want to know if you are genuinely going through with this plan?"

A dozen cutting or dismissive comments rose to Radoq's lips and if it were Sijun or Evie perhaps they would have seen the light of day but the Sheriff had never spoken lightly on matters of importance and so he checked his barbs.

"I don't see any other way." he spoke slowly "The moment we entered the facility in Khafon we were committed. The moment for doubts, Tricial, was before we committed treason."

The Sheriff nodded "I know that, Radoq and I came with you, didn't I? Stood by and played my part." his face creased into a frown "I hope it isn't my commitment that you doubt."

Radoq realised he'd offended his friend and made an apologetic gesture "I would have you speak freely to me."

Tricial nodded "This deal you have made with the Dark Ji and the virals. It goes against every principle our kind –" he shot an apologetic glance at Evie who shrugged "- has stood for in our history. Intentionally leading virals towards a settlement, *the* settlement that your tritus protects is…" his voice tailed off, not wanting to label the action.

"An unspeakable crime." Sijun finished, holding Radoq's gaze with steel.

"A heinous act." Radoq agreed "But only if the virals reach the town. Remember, we will draw Juraj and his 'army' out and watch them break themselves on the virals. That is all we have to do! And then the virals will return to the Dark Lands with the nuklera."

"Do you trust Guysil?" Tricial asked flatly.

"I trust the people in this room." Radoq responded in the same tone "That is why I've involved you all in this scheme."

"Do you think he will keep his word, though?" Tricial leaned forward.

"Yes."

"Why?"

"Because he is, or was once, a Domerus and a Ji. And the word of a man like that is not given easily." Radoq frowned at Tricial

"You know this as well as I do!"

"I have a question." Sijun raised his hand "Tricial is right to question you, Radoq. We will follow you, no matter what but he's right to know that you are not throwing our lives away in vain." Radoq began to speak but he shook his head "That's all I have to say on that. My question is after the nuklera has detonated. Guysil told you the glow would help the virals and by that we can assume he means create more of them."

"I think that's true."

"Then what of your duty as Po of tritus Fortisun? The Western Hills stand as the border to Wallanria and you – you, Radoq –" he pointed a finger at Radoq's chest "- are charged with their defence. You are making the rest of your life harder than it ever needs to be."

Radoq nodded "Yes, and of course I've thought of that." he glanced at Evie "It depends how you look at it. On the one hand, there will be more virals but on the other this will free Fortisul, remove Juraj and my tritus will be free to fulfil their duty. Now we have Oprain as our friend we can stand against the virals. What more would we do, Sijun? What other task is there for us than to fight the virals? If nothing else this legitimises our existence for perhaps centuries more!" Evie stirred but Radoq ignored her.

"What if the Crown Prince discovers it was you who stole the nuklera?" Tricial asked.

"That is inevitable."

Sijun stared in horror "I thought – *what?*"

Radoq nodded "I assume he will. At some point the blame will come to me and I will shoulder the burden."

"He'll have your head!"

"Perhaps not. If the threat of the virals can be met by Fortisun then we – I – can prove my use to Admirain. The Crown Prince is hardly going to weaken his eastern border over a petty theft!"

"You plan to make yourself invaluable?" Tricial asked sceptically.

"Think about it!" Radoq stood and began to pace the bridge

"I am already the Po. My father is young enough to fight but he is no longer my equal. I fight better than any in my tritus and we are a large tritus! If I am seen as the General of the eastern border, winning battle after battle then public opinion will be behind me! Should the Crown Prince question me I will confess to the crime and beg for forgiveness. It would be politically advantageous for him to leave me where I am!"

"Until you fall foul of him for some other reason." Sijun pointed out "Then he'll use the theft against you and –"

"Have my head, I know." Radoq turned to stare out the windows "It's a risk. But it's my risk to bear."

Sijun grunted, Tricial said nothing and Radoq gave them a moment before he turned back to face them "This is it! This is the end of everything we've been working towards! One deal, a final battle and then Fortisul is liberated, Juraj is dead and in the process I can bring Argan to justice! It's an adventure!"

Sijun gave a nod. No smile.

"What about Guysil. I mean in the future? After this he will be your enemy." Tricial pointed out "I can hardly see a future where you invite him to Fortisul to play Sagalm."

Sijun snorted.

"He's a viral – he's already my enemy. I suppose I will fight him another day. I know he's real now, at least and his control over the virals is real. That's something to be studied and tested." Radoq shrugged "Perhaps if we understand more about them, we'll be able to fight them better."

He began to say more but Tricial held up a hand "If I can offer advice, Radoq, it is that you yourself must be comfortable with your reasons for doing this. Yes, perhaps this may legitimise the divide between Domerus and lun'erus for a thousand years to come but that's not your motivation. You're doing this to free your people and our home. That must be clear in your head if we're to attempt this."

Radoq took a breath to argue but let it out slowly instead, nodding at the sense of Tricial's words "You're right, of course."

"Sounds better that way, anyway." Evie put in, speaking for

the first time "Not that you need legitimising anymore." there was venom in her tone and Sijun looked at her in surprise.

"Is that what the two of you were whingeing about?" he asked in surprise "Lun'erus and Domerus? Chox, Evie, Radoq! Haven't you more important subjects to fight over?" the big man began to chuckle.

"I'm glad you think it so funny!" Evie snapped, colour flushing into her cheeks.

"Oh!" Sijun waved a hand and shook his head "Don't think I'm being disrespectful, friend Evie! If you think your lot in life is so badly cast then fine, I'll not try to change your thoughts but for Chox' sake, woman! We just made the greatest heist in the history of this country and you're bickering about nonsense neither of you can change?"

Evie began an angry retort and Radoq opened his mouth to stop Sijun but the big man stepped forward, dropping to kneel beside Evie in the engineer's chair. He pinched the flesh of her forearm between his massive finger and thumb, offering his own bare forearm to her. Warily, she mirrored the action, scooping a portion of his flesh between her own digits "Does this make us so different, Evie? Does my skin feel so different to yours? And what use is my size, speed and strength when the engines fail? When we break into a nuklera storage facility? Who got us in there and got us out? Who saved our crew in the Dark Lands? Who, in every situation that life has thrown at her has simply nodded, cracked a joke and then got on with whatever needed doing without complaint, pauses to rest or concern for personal injury? You sit there, Evie, wanting to kneel where I kneel but I tell you if you didn't sit there, there would be no Sijun to kneel before you!" he shook his head as though working thoughts to the front of his mind "I live a life of adventure, Evie, brazenly and unashamedly but do you see me doing anything different to you? We sit in the same ship, visiting the same places, fighting the same fights together! There are different principles that govern us sure enough but in the end they've brought us to the same place!" he squeezed her flesh again "We're different in a lot of ways, I'm funny, you aren't, you're clever, I'm not, you're short, I'm huge but if we sit here arguing over our differences we'll do nothing but fight! Our differences are not what bring us together, it's the things we have in common! But when we come together, our differences are what make us valuable! If we were all the same here we'd achieve nothing. Tricial would be penned in a cell somewhere in his own keep, I'd be bored kow-towing to Juraj in Fortisul and you two would be in chains in a market in Xeonison!"

There were tears in Evie's eyes as she stared into Sijun's but she said nothing.

"We will always have our differences, Evie but if we spend our time looking at others and noticing only how we are different then we'll never be satisfied! We are what we are, and there are precious few ways to change that! What we do is look inside ourselves for *who* we are because that is ultimately the greatest freedom that any of us have. To be who we *know* we should be. Not to try and be someone else."

An embrace, one side fierce, one side tender but both burning with emotion as the two of them openly wept. Evie clenched her hands into small, angry fists whilst Sijun let tears roll freely down his cheeks. Tricial cuffed at his own eyes and Radoq bowed his head, ashamed of his earlier anger as they waited for the storm to pass.

Finally, all tempests come to an end and Evie leaned back, hiccupping slightly and cuffing at her eyes. Sijun crossed the bridge and removed a bottle of sky spirit from a cabinet marked 'MEDICINE'. He poured four glasses and they drank, all of them hissing at the harsh liquid.

"Thank you." Evie said to Sijun.

He nodded.

"I'm still mad at you." she shot at Radoq, some of her vigour returning.

"What's new."

"I'll tear you something new if you don't –"

"Children!" Sijun called in a matronly voice and they all

dissolved into laughs.

"I'm with you." Evie said after the mirth had settled, looking hard at Radoq "All the way."

"I know."

"We all are." Tricial stood and raised his glass.

"Yes." Sijun mirrored the action.

Evie stood too and then they realised their glasses were empty so Sijun filled them again.

"To Radoq."

"Radoq."

"Chox'd Domerus... To Radoq!"

A wary glance at Evie and then "To me."

"So arrogant."

"Got to be to do this job."

"... *Golden Kote. Come in...*"

"The communicator!" Tricial hurried to the console and pressed the talk button.

"*Eyrie... this is Oprain.*"

"Oprain? This is Radoq." Radoq had crossed the bridge, setting down his glass.

"*... land immediately when here. Urgent...*"

"The signal is weak." Tricial explained "We're still a hundred miles from them."

"Oprain? What's happened?" Radoq demanded.

"*Can't explain over this. Land immediately... here.*"

The signal dropped out and Radoq turned to the others, eyebrows raised "Something's wrong."

CHAPTER 25

The Eyrie patrol ship led them in, both vessels rocking slightly in the strong winds as their speed dropped. The floating beacons that marked the sky lanes pulsed a familiar greeting and Radoq thought guiltily of the terrible weapon that was concealed inside *Golden Kote* and the risk to everyone in the craggy city he was creating.

"Nothing more from Oprain?" he asked Tricial as the patrol ship banked sharply to the north to join the incoming lane.

"No. All very cryptic."

"It could be –" Sijun piped up but Evie let out a groan.

"It could be the end of the world, Sijun or any of a thousand other things. Let's let the Domerus land us then find out for ourselves."

"– a horde of virals, the Crown Prince finding out, Juraj being ascended or our spies in Fortisul have sent a report!" he finished, pointedly ignoring Evie.

The easterly winds caught the ship hard as Radoq turned into the sky lane, the broad flank of the battle ship providing a firm grip for the tempestuous gusts and there was silence for a moment as he wrestled with the fine adjustment controls.

"There's Oprain." Tricial pointed ahead and Radoq adjusted his aurae to see the elderly Domerus with a small crowd of attendants on the dock. The communicator crackled, directing them to moor beside him and behind a sleek racing yacht not unlike the craft Evie had enthused over in Volanbuta.

"That ship has Fortisul markings..." Radoq pointed but was distracted by the docking procedures. As the ship moored, more time was taken in ensuring the crew who were visiting the Eyrie did so in small groups under the supervision of either Staph or Rakr who Radoq knew he could trust to keep the soldiers and airmen out of the taverns and their mouths shut. Radoq made his way down the gangway and turned towards Oprain, impatient to know what was so important that he had to stop his mission at such a critical juncture but the old man made no move towards him and he frowned as a Domerus standing close by detached herself from the small group and stared at Radoq with shock, disbelief and then tears and suddenly he was sprinting forward down the length of the dock, the Domerus given speed in his legs so painfully slow it felt like he was running through wet mud and then there was no time for thought or speech save for one word which her lips muffled inside his own.

Malain

*

"I'm sorry-"
"I tried to-"
"How are you-"
"I knew-"
"It's so-"

They spoke over one another, breaking apart for a moment to laugh and then try to speak again only to talk over one another all over again and the laughter was deep and happy. Tears poured down both their cheeks and Radoq staired at her dark haired beauty, drinking in her face as if he'd never been satisfied basking in the glow of her presence.

"He has my family." the tears were agonising now "I had to pretend – it was the only way."

"I know – I heard everything."

"When I saw you there in his house I thought I would kill him-"

"There was nothing else to do-"

"You came back for me-" she squeezed him tightly, crushing him against her warm body, the best feeling in the world.

Throats cleared pointedly behind him and Radoq turned, still grinning wildly and with his arm still firmly around Malain's waist to see Tricial looking awkward, Sijun beaming and Evie with an expression of disgust on her face. Behind them, every porthole and the wide glass of the bridge was lined with faces as the entirety of the crew stared enraptured at their Captain. Radoq distinctly saw Staph and Rakr in the best spots, unashamedly gawping with the rest and he roared with laughter.

"Do you need a bit of space, Domerus?" Evie asked sarcastically as Sijun chuckled, elbowing the skinny lun'erus aside and making a fluttering, floor level bow.

"Sijun Kaymsus Su-Camrouak, an honour to meet you good lady!"

"Malain Saxodas Po-Hammun." Malain gave a small, polite curtsey "Oprain here has told me a lot about you."

"And Radoq here has not stopped talking about you." Sijun smiled "I'm pleased to finally see that his storytelling has done you little justice."

"Oi!" Evie piped up and Malain turned in surprise.

"This is Evie, our chief Engineer." Radoq explained but Malain stepped forward to shake the lun'erus' hand with a smile.

"Oprain told me a lot more about you. Is it true you trained in Admirain? And you fixed the *Golden Kote* in the middle of the Dark Lands?"

"Well, tried to, didn't I? The Domerus here was off trying to score his new bromance."

Malain let out a roar of laughter and a moment later the two had stepped to the side and were chattering away like old friends leaving Radoq to roll his eyes at the mysterious ways of women.

"Back to my house, I think." Oprain was watching with a small smile on his lips and Radoq allowed him to lead them back to the higher tiers, his hand never letting go of Malain's.

"But how are you here?" he managed to ask when Evie had

paused for breath.

"Juraj sent me." Malain saw the look on his face and squeezed his hand "We've a lot to talk about but he sent me to taunt you."

"In what way?" they reached Oprain's study and drew up chairs while Oprain called for refreshments.

"Well –" Malain looked around at the enraptured faces "Juraj has built what he calls an army. Really they're a band of cut throats, most of them are of questionable fighting ability but there are enough of them to really cause trouble."

"What manner of trouble?" Oprain asked with narrowed eyes but Malain's quick mind sensed the question behind his words.

"Argan is with him in Fortisul. They took him from an airship crash and Juraj has been trying to bargain with him ever since."

"Have they attempted the ascension?" Radoq asked.

"No. Not yet. Argan has stipulated that Juraj help him take over the Eyrie." She looked at Oprain "He wants your head."

"Are they going to attack us?"

"Yes, I think that's their ultimate plan. As it stands though, they sent me to tell you their strength in the hopes that you would attack Fortisul." She directed her last words to Radoq who nodded.

"It makes sense. If we attack and he defeats our fleet then he is free to attack the Eyrie."

"Also, any hostile move by us would kill some of the inhabitants." Tricial pointed out "Any act of war would further legitimise his claim to Fortisul. If he can be ascended." he added as an afterthought.

Radoq turned to Malain, her hand still held tightly in his "Is he a half blood?"

She shrugged "I don't know. I don't know that there is any way to tell other than to attempt the ascension. He is utterly convinced though. He talks of little else. It's become an obsession."

"And what does Argan think?" Oprain's voice had a note of steel that Radoq hadn't heard before.

"I didn't see him much. I think he avoided other Domerus."

"Probably ashamed." Sijun opined "The man has no honour to speak of."

"Agreed." Evie surprised everyone by speaking up "What? He's a snake. Can't trust him."

"I like this one." Malain turned to Radoq.

"She's gold." he agreed.

"I'm a lot more than that." Evie grumbled but smiled at the compliment.

"I'm curious –" Tricial spoke up "What taunts has he sent you with? So far I cannot see that we are being convinced to attack Fortisul."

Malain sighed "There are a number of prisoners, yes? Mostly the Domerus, our two families and the others that live there. Now he has Argan he is able to restrain them a great deal more effectively and they've all been moved to the keep. There are also some lun'erus who dissented, a few of the city Guard tried to overthrow him and a couple lost their heads but the rest are in the dungeons with our tritus'." She turned to Radoq taking a deep breath "For every day that you don't attack, another prisoner will be executed."

There was a painful silence in the dusty office.

"Chox!" breathed Sijun "And this man thinks to become Domerus? A madman!"

Radoq shook his head sadly "He leaves us with little choice."

"No!" Malain shook his hand "The place is a fortress! They've got ships, men and the walls are stuffed with pinzgats!"

"We've got pulse torpedoes." Sijun retorted "We could take out half his men in a few hits and storm the town."

"And slaughter half the population?" Radoq scowled "No. We've already got a plan."

"What? Tell me!" she urged but every eye had turned to Oprain who rolled his own.

"Fine." he stood and headed for the door "I heard nothing."

Radoq began to speak. He told her about their flight across the Dark Lands, the sighting of the captured *Golden Kote* and the fight aboard the ship. Sijun began to interrupt with details of the duel but Radoq hushed him, moving to the part where Guysil had appeared out of the darkness.

"He caught you unawares?" Malain frowned "That's impossible."

"Yes, isn't it?" Radoq nodded "Then he ran, faster and further than I've ever run in my life. Remember when Gellian and I had that instructor? Guysil didn't even break a sweat and it was all I could do to keep up."

He related the conversation it the cave, watching her face as he told her of the deal he'd struck with the madman.

"And you..."

Malain stood, finally letting go of his hand and striding to the window to look down at the skyport, tiers below them. She turned back to Radoq "Is it in there? You stole one?"

He nodded "Yes."

A deep sigh rocked her and she turned to the rest of the group "Would you give us a moment?"

Evie leapt to her feet and chivvied Tricial and Sijun from the room almost immediately. Radoq could tell by the way Malain appeared unsurprised by the lun'erus lack of manners that she was not seeing the comedic scene. When they had gone she turned to him, taking both his hands in her own.

"Radoq, do you remember decades ago when the slave trade first started crossing Fortisun lands?"

Radoq agreed that he did.

"And your grandfather sent to Admirain for help with those that they were liberating? There were too many to settle in our lands but most didn't want to return to their own homes. Or they had no way."

A nod.

"And the King said that he would deal with it and the freed slaves were all shipped away and we assumed they were being settled into the four cities but then it came out that he'd made a deal with Xeonison and they were all going across the Wallanrian sea?"

"I don't-"

"Hush." she smiled and squeezed his hands "How do you think the King came to the conclusion that this was a better course of action than just giving them employment?"

Radoq didn't like it when she set out these thought experiments for him but she was making a point and he wanted her opinion so he played along "I suppose he and his advisers talked about it."

"But it cost a great deal of time, money and bother for them to ship them away. It would have been cheaper and more practical just to house them here in Wallanria. But they didn't want to be seen to be soft so they took a decision."

"What's your point?"

"My point is that it took them a long time to come to that decision. And, knowing Domerus as we do I think it's clear that they genuinely believed that what they were doing was the most practical and ethical thing to do. They believed that because they'd talked through all the options and to them that was the most logical route."

Radoq nodded.

"But on the face of it 'Shipping freed slaves to a slave owning country' sounds ludicrous. Worse than that, it sounds monstrous and any uneducated, clod brained fool would tell you that."

"But they hadn't followed the King and his advisor's logic." Radoq pointed out.

"No." Malain paused, trying to make sure the point came across correctly "But the clod brained people were right."

"How so?"

"Because when you overcomplicate a clear ethical question, you start to create twists and turns in the logic. Ethics are very clear, there is right and there is wrong. And when you – when one twists and turns, they begin hiding behind things that are wrong in the aim to do things that are *right*."

Radoq sighed "I know what you're going to say."

"Yes, because it's obvious." She nodded at him, holding his gaze firmly with hers "When you describe a situation that you want to judge ethically and from the moment you hear it you instinctively know 'good' or 'bad', there is no changing it."

"But-"

"Shipping freed slaves to a slave owning country is bad."

He waited, resigned.

"Creating more virals is bad."

"I know!" he shouted, almost pulling away from her but stopping himself "Don't you think I know that? I don't want to help the virals, Chox knows I've fought them my entire life but there is something different about Guysil and his way with them! Here is an opportunity to do good!"

"Yes." she placed her palm on his cheek "Freeing Fortisul is a good thing, my love. But creating more virals is not. And it will never be. It will only lead to more evil, more death and more war. There is no good to come out of this."

She was right. Of course, she was right. Radoq had long ago learned that in questions of logic, the women in his life were almost always right. That didn't mean he had to be happy about it though and he looked away from her for a moment before realising that he was sulking and looking back.

"I stole a nuklera from the Crown Prince."

She took a deep breath "I know."

"I have it in *Golden Kote.*"

She nodded.

"What should I do with it?"

She shook her head abruptly "You aren't asking me for answers. That isn't how this works. We discuss and come to conclusions, remember?"

Radoq turned away and began to pace up and down as though deep in thought but the truth of the matter was that there was no depth. In reality, there was no decision to be made. That didn't mean that *not* making it would be any easier though.

"I made a promise to Guysil." He pointed out.

Malain thought about it "Yes. And honour dictates that you carry out your side of the bargain. But honour also dictates you don't detonate a nuklera in the Dark Lands to help Guysil breed more virals."

"I'm not sure that's how it works – anyway." he hurried on seeing her roll her eyes "That's not the point." he sighed, stopping his pacing "I need to make a decision, don't I?"

He called the others in and told them what was going to happen. He expected Tricial to question his honour, Sijun to refuse and Evie to agree but to his surprise and pleasure, they simply nodded.

"I'm in." Sijun said simply.

"It's the right thing to do." Tricial nodded.

"What about my promise to Guysil?"

"That's your business." Sijun said slowly "But the ethical choice overrides it, if you want my opinion."

Tricial simply nodded.

"Evie?"

"Yeah, yeah. Whatever you say, Domerus." she waved her hand as though plans and fortunes changed at such a whim every day "I'm glad she's here to set you back on the straight and narrow. Either way, still doesn't answer what you're going to do about matey-boy back in Fortisul." she paused for a moment "Unless you want to drop the Chox'd thing on the city, hit the reset switch?"

Dead silence filled the room.

"What? It was a joke!"

The day wore on as they sat in Oprain's house debating, arguing, making plans, wiping them out and scratching their heads. Radoq felt as though a new energy burned inside him. A great weight had been lifted from his shoulders at his decision but it was Malain's constant presence that filled him with vigour and life.

"I have to return to Fortisul." She told him as they ate, hours later. Evie snored in a chair that was far too big for her beside Oprain's table.

"I know." Radoq sighed "When?"

"First light tomorrow. I can't risk *him* hurting my family." she sneered at the thought of Juraj's name.

"I'm going to take him out into the Dark Lands and feed him to the virals, one limb at a time." Radoq swore.

"You'll have to beat me to him." Malain promised "Ugh. Why can't we work this out?"

"We're overcomplicating things." Radoq guessed "All of us are tired, Evie has the right idea. She's taking a break, letting her mind clear."

"Hmm? Who said my name?" Evie jerked awake with a comical rising snore and blinked stupidly at Malain for a minute "Was he talking about me?"

"Yes."

Radoq tutted in exasperation as the two women dissolved into giggles.

"Anyway –" Evie stretched like a cat, looking around the room "Have you lot worked it out yet?"

"We've been thinking of doing –" Tricial began but Evie spoke over the Sheriff as though he hadn't said a word.

"'Course, this is why you need me. S'just like Sagalm all over again. Did he tell you I beat him? Bet he didn't. Anyway, simplest is always best." Evie gave Radoq a huge wink.

He had to laugh "Go on then, oh mighty sage!"

A minute later, they stared at Evie as she beamed around the room.

"Like I say, simple!"

Oprain stared at her "You want me to fly my entire fleet away and leave the Eyrie exposed? You know there are brigands that patrol these skies? Slavers? Air Pirates? It isn't just Juraj we fear."

"No, you aren't listening!" Evie sounded exasperated "You spread the word through your little blokes on the ground in Fortisul that you've found a viral nest and you're taking *almost* everyone out to – I dunno, blow it up? Whatever you do with viral nests."

"I've never even *heard* of a viral nest." Oprain muttered.

"So? The point is, you fly out of sight, get above the clouds and then matey-boy Juraj comes swooping in with Argan and *then* we get to use those pulse torpedoes!" she beamed again.

"I'm in!" Sijun jumped to his feet "I'll go and tell Armlu the good news!"

"Can everyone-"

"Stop talking about the pulse torpedoes!" Evie finished, rolling her eyes "The point is, this could work."

Radoq sighed but Malain was nodding and Tricial was looking quietly impressed. Sijun was practically drooling at the thought of blasting Juraj from the skies with the pulse weapons.

"Oprain?"

The older man had leaned onto his desk with both hands, looking old and weary. He rocked his head from side to side as though considering the possibilities but finally he looked at Radoq "If we can notify our people in Fortisul –"

"I can pass the messages." Malain nodded "I need to return anyway."

"Then I can see no reason why it won't work. Of course, I'll have to leave most of the Marines in the town in case there are raiders."

"It's the ships we need." Evie explained "Once the mercenaries see Juraj is dead they'll most likely drop away."

"You hope." Oprain warned and the small lun'erus shrugged.

"Fine." Radoq nodded "We'll go with Evie's plan." He made to stand up and headed with Malain towards the door.

"Where are you going?" Sijun demanded "Armlu will need briefing!"

"A fine job for you, Sijun!" Radoq beamed and Malain tugged him harder towards the door "We're going to find a bed!"

Sijun's booming laugher followed them from the room.

CHAPTER 26

An emptiness followed Malain's departure but not as acute as the one that had preceded it. Radoq felt a burning energy that filled him from when he'd awoken next to her. She was leaving, but she assured him it was only temporary and there was plenty to do. Oprain busied himself filing false reports of viral sightings whilst Radoq gave Armlu and Sijun free reign over filling and sighting the *Golden Kote's* armaments. The two men, one huge, one small chattered at a speed so great most could barely hear human speech let alone decipher the complex technical data that streamed from their lips but they seemed happy.

"Sir?" Staph approached Radoq as he turned from another query from an airman.

"What is it, Sergeant?"

"Lads want to know if there's gonna be a proper scrap."

"Yes." Radoq turned to fully face the man "As big as it gets."

Staph nodded "That being the case, Sir, perhaps you might make a speech?"

Radoq made a face but the Sergeant was implacable and he dipped his head in acknowledgement "Any ideas what I should say?"

"Me, Sir? No, above my paygrade to make officer speeches. Usually just full of nonsense and patter anyway. Officers never really get to the point when they open their mouths. The lads never want to hear his opinion on stuff, they just want to know if they're gonna survive the next battle and be richer at the end of it." Staph shrugged "'Course, me and Rakr don't mind. Just another day for us."

"I see." Radoq nodded at the Marine "I'll make it when we're underway, alright?"

"Lads don't like it when theres a lot of waiting before a fight." Staph sounded almost as though he was thinking out loud "Waiting's the worst bit, you see. Once we're in the scrap its alright but when they see the enemy? That's a bad time if they don't get a word or two of encouragement. If you catch my drift, Sir." Staph turned and marched away, his sharp tongue lashing the crew around him. Radoq watched him go, shaking his head at the verbal contortion the Sergeant was capable of. He began running words through his head as a dozen tedious tasks immediately presented themselves.

"Issue phasrs, Sir?" a fresh faced young soldier was clutching a handheld and looking at Radoq expectantly.

"What? Of course we need phasrs!"

"What about coltacs and berretts, Sir?"

"Erm – isn't there a ratio for these things?" Radoq asked, distractedly "Ask Sergeant Staph. Or Rakr."

"I did. They sent me to ask you." The soldier looked miffed at Radoq.

"Well –"

"Sir? Problem with the pulse tubes." Nimel, the local of Khafon was tapping Radoq on the shoulder.

"Send Evie."

"She sent me, Sir. Said you need to take a look."

Rolling his eyes, Radoq hurried through the narrow corridors and down through the decks to the cramped weapons deck. Sijun and Armlu were now arguing over payload strengths and Radoq hastened past them, avoiding yet more work.

"Evie?"

"Domerus? Think I've fixed it. Nothing to worry about."

"Chox, Evie. Can't you see how busy I am?"

She made a pained face "Looks like you're standing around moaning at me, Domerus. Time must be plentiful!"

Radoq swore colourfully bringing a grin to her face and headed back towards the stairs.

"Radoq! This Xeonison scum thinks our torpedoes should fire on a reduced payload!" Sijun was irate.

"The payload has to be reduced or it'll blow us out of the air at close range!" Armlu thundered, seemingly unaware of the towering Domerus "It's standard operating procedure –"

"It's Chox'd cowardice!"

"You calling me a coward, you overgrown corflye?"

"I –"

"Perhaps a trial on the field of honour?" Radoq shouted over the rising voices. Both men looked at him in bewilderment for a second before bursting out laughing and a moment later, had settled on a payload and were on to the next task. Radoq left the deck feeling a rising knot of frustration in his chest.

"Sir? The rations are lower than they should be."

"Sir? The fuel is here."

"Sir? Have you –"

"Sir?"

"Sir?"

Slam

Radoq shut himself in the bridge, standing with the door closed behind him as he willed himself not to lose his temper. A moment's respite and then Tricial's voice.

"Alright? Busy out there, I expect?"

"Busy in here too, no doubt."

"Actually..." Tricial had his feet up and was perusing a handheld with leisure "See, I think this sort of time is when an officer should be out of the way. Your two chaps Staph and Rakr have things under control. You being out there just gives people something else to do. Take my advice and keep that door shut. You've got some preparation to do anyway, if I'm correct?"

Not a little relieved, Radoq ensured the door was shut and took a moment to breathe deeply before stepping across the bridge to the small door marked 'DOMERUS'.

"Captain's authority." he called to the security system and with a clank, the door retracted in on itself to reveal a cabinet stuffed with dark coloured panels in a pile.

"That doesn't look right." Tricial had leaned forward and was frowning.

Radoq sighed "Urgh. I haven't opened this since we took the ship back from Correlius. He must've tried to put it on. Chox'd thing would've been far too big."

"I suppose he thought it too valuable to discard?"

"It is." Radoq removed a wide black object shaped like a thin circle "Adamantine, all of it and based on the retracting design the Crown Prince wears." He raised the circle to his neck where with a sudden hissing sound it leapt around his skin, forming a snug but comfortable bond.

"Not good if you've gained a few?" Tricial joked, patting his belly.

"It adjusts. Here." Radoq brushed the circle and at once the components inside began to crawl at a rapid rate over up his neck and onto his head, forming a tightly fitting helmet.

"Mighty fine." Tricial nodded in appreciation "Is it comfortable?"

"Not really." Radoq's voice was magnified by the armour which removed all facial features, replacing them with a flat, black nothing "It's better than a berrett to the head though."

"Indeed."

Tricial watched as Radoq sorted through the pile, adding gauntlets, vambraces, hauberk, cuisses and greaves. Finally, he stood enclosed in the adamantine armour, only his palms remaining bare beneath the armoured fingers. He examined himself in the reflection of the bridge windows and nodded.

"Tricial?"

Oprain's voice crackled over the communicator and the Sheriff leaned forward to pick up the message.

"Chirruf is out of danger."

"Excellent!" Tricial was on his feet, beaming with joy "Oh, that's excellent news, Radoq!"

"A flight of mercenary ships is preparing to leave Fortisul. They're waiting until they have word that the Eyrie fleet has left. Everything is being moved up. We're leaving now."

Tricial confirmed as Radoq felt his heart leap. It had worked! Juraj and Argan had fallen for their lure and he dashed to the communicator console where Tricial sat, snatching up the control that would carry his voice across the ship.

"Crew, this is Radoq. Timings have been moved up. We're leaving now. Everything stowed immediately, and all provisions brought on board." he paused, searching for the words "This is it, troops. The big one." The words sounded lame even to him and he cringed. Knowing the message needed finishing he blurted out the only thing he could think of "We're going to win!"

He turned to Tricial, wincing at the clumsy sentence but before he could speak, the sound of cheers from beyond the closed door erupted and he felt relief wash over him.

"I thought I'd made a Chox'd mess of that."

"They like you, Radoq. They like following you. Remember, you're the man with the golden kote! They all want a piece of the action!"

Radoq grinned and fired up the engines, seeing the final crew scrambling up the gangway and sealing the hatches. He thrust the throttle open, merging into formation with the other ships of the Eyrie's fleet. Oprain was aboard a narrow cutter, he knew and he spotted the smaller ship safely in the centre of the pack with its name *Terminal Sky* stencilled in no-nonsense lettering along the side.

"Here we go!" he called as the vanguard, flight lanes forgotten for once, punched their engines and leapt out into the sky, banking in a wide turn around to the east and climbing swiftly through the scudding clouds.

The door to the bridge burst open to reveal Sijun, practically bouncing with excitement "Radoq! You're armoured! I must join you!" and he began pulling on armour pieces, muttering something under his breath in his own language.

"What's that you're saying?" Tricial called and Sijun raised his voice to reveal a battle chant. After a moment of pause he translated it into Wallanrian.

A day to fight, a day to die

Blood across the shining sky
Warriors blazing like the sun
Fight for honour, beat the drums

"Sounds better with the drums beating." Sijun fiddled with his biom, finding a likeness and playing the music for them all to hear as *Golden Kote* streaked across the sky.

"It's good." Radoq nodded along as Sijun repeated the lines "Can we play it around the ship? A soft version, just enough for the crew to hear the drumbeat?"

Tricial, pleased to have something to do busied himself with the task and a few moments later Radoq felt the thudding percussion beating through the hull.

"This is a sight!" Sijun's voice came from the far side of the bridge where he stared out of a window as they completed the wide turn to the east. Radoq looked and saw behind them, strung out in a shining formation across the sky was the fleet. Ships, bristling with weaponry hung in the air in tight groupings as smaller escort vessels raced around in a patrolling pattern.

"By Chox!" Tricial boomed "I never thought I'd see such a thing!"

Radoq had seen it before and he recalled the last time he'd sat in this seat at the head of a great fleet. None of those ships now flew with them and he was the sole survivor. He swallowed at the sudden bad omen and forced himself to concentrate.

Minutes passed as the Eyrie faded to a dark shape in the distance and then they climbed higher still, the life support system in the *Golden Kote* kicking in to flood air to the crew.

"How long? How much longer?" Sijun wondered out loud and Radoq shot him a hard look.

"Long. We have to wait for them to leave Fortisul. We may be waiting for hours."

"But it's not far to Fortisul." Sijun seemed barely aware that he was speaking. His gaze was fixed on the fleet out the window.

"They will be coming cautiously, travelling in formation."

"I hate the waiting."

"Go and see the crew. Walk around, smile, show off your armour. You look Chox'd invincible in that stuff." And he did. Sijun looked like a monster from legend, the extra size the armour added and the shining black surface giving him more in common with a boulder than a man. He shot Radoq a grin and headed out.

"The big man is nervous." Tricial observed.

"Aren't you?"

"I'm old. We hide it better." Tricial glanced at Radoq "Are you?"

Radoq nodded "Yes."

"I suppose you'd be mad not to."

Radoq gave a humourless laugh "I can't stop thinking about the last time I led an army."

"This time will be different."

"Yes."

"No more mistakes?"

"No." Radoq nodded in time to the faint drumbeats.

Blood across the shining sky

"Today is the day, Radoq. Today we'll take back our home."

"We will."

"By tonight, we'll sleep in our own beds."

"By tonight, we'll drink gallons of sky spirit in our own homes. And our own beds will be filled with beautiful women."

"Just the one, I think?"

"Hah! One will be plenty."

They laughed.

"Enemy fleet sighted."

"Chox!" Radoq locked the controls and raced to the window, priming his aurae.

"There!" Tricial had spotted them on the screen and now pointed directly. Radoq flicked frantically through his vision, bringing the vast distances to his eye as if they were nothing.

Silence filled the bridge.

"There's fewer than I thought."

"More of them than us."

"Yes, but they're mercenaries, not used to fighting together.

Oprain's men have fought together for years."

"Yes." Radoq nodded but his blood had run cold. It was a *lot* of ships.

He crossed to the communication console, pressing the command to echo his voice across the ship. He tried to remember Staph's confusing advice.

"Troops, this is Radoq. The enemy is in sight. And what an enemy! Today we'll take so many prizes we won't be able to fit them in the dock! There'll be fortunes aboard them, gold, weapons and goods. Every warrior who does their duty today will be rich by sundown!"

A weak chorus of cheers through the open door. What else had Staph said?

"The enemy looks tough, but for all their bluster they're men fighting for a cause they don't believe in. A usurping criminal gang is all they are. Those are not soldiers! Those are thugs with gold plated coltacs!"

Shouts of agreement.

"But we aren't just soldiers either! Soldiers was yesterday! Today, we don't just follow orders. Today we aren't just men and women in a training yard, sweating whilst Sergeant Rakr bores us with a story about the night he spent in the Dark Lands!"

Chuckles.

"Of course, he never told you about his viral girlfriends..."

Bellows of laughter now. Tricial smiled.

"But soldiers are for peace time. This is war! Today, we are warriors!"

There were cheers coming now. Radoq looked through the door to see a cluster of soldiers and airmen watching him with such fervour on their faces that it brought a lump to his throat.

"Warriors!" he shouted the word and the men roared their approval, punching their fists into the air "Your enemy is made up of thieves and bullies! They have never met our like! They have never fought us!"

"Warriors! Warriors! Warriors!" it had become a chant and he heard it echo through the corridors of the ship and beamed.

"Fight with me today! Stand beside me as warriors! Today, we are all brothers! Today, we are all victors!"

Movement in the corridor. Rakr, making a cutting sign across his throat and holding up a thumb with a sharp nod.

Done.

Radoq pumped his fist in the air and turned away, hearing the raucous shouts fill the ship. He gripped the controls as Oprain gave the order to advance. Evie opened up a communicator line from the engine room where she would stay for the battle.

"Nice job, Domerus." was there a hint of fear in her voice?

"Standard, isn't it?" Radoq jibed.

"Don't get me started." the banter was weak, but it was there and Radoq nodded to himself as the fleet turned as one, moving in an instant from a stretched out column to a wide, fighting line and they dove down through the long miles of open sky that separated them from Juraj's ships.

"All ships, move to attack bearing."

Oprain's voice was characteristically calm and Radoq remembered Tricial's words about the older generations being able to hide their fear. He forced himself to mimic the Sheriff, affecting an unconcerned look.

Crew began to pass in and out of the bridge, passing him reports and Radoq nodded to each one, giving a hard look where needed or a smile of encouragement to a pale face.

"Distance, forty eight miles. Closing."

Closing? Of course they were closing. Why did Oprain need to say that?

"All good up there, Domerus?" Evie's voice crackled over the communicator.

"All good. You alright?"

"Smashing. How far?"

"Forty seven miles.

Evie swore and went quiet.

"Radoq?" Sijun re-entered the bridge, flushed with shining excitement "The troops are riled up. Best hope we can keep them like this." he eyed the distant fleet warily.

"Forty five miles. Closing."

"Why does he keep saying closing?" Sijun wondered out loud.

"They're turning!" Tricial leapt to his feet, arm outstretched and indeed, Juraj's fleet of mismatched ships had turned sharply towards them and was deploying into a wide battle line.

"This shortens the wait a bit!" Sijun rubbed his hands together with glee. After a moment of silence he looked pleadingly at Radoq who rolled his eyes with a grin.

"Now we can use the pulse torpedoes!"

"I'll call Armlu! He should see the first at least." Sijun vanished to find the Gunnery Sergeant who appeared a minute later, eyes feverishly bright.

"Thirty five miles. Closing."

"Does he need to point that out, Sir?" Armlu wondered, one eyebrow cocked.

"Everyone needs a hobby, Sergeant."

"Aye, Sir."

"Who fires the first shot then?" Radoq glanced at Sijun and Armlu who looked at each other in surprise.

"You, Domerus." Armlu addressed Sijun.

"No, no. I couldn't possibly take the honour from you."

"It's not my position…"

"I wouldn't dare…"

"By Chox!" Tricial stared at them in shock "I thought we were all warriors?"

Armlu blushed and Sijun turned away.

"Ji, viral, berrett?" Radoq suggested and Sijun frowned.

"What is that? I've never."

"It's easy." Armlu explained "You do one of these three gestures." he demonstrated "You both go at the same time and you don't know what the other is going to do."

"But who wins?" Sijun was confused.

"Here. See, Ji kills viral, viral smashes berrett, berrett blasts Ji. Simple. Ready?"

They played. Sijun lost with much cursing and bad grace whilst Armlu began adjusting the weapons officer's chair to his height and pulled up the pulse torpedo screen "All set, Sir."

"Twenty two miles. Closing. All craft prepare to fire."

"Prepare to fire!" Radoq echoed the order.

"Way ahead of you." Armlu grinned over the control lever, sighting on a distant ship. Sijun gripped the back of his chair so hard it began to creak under the pressure.

"Twenty miles. Standby."

The fleet ahead seemed to be racing towards them, what was Oprain thinking? Surely Juraj's ships would fire first?

"Nineteen miles. Standby."

"Come on!" moaned Sijun. Even Tricial was looking strained now.

"Eighteen miles. He'll have to call it at eighteen." Armlu was muttering.

Silence.

"They've fired!" Tricial pointed and Radoq saw torpedoes, these the ordinary plasma variety streaking toward them from one of the mercenary ships.

"Well out of range." Armlu shook his head "Easy target, that ship."

"Eighteen miles. All craft, fire!"

"Fire!" bellowed Radoq.

"Fire!" bellowed Sijun.

"Firing!" roared Armlu and rammed the trigger home.

With a whoosh and a violent jerk in the motion of the ship, the two weapons erupted from the nose of *Golden Kote*. Streaking with aquar, they left a wake of crackling blue rings in the air behind them which made the ship shake alarmingly. Radoq felt his eyes lock onto them, seeing them shoot across the empty sky eating up the distance that the airships would take minutes to traverse and then...

"A hit!" Sijun roared a victory cry and in the distance, now fifteen miles away by Oprain's count Radoq saw the weapons strike a mercenary ship, smashing into the bridge and then the ship vanished in a cloud of aquar lightning, unnatural blue light exploding out in jagged lines until Armlu flung up his hands in victory.

"It's going down!"

And Radoq saw the enemy ship was spinning furiously, nose pointing directly down and a visible fire erupting from the stern. Even as they watched, it plummeted into the black rocks of the Dark Lands and exploded in a great burst of flame.

He joined in the cheers, bloodthirsty as they were. Now was not a time for morals and he heard Tricial roar the victory to the crew over the communicator. Other airships from Juraj's fleet had been hit and more were spinning out of control. Some had recovered and were charging onwards, now almost level with the Eyrie fleet.

"Eight miles, prepare for boarding."

"Ready the pinzgats!" Tricial called and Radoq fancied he heard Staph bellowing at the troops on the fighting deck above them.

"Fire again, Sir?" Armlu called and Radoq nodded, seeing another pair of torpedoes strike a heavily armoured cruiser, this time impacting on the protected flank so the ship did not crash but even from this distance they could see the jagged hole in the side of the craft, blue aquar still radiating around it.

"That's our baby!" Sijun pointed "Prepare to board, Sir?" he shouted to Radoq.

"No!" ignoring Sijun's shocked expression Radoq stayed firm "Our task is to find Juraj and Argan! The rest are for Oprain and his men! Look, that ship is turning away even as we speak!"

It was true. The damaged ship had turned back towards Fortisul, leaving the battle. Sijun spat in disappointment but contented himself shouting insults after them as they fled.

"How will we find him?" Tricial called as Armlu raced back to the weapons deck where he was needed and Sijun took his place with relish although they were now too close for torpedoes.

"We'll find him." Radoq reassured him "The entire fleet is looking for him!"

But then the line of mercenary ships drew level and suddenly there was no time for talk, only to fight and to die as the battle lines crashed together.

CHAPTER 27

Radoq cursed, swinging the controls wildly as a mercenary ship loomed before them. Sijun fired the forward facing pinzgats and the entire starboard side of the enemy airship crumpled as Radoq raced *Golden Kote* overhead. He had a fleeting glimpse of the enemy flight deck, terrified lun'erus faces staring up at him and then they were past and there was only empty sky before them.

"Back! Take us around!" Sijun was urging but Oprain had already given the command and the line was slowing, turning to bring the rows of gats on their flanks to bear.

"Steady! Everyone look out for the lead ship!" Radoq called even as he heard the pinzgats on the fighting deck begin to blast and the air between the two lines filled with plasma. *Golden Kote* was now sideways on and Radoq had to turn to his left to see the enemy fleet which had turned more slowly than the professional flyers of the Eyrie and was taking a pounding as a result. Two ships were already falling back, one smoking badly and another appearing undamaged but as Radoq watched, it suddenly dropped to the black rocks below and he guessed the vakkor engine had been damaged.

"Over there?" Tricial was pointing and Radoq left the controls to peer to the furthest right of the enemy line, their own left where a solid looking destroyer hung back from the main line of ships.

"Could be! It's a *bolerion* destroyer, old fashioned but I could see Argan using it!" he hastened to identify the ship to Oprain whose response was delayed, given he was directing the battle.

"*It could be. Break formation,* Golden Kote *and observe.*"

"Here we go!" Sijun roared as Radoq hauled the ship out of the firing line, moving back and around their own ships to race towards the destroyer.

"Can you see her name?" he shouted to Tricial who flicked through his aurae, his face pressed up against the glass.

"*Days End.*" he called back.

"How can we be sure?" Sijun called back.

"Chox to being sure!" Radoq snarled and rammed the throttle open, at the same time punching the control that slammed the protective shutters down over the bridge "Sijun! Prepare to board!"

"Aye, aye!" Sijun leapt to his feet and sprinted out of the bridge, yelling for Rakr.

Oprain's voice demanded an update as Radoq tried his best to aim with the small space he had left to fly the ship with.

"Tell him we're ramming that destroyer!" he snarled at Tricial who chose to laugh in response.

CRASH

The first in a flurry of pinzgat bolts erupted onto the shutters and Radoq lost his visibility in a sea of green. He cursed, punching the aquar charge that kept the battle sights clear and a second later, saw the *Days End* swinging hard away from them, clearly well apprised of their intentions.

"*Boarding party prepared, just waiting on you!*" Sijun had found a communicator and Radoq bellowed an acknowledgement.

"Tricial! Be ready to take the helm!" he shouted and the Sheriff nodded, his face suddenly pale as more bolts made the shutters rattle.

There

A face at the bridge of the destroyer, visible only because it was distinctly Domerus in shape and Radoq heard an animal snarl leap from his lips "Argan!"

CRASH

The bows of *Golden Kote* impacted with the flank of *Days End* and Radoq sensed, rather than saw the grappling lines shoot from the fighting deck and he shouted to Tricial to take over, backing the engines to a stop and racing out of the bridge after Sijun.

"Here we go!" he roared to the boarding party who bared their teeth at him, Rakr at the head with a coltac in each hand, a snarl on his face and the rest fairly bristling with weaponry. Radoq closed his helmet, feeling the energy fill his body as the boarding hatch swung open. Almost at once plasma rounds poured in, glancing off his armour and he snatched a phasr from the nearest soldier, emptying the weapon into the face of a woman on the lower fighting deck of the destroyer.

"Charges!" he bellowed and two techs ran forward, pulse satchels in their hands which they swung through the air, risking the gat fire to stay and watch their handiwork as the devices locked onto the hull.

A blinding flash, then a cheer and the breach yawned before Radoq, a dark hole of twisted metal in the flank of the enemy ship. With a snarl, he leapt forward, anchoring himself on the outside of the hull and tearing at the sides of the breach to enlarge it. A crash beside him announced Sijun's armoured form joining him and the two Domerus wrenched the twisted metal aside and then enemy airmen were there, firing coltacs and Radoq grabbed the nearest, a skinny looking woman and dumped her over the side, leaving her to plummet to her death below. Then he was through, finding himself in a dim storage room into which enemy fighters were now pouring and a burst of gat fire from behind him announced Rakr exploiting the breach and pouring through.

"Pulsan!" roared a voice and, trusting his armour, Radoq simply knelt, lowering his head as the explosive sent three mercenaries flying backwards in a burst of aquar.

"*Hast!*" he roared a challenge and sprang forward, holding both hands out to the side and shattering the lun'erus that were firing at his men. Battle madness filled Radoq and he had no sense of danger, tearing mercenaries apart and flinging parts of their corpses at the others. His own troops were not idle and even as he reached an enemy, a shot from behind him would drop the man or woman and he would bound forward, always moving, clearing the deck for his men.

"On the right!" Sijun's voice roared through a communicator and he turned to see a squat, ugly looking man aiming a huge quadgat down into the room from a narrow doorway. Radoq flung himself forward even as the first burst ripped through the air. The front of his armour grew white hot and burned the skin below and Radoq turned his bellow of pain into a shout of fury and saw the mercenary's eyes widen in shock then fear and then he was dead, Radoq's thumbs in his eye sockets.

"Move!" Rakr's voice filled his ears, urging the men forward, out of the killing zone and into the rest of the ship. Their training took over, the long hours in Oprain's yard aiding them as they moved in tight formation down unfamiliar corridors, blasting mercenaries and driving the enemy back.

"Onwards!" Radoq roared encouragement but Rakr waved him off, impatiently.

"To the bridge, Sir! Get to the bridge!" and Radoq saw the sense, leading Sijun on a wild charge up a flight of stairs, ducking a burst of gat fire and killing two more men with precise Tal-Kan strikes to exposed necks.

A third man reeled back before Sijun, dropping his phasr and throwing up his arms in terrified surrender. The big man seized him by the throat, ramming him against the wall.

"Where is the bridge! Tell us!"

"There! Up there!" the hapless mercenary pointed up a narrow flight of stairs Radoq hadn't seen and he shouted to Sijun who nodded, casually killing the man with a single blow. Radoq winced but knew it was the practical thing to do. They could not afford prisoners at this point in the battle.

Up, up, up, twisting flights and Radoq urged Sijun to be silent, trying to gain the element of surprise. Rakr over the communicator reported taking corridor after corridor and Staph on the fighting deck requested permission to board from the top which Radoq gave readily. There was no time to be amazed at the speed and ferocity of the assault but later, he knew, he would sit and remember small details, wincing at close blows and lucky escapes.

"There!" Sijun pointed and Radoq saw a small red door. Surely that didn't lead to the bridge? But Sijun was surging past eagerly, using his body to cover Radoq and he tore the heavy iron off its hinges, stepping through into what looked like an emergency escape route from the bridge –

Only to be torn back by a blast from a berrett which shattered the helmet of his armour, spinning him backwards in a spray of gore and a bellow of agony.

"Sijun!" Radoq grabbed his friend, dragging him out of the line of fire as a second and a third blast filled the space where the big Domerus had been just a moment before "Report! What's your status!"

"Chox'd painful!" Sijun seemed to grin as though this were a fine thing but Radoq saw the bolts had torn through his right cheek, cracking the jaw and the whole side of his face was now hanging in a torn mass of flesh and shattered flecks of bone.

"Turn!" he patted down Sijun's neck, seeing the deep wounds there but already the biom was stopping the bleeding, sealing the breached artery and Sijun would live. He was pale though and he slumped backwards as Radoq watched.

"Two men." he tried to describe what he'd seen through the door, his voice distorted by the terrible wound "One there –" he pointed to the left of the entrance "A second to the right. Domerus." Then he lost consciousness. Radoq spared a second to summon a medic to the spot and then he crouched, lowering his body into a powerful spring.

I'll come back to you

If Juraj was on the far side of that door then Radoq knew he'd face any danger just for a chance to tear him apart.

He sprang.

The berrett fired, a modified double burst of plasma bolts, concentrated into a small spread which explained the damage to Sijun's armour but Radoq was already past the danger, turning in mid-air as he bounded down the length of the bridge, his eyes coming to rest on the shooter who was still staring dully at the doorway.

Juraj.

Wrapped in bulky armour, cradling an enormous berrett and curiously, an odd looking handheld lashed to his chest with thick leather straps. He looked ridiculous.

He looked deadly.

But it was not towards him that Radoq sprang. It was to the right, towards the Domerus who stared at him with eyes widening in shock and a desperate step to move into Radoq's path but then Radoq had landed, wishing with all his might that Sijun could see him as he stepped perfectly, no stumbles or slips, kicked Argan's leg from under him and wrapped his right forearm in an impeccable soul grip around the Domerus' neck.

"I have you!" he bellowed his victory but Juraj fired again and the blast tore a chunk from the ceiling above Radoq sending wind and dust into his face.

His grip remained absolute though and Argan bellowed for his lun'erus partner to stop, to allow the duel to continue.

"This is how Domerus duel, Juraj! If you want to be one of us, you'll let this happen!"

Juraj had closed on them, now standing level with the door. Radoq saw movement and that to his shock, Sijun had hauled himself upright and was crouching behind the door. He shook his head at the big man who was covered in blood.

"I'm not one of you yet, Argan!" Juraj roared over the rushing of the wind. In his ear, Radoq heard Staph reporting the upper decks were theirs "One last act of lun'erus defiance before I am ascended!"

Radoq flicked through his aurae almost by habit. He locked onto Juraj's face, searching for the tell-tale signs that would betray him pulling the trigger and give him the second he needed to twist out of harm's way and he saw the lun'erus' eyes widen in surprise as Radoq extended his left palm towards the man, seeing the green glow of plasma there and then the fear at this unknown weapon and then Juraj moved, faster than any lun'erus Radoq had ever seen he dived to the side but not faster than the bolt from Radoq's biom which caught his shoulder, spinning him around and flinging him to the ground.

Argan broke the soul grip.

It had never happened, never been seen in the fields of Tal-Kan nor in the heat of battle. As Radoq felt his arm move and saw the ground rush up to meet him as Argan threw him, his only, ridiculous thought was how glad he was Sijun was able to see it.

He hit the ground and slid as Argan took several quick steps forward, moving to strike but Radoq spun in place, kicking the man's leg, and seeing Argan fall in a vulnerable position but it was a sham and Radoq skittered backwards, avoiding Argan's scything blow.

Movement, and Sijun was there, moving slowly towards Juraj. That he was able to move at all was testament to his strength of will because he looked as though he should be dead. Juraj, his own blood visible on his armoured shoulder and his deadly weapon gone hastened past Radoq to plead with Argan.

"Do it! Do it now! Ascend me and we can fight them!"

Argan turned with disgust on his expression and Radoq saw then that the Ji had perhaps never intended to ascend Juraj. Juraj seemed to sense this too and he leaned in, the same charm that Radoq remembered layering his voice.

"Argan, this is your chance! A victory here, kill Radoq and this fight is over! Only Oprain stands before you and we have a fleet! We can break from battle and race to the Eyrie! Think, two Domerus will be able to stroll in and own the place! Oprain will never get close! Do it now! Act now!"

"Fine."

Argan reached out and pushed Juraj to his knees. Powerless to stop them, Radoq could only stare in horror as Argan placed his left hand on Juraj's head, seeing the bright glow that he remembered from his own Ji's biom begin to brighten and burn and he saw his undoing in that light, the understanding that Juraj would ascend, would claim the Eyrie and Fortisul and his family would never be free and he, Radoq, would bear the blame for his many failures.

Juraj screamed.

The process, Radoq remembered, was agonising. But he hadn't screamed. His father had expressly forbidden it, threatening to stop his ascension if he did and Radoq had endured in silence.

Juraj's scream was beyond agony. It was beyond control and even as Radoq listened, it became more of a wail, curling and screeching in octaves as Juraj clamped his hands to his own head, his eyes burning bright and Argan looked on in horror at what was happening to his erstwhile ally because Juraj's mouth was now filled with light, not a bright light but a burning light because flames had formed in his mouth and now in his eyes and now his whole body was bursting with little fires and the scream cut off abruptly, his head snapped back, pulling Argan's hand from him and he pitched sideways, smoke pouring from his corpse to be snatched away by the wind gusting through the hole blasted by his own weapon.

There was a moment of shocked silence and then the strange device strapped to Juraj's chest let out a shrill whine, the screen lit up and then it went blank and silent.

Argan regarded the corpse coolly for a moment before murmuring to himself faint words that Radoq's biom picked up and relayed to his ears.

"Not one of us after all, then."

Radoq shifted forward and Argan registered the move, turning to meet it. Sijun moved to stand beside Radoq and Argan grimaced at the sight of him.

"A duel, perhaps, Radoq? Two champions in an epic struggle to the death?"

It was tempting. Radoq could feel his blood rising at the challenge, could see the golden kote on his biom that matched his own but this was a battle and his duty was to end the fight and re-join his men.

And Argan had *broken* the soul grip. No Domerus had ever done that.

"This is war." Radoq grated "Enough playing."

Argan's mouth thinned into a hard line "As you wish."

He swung such a fast blow that Radoq barely had time to block it, a hammer fist that might have broken his neck had it connected but Radoq stepped sideways seizing the wrist and turning it with his body, locking the joint. Argan snarled and turned his own hips, whipping his hand out of Radoq's grasp and cuffing him across the face. Agony exploded across Radoq's forehead and hot blood poured into his eyes. A second of blindness before his aurae adjusted and he instinctively raised both hands to block the blow he knew was coming but Argan swung a kick into his thigh and then the aurae cleared his vision and he could see Sijun leap...

Argan tried to turn his hips but he had seen the attack too late and he landed beneath the huge Domerus who wrapped his arms around Argan's torso, crushing the older man to him. Blood gushed from his ruined face and spattered his enemy's eyes and Argan cursed, twisting his head frantically.

Then Sijun's strength failed him and he could do nothing to prevent Argan bringing up a leg beneath him and levering an inch of space between their locked bodies and for a Domerus of Argan's skill it was enough and he launched Sijun back, breaking the hold around his neck and rising to one knee.

Radoq did not risk a soul grip. He caught Argan's chin and the back of his head and with all his Domerus strength he wrenched.

A sickening, appalling sound and Argan collapsed in a nerveless slump. His eyes stared wildly, locked in the final fear that had gripped his features. Radoq bared his teeth in a savage grin of victory as Sijun panted weakly from the floor.

"That throw." Radoq's voice came in bursts, he was suddenly aware of his chest was heaving "How?"

Sijun shook his head, blood spattering the floor beneath him "I've never seen that."

"It's impossible."

The fear that passed between them was palpable but a crash and the main door to the bridge exploding inwards announced the arrival of Staph and Rakr who were apparently calm and unflustered by the battle. They quickly directed their troops to secure the bridge, signalling to Tricial their victory.

"His kote –" Radoq pointed "Yours if you want it."

Sijun shook his head "No. You killed him."

"I have one." Radoq reminded him but Sijun would not take it and so Radoq placed it on his own biom, watching it fit itself next to the award the Crown Prince had given him.

"Radoq to *Golden Kote*." He spoke into his communicator.

"*Tricial here.*"

"Broadcast to all ships that Juraj and Argan are dead."

Tricial spared a moment to cheer before beginning to broadcast the message on all signals he could find from the bridge of *Golden Kote*.

"Sir?" Staph approached the two Domerus, looking uneasily at Juraj's burned corpse "The ship's ours."

"Good. Add our sigil and we'll get back to the battle."

But the battle was over. The mercenary ships had fared badly against the superior firepower of Oprain's fleet although wrecks on the ground below the Eyrie line marked his own casualties. The mercenaries had lost twice as many ships and Oprain had captured nearly a dozen which now hung listless around the battlefield. At the sound of Tricial's broadcast, Radoq could see mercenary ships disengaging and racing eastwards, away from the battle.

"Cowards." Sijun had risen to a kneeling position and was being treated by a medic.

"Their employer is dead. There's no more reason for them to fight." Radoq shrugged. It was the reaction he'd hoped for and he wondered why he didn't feel elated at the victory.

"Any idea what this is?" Rakr was checking Juraj with the professional curiosity of a soldier. Radoq noticed the grizzled Sergeant had already claimed Juraj's modified berrett. But it wasn't the weapon or the bulky armour that held his interest. Instead, it was the curious device strapped to his chest that was now dark and silent.

"It made a noise just after he died." Radoq remembered "I thought it was from the flames."

"Looks like a signalling device." Rakr pointed out a few components "Must have sent a message in the event he died."

"Probably why the others disengaged so fast." Staph interjected "Mercs often run with that as an arrangement so if their employer is killed, they know not to waste lives."

Rakr spat in derision at such an arrangement but seemed satisfied.

"Sir?"

A soldier drew Radoq's attention to the sigil now visible from the bridge across *Days End*. A pair of golden kotes to replace the single that had marked Radoq's banner before. He nodded and forced a smile which brought a cheer from the crew.

Sijun was carried back on a vakkor stretcher to *Golden Kote*. The bleeding had stopped though and he was stable, even beginning to be in fine spirits as the full weight of their victory settled in.

"Forgive me, but you don't seem thrilled with the victory?" Tricial asked as Radoq slumped in the bridge on *Golden Kote*, exhausted.

He let out a deep sigh "I am. Believe me, Juraj and Argan are dead and we haven't lost a single soldier. I couldn't be happier."

Tricial, wisely, said nothing.

"But I have unfinished business."

"In Fortisul?" Tricial made to plot a course.

"No." Radoq stood up, pointing eastwards across the Dark Lands "Here. I have a deal to keep."

CHAPTER 28

"See –" Evie strolled nonchalantly into the bridge turning a small object back and forth in her hands "If he had this on his chest, it suggests it was for a reason." She looked up, surprised at the silence that greeted her "What?"

"You're awfully cheerful." Radoq murmured.

"So? No-one died, did they?"

"A great many people just died." Tricial mused.

"Yeah, but no-one on our side, right?"

Radoq shook his head.

"Right! So why don't you start looking like you just won the war instead of like you're about to jump out the boarding hatch?"

Road turned back to the Dark Lands and Evie scowled.

"Point is, if he was wearing it, it was tracking his heartbeat or something. When he died, it sent out the signal."

"We thought that was what called the mercenaries off." Radoq turned back to her.

Evie looked surprised "No! That was him –" she indicated Tricial "- banging on about Juraj and Argan being dead! They scarpered right after that, no point hanging around to die."

"Where did the signal go then?" Radoq asked.

Evie looked triumphant "Exactly! No idea!"

"Okay." Radoq turned away again.

"Oh, Chox! Whats the matter with you all?" she demanded.

Radoq gestured out at the black rock that stretched to the horizon and she nodded.

"Ah. Having second thoughts?"

"No."

"Having dark thoughts, then?"

Radoq nodded.

"Best place for it." Evie strode forward to peer out the windows "We nearly there?"

"To tell the truth, I'm not quite sure." Radoq set the controls to maintain their course and heading and moved over to the navigation chart "Here's where *Golden Kote* went down and I went... this way." He stabbed a finger down on the map which was empty of all detail.

"So... You're thinking it might just say on there 'Dark Ji lives here'?" Evie teased.

"Hmm." Radoq would not be provoked and after a laborious eye roll, she abandoned the attempt at humour.

"I think we-"

"Haven't you got work to do?" Radoq asked abruptly and Evie raised both her eyebrows so high they were in danger of vanishing into her hairline.

"That I have." she muttered and stalked out of the bridge, clearly affronted.

"Can't be far now." Tricial called when she had gone "Was there anything distinctive about the place?"

Radoq grunted and thought "Just the hatch he led me through."

"Was that something he built?"

"I don't know. It could have already been there."

"You mean from before the virals?"

"Mmm."

The ship flew on as the crew rested. Tricial even stole a rare moment of sleep, leaving Radoq alone with his thoughts.

Movement suddenly caught his eye and he crossed the bridge, staring down into the wasteland below in wonder.

Virals, thousands upon thousands of them, all streaming towards one place and Radoq concentrated his aurae, watching the odd patterns of their behaviour. Some moved alone, others in small pods of two or three but most were in large groups, hundreds or even thousands. They mystified Radoq. Nothing existed out here but the glow, was that all that sustained them? How had they become these monsters, so different from the rest of humanity? He concentrated on their form, seeing the pale skin, the distended limbs and wild look in their eyes. Was there intelligence there? He thought not, seeing only animal instinct.

His eyes met Guysil's quite unexpectedly making him jump. Accounting for the aurae, the Dark Ji was still some miles away but he clearly saw Radoq and a small, knowing smile played around his lips. Overcoming his shock, Radoq raised a hand in greeting and turned his ship towards the man.

Towards the place where the virals were streaming as though following a hunting call.

"Evie? Are you ready?" he called over the communicator.

"Yep."

"Meet me at the hatch when we stop."

"Yep."

Radoq had no time to waste on apologies as he brought the ship to a halt and handed the controls over to Tricial, making his way back through the narrow corridors.

Evie met him at the hatch, wrapped in her protective suit and with a huge vakkor case before her.

"You had to bring this?"

"It contains it. Stops the glow getting all over the ship." She shot him a poisonous look.

"Fine. Get back." He swung the boarding hatch open to admit a blast of strong wind and cold air. Immediately the sound of the virals was deafening, the hunting cries tearing through the air and he felt Tricial raise the ship a few inches in response.

"Hello, Radoq. Hello, hello, hello!" Guysil spoke at a normal volume but Radoq heard him clearly enough. He nodded to the man who looked odd in the daylight, pale and unnatural.

In response, Radoq held up the case and jumped from the ship, landing easily on the hard rock. A viral snapped at him and he turned to it but the beast moved on, surging towards Guysil who stepped through the massing bodies, their forms parting before him.

"Our deal is done!" he grinned, white teeth contrasting with the rock behind him.

"I don't need you to attack Fortisul anymore." Radoq was tired and already sick of this madman. Manners did not occur to him.

"Then it is not a deal anymore." Guysil was still smiling that insane smile.

"Then take it as a gift." Radoq opened the case, scooping the small nuklera out and extending his hand. Guysil's eyes locked onto the device and he stepped forward but moving around the object as though afraid to touch it.

"The glow. The glow, the glow, the glow!" he cackled to himself, Radoq's presence seemingly forgotten.

Radoq made to hand it to him but his eyes caught the top of the metal hatch that led to Guysil's home. It looked ancient, he thought, clearly something the Dark Ji had discovered, not made.

"And what favour will I owe you?" Guysil suddenly snapped, the madness gone from his tone "No object such as this is given freely. Tell me, and do not lie, Radoq."

Radoq had expected the man's suspicion and he nodded "I will ask a favour of you but I will not tell you it now."

A frown and the dance of mad lights in the Dark Ji's eyes.

"It is a complex favour, one that I have fought with myself over asking of you. At times it seemed dishonourable and I have wrestled with my conscience."

Guysil was intrigued, Radoq knew. That was good.

"I ask you this. When the time is right, you will know the favour and I ask you then to act on it in all good faith. In return, I give you this weapon. Freely."

Guysil snatched the nuklera from his hand, cradling it close. Suddenly, the virals all around them went perfectly still, every diseased eye locked on Radoq. He looked up to *Golden Kote* hanging in the air above them, wondering if he could leap from here before the virals surged forward.

Guysil laughed again, a long, cackling burst of joy as he shook his head "Go then, Radoq! Go, go, go. And take your mysteries with you." He smiled, shaking his head as though Radoq were the mystery that he, Guysil could not solve.

Radoq nodded and stepped towards his ship but Guysil snaked out a hand, grabbing his wrist and pulling his head close to whisper.

"Take your mysteries, but leave me here with mine."

Did he know? Was there understanding in his eyes? Radoq could not tell but he tore his gaze away from Guysil's hypnotic sight and shook his head.

Aboard the ship Evie greeted him, still wearing the protective suit. Tricial was already climbing, widening the throttle as the boarding hatch clicked shut.

"All good?" Evie asked, her earlier animosity apparently forgotten.

"Better than the alternative."

They made their way to the fighting deck and the rushing air. Already, the sea of virals was receding in the distance. Evie stood behind a quadgat, leaning out around the armour plates.

"Are you certain it worked?" Radoq asked.

She shrugged, still not happy about finding an area of mechanics that was not her expertise "Baxl had some bright ideas. We can hope that-"

Bright, impossibly white light erupted in the Dark Lands scorching the surrounding rock with its brilliance and deepening the burned layer. Radoq's aurae compensated almost immediately but still he felt the stabbing pain in his head. He forced himself to watch, seeing the shockwaves travel out across the flat ground, stirring up dust and debris that had lain dormant for generations. Evie shrieked in fear but the suit protected her and Radoq stared in awe at the appalling destruction.

Great rings of brilliant white were now racing away from the centre of the explosion whilst the burning fireball, miles in diameter was rising fast leaving a vast column of white smoke in its wake. Then it was widening, forming the distinctive cloud that Radoq knew would be seen across the entire Kingdom.

"Chox! Chox'd Chox!" Evie was swearing, staring through the visor of the suit, knowing that she was being treated to a sight so few of her kind could ever experience.

Now great halos of light were forming over the Dark Lands, stretching out at impossible speeds and Radoq saw one approach them, racing to catch the ship and he grabbed the side of the quadgat as the shockwave struck and *Golden Kote* was tossed like a leaf in a storm. Evie screamed but Radoq held her firmly, never once taking his eye off the towering pillar of destruction that he had unleashed on the world. He felt sick, guilty like a naughty child that could not take back its trespass. Tears formed in his eyes, swiftly evaporated by his aurae and he could only shake his head as the destruction passed and the halos began to fade leaving only the mushroom shaped cloud that hung over the Dark Lands.

"No more Dark Ji." Evie tried to joke but her voice was hoarse.

"No-one could have survived that." Radoq shook his head but there was no conviction in his voice.

"No-one." Evie agreed, turning to nod to him.

There was no question. For miles around the site, only death and destruction held. Radoq imagined the bodies of the virals, utterly vaporised by the awesome power of the nuklera. That, he reassured himself, was a good thing and that reminded him of the favour he'd asked of Guysil which he now asked the empty lands.

"Die for me, Guysil."

A favour he prayed would be fulfilled.

*

They left one column of smoke behind them only to see another rising from the horizon before them. Miles from Fortisul, Radoq could see his home burning and all thoughts of virals and nuklera fled as a pounding fear filled his heart.

Silence filled the bridge. Sijun, his head swathed in dressings slumped in a spare seat but even he fidgeted nervously. Evie was silent for once, seeing the strain in Radoq's face as he once again pulled on his armour, preparing to fight an enemy whose identity he didn't know.

Tricial tried to signal Fortisul but there was no response. Radoq tried not to race through scenarios in his mind where such an eventuality would come to pass but fear and dread threatened to unman him and he pushed *Golden Kote* to her limits, diving towards home and to the woman who waited for him there.

I'll come back to you

But would she be there? Would anything?

The smoke billowed in the irregular gusts of wind between the mountain peaks. Forcing himself to be cautious, Radoq reduced their speed and posted lookouts, not wishing to collide with a fleeing ship in the thick smoke. Through sudden gaps blown by the wind they caught snatches of burning buildings and running lun'erus.

"Some are alive at least." Tricial pointed to a group of small figures working a pump at a fire "The keep is burning. The Domerus tiers too." He turned to Radoq "The sky port looks safe. Start descending."

Radoq lowered the ship cautiously, suddenly finding that they were below the smoke. Ahead, the docks loomed but they were empty. A pile of debris lay across the stream that formed the bottom of the port, some of it still smoking faintly but no fire raged here.

"Explosives." Evie was pointing "They tried to take out the port master's cabin there but it fell into the water. You can see where it happened."

"Now we know what Juraj's signal did." Sijun growled from his seat "That Chox'd dishonourable –"

"Tricial!" Radoq snapped "When we dock, you organise the lun'erus to fight the fires. I want you to report to me on which buildings can be saved. Evie? Stay with the ship and make sure the sky port remains open. Sijun, you'll stay and protect Evie if there are still enemies in the town."

The flurry of orders silenced them and a moment later, Staph and Rakr appeared in the bridge with Armlu.

"Get the crew off and help with the fires." Radoq ordered them "If we need to evacuate, get people down to the sky port and we can shuttle them down the slope below the smoke in *Golden Kote.* Take your weapons with you! There may still be enemies here but our priority is the locals. Protect the townsfolk!"

He docked hastily, knocking the hull against the thick buffer plate of the dock a small error he cared nothing for. Racing down the gangway he leapt ahead of the lun'erus, plunging into the smoke filled streets and racing through the main square, past a soot choked fountain and the corpses of beggars and then up the steep streets, through the cloud park where frightened lun'erus huddled and into the Domerus tiers.

"Radoq!" she was there, she was alive and he flung himself towards her but she was shaking her head, tears streaking down her face.

"Your family? Are they safe?" he demanded, fear gripping his heart and she nodded.

"Radoq Loxelsus!" a silver haired and ancient woman of Domerus stature was walking towards him with slow, painful steps. Her face was grim and her clothes were stained with fire "The granary is burning, the keep and the justice building but most of the lun'erus homes are safe. The Domerus tiers are almost all destroyed. Your tritus home is safe and we've moved people there until the smoke passes.

"Saxo –" he began but Malain's mother was standing formally before him, the composure of the Ji on her face and he fell silent, understanding suddenly filling him.

"No-"

"Radoq Loxelsus, it is my duty to inform you that you are now the Ji of tritus Fortisun." Her eyes shone with repressed grief "Your people need you to lead them-"

"Where are they?" he choked as Malain put her hand on his arm.

Saxo shook her head, trying to direct him to the lun'erus who fought the destruction that Juraj had sown.

"WHERE ARE THEY!" he roared in a voice that echoed from

the mountain peaks.

Saxo bowed her head and gestured. Radoq stumbled forward through the smoke as Malain followed. Down the street, past the shattered remnants of a tritus mansion and along another, round a turn and down the street that led to the keep, the same road he'd walked with Juraj and there...

Two figures, their heads distorted at odd angles, hanging by ropes from the wall of the keep, their skin stained by ash and their eyes wide and staring...

"No-"

But no denial would hide the fact that Loxel and Gellian were dead, murdered by a hand that could only have been Argan's. A man who Radoq had already killed. Vengeance was his, had been for hours but now it felt hollow and empty and he fell to his knees, Malain wrapping her arms tightly around him and whispering in his ear but he heard nothing of what she said. Instead, Oprain's words about self-pity seemed to taunt him as he smelled the smoke and felt the grief of his people around him as their home burned whilst inside him, something less tangible burned away with it.

Dimly, he recalled struggling to his feet and taking command. He was now the Ji and people needed him. Malain was there, watching him, helping people but watching him all the time and he remembered as though it were a thousand years ago her telling him that Gellian had challenged Argan, the elder Domerus killing him in the duel. Loxel, defending his tritus had flown at the disgraced Ji in a fury but could not hope to defeat the man who bore the golden kote and so father and son had ended their lives in Argan's soul grip. Radoq found himself daydreaming, wondering how Argan had broken the impossible hold and then wishing he had stormed Fortisul, that he'd had the courage to take the risk and that the fires around them that he now fought to extinguish had been caused by his own fleet, not by Juraj's murdering hands.

"Radoq, we must -"

"Sir, there are -"

"Domerus, you –"

"I need –"

"We have to –"

"The *town* needs –"

Everyone needed something. And Radoq had to give it to all of them. This was his purpose in life, not to live as a free lun'erus but to serve them, to serve the people who looked to him and to be the leader. He reassured people in an empty voice that they would rebuild, that this was not the end but how did you rebuild a murdered father and brother? They could not simply be reconstructed. They were gone.

Gone.

Gone

CHAPTER 29

Days passed. The smoke dissipated. People began to clean and scrape away the evidence of death but to Radoq the stench of it still hung in the air. He could not weep. He knew that if he gave in to his grief on any level it would overwhelm him and the guilt and pain he felt would drown the whole town. People needed him and he needed them to flee the nightmares that plagued him on the rare days he dared to sleep.

Oprain sent help from the Eyrie, six ships arriving with builders and materials and almost at once the rubble began to be cleared and new buildings went up. The progress was like nothing Radoq had ever seen but he took no pleasure in watching it nor in the thousand small tasks that took up his days.

He knelt each day by the bodies of his family. Domerus flesh did not decay like that of the lun'erus and custom dictated that they lay in state for the town to file past. He'd tried to skip this ceremony, arguing that the people were too busy to care but Tricial and Malain had persuaded him and he knelt as what seemed like the entire town, all of them weeping, filed past. Some came twice. Others came more. Some placed hands on his shoulders, remembering the Domerus who had left for war and seeing the haggard warrior who had returned, aged and worn.

It helped.

Then came the funerals. First, the lun'erus and Radoq's crew formed the honour guard for the dozens of hastily made litters that the dead were laid on. Sombre soldiers, dressed in black cloth carried each man, woman and child past silent crowds up through the town, breathing the still lingering stench of smoke to the edge of the valley. There, the Domerus that survived formed pairs and they carried the dead high into the three peaks that surrounded Fortisul. The bodies were laid bare and soon great clouds of prey birds wheeled and screeched as the corpses were stripped bare.

There were a lot of dead and the birds grew fat, swooping down to waddle to the channelled streams that watered the town, desperately drinking to wash down the flesh that distended their bellies.

Finally, the Domerus dead and Radoq, ignoring the traditions slung the pale bodies of his father and brother, one over each shoulder and set off, remembering a day when he and Gellian had run up this very slope so many times they'd passed out. He bared his teeth at the memory, driving himself forward and ignoring the pain.

The mountains were steep but Radoq's grief was stronger and it propelled him to the highest peak where already white bones were stripped bare to the cold winds. People in the town said that the birds took your flesh whilst the wind took your spirit to blow forever in the heavens. Radoq hoped that was true as he reverently laid his family down to rest, side by side and stood, bowing his head.

She was there, of course she was. As he finally allowed the tears to run freely down his cheeks, he realised that she would always be there. He would never leave again. He would never let that happen, no matter what enemies faced them.

The eye of Admirain was strong and even in this sanctuary as he turned and stared across the lowlands, Radoq felt its gaze upon him, the promise of retribution to come. To the south and east, the Dark Lands stretched with the crag of the Eyrie a distant beacon of friendship and hope. There, Radoq knew, he would always find help. In the east, beyond the black rocks that met the horizon there were whispers, sightings of virals moving in numbers never seen before. Rumours of the Dark Ji and Radoq tried not to think of the towering pillar of smoke that had hung for days.

A bird flapped down from the sky to land at his feet, staring at him with one beady eye before looking to the pale skin of his father. Acknowledging the creature's right to the feast, Radoq gazed one last time at their faces, feeling Malain's warm arms around him and he bowed to them, wishing them fair flight on the gusting winds of the heavens. A final goodbye.

As they turned to descend towards the town and the endless work that it promised, Malain stopped him and placed her hands on his shoulders, looking deep into his tear filled eyes.

"We have each other now. We won't let them take that from us again."

"Never." he swore and leaned his forehead against hers as behind them the birds screeched and gorged.

"Whatever they do, we'll face it together." she murmured, her lips against his ear as they held each other tight.

And she was right.

THE END

Printed in Great Britain
by Amazon

33752285R00165